I0764350

King Juba's Chest

Leander Jackie Grogan

Publishing Services Worldwide

HARDBACK EDITION

For information on permissions, email:
grogan007@live.com

Visit website at: https://groganbooks.com/

Printed in the United States of America
Seventh Edition: August, 2018
ISBN-978-1-62620-215-3

BOOKS BY LEANDER JACKIE GROGAN

Orange FingerTips

Exorcism At Midnight

Baby, Put That Gun Down

Layoff Skullduggery: The Official Humor Guide

King Juba's Chest

Black Church Blues

The Bible Gobbled Up My Big Sister [Not yet released]

What's Wrong With Your Small Business Team? [Nonfiction Bestseller]

The Blood Tears of Jesus

Dedication

This book is dedicated to my devoted wife, Brenda, whose tenacity, strength and love have taught me a thing or two; to my adventurous son and brilliantly inquisitive daughter who have made me so proud, to my admirable son-in-law (second son); to my ever-believing friends who have been so supportive over the years, and now, most recently, to my two beautiful little grandbabies who will probably be reading this when I'm dead and gone. Study Lola's character closely, my little ones. There is valuable wisdom and folly immersed in her life decisions that no book can teach. Only the eyes of the soul can see them.

About the Author

Leander Jackie Grogan is a native of Houston, Texas, graduate of Texas Tech University and novelist for twenty plus years. His excellence in writing extends over a multiplicity of genres with seven novels having been distributed in eleven countries and five different languages. Both, *Exorcism At Midnight* and *Black Church Blues* have become best-sellers with worldwide distribution and popular choices for discussion on national talk shows. He has won numerous local and national awards in creative writing for radio, print and the web.

Besides having authored a number of nonfiction articles in such national publications as the Houston Business Journal, AdWeek, Dallas Weekly, Jet and Business info Magazine, Grogan is author of a current business bestseller, *What's Wrong With Your Small Business Team*; at one point in 2011, holding the #44 spot in the small business category on Amazon.com. Grogan also serves as a guest blogger for the national crime/suspense writer's website, *Murder by 4*, has written and produced three local spiritual comedies, and some years ago, had a work of fiction published in Hustler Magazine.

Grogan's popularity continues to grow exponentially as a member of the new breed of storytellers unencumbered by the dictates of old world cookie-cutter characters and a narrow spotlight perpetually shining on the rich side of town. His characters are bold and edgy and unpredictable, and invariably in conflict with traditional values. His writings go out of their way to explore spiritual unknowns and the deep crevices of the mind that harbor raw insight and truth.

Grogan's favorite writer, and most preponderant upon his current style, is the late Sidney Sheldon. Specific works such as *Polar Shift* by Clive Cussler, *Dead Zone* by Stephen King, *Song of Solomon* by Toni Morrison, *Deep Cover* by Michael Tolkin and *The Rainmaker* by John Grisham have also had a great influence on his commitment to rich, multi-layered characterization and intricately crafted plots.

The Quest for Freedom

If you can avoid the scorching heat and desert rattlesnakes, the ruthless Los Zetas gangs and US ICE patrols, the patriotic crazies that roam the border with shotguns and baseball bats, and the rape camps outside of San Diego where they hang your panties in the trees, then you are ready to embrace the darkness of a collapsing drug smuggler's cave. Crawl to the light of freedom, my innocent one. Crawl to America.

Prologue

It was early fall when Professor Timothy Broadson's international flight landed at the Pokhava Airport in the remote mountain country of Nepal. Nestled enigmatically between the steamy dark jungles of India and the frigid river valleys of China, Nepal was an ancient experiment in contradictions.

Within its strange and mystical religious traditions, Nepal's showcase city of Pokhava glimmered like a precious jewel. Centuries of sacred Hindu rituals and Sanskrit songs of meditation had polished its outer shell. Legions of devout Buddhists meandered through the crowded streets, searching for spiritual enlightenment and keys to the reincarnated life to come.

This was the ethereal coating that glazed over the class poverty and political corruption and black market crime. This was the tapestry of peace and tranquility that concealed the sale of cheap Hashish and skillful exploitation of tourists.

Twenty years earlier, the glazed-over coating had brought a younger, more idealistic Professor Broadson to Pokhava. Now, the dark faces of crime and class and poverty had brought him back again.

Brahma, the Hindu creator, had placed many restrictions on the poor, lower class *untouchables*. There were many sacred monasteries and hidden chambers they could not visit. Only the highest ranking monks could enter the sacred mountain caves above the city. That's where Professor Broadson was headed, to a secret cave where no one else could go.

Following the steep, rocky mountain path toward the snow capped peaks of Machhapuchhre, Professor Broadson quickly realized he wasn't the man he used to be. The puffy blue thermal jacket and polar fleece mask covered his portly body and black, bearded face. Still, they seemed grossly inadequate to buffer the icy wind gusts, slithering across the dark canyon walls.

At five thousand feet above sea level, in a place the Asian explorers called the *Roof of the World*, the frigid air was stingy and raw, currents of invisible daggers that sliced his throat. The footing grew more precarious with each grueling step. Precise vision was a fading enigma, swallowed up by the blinding white of the snow.

The old Hindu monk that had led him up the holy mountain was surely dead now. Yet, Professor Broadson could still hear his withered voice, echoing through the deep cavities of his mind. "Against all the sacred teachings of *Vishnu*, I bring you to this place. The supreme voices of the universe have told me. One day, you will need to come again."

Just as the old monk had prophesied, Professor Broadson was back ... back to this place of desolation and forbidden access, an exalted fortress in the sky. There was no better place to hide a terrible secret from mankind; no better place to house the most dangerous chest in the world.

The cave was located between two jagged mountain ledges, connected by a flimsy rope bridge that bucked and swayed and whistled in the wind. With no local guide, no radio and no archaeological team members aware of his location, the professor could only hope his good intentions were enough to keep the ancient conduit in place. There were no other options. There was no turning back.

With a pounding heart and wobbly feet, Professor Broadson crossed the twisted mangle of shredded ropes, dried vines and rotten plank boards. A single sharp boot through the icy buildup quickly exposed the outer extremities of the cave's tiny mouth. Professor Broadson took a deep breath of chilled mountain air, then plunged into the narrow darkness.

Removing the huge incandescent flashlight from his safety belt, he cautiously surveyed the room. It was a dark, cramped, semi-circular chamber with spiked rocks hanging a few inches above his head. Ancient figurines, rare artifacts and precious trinkets of gold and silver aligned the stone shelves that had been adeptly carved into the rugged black walls. Life size replicas of a holy cow and King Cobra snake peered out from the darkened corners. Tattered hand stitched satin prayer flags covered the entire back wall.

In the center of the cave, like an elongated thumb with a recessed capstone on top, a stone altar rose from the floor. Within the capstone lay a tattered copy of the *Vedas*, the most sacred Hindu text in existence.

After spending a lifetime uncovering archaeological civilizations, Professor Broadson's exploratory instincts enticed him to look further, to examine more closely, to soak in the inate value of earthly treasures undesicated by the modern world. But with the snow flakes thickening and wind squalls, screaming their relentless warning, there was no time for professional liberties. He needed to be about the business at hand.

He unzipped his sturdy backpack and carefully removed the small wooden chest. He placed it inside another trunk, a larger copper container, etched with sacred Hindu markings.

Since Nicholas Hartman had handed over the Juba Chest a few weeks earlier, a daunting, troublesome, unspeakable dilemma had bounced around in his mind.

Would it better serve humanity to hide the chest as he was now doing, or completely destroy it so no one else would be privy to its deadly powers?

It reminded him of one of those profound rhetorical

puzzlers he had often presented his students at the university. Of course, this was no puzzler. It was a paradoxical nightmare affecting the entire world.

Should one man take it upon himself to destroy a powerful instrument that might one day be needed to save the world?

He was certain the creators of the atomic bomb had asked the same question. They were all honorable men, wanting what was best for humanity. But humanity had a horrible track record, a dismal account of making bad choices and pushing mankind to the brink of extinction. Would it be morally responsible to ignore humanity's ruthless tendencies, or was it his sole obligation to declare the human race incorrigible and hopeless and void of any future capacity to do the right thing?

Professor Broadson did not feel worthy to make such an immutable decision. And so he chose the venturesome second option; to leave the chest in play.

King Juba's Chest would exist in an isolated chamber of secrecy, a place where no ordinary human would stumble upon it. Perhaps it would resurface a million years from now, just in time to keep the sun from burning the earth to a crisp. Until then, mankind would have to learn to live without it. That was the precarious, redeeming virtue in his simple holy mountain plan.

Professor Broadson zipped up his thermal jacket, strapped on his backpack and prepared his frost-bitten mind for the long trek back down to Pokhava.

Outside the dark cave and into the blinding light, he eased gingerly onto the old bridge. Weeks of consternation were behind him now. The world was safe again, at least, for a while. It was time to go home.

He took a single step onto the old catwalk. Immediately, the bottom suspension vine snapped. The sudden shift in weight sent a powerful whiplash through the system, ripping the stabilizing pegs from the ground on the opposite side and slamming the hapless contraption against the rocks beneath his feet. In a split second of ill-fated providence, Professor Broadson found himself clinging to the splintered rope, tied three hundred years ago to the rotten wooden pegs in front of the cave.

Though stunned and frightened and losing his grip, Professor Broadson never veered from his uncanny sense of reasoning and scientific deduction. He quickly realized his weighty backpack, which contained his only rations and survival tools, was an agent of death, dragging him further down the slippery rope.

Lose the weight, he told himself. *Lose it or die.*

He wriggled his left shoulder, allowing the sturdy nylon straps to slip into the folds of both arms. Finally, he mustered the courage to release his left hand, completely freeing the strap from his arm.

The backpack's shifting weight yanked him further down the rope. He quickly removed his right hand, and then gazed in silent horror as the bulky container tumbled into the dark gray abyss.

He was now dangling an exasperating three feet below the icy ledge. The more he dangled, the more he realized his fifty-two year old flabby frame demanded much more tenacity than his frail fingers had to give. If he was going to make a move, he needed to make it now.

The mind is a terrible thing to waste....

He suddenly recalled the familiar slogan from his many years as regional sponsor and fundraiser for the United Negro College Fund in Missouri. Like a complex, all-knowing, ever-vigilant vault, the mind retained every life experience and every thought. At that moment, Professor Broadson's mind regurgitated a forgotten scene from his childhood, a transformative moment that had changed his life.

At six years old, fragile, fearful and struggling to make sense of the world around him, Professor Broadson had fallen out of his small tree house in the backyard. Lying there on the ground, he had moaned and cried and sworn never again to go back into his deadly playhouse. But his father made him go. He stood there with a thick belt in his hand and demanded young Timothy grab the flimsy rope ladder and climb back up the tree.

It was the longest, most painful climb Professor Broadson had ever made. But he made it. He did what he was sure he couldn't do. Now it was time to do it again.

It required every ounce of his waning strength to shimmy up the rope and onto the icy ledge. But like the timid six-year-old who didn't have a choice, he did what he had to do.

Once inside the cave, he allowed his racing heart to simmer. Although it took a while to collect his thoughts, they soon became crystal clear.

No one was going to find him inside the remote ice walls of the Himalayas. That's why he had chosen the sacred cave in the first place. He had no rations. Eventually, he would freeze from the bitter cold or starve like an abandoned dog. He was trapped in a frigid skyscraper of death. And there was no way out.

Except....

He looked at the copper trunk and turned away. He had promised himself after the *Le Joola* ferry disaster in Africa never to use the chest again. But how long would it take before the ravaging pains of his bloated stomach or his frostbitten toes, breaking off one at a time, changed his mind?

He thought about it for a long time. He would do what he had to do. He stood up, walked to the mouth of the cave, closed his eyes and sailed outward, into the bone-chilling sky.

"Do not follow where the path may lead. Go, instead, where there is no path and leave a trail."

-Ralph Waldo Emerson-

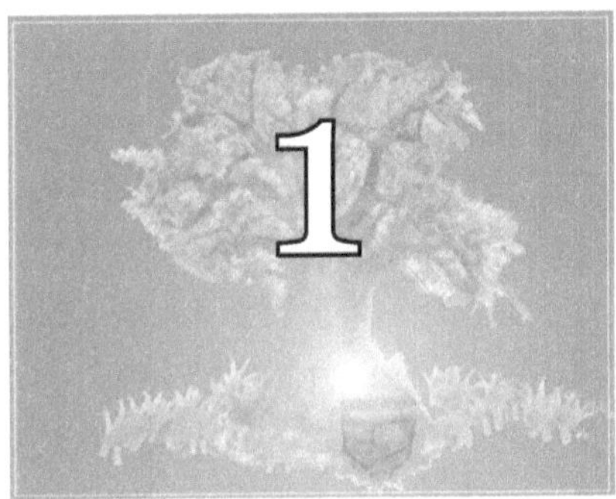

Lola had to face reality. The big yellow machine was out of control. Like her famous boxing uncle from Guadalajara, Jesus "Hitman" Becerra, the hydraulic boom on the old Caterpillar backhoe had gone into a zone ... a wild killing zone, bouncing and growling and landing vicious hay-makers on everything in its reach.

One lick from the two-ton, jagged-mouth front loader bucket reduced a brand new electrical transformer into a mangled mass of angry sparks and scorched metal. Another wild swing took out the building's stately white columns, vaulted entryway and red brick exterior. Finally, the gigantic boom slammed into a nearby aluminum light pole, unleashing a hailstorm of shattered glass on Emilio's wheelbarrow, water buckets and lucky coyote gardening hat. The pudgy, panic-stricken landscaper and three-man crew quickly abandoned their green thumb duties in courtyard's lovely geranium beds to run for their lives.

The large blue sign in front of the construction site still read: FUTURE HOME OF COLONIAL HEIGHTS ASSISTED LIVING.

It was the second two lines that had suddenly become a lie:
ANOTHER OUTSTANDING PROJECT
BY ALLEN BROTHERS CONSTRUCTION.

Lola didn't panic. In the scheme of things, what was a mere two hundred ton, thirty-foot steel boom and claw mouth bucket swinging recklessly in the wind? During her twenty-six chaotic years in two countries, five cities and four states, she had managed to escape from the ruthless *Zetas* cartel in Juárez, elude immigration officials in Arizona, eat out of the fancy hotel food dumpsters in San Diego, coexist with rats and roaches in the condemned *colonias* of New Mexico and dodge repeated blows from an abusive, carjacking, paint-sniffing boyfriend in Amarillo. If life had taught her anything, it was that timid crybaby whiners didn't get very far. Back in Mexico, her little sister had been one. And now she was dead.

For Lola, exploding transformers and crumbling brick walls served as a wake-up call to her brain, an encrypted code that triggered her robotic, trance-like, hyper-analytic, self-induced methodical mode. With one smooth motion, she locked the dipperstick, killed the hydraulics and leaped off the grungy machine like a sturdy cowgirl dismounting an angry bull. She walked a few steps to the edge of the construction site and flipped out her cell phone. Tiny Johnny was the first number on her speed dial.

"Daddy, I don't want to tell you but I screwed up bad this time." She confessed her sins with a heavy Spanish accent. "Can you come and get me?"

She already knew the answer. Tiny Johnny was always at her beck and call ... that is, unless he was up in Chicago, breaking bones for the mob or delivering a shipment of methamphetamines to distributors down south.

If all went well, he'd be there in thirty minutes, just enough time for Lola to grab her metal lunch kit, rubber boots and bright orange safety vest from the storage shed. These would be her personal mementos from eleven months of anguish and hardship and a payday Friday that had suddenly been flushed to hell.

A slow stampede of wide-eyed construction workers congregated in front of the building and gawked at the damage. They spoke in "panic Spanish", the same incoherent gibberish they would use to try to explain what had happened and proclaim their total lack of involvement in the matter. They would try to explain. But only Lola could tell the whole story.

Of course, she wouldn't tell the whole story, not a single tearful explanatory word of it. By the time the Allen brothers returned from their loansharking exploits at the Marina, she'd be long gone.

Spoiled, greedy, manipulating gringo bastards.

The whole ordeal had started when the two blonde-haired, sun-baked Texas twin owners loaded all of the Mexican laborers and one trailer-trash white man named Goodboy into their two diesel crew cabs and headed up to Lake Lou Yaeger's Marina to cash their checks. Though they brainwashed everyone into believing the trip was a courtesy to the workers, it was nothing more than a sleazy ploy to make sure the financially strapped wetbacks paid off the high-interest loans the brothers had extended during the week.

Before leaving, one of the brothers, Morris "Gator" Allen, known for his fancy alligator cowboy boots, had made a lewd comment about Lola's breasts.

"Little water cups," he had called them.

With the exception of Goodboy who never made fun of her, the entire truckload of spineless migrants hooted and howled and back-slapped to their boss' approval. It was more than the perpetual hazing she had come to expect as the only female employee at the job site. This time it was personal.

In the past few weeks, Gator had twice asked her to meet

him after work for drinks. Twice, she had turned him down. Now it was his turn to dish out some Texas-style retribution, a crude, well publicized calf-branding session in which she was the only little ornery heifer on the list.

Stupid, juvenile, womanizing, gringo bastard.

Everyone who hadn't lost their eyesight to a nail gun or hot roof tar or some kind of banned chemical pesticide most construction companies used in spite of the law, could see his off-colored remarks were nothing more than a sour grapes vendetta. Although she was not in the same league as the strip club floozies that rocked the Allen brothers' little white trailer two or three lunch hours a week, she could hold her own. Men still gawked at her short curvy body and glazed brown eyes. Her dark smooth face, framed in a bushel of silky black shoulder-length hair, was an intriguing puzzler to most suitors trying to pin her true origin. Was she Mexican, Indian, Pakistani? They all wanted to know.

Born in Juárez, she was Mexican of sorts, fluent in Spanish but surprisingly adept in English, compliments of the local *Lady of Guadalupe* English-speaking program her great Aunt Conchita managed in San Elizario. Even without her bilingual prowess, there was something different about her, something that made her stand out from her other siblings.

She was twelve when her mother finally told her. "Your real father is *un hombre Negro*. I met him while your Papa Jose was in prison."

Lola's American father was Tiny Johnny, a flashy young Chicago street hustler, trying to make a name for himself. He had followed a Latino bail jumper across the border into the dangerous Juárez underground. There, he had met Ruby, a beautiful young street vendor selling flowers outside the Radisson Hotel Casa Grande.

The sultry two-week affair was never intended to bolster international race relations. No multicultural committee monitored their palpitating hearts. As Johnny and Ruby danced under the moonlight on a Rio Grande party boat, rode mules along the beautiful Tarahumara Canyons and raced back to his hotel room for another drunken night of margaritas, it never occurred to them they were altering history, adding a new name to the universal roles. It was just an affair, an unexpected misadventure facilitated by Johnny's ridiculous attempt at international sign language and Ruby's enduring smile. That's how Lola had come into the world.

Nine months later, Ruby had mailed photos of baby Lola to Johnny's Chicago apartment. He never saw them, however. Peaches Vastine, a wild-eyed, psychotic hairdresser who had recently moved in with him, intercepted the letter and threw the photos in the fireplace.

When Johnny didn't respond, Ruby took that to mean he wanted nothing to do with the baby. When Ruby didn't call or employ her sister, Conchita, to write any more letters, Johnny took that to mean Ruby's husband was out of prison and all bets were off.

It had taken twenty-six years for the true story to unfold. Lola had inadvertently been the ... *unfolder.*

As soon as she reached America, she had begun searching for her father. A disconnected number and an old Christmas card had eventually led her to Litchfield, Illinois, a quiet, dead-end city just south of Springfield.

Even in Litchfield, Johnny had been impossible to locate.

One night outside a small restaurant where Lola worked as a part time waitress, he approached her. "I hear you were over at BIG EASY Burgers asking questions about me. Unless you some kinda underground census taker, you best have a good reason why."

She should've been intimidated by his dark, minicing eyes and towering frame. Instead, she stepped toward him. "I am your lost daughter, your Juárez child. I had to find you, *sí*? I had to find me in you, *sí*?"

Her mother had warned her about Johnny's suspicious

nature, his preoccupation with the sleazy con games of life. Knowing this, Lola insisted on a blood test to set his mind at ease.

Yet, long before the results came back, Johnny already knew. The keen instincts he trusted to keep him alive whispered to the innermost crevices of his mind. The unmistakable familiarily in her round face and hazel brown eyes stirred a sense of rejoicing in his battered spirit. No blood test had to convince him. Johnny knew she was his child.

When he found out her paint-sniffing ex-boyfriend had followed her from Amarillo, Johnny moved her into his apartment right away. A few weeks later, the harassing phone calls stopped and the boyfriend ... disappeared.

Lola was quite certain Johnny could make Gator Allen disappear too. But it just wasn't worth it. After her disastrous, ten minute career as a Caterpillar backhoe operator, she was done with the Allen brothers, done with the daily catcalls, degrading work assignments and condescending remarks. Soon, Johnny would be there to take her away from the hell hole she had endured for eleven agonizing months.

There was just one more thing she needed to do.

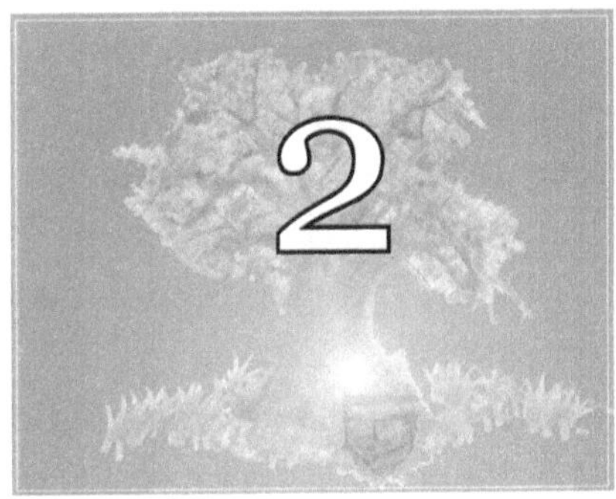

Before she left Juárez, Lola's mother had taught her many rules about life. At night when the drug cartels clashed and the gun battles reached their street, she and her two sisters were to dive on the floor, close their eyes and say three Hail Marys so the Saints of heaven would surround them. Although he was much younger, her brother received explicit instructions to lay across them in case a stray bullet came through the walls. On Sundays, when they visited their Aunt Conchita's house for dinner, they were to always arrive thirty minutes late. At the table, they should keep both hands in plain sight and leave some food on the plate as a show of good graces. At the market, girls were never to greet other girls with a handshake, but rather, extend an affectionate pat on the right forearm or shoulder.

There was another unbreakable rule her mother had taught them to follow. If ever a stranger performed a good deed on their behalf, they were to give him or her a small gift, perhaps, some flowers or a card. At the very least, they should offer a blessing of thanksgiving through the sign of the cross.

Goodboy was that deserving stranger, the only coworker who treated her with respect and intervened on her behalf. She would leave him a note and maybe some flowers from the assorted beds of blue poppies and white geraniums Emilio's landscaping crew had just set in the ground. That way, when the exaggerated accounts of her destructive nature finally subsided, he would remember her gratefulness. This would be her final obligatory deed, an epistle of thanks and goodbye, hidden beneath his spare blue overalls in the dressing shed.

Finding her way to the rear of the building, away from the swelling crowd of onlookers, past a line of dump trucks and mixers and toward the smelly portipotties that guarded the dressing shed, Lola paused along the gravel walking track to survey the narrow creek below.

Crystal Creek.

They named it for its pristine waters and sparkling reflection against the noonday sun. One day the elderly residents of Colonial Heights would hobble along its banks, admiring its sleepy oak trees and dark green lily pads. Its peace and tranquility would fill them with thoughts of eternal rest, forever hiding them from the miseries of life and cloaking their weary days in the hemlocks of nature's sacred place.

In the distance they would see a few scattered mounds of dirt and random dredges into the rich, black soil. They would speculate about those shallow pits, offer a few preposterous theories for their mysterious origin. And then as the thick underbrush swallowed the landscape, the old timers would completely forget the mysterious holes were there.

But Lola would never forget. Those shallow pits represented her sacred training ground, the place where her hopes for a better life had arisen ... and now were buried. They had been her reason to endure another day of scorn and heckling and fabricated accounts of her incompetence. Now, they were nothing more than a graveyard of memories and the future that could have been.

She stood there with churning emotions, remembering how it had all begun.

Three months earlier, on a rainy, wind-chilled morning, Lola had sat on the edge of the creek bed, crying her eyes out. Her clothes were soaked and dirty. Her hair was full of mud.

Goodboy had walked over and taken a seat on the wooden bench next to her. "It's lunchtime, Lola. Why aren't you eating?"

Without saying a word, she had handed him her lunch kit. Opening it, he had found a clump of angry red critters crawling around inside.

As it turned out, she had been the victim of the work crew's perpetual boyish pranks. Someone had gone into the shed, found her container and dumped a small mound of fire ants on top of her tamales.

Goodboy strolled over to the creek, dumped the tamales and dipped the container into the crystal flowing waters. When he returned, the kit bore an immaculate silver gleam.

"Here you are, good as new." He placed his own Philly cheesesteak sandwich inside the kit and set it on the bench beside her.

She shook her head vehemently. "I no need it no more. I quit! I quit today!"

"You can't let them get the best of you, not behind a silly lunch prank."

"You think it is just the lunch?" She pointed to her orange safety vest, drying out on a nearby rock. "Look at my clothes. Look at my face. Look at my hair."

He smiled gently. "I have to admit. Right now you probably wouldn't win my vote for homecoming queen. But you have to remember, Lola. You are the flagman ... well, flag woman. Standing out there on the highway in this kind of weather is going to take its toll."

"I do not mind the weather. Bringing the big trucks into the site is my job. But is it my job to stand there while they throw mud and water buckets at me whenever they pass by?"

He dropped his head. "I'm so sorry, Lola."

"They yell at me, call me names. Why do they hate me so?"

He paused a long while, pressing his thoughts with compassion. "I'll tell you. But first you have to stop crying. Never let the enemy know they've gotten the best of you."

Lola took a few moments to regain her composure.

Goodboy explained, "They hate you because you're a woman earning the same wage as a man."

"You don't think I deserve $7.50 for the hour?"

"I think you deserve more, with all the crap you take. But these men see themselves as breadwinners for the family. You're not a man. You don't have a family to take care of. In their minds, you don't deserve to be paid the same."

"So a woman should not want to get ahead? She should stay home and have the babies and wait for the man to bring the $7.50 check to them?"

"Something like that," he confirmed.

"Then they are stupid men, Goodboy. They are very small stupid men."

He nodded. "We certainly have a history of that."

"I don't care what they think. I want to get ahead. Can you tell me how?"

An older man with tattered overalls, mangled reddish hair and a perpetually stubble chin, Goodboy was not like the others. He was white, but kept a safe distance from the white chauvinistic *gringo* pigs that ran the place. Obviously poor and often needing a shower, he never acted *poor*, not like the classless migrants that danced a jig whenever they were told. He kept a low profile and did his job. As the only certified backhoe operator on site, no one did it better.

On that rainy day by the creek, with a mischievous sparkle in his eyes, Goodboy had made her a promise. "If you're willing to learn, I'll teach you a valuable skill."

That's how Lola ended up pushing buttons and pulling levers inside the big yellow machine.

In hopes of sniffing out new business, each Wednesday the Allen brothers drove over to the Chamber of Commerce business luncheon in Springfield. With both owners away, Lola and Goodboy arranged their own covert luncheon, an intense one hour session on the far side of the hill. Obstructed from view by the thick brush and sloping landscape, the grassy knoll adjacent to the creek became the perfect training ground.

In order to observe Lola's secret apprenticeship in action, her small minded antagonistic coworkers would have to forsake their pushing and shoving ritual in front of the food trucks, blow through their spicy Tex-Mex fajitas and chicken corn wraps and abandon their after-meal card games and bloated *Cantina* stories.

Such an unthinkable heresy was simply not going to happen, not for the sake of investigating the distant growl of a diesel engine and some dumb *tonto*, working through the lunch hour. Lola's secret was safe ... safe with Goodboy, safe with Crystal Creek and safe with Little Blue.

Little Blue.

That was the name Goodboy had given the company's little blue and white four-cylinder, eighty-six horse power, thirty thousand pound turbocharged Komatsu excavator. Compared to the big yellow Caterpillar 5130 which weighed in at four hundred thousand pounds, Little Blue was a baby.

Yet, for twelve glorious Wednesdays, it was her baby. She caressed its levers and throttles and floor pedals by day; stumbled through its complicated English instruction manual by night. In her dreams, she would often hear Goodboy's gruff voice, barking out instructions with military precision. *Stabilizers down! Stick in! Boom up! Stay at grade!*

On the seventh Wednesday she had finally managed to dig the perfect hole ... perfect dimensions, perfect grade, perfect allotment of time. Goodboy had rewarded her with a musky hug and a blue icy from the food truck. Though they watched from afar, none of the spineless workers had been able to figure out Lola's reason for celebration. That had made her triumph all the more rewarding.

Now, standing on the ridge, overlooking the creek, she spotted her perfect hole in the distance. It was a beautiful black rectangle, a gift box without a top. She would tell her story to Johnny, and in a letter to her mother and Aunt Conchita back in Mexico. But without seeing her magnificent accomplishment, they would never understand.

And then it dawned on her. They *could* see it. Perhaps, she could make them understand.

She flipped out her cell phone again, turned on the powerful sixteen megapixels camera and headed down the ridge.

A few minutes later, she stood over the hole. It was still a perfect twelve yards long and six yards wide; but much deeper than she remembered. Staring down into the dark, grave-like chasm brought back painful memories, terrible thoughts she had tried to erase from her mind. Suddenly, she became nauseated and had to back away.

This is not that place of death, she told herself. *This is your perfect hole.*

With time running out, she finally stepped forward again.

She had snapped a couple of wide angle pics before she discovered it ... the remnants of an object, square-edged and shiny, bulging ominously from the thick clay.

Her natural curiosity prodded her forward. But further investigation required a five foot woman to climb down into a six foot trench with unbraced walls and a slippery, implausible climb back to the surface. Of course, there were snakes in the hole. She had heard the men talking. Every hole near the creek was a water moccasin haven. Sometimes a hundred of the slimy creatures wrapped around each other in a mating orgy. They would not take kindly to being disturbed.

Lola was fully aware of the inherent dangers of construction work. At a construction site in Atlanta, a distant cousin had been working under a house when the jacks collapsed and crushed him like a pancake. A few weeks earlier in nearby Hillsboro, another Latino worker had been run over by a bulldozer. At $7.50 an hour, it just wasn't worth the risk.

That's when she spotted the carpenter's ladder propped against a small utility shack. The ladder should have been locked up with the rest of the tools. But there it was in plain sight, fifty yards away, accessible to anyone who needed it.

Could it be a sign from God?

The priest always said that God worked in mysterious ways.

With so much carnage in front of the building, the Allen brothers would surely keep her paycheck for the week. Maybe, whatever was down there in her perfect hole would make up for the wages she would never see.

Time was running out. The Allen brothers would soon return from the Marina. All hell was going to break loose.

She dashed up the ridge and across the gravel walking track. She grabbed the light weight aluminum ladder and returned to the hole.

Her descent into the darkness was horrifying. A stiff nausea engulfed her soul, so much worse than before. She closed her eyes until both feet were firmly planted. And then she waited to feel the sharp fangs of a hundred deadly moccasins, striking through her leather boots.

Nothing. Just the muted silence and black walls closing in on her.

With trembling fingers and a pounding heart, she plowed into the clay. Slowly, she unearthed an old Birchwood steamer trunk trimmed in black vinyl with a rusty copper plate across the top. Snapping open the corroded latches, she peeked inside.

To her surprise, a smaller chest hibernated inside the larger trunk. The adorable little box was about fifteen inches long and ten inches deep. There were three silver bands across the top and two silver latches on the front.

Unlike the old rusted trunk, the small chest was far more decorative, with embossed corners, hand-painted animals, flowing rivers and husky tree trunks. Between the two silver latches, within a circle of Roman and Hebrew inscriptions, two Egyptian kings sat gracefully upon their thrones. An eerie elongated African mask rose above their miniature kingdom, as if having power and dominion over the kings, themselves.

Although the small iron padlocks on both latches prevented her from looking inside, the fact that the chest was locked reassured Lola of its value. She tucked the fancy box under her arm and scooted up the ladder. A mad dash to the storage shed to leave her goodbye note and secure her other mementos, and she would be long gone.

The birds took flight in horror. A family of stray beavers retreated to their underwater den. The ground beneath the parking lot quaked and trembled, as if a thousand kettle drums terrorized its porous asphalt skin.

Tiny Johnny was in the house.

As Lola rounded the corner of the building and scurried toward the main gate, the site of Johnny's fancy getaway machine invited her racing heart to simmer. Only a handful of day laborers from the landscaping company stood between her and her glorious escape from the Allen brother's torture chamber.

Lola was always amused to see her clueless cohorts, gawking with envy each time Johnny picked her up. Watching his shiny blue 1999 Cadillac Deville cruise into the parking lot, chrome wheels glistening and oversized Bose trunk woofers, spraying deadly shock waves through the air, everyone knew Lola's big black sugar daddy had arrived. Though his broad shoulders and thick razor-shaven head were an antonymic play on his name, his diamond earring and shiny Rolex made his profile a perfect fit for the dimwitted imagination of onlookers.

They had no idea the uppity young twenty-six year old Mexican *fulana*, jumping into the car with the forty-nine year old black candy man, was really the distorted visual of a father and daughter, carrying out a more elaborate plot.

Lola and her father wanted to move from their cramped apartment on the north side of Litchfield to a more spacious location, perhaps, a no-frills, single story starter home they could call their own. Johnny had more than enough for the down payment. But his untraceable cash income invariably flowed under the table. In order for the mortgage company to finance the loan, someone needed to have W-2 income for a minimum of twelve months, something the lender could trace back to a legitimate source. The lender didn't care about her $7.50 per hour. With a big enough down payment and a government subsidy to move families of Hispanic origin from rental apartments to homes, the lender was happy to push the deal through, no questions asked.

That's why Lola had taken the construction job in the first place. The Allen brothers needed at least one female at the job site to satisfy the State Labor Board and federal government's equal opportunity gender clause. Lola and her father needed at least one year of wage income to satisfy the mortgage company's lending requirements. Now, eleven months into the arrangement, with the front of the Colonial Heights facility in shambles and a pink slip on the horizon, Lola and her father would have to come up with a whole new scheme.

As Lola approached Johnny's Deville, the door of the Allen brother's construction trailer swung open. A hard-faced Mexican straw boss named Miguel stormed down the wooden ramp.

"Hey! Hey! *Esperar!* Wait one damn minute," he shouted. "Where do you think you're going with that equipment?"

Lola clutched her rubber boots, safety vest, lunch kit and

fancy chest tightly in her overloaded arms. "This no equipment. This my stuff. This belong to me."

"Says who?" he pressed.

"I paid for it," Lola insisted. "They take the money out of my check."

Miguel was fully aware of the policy. Each worker had to pay for his own safety hat, boots and in her case, vest. Still, he persisted. "Maybe you did. Maybe you didn't. The point is nothing leaves this job site unless Mr. Gator say its okay."

Johnny killed the engine and got out slowly, a subtle limp from an old gunshot wound in his leg. He walked around the front of the car and stood between Lola and Miguel. "Is there a problem?"

"You see it, plain and simple. She try to steal company property," declared Miguel.

Lola shook her head. "I no steal nothing, Daddy. This is my property. They take the money out of my check."

"Is that true?" Johnny's stare was ice cold.

"This does not matter," Miguel defended. "It is still company property until the boss say different."

Johnny took a short step forward. "Then I have another question for you about property. When I hang my foot up your ass, will these new Stacy Adams loafers still be my property, or will they belong to you?"

Miguel started to back peddle. "I-ah, I don't want no trouble, *amigo*."

"Maybe, you shoulda thought about that before you called her a liar and a thief."

Lola grabbed Johnny by the arm. "No, Daddy. We must go."

"Somebody needs to teach these people some respect around here."

Lola couldn't have agreed more. But as she spotted the

Allen brother's pickup trucks coming down the highway, she realized the lessons would have to wait for another day.

Johnny helped her load the curious bundle into his trunk. "What's all this crap? Some kinda fire sale?"

"I explain to you later, Daddy. But now we need to go. *Apresurar!*"

****

A few miles down the highway, he shook his head disgustedly. "So you wrecked that big Caterpillar tracker trying to show them you got skills?"

"I no wreck the tracker. I knocked down the light pole and the wall. And *si*, they must know I can do more than fill up water buckets and flag trucks on the highway."

"You think they don't already know?"

She paused, "I do not understand?"

"You'd better understand if you expect to survive on this side of the border," he warned. "But hold that thought for now. I got some other business calling for my undivided attention."

Johnny whipped his blue Deville around a corner and into BIG EASY Burgers, the local greasy spoon cafe where he and Lola had first met. He skidded to a tire-squealing hault in the drive-thru lane and shouted into the speaker.

"Hey, give me one of them triple meats with a lot of Cajun spice and onions and hot pepper fries. I'm hungry and I'm mad. But I'll deal with the mad later."

A familiar baritone voice came over the speaker. "Is that you, Johnny? I need to know so I can double the price."

"Bumpy, you New Orleans shyster. Don't start nothing and I just might let you live another day."

"Cool. I was about to add a free drink to wash down those pepper fries, but since you've got a bad attitude..."

"Johnny quickly acquiesced. "Ahh, you know I got nothing but love for you, my man."

"That's better. Now you need to teach your Chicago Bears to suck up to my Saints like that. Maybe they'd win a few games."

"Now you've started some mess. Let me tell you about your dirty cheap-shot Saints."

Bumpy crumbled a loud paper bag in the microphone, drowning out Johnny's response.

"I can't hear you, sir. Is that all you're having today, sir? Please speak up."

Johnny looked over at Lola. "You want a burger from this fool?"

"No. And you should no want it too. This is bad for your blood pressure."

To drown out her nagging, Johnny started to sing an old slavery song: "NOBODY KNOWS THE TROUBLE IZZ SEEN, NOBODY KNOWS BUT JESUS...."

Bumpy quickly realized his incessant bag rustling was no match for Johnny's discordant, off-key serenade.

"Don't know if you're singing or throwing up in my drive. Either way, it's bad for business. Pull up to the window with your $9.55 in hand so I can get you off my property."

A few minutes later, weaving in and out of traffic, Johnny chomped on his greasy burger.

"Like I was telling you, these white folks ain't crazy. They hire Mexican laborers because when it comes to construction, you're the hardest working people in show business. You work these suicide jobs from sun up to sun down for little or nothing. And if they teach you something worthwhile, they know you'll soak it in and be good at it."

"Those scumbags no teach me nothing! Goodboy teach me what I know. Not them."

"Because that's not your purpose. You've been with me almost two years and ain't learned diddly-squat."

"I learned a lot from you, Daddy. You help me study for my GED. You send me to classes at the community college. You teach me about the trails...."

"*Streets!* I'm teaching you about the streets," he corrected her.

"*Si*, the streets," she corrected herself. "But now what do you teach me?"

"About life, Babygirl, and knowing your purpose."

Johnny stuffed a few pepper fries into his mouth, then guzzled his drink. Finally, he told her the story of his older brother, ArchieV.

"Back in the day, maybe '69 or '70, the government was putting the clamps on these companies to hire some Niggahs. They gave it a pretty name: *Affirmative Action*. In other words, we affirm we've been screwing black folks to the wall for a long time. Now we gotta take some action."

Lola frowned. "How you mean to the wall?"

"Locking us out of the system. Paying us substandard wages. Making sure we couldn't move up. Keeping our backs to the wall."

"This is what they do to me," she whined.

"Pay attention. This story is not about you, at least, not right now."

"Okay, I listen to your story."

Johnny continued. "Straight out of Grambling State, ArchieV got a job at a big oil company in Dallas. Glass office, secretary, nice piece of change. You know what he was doing?"

"What?"

"Not a damn thang. They had him in that glass office to be seen and not heard; a token Niggah, just in case the government people came by. That was his purpose, knowemsayin'?"

"I don't want that purpose," she protested.

"He didn't, either. He kept trying to get in the mix, writing these reports, speaking out in meetings on how to improve the company, just Powerpointing his skills to the good ole boys in charge."

"What happened to him?"

"They got rid of his ass ... got themselves a new Niggah, a cowardly, foot-shuffling Niggah with a better attitude; somebody who understood his purpose."

"Screw that job, Daddy. I don't want to shuffle. I find me a new purpose."

He grinned precociously. "Yeah, I guess you will, now that you've trashed the whole damn job site."

"I'm sorry I messed up the plan for our new house."

"Don't worry about it. We'll find another way."

"Maybe I get a better job with my new skill, yes?"

"New skill?" Johnny finished off the last of his burger.

"*Si*. I no tell you, but I've been practicing." She pulled out her phone to show him her perfect hole. "Goodboy told me I will make good money this way. And then we will get our house."

He eyed the photo with approval and then began to laugh. "Good job, Babygirl. But from what you've told me, I think your future is headed in only one direction."

"What's that, Daddy?"

"Mexican demolition."

"You not funny, Daddy." Lola tried desperately to hold back her laughter. But as she imagined the panic-stricken look on Gator Allen's faces, she let out a loud cackle and continued all the way home.

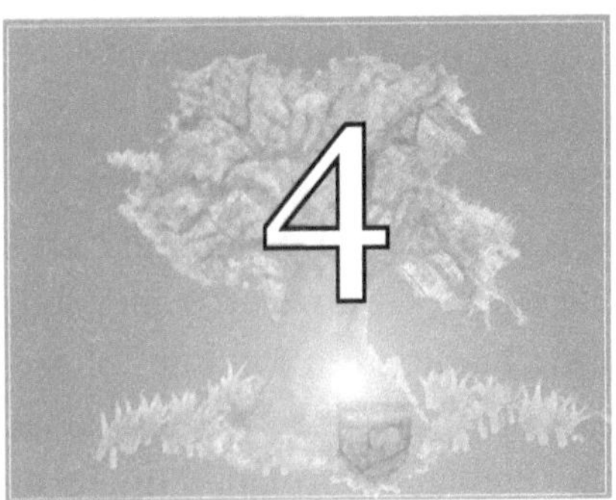

Ten minutes later, Johnny wheeled into the parking lot across the street from their apartment. Retrieving his fancy Samsung Android cell phone from the center armrest, he dialed the security company, punched in an elaborate passcode and began reviewing live streaming video of the entire apartment.

He turned to Lola. "Did you leave your closet door open this morning?"

She thought about it. "Maybe. I was kinda in a rush."

"Babygirl, if I've told you once, I've told you a hundred times."

"I know, I know. Close every door before you leave."

"If you know, why don't you do?" he scolded her. "And stop leaving those jelly bean packages all over the counter. You want to invite the neighbor's roaches to our place?"

Lola loved jelly beans. They seemed to calm her nerves. In a rush, she'd grab a few cellophane mini-packs to stuff in her pockets for class. The rest of them invariably ended up on the counter, waiting for her to clean up when she returned home.

"Sorry, Daddy. I be more careful next time."

Johnny took a few extra minutes to make sure nothing else appeared questionable or out of place ... a kitchen drawer left open or rug flapped over at the edge. He knew where everything was supposed to be. The slightest rearrangement was sure to catch his eye.

Eventually, he exited the screen, punched in a few more codes and summoned a special green screen with red squares. Each square displayed a still shot of designated areas in and around the apartment: the parking lot, stairwell, outer hallway and courtyard. Each still was time stamped, allowing Johnny to know the exact minute of the day an intruder ... he called everyone an intruder including the other tenants ... invaded his space.

This was his daily ritual, strictly adhered to each time he went out. His strategically placed network of security cameras kept him abreast of any suspicious activities around the small complex. For Johnny, *suspicious* had one definition: sent by the mob.

Over the years, Johnny had done a ton of work for the Chicago Mafia. Although he wasn't a hit man in the true sense, he had killed before. One of the men he had killed was Little Vinnie "Meatball" DiVarco, a popular member of the mob's adult bookstore operation. A misunderstanding about some counterfeit plates led to a shootout between the two. Johnny got hit, but Vinnie got dead. The word on the street was that Vinnie's boss, Joey the Clown, had put out a contract on Johnny, a grim prospect that kept him looking over his shoulder and living underground.

Johnny didn't take any chances, the only reason he was still alive. If a man wanted to keep breathing with a killing machine on his trail, he needed to find a faster machine that gave him an edge. Technology was that faster machine. The cutting edge assortment of cameras and relays and remote wifi controllers kept him alive.

After examining still shots of the postman, maintenance man, pizza delivery girl, FedEx driver and other familiar intruders going about their daily task, he turned off the screen.

"It's all good," he assured Lola as they pulled across the street and through the gate. They parked beneath the aluminum carport and headed up the narrow wooden steps.

Johnny's second floor apartment was a cramped two-bedroom shoe box with drab gray walls and a brown linoleum floor. The lighting was dim; the furniture, a combination of bargain basement throwbacks and flimsy leftovers from renters being evicted. Though Lola had hung a couple of Mexican bullfighter pictures on the walls, the place had a hardness to it, like a house that had never really become a home.

For Johnny, it was never intended to be a home. He had sent word to a Southside mob lieutenant, explaining his run-in with Vinnie, hoping to get back to Chicago under an official decree of amnesty. But in the shadowy world of Costa Nostra, one never knew if forgiveness was authentic or just a slow road to a bullet in the back of the head.

Johnny had decided to wait until Joey the Clown was either killed or arrested. Then, when the timing was right, he would plead his case again.

Safely inside the apartment, Lola guzzled a large glass of orange juice, then started toward her bedroom. "Don't forget. Tomorrow is your doctor's appointment. No more excuses."

"Yeah, yeah I hear you," he groaned, flopping into his leather arm chair in front of the television. He waited until she left the room, then poured himself a shot of Johnny Walker Red.

****

During the early morning hours, Lola tossed and turned, trying to wake up from a terrible dream. The Allen brothers had driven her to a wooded area below a steep hill and pushed her off the back of their pickup truck. As she ran through the brush trying to get back to civilization, two ferocious lions had begun to stalk her. She struggled to climb a concrete wall to get away from them, but kept slipping back down. Goodboy, who stood at the top of the wall, tried to pull her up with a tree limb, but to no avail.

As the two hungry lions stood over her, she awakened. Her pillow was wet with sweat. Yet, in her groggy, panic-stricken mind, she continued to hear the echo of their faint roar.

Dreams were a serious topic back home in Juárez. Her mother and Aunt Conchita often talked about the prophetic power they embodied. Though Lola had pretended to listen to them, in the back of her mind, she relegated their family discussions to folklore and superstition.

In a vision, Lola's grandfather had visited the place of the seven caves in Chicomostoc. Her uncle had seen the Virgin Mary in his back yard, releasing colorful butterflies. Her mother had heard the voice of God in the clouds. There was always some weird visitation or spiritual journey haunting the family tree. None of it added up to a hill of chili beans.

Lola flipped her pillow to the dry side and went back to sleep.

The next morning on the way to the doctor, Johnny barely made it across the railroad track before the crossing arms came down. A few minutes later, he swerved into the oncoming lane, then back again.

Lola pressed hard against her pounding chest. "What's wrong, Daddy?"

Johnny rubbed his tired, red eyes. "Didn't get much sleep last night."

"Worried about the appointment?"

"Not really. I mean, if this quack gives me a bad report, I'll just pistol whip every useless bastard in the whole freakin' clinic until they get it right."

She smiled at his perpetual tough-guy veneer. "Then why you no sleep?"

"I-ahhh, I don't know. Kept hearing these freakin' animals."

Lola's heart stopped. "A lion, maybe?"

"Lion, tiger, something. You heard it too?"

"Mine was a dream."

"Yeah, well mine was more like the city zoo in the parking lot. The lease says no exotic pets. But apparently some of these jokers never learned to read."

They finally pulled up in front of the small medical clinic in Springfield. Johnny pressed a console button to pop the trunk. "Get my brown folder. I've got special ID to keep this visit under wraps."

Lola jumped out of the Deville. Scouring inside the trunk, she realized she had forgotten about the fancy chest. She sniggled at the crude etchings of lions, tigers and elephants on the front. Maybe they were the restless creatures making the nocturnal fuss.

Inside the clinic, Johnny presented himself as Johnny Fountain. The fake Illinois drivers license was the best Lola had ever seen. After filling out a few forms, they called him to the back.

Lola stood up. "I want to come with you, Daddy."

"Oh, hell no. You think I want you back there when the doctor rams his elbow up my ... private parts?"

"Okay, but you tell him everything, *si*?"

"Yeah, yeah."

"You promise, *si*?" she persisted.

Everything meant his foamy urine laced with blood, the swelling in his bad leg, his shortness of breath when he climbed the stairs and the increased nausea whenever he ate solid foods.

"I'll tell him, okay." He finally disappeared behind the large cherry wood door.

With time on her hands, Lola's mind drifted back to the

fancy chest. She retrieved it from the trunk and took a seat in the corner of the crowded waiting room. Using a stray paper clip from the coffee table, she began picking at the iron padlocks.

She had tinkered with the chest a few minutes when a tall, blond lady with a sculptured movie star face sat down next to her.

"Are you a connoisseur of the arts?" The lady finally inquired.

Not knowing what *connoisseur* meant, Lola offered a bashful smile.

She pointed to the African mask on the front of the chest. "I believe I recognize that symbol. It's from one of the permanent exhibitions at the Museum."

Lola's face brightened. "This mask, you know it?"

"I'm pretty sure. And look at those exquisite green and brown etchings along the bottom. The color scheme is the same as the collection at the Springfield State Museum."

"You think it's worth a lot of money?" asked Lola.

"Well, I'm no expert. But I'm sure they could tell you. Do you know where the Museum is?"

"I'm not from here."

"And I don't remember the exact address," the lady confessed. "But here's what you can do."

She reached into her purse and pulled out a business card. "This is my son, Nicholas. He manages the hardware store right down the street from the Museum. He'll know the address."

A few minutes later, the woman faded behind the cherry wood door. Lola continued picking at the locks. For two hours she picked and pulled and shook the little box until Johnny reappeared.

He wasn't happy. He paid the clerk at the window $400 in cash and headed for the door.

"Mr. Fountain, you have some change coming," the young window clerk shouted.

He brushed his large hand through the air. "Don't worry

about it. Buy yourself a pretty black dress for my funeral."

They rode in silence for about twenty miles. Finally, she broke the ice. "You might as well tell me, Daddy. I won't leave you alone until you do."

"Two words, Babygirl ... kidney disease."

She paused a long time. "They will cure it, *si*?"

"Too late for that. They're telling me I need a transplant."

"Okay, so they transplant it, *si*?"

"*Si.* So long as you got a $120,000 for the transplant and another $44,000 for the maintenance. Do you have that, Babygirl? Because I sure don't."

"We will get the money. I know we will."

"From where? Out of thin air? Maybe some golden goose is gonna fall from the sky, or some Brinks truck driver is gonna dump his load at the bottom of our stairwell? How in the hell am I supposed to come up with that kinda money?"

"I, ahhh, I don't know yet. But we will."

"Well, until you do, I don't want to hear nothing about it, knowemsayin'? Keep your medical opinions to yourself."

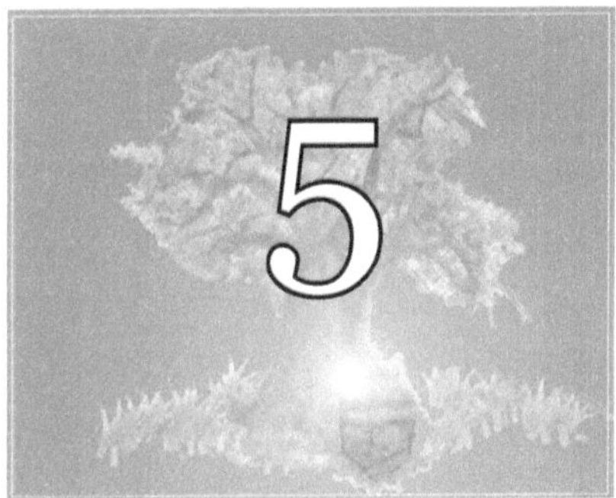

A whole week passed without either of them mentioning Johnny's deteriorating condition. Just as he had requested, she observed his bloated ankles, diminished appetite and multiple trips to the bathroom, but made a conscious decision to look the other way.

She dreamed of the diamonds and rubies and priceless gold coins waiting inside the fancy little chest, treasures that could rescue her father from his dreaded illness and give him a new lease on life. But no matter how hard she tried, the old padlocks wouldn't budge.

In a moment of frustration, Johnny offered to shoot them off with his .357 magnum. But she was afraid the damage might reduce the value of the chest, especially if there was nothing tangible inside.

One morning she awakened to Johnny's deep voice, bellowing into his cell phone. He paced the floor like a stockbroker on Wall Street, closing a big deal. When he finally hung up, he turned to her with a boyish smile. "I got a chance to make a hundred grand."

Because of his temporary split with the Chicago mob, he depended more heavily on assignments from his other clients. One of them was the notorious Jamaican Rude Boys, a Caribbean cartel far more ruthless than the mob. One slip up with them and they'd murder your entire family.

Johnny trusted a posse leader named Calypso. He was currently the cartel's point man for getting a Jamaican Diplomatic Ambassador's son, accused of being a drug mule, out of jail. The FBI agent in charge of the case was supposedly open to a $250,000 bribe. But because of so many recent FBI sting operations, no one was willing to meet with him face to face.

Johnny remembered the agent's name coming up years earlier, during several Southside mob deals. Long before he became a federal agent, the cocky Chicago street cop fraternized with underworld bosses and enjoyed the lavish perks of an insider. If anyone was legitimately dirty and open to a bribe, G.G. Stockman was. With that privileged historical information at his disposal, Johnny agreed to act as the Rude Boys' go-between.

"I'm leaving for New York tomorrow, Babygirl. If this goes well, the kidney thing is in the bag."

"But what if it no go well?" Lola's eyes watered with morbid speculation.

He shook his long, condemning finger at her. "You see. That's why I never got married."

She grabbed him around his waist. "Okay, okay, you say it go well. I say it go well. But you call me as soon as it go well. *Si*?"

That's a fair deal," he agreed. "But I need you to do something for me."

"I will do it. What is it, Daddy?"

He stroked her silky black hair. "Take care of yourself. I'm leaving you the car so you don't miss your classes at the college.

Don't go anywhere unless you have to. And if you go, keep your eyes open and follow the routine. Here are the new security codes. And remember, Babygirl. The cameras don't lie."

Johnny was a meticulous planner. He left her food, money, the Cadillac and instructions to keep her safe. Still, it was not enough to control her insatiable curiosity.

For the first few days, Lola followed her minimalist security routine to the letter. She went to class, did her homework, cleaned up the apartment, watched a few soccer matches, listened to English/Spanish tapes, wrote a letter to her mother in Mexico and cooked a new diet tortilla dish that tasted like cardboard. But by the end of the week, with summer classes over and no Allen brothers to antagonize her, Lola's curiosity ran wild. She called the number on the business card to get the address to the Springfield Museum.

"I don't know it off the top of my head," admitted Nicholas Hartman, son of the blonde lady Lola had met at the clinic. "But by the time you get here, I'll have it."

****

A few hours later, Lola entered Bishop Hardware's red brick building on Edwards Street in Springfield. A tall, slender white boy with blonde hair, pointy ears and a thin mustache stood behind the register. He was talking on the phone in a loud voice, while simultaneously whispering to a nearby employee.

"Yes, sir, that unit is the top of the line. It costs more, but it's going to last a lot longer," he said to the customer over the phone. And then he whispered to the employee, "Pull all of those bags off the shelf. There's a recall and we don't want our customers getting involved with that fiasco."

He eventually noticed Lola in her tight blue jeans and snugly fitting red blouse, standing in front of the counter. "I'll be with you in a minute."

Finally, he stepped from behind the counter and flashed a broad smile. He glanced at the fancy chest under her arm, then playfully announced, "If you're trying to exchange it, you're out of luck. We discontinued that model about four centuries ago."

"No. No exchange," responded Lola in a serious tone.

He chuckled. "Just giving you a hard time."

Lola final offered a reciprocal smile.

"May I see it?" he requested.

Lola slowly, reluctantly handed it over.

He studied it for a moment. "Mother was right. This does resemble the *Juba Collection.*"

"Juba?"

"Yes. King Juba II. He was a great King in Numidia, Africa. They have a standing exhibition of his artifacts at the Museum down the street." He reached into his shirt pocket and handed her a slip of paper with the address.

"So if this trunk belonged to a king, it must be worth lots of money, *si*?"

"Is that all you women ever think about?"

She smiled, sheepishly. "No. We think about how to spend it too."

Like high school steadies, they both began to giggle.

He held the chest up to the light. "Do you know what's inside? That would probably give us a clue about its true value."

"I no can get inside," she sadly confessed.

He tinkered with the padlocks a moment. "Come with me."

They made their way down a long aisle to a makeshift utility room at the back of the store. There were several different workstations with a variety of strange tools. One of the stations contained a huge set of bolt cutters with electric wires that extended from the handle and plugged into the wall.

"The locks are jammed with rust and corrosion. They'll have to be cut with these heat-inducing blades. Do you give me permission and promise not to sue?"

She nodded, affirmatively.

Though the old locks resisted, Nicholas managed to slice them in half. He lifted the silver latches, allowing Lola to peer inside.

Like anxious treasurer hunters, they both stood there a long time, staring at their loot. Finally, Lola started to cry.

She had spent days dreaming about the gold coins and precious jewels she would find inside. Now, all her teary eyes feasted upon was a musty pile of splintered wood. How was she going to pay for Johnny's transplant with useless chips of wood?

Nicholas gently draped his long arm across her shoulder. "Hey, don't throw in the chips so quickly."

When he said *chips*, Lola took another look at the wood and began to boo-hoo.

"Okay, okay, maybe that wasn't the best choice of words," he admitted. "But there's still hope."

"What hope do you see in rotten wood?" she whined.

He picked up a few pieces to examine. "First of all, it's not rotten. It's more like tree bark. And secondly, it may have nothing to do with the value of the chest."

She slowly perked up. "You think the chest is worth a lot by itself?"

"Maybe. Where did you find it?"

"In a hole."

"Can you be more specific?"

She shook her head. "No."

"Okay, there may be a problem."

"What problem you speak of?"

"If you go waltzing down to the Museum with a stolen

artifact, they might take it from you and then turn you over to the police."

"I no steal nothing!" she snapped.

"Calm down. I never said you stole anything. I'm just saying. Whether it's valuable or not, there may be a question of ownership."

"Then maybe I don't go to the Museum."

"Then maybe you'll never find out what it's worth." He paused for a brief moment. "Unless..."

He walked over to one of the cabinets and pulled out a digital camera. He took a picture of the chest and printed out a hard copy. "We'll show them this photograph. How can they arrest us behind a photograph?"

Handsome and clever too, Lola thought to herself.

They walked out of the store, deposited the chest into the trunk of the Deville and then headed toward the Museum.

Inside the towering marble walls and vaulted ceiling of the Springfield, Illinois State Museum, Lola discovered a phenomenal treasure trove of exhibits. Leading her down a long hallway, past the busy gift shop and exquisite collections of rare paintings, sculptures and photographs, Nicholas escorted her into a room filled with African artifacts. With a subtle sense of intrigue in his voice, he announced, "This is it. This is the mysterious collection."

The first thing Lola noticed was the ominous African mask with half closed eyes, towering from an overhang near the back wall. It was the same mask on her little chest and the backdrop for a series of glass cases that contained a variety of gold statues, spears, helmets, sarcophagi, coins and medallions, uncut diamonds and inscribed scrolls.

When she observed the small sculptured animals lining the green turf of one of the cases, chills ran down the back of her neck.

The lions were identical to those on her fancy chest and the splitting image of the two that had chased her in her dreams.

"I take it you're into the Juba thing." A distinguished baritone voice with a proper Boston accent clamored over their shoulders.

They turned to find a plump, ruddy faced man with red hair standing behind them. His protruding chest proudly displayed an official green museum badge.

"Yes, of course," said Nicholas. "But we'd like to learn more."

"Tell me what you know so far."

"I don't know nothing," Lola truthfully confessed.

"Ah, a rookie," he observed. "You're the best kind. Unfamiliarity opens the channels of possibility, don't you agree?"

The man began a long explanation of the exhibit's unique history.

The Lost Treasure of King Juba had been discovered in 1982 in a remote cave in southern Illinois by an obscure treasure hunter named Russell Burrows. The discovery had set off a firestorm in the archaeological community because it provided evidence that a little-known African tribe called the Mauretanians had come to America long before Columbus or any of the Viking explorers.

"In a way it finally explained the mystery of the Washitaws, an African tribe first encountered by the Lewis and Clark Expedition and many other explorers. These four thousand artifacts threatened to force historians to rewrite the history books and make Columbus take a back seat to the Mauretanians. Of course, it never happened that way."

"Why not?" asked Nicholas.

"Too much controversy. Too many naysayers and fault finders. Too many people wanting to hold on to a more familiar truth," he reported. "With so many accusations of fraud and historical manipulation, Burrows went back and sealed up the cave. I suppose it was his way of leaving us to our ignorance. What you see here is all we have left."

"Where is this Burrows man now?" asked Lola.

"I'm afraid he's quite deceased. You might say he took the secret of King Juba's Treasure to his grave."

Nicholas handed him the printout of the chest. "Is there anyone who can tell us about this?"

The man was visibly shaken. He walked over to one of the glass cases and compared the markings on the printout to several artifacts in the case. "Wh-Where did you get this?"

"Let's just say it came into our possession," Nicholas replied, coolly. "Can you tell us whether it's part of this King Juba Collection?"

He continued his meticulous comparison. "Could be. Could very well be. Of course, I'm not the expert."

"Do you know the expert?" Lola asked.

"That would be Professor Broadson, a former curator. He's responsible for our involvement with the collection. He actually spoke at great length to Russell Burrows before he died."

"Where is he?" pressed Lola.

"Oh, that's a hard question to answer. Since he retired from the university, he could be almost anywhere; India, France, Egypt. He does, however, come by from time to time."

"Can you get this picture to him?" asked Nicholas.

"No problem. He's an email junky. I'll just scan it in and send it to him. How can he reach you?"

Nicholas handed the museum official his business card. "Here's my number. I'm at the hardware store down the street."

"Very well. I'll pass it on."

A few minutes later, Lola and Nicholas stood outside the hardware store next to Johnny's Cadillac.

"Fancy set of wheels you got there," observed Nicholas. "I guess your husband keeps you riding in style."

I'm not married," she happily reported. "This car belongs to Daddy."

"Wow. That's a relief. Usually, every time I find myself interested in someone, she's already taken."

He's interest in me, Lola thought to herself, her heart, racing with anticipation.

"Would it be out of place if I offered to buy you lunch?"

"*Si.*" She waited a long time, allowing his disappointment to set in. And then she added. "Because you have helped me, I should buy your lunch."

She reached into her pocket to pull out a couple of crisp one hundred dollar bills.

"Rich AND beautiful!" He announced his glowing assessment of her. And then, he looked up toward the clear blue sky. "Oh God, if I'm dreaming, please don't wake me up."

In a dark alley off West 42nd Street, a few miles from the Lincoln Tunnel, Tiny Johnny was in trouble. He could smell it with his invisible nose. He had spent a week setting up the details of the payoff to the rogue FBI agent, G.G. Stockman. But now seeing the muscular white man in the dark suit, sporting a crew cut, horn-rimmed glasses and red cashmere scarf, Johnny realized that everything was unraveling right before his eyes.

He had met with Calypso at the Hilton Times Square Hotel in Manhattan. The Jamaican cartel leader had given him $250,000 for the FBI agent and another $50,000 in advance toward his fee. Johnny would receive the remaining $50,000 when the Diplomat's son was released.

With cold, staring eyes, pushing out from a maze of dreadlocks, Calypso had warned him. "Here is de problem, my friend. This case is on de FBIman's desk. This guy can spit on de folder and let de bwoy go free. But next week de guy is retiring. A new FBIman will be at that desk."

"I understand." Johnny had tried to reassure him.

"No, I want to express myself in a way you truly understand," Calypso insisted. "De people I represent do not play. If we fail to get de money to this FBIman in time, we are dead men. If this FBIman, he takes de money and does not release de bwoy, we are dead men. If we get our wings clipped in some kind of undercover scam, don't bodda to cry. They think we will talk. In jail, in prison; they will find us. We are dead men."

When Johnny turned into the alley and saw the wrong man wearing the red scarf, he could hear Calypso's prophetic voice. *We are dead men.*

Johnny knew how Stockman looked. He had been around during the early years when Stockman was a mere street cop, taking bribes from the Chicago mob. Stockman was supposed to wear a red scarf to identify himself. But the man in the alley, wearing the red scarf, was someone else.

Johnny was aware of another deadly reality. One of Calypso's Trench Town goons had been shadowing him the whole week. If he turned to walk away from the alley, his actions would be interpreted as a double cross, an attempt to take the money and run. Johnny had worked with Calypso long enough to know what they did to double-crossers.

Johnny continued down the alley, toward the red scarf. Underneath his bulletproof vest, he wore a black leather pouch, strapped to his chest. The pouch was stuffed with $250,000 in one hundred dollar bills. He was about to give it to an imposter. And now, he was a dead man.

Think! Think! Think! He hammered himself. And then his PhD from the gritty streets kicked in. If Stockman set up the sting, then Stockman was sitting in some nearby sound truck, listening to the wire. What Johnny desperately needed to do was talk directly to Stockman, let him know that going out in a blaze of retirement glory on a headline-grabbing undercover operation was going to be a lot harder than he thought.

Johnny stood directly in front of the man wearing the red scarf. Without saying a word, he lit up a smelly Swisher Sweets Cigarillo with a long plastic tip.

The man with the scarf spoke first. "You have the money?"

Johnny blew a white plume of smoke directly into the man's face. "Who are you?"

"Who do you think I am?" he snapped.

"A faggot in a red scarf." Johnny snapped back.

"Look, I'm not here to play games. Either you want your little mule boy to walk or you don't."

"I don't have the slightest idea what you're talking about." Johnny replied, nonchalantly.

"Okay, we'll see who has the last laugh." The man began to walk away.

"Hey, sometimes these first dates don't work out," Johnny taunted him. "Maybe we can try it again in, say, twenty-four hours exactly."

The man stopped to turn around. "What do you mean?"

"Who knows? By then my memory might come back to me. I know a little redhead on Rush Street that helps me to remember things, a whole lot of things. You and me might end up with something to talk about after all."

"What the hell you mouthing off about?" The man in the red scarf growled. "I don't know anything about a redhead."

"Then I guess you and me got nothing else to say."

Johnny waited until the man had cleared the alley. Then he walked to the corner and stopped. He wanted the goon to see him making the phone call to Calypso. He knew Calypso would call the goon to let him know Johnny was not attempting to run with the cash.

Johnny was certain the undercover agent in the red scarf was wearing a wire. Consequently, he had spoken in code that only Stockman could decipher.

Part of Stockman's early Mafia payoffs had included the sexual favors of a red headed blackjack dealer at the Lake Underground Casino on Rush Street. Stockman would realize there was someone out there who knew about his past, someone fully capable of spoiling his little FBI retirement party after all.

It was a long shot. But it was the only shot Johnny had. If all went well, Stockman would meet him in twenty-four hours at the Lake Underground Casino in Chicago.

When Calypso answered the phone, Johnny informed him in a confident voice, "We're not dead men. We have twenty-four hours left."

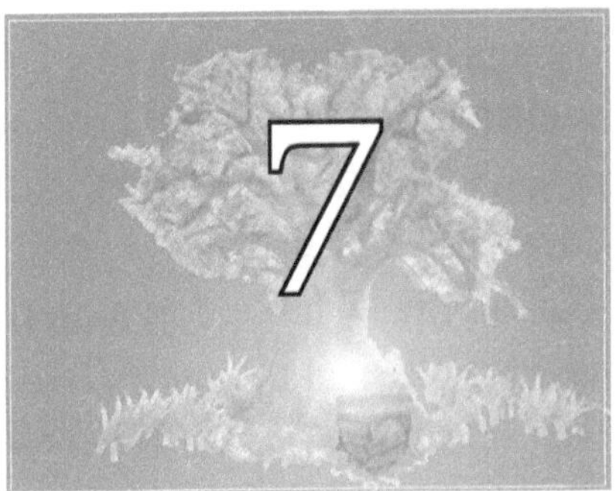

Lola hated herself. She never should've spent the night at Nicholas' apartment. She barely knew the most handsome, caring, honest, sincere, affectionate man she had ever met in her life. Yet, there she had been, dancing to his soft seductive music, eating his specially prepared shish kabobs, sipping his Carlisle Zinfandel and shouting sweet nothings in his bedroom, all night long.

Sitting on a bench by the lake in the park, gobbling down jumbo hot dogs and watching the small sailboats gliding by, should've been enough. Instead, she had agreed to take in a movie after work and listen to a jazz band at a neighborhood bar. She was twenty-seven years old. She knew what an invitation to his apartment could lead to ... did lead to.

Now she was nothing more than a little Mexican slut he had conquered in no time flat. He wasn't going to call her back. He had other beauties to seduce, other trophies to put on his mantel. The most she could expect out of the incident was an enduring memory, a night she would cherish the rest of her life.

And then, her cell phone rang. The caller ID read Bishop Hardware Store. Her heart began to race as his soothing voice came on the line.

"I wanted to make sure you got home safely. I guess waiting until 1:00 pm in the afternoon to call is some pretty sorry detective work."

"*Si,* pretty sorry," she agreed. And then she began to giggle. She had barely crawled out of bed.

"I want to apologize," he said in a more serious tone.

Lola braced herself and thought: *Here it comes. He wants to apologize for not telling me about his wife and kids.*

"About what?"

"About last night. I put you in a compromising position. You're a beautiful lady and I didn't mean to ... well ... take advantage of you."

I'm a beautiful lady, not a Mexican slut, she thought to herself. And then she began to cry.

"What? What did I say *this* time?"

"Everything. Everything that you needed to say," she reassured him.

That night when she fell asleep, she expected to dream of the two of them making love in some enchanted tropical garden where the fluttering wings of green butterflies pushed a misty breeze through her hair. Instead, she found herself engulfed in a sinister, teeth-grinding nightmare filled with gigantic man-eating snakes. One huge python sucked in the lifeless body of an African tribesman it had just crushed. An old woman in a flowered green dress, multi-colored orange headwrap and chunky necklace made of black death-head skulls stood by, screaming for help.

Again, Lola awakened to a pillow soaked with sweat. Again, the screams persisted beyond her dreams. Again, the sounds came from the parking lot.

Pulling back the curtains, she was petrified. The gruesome scene she had just witnessed in her dream was playing out in real life, right next to Johnny's Deville. The hysterical woman, hungry snake and half-eaten man had all somehow manifested into skin and bones. Even more disturbing was Lola's realization that the old woman was now looking toward the window, directly at her.

Lola snatched the old yellow drawstring curtains together and leaped back into her bed. Just as she had done as a frightened little girl when fierce lightning storms sequestered her room, she threw the covers over her head and prayed for Mother Mary to take it all away.

She needed to wake up ... really wake up. Obviously, she was still asleep, still caught up in a screwy nightmare inside of a nightmare that was playing tricks on her mind.

Dawn's early light finally coaxed her from the safety of her bedspread cover cave. A procrastinating trip to the bathroom and then she would face the surreal visitation of old women and killer pythons. It was, no doubt, a continuation of her family's weird spiritual legacy, the foolish folklore she had cast aside.

Finally, she mustered the courage to peep outside.

Nothing. Except her sigh of glorious relief.

Scanning the parking lot, she observed a young secretary type in high heels and stockings, sliding into a red sports car. No old woman, no snakes, no nothing.

Dreams were like movies. They seemed so real. But the moment you left the theatre, you realized they were just movies, no connection to the truth.

She would've stood there at the window a bit longer celebrating the conquest of her fears. But her cell phone went off. Johnny's number came up on the ID.

"I'm in Chicago, Babygirl. I don't have a lot of time to talk.

I just needed to know you're alright."

"No, no, New York. You NO suppose to go to Chicago!" Lola envisioned Mafia gangsters with Tommy guns, hiding in every back alley.

"Didn't have much of a choice. But don't worry. I'll be in and out before anybody knows the difference."

"You be home soon?"

"Yeah, soon as I'm done choking this bastard with a red scarf. I gotta go now." He hung up the phone.

She wanted so much to tell Johnny about Nicholas. But she knew better than to call him back. The last thing he needed was a romantic mush mouth pulling him away from his business. Nobody had time to listen to her meaningless chatter about her new-found ... friend.

At 11:00 am, her new-found friend called. There was an unmistakable urgency in his voice.

"That professor contacted me, the one that's an expert on the Juba Collection. He'll be in town this afternoon and wants to meet us at five."

Lola and Nicholas made their way to the back of an old Greek restaurant located in the quaint Adams Street District in metropolitan Springfield. A distinguished looking black man with thick glasses, a balding head and peppered gray beard ushered them to his table.

He pointed to the stark gray menu. "The Lamb Fricasse is excellent. But order your heart's desire. I'm picking up the tab."

After an appetizer of chewy grilled octopus and dry *Cabernet*, he inquired, "So you're the couple that found the Juba Chest?"

Couple. He called us a couple, Lola thought to herself.

"We're really not sure what we have." Nicholas responded, coyly.

"Well, I'm sure, as sure as one can be without seeing the actual artifact." He pulled out a copy of the emailed photograph and re-examined it with a strict ardent gaze. "You see these inscriptions at the bottom?"

They both leaned forward.

"The combination of imagery is unmistakable. We've never seen this particular cultural miscegenation in any other collection. Even without the Roman, Hebrew and Numidian inscriptions, the North African mask is most definitive to the region."

"What is this mask?" asked Lola. "It gives me the creepies."

"It's the ceremonial Mask of Deities, the ultimate symbol of power and wisdom during Mauertanian times."

Nicholas squinted. "What was it used for?"

"Nothing less than to decide the mortal fate of men, whether they lived or died."

The professor went on to explain that around 45 BC, Mauertania, now modern-day Morocco, was an advanced civilization in Africa presided over by King Juba II and his devoted wife, Queen Cleopatra Selene.

"I'll pause there because only recent findings have given us the full story."

"What do you mean, *full* story?" asked Nicholas.

"Recently discovered artifacts have confirmed there were two King Jubas', twin brothers that carried out an elaborate identity ruse, distorting our sense of history. There is the conventional, romanticized account of King Juba and his peaceful coexistence with Julius Caesar. And then there is the more accurate account of tyranny and war that drove the surviving King Juba from his kingdom to a mysterious land of exile."

"America?"

"Indeed." Professor Broadson explained that because of its rich forestry and precious minerals, Julius Caesar invaded Mauertania and made it a Roman Province. The Mauertanians, however, led by the more defiant twin brother, refused to relinquish their freedom. Under the cover of the dense forest and pitch-black nights, they built large ships and escaped to the new world, the perennial promise land that freedom seekers always seem to find.

The professor's crow face slowly intensified. "You must understand. Freedom wasn't the only reason they fled their homeland. They left Mauertania to protect a great secret."

"What secret?" probed Nicholas.

"The secret of the Juba Chest." The professor's voice thundered with the authority of a great storyteller.

"This secret makes the chest worth a lot of money, *si*?" Lola pressed.

He took a vociferous gulp from his wine glass. "The chest is worthless to some; priceless to others."

"Okay, okay, what is the secret?" asked Nicholas.

"You would have to understand the complex rituals and protocols of the Mauertanian civilization. Their system of life was governed by a council of two. Two appeared to be a sacred number to them."

"Let me guess. The council of two kings; the two rulers on the front of the chest, right?"

"A logical guess, but quite incorrect," the professor admonished. "The council of two were the two great *Nous* Spirit Men who wore the mask. Two kings appointing two Spirit Men, get it?"

Nicholas frowned. "Kinda."

"Think of it as a system of shared power, equal representation of the twins' dissimilar core values. These Spirit Men settled all disputes and passed judgment on all transactions. Both brothers had the right to intervene, but seldom did. After all, these Spirit Men were deemed to be, well, *Spiritual,* of the highest integrity with mystical connections to the universe. Their decisions were based on the will of the gods."

"These gods talked to them from the sky, *si*?" Lola suddenly recalled her grandfather's account of their spiritual Aztec ancestry.

"Who can say? The point is, sometimes the two Spirit Men

disagreed. When that happened, the only solution was to let the gods decide directly."

The professor gave them an intriguing example.

"Let's say a man was accused of stealing. One Spirit Man believed he was guilty; the other believed he was innocent. They would take the accused into the bush to the sacred Baobab tree and tie him up. If he survived for three days they would set him free. But if the animals came along and devoured him, then he was deemed guilty as charged."

Lola's voice quivered. "Animals lah-lah-like lions?"

"Lions, tigers, snakes, spiders. There was an abundance of executioners in the lush jungle."

Lola fell into silence.

Professor Broadson continued. "Legend has it this tree had been planted in the center of the mysterious Mzorz Stonehenge in Morocco, thousands of years ago."

Nicholas squinted. "Wait. Morocco? I thought the great Stonehenge was located in England near Salisbury."

The professor nodded, graciously. "That's a common misconception. The truth is Stonehenge configurations are located all over the world ... *Zorats Karer* in Armenia, *Puma Punku* in Bolivia, *Gobekli Tepe* in Turkey. They seem to have been placed in every strategic corner of the globe."

"What is this stonehenging?" asked Lola.

"Stonehenge," Professor Broadson corrected. "In the crudest sense, they are circular patterns of huge stones, precisely erected in combination with other Neolithic and Bronze Age earthworks."

"Big rocks," Nicholas simplified.

"Gigantic, indeed. Some are thirty feet high, weighing three million pounds."

"What are they for?" asked Lola.

Shaking his finger at her, Professor Broadson offered a

discerning smile. "Now that is the operative question, my dear. Indeed, a paradox that could keep us here for the rest of the week."

Lola looked at Nicholas with pitiful eyes. "I no can stay that long."

Professor Broadson appeared amused by her charm and naivety. "Then, perhaps I should get to the point. Each Stonehenge is different, and yet, the same. Some configurations are instruments of ancient astronomy, stargazing laboratories if you will, capable of mapping out distant constellations with 99.9% accuracy. Others are crude calendars that track the summer and winter solstices and annual movement of the sun. Others, such as the one near Salisbury, are built to tap into the earth's geomagnetic fields to produce advanced energy grids, the usage of which we have yet to comprehend. Still, others are sacred religious sites used in ancient rituals, but more importantly, as a means to communicate with God."

Nicholas pondered a moment. "What about the one in Morocco, the one where they performed this so-called tree ritual?"

"Mzorz?"

"Yes. I take it that was a religious site?"

The professor appeared pleasantly surprised by Nicholas' quick interpolation.

"You take it correctly, Mr. Hartman. I do regret not bringing my grade book to record your rare acumen. Usually people take much longer to get this."

"What I don't get is how all of this is connected to the chest?"

Professor Broadson took a deep breath. "When you've studied the Stonehenges as I have for decades, you come to realize there is no logical explanation for their existence. In some instances, these million pound stones were transported hundreds of miles. They were cut at precise angles requiring tools that didn't exist back then. Some angles display explicit use of the pythagorean theorem which did not come into being for thousands of years. Some rock formations harness light, sound and geomagnetic waves that not even today's scientists can reproduce. Only a fool would say these ancient cave people accomplished these magnificent feats using conventional knowledge."

"How do you define conventional?"

"Tangible, scientifically based practices tied to their particular periodization," Professor Broadson explained. "We can assess a civilization's overall intelligence quotient based on many things including manuscripts, tools, food consumption and so on. There's no way these Neolithic dimwits accomplished these things on their own."

"Then how did they do it?" asked Nicholas.

"I believe they stumbled onto some kind of transcendent metaphysical power," the professor conjectured. "Something beyond their ability to describe or comprehend. And yet, they were able to use it to accomplish tasks far beyond their imagination."

Lola shook her head. "I do not understand."

"Think about spiritual healing," said Professor Broadson. "Respected physicians have documented thousands of cases of successful, permanent, miraculous recovery by patients, some on their death beds. A person of great faith walks into the room, prays, touches, counsels, and reads from the Bible and suddenly the cancer disappears. Who can say how or why? Who can explain to future generations the unseen, imperceptible framework in which this phenomenon has occurred?"

Nicholas' mind began to race. "Okay, okay, let's say we accept your explanation that some unknown power source played a role in these Stonehenges. What does this have to do with the chest?"

"Yes, of course, the chest." The professor took another extended sip of wine. "As I explained earlier, the tree was planted in the center of the Mzorz sacred circle. I suppose we could think of it in terms of the tree in the center of the Biblical Garden of Eden. In the spiritual sense, it was the focus of attention, and according to the records left by the Mauertanians, held special powers."

Remembering his many Sunday school sessions at the local

Methodist Church, Nicholas nodded, fondly. "The tree of good and evil. I know the story well."

"Legend reveals a metaphysical transition by the great tree."

Lola shook her head. "This word ... medda-how-you-say?"

"Metaphysical," clarified the professor. "It means to defy the laws of nature. In the Gospel of *Luke*, Jesus refers to the rocks crying out ... although in nature, they were created with no mouth, no speaking capacity.This would require a metaphysical change ... do you see?"

Reluctantly, she nodded.

"Thus, with the tree being a part of so many life-and-death struggles, witnessing so many hours of the human spirit, toiling to survive, the tree, itself, gained the power to grant life and death. Of course, I don't believe that part."

"The part about the tree having the power to grant life and death?" queried Nicholas.

"No," said Professor Broadson. "The part about how the tree acquired the power. I believe, from its very origin, at this particular site, the configuration of the stones unleashed some kind of energy within the tree, something very ancient, very powerful and perhaps, very deadly."

"Whouuuh!" said Nicholas, trying to bring Professor Broadson's runaway supernatural stagecoach to a halt. "That's a bit of a stretch, don't you think? I mean, where's the evidence of this so-called ancient tree energy?"

The professor displayed a facetious smile. "Many years ago I went to see The *Curse of the Mummy's Tomb.* After the movie I wrestled with that same question of *evidence*. In fact, I decided to do my own research, just to dispel any lingering doubts about the ridiculous notion of dark powers and some kind of curse. No need to torture the archaeological side of my brain with bad dreams if I didn't have to. Right?"

Thinking of her own troublesome nightmares back at the apartment, Lola nodded, vigorously.

"What I discovered was, in real life, two archaeologists and an assistant associated with the removal of that Egyptian tomb died prematurely and under questionable circumstances. In fact, one died as the result of a mosquito bite. Now, I ask you. Is that evidence?"

Nicholas thought about it. "Maybe, maybe not."

"I'm going to say *not*. You know why?"

Nicholas shook his head, unknowingly.

"Because I won't let it be evidence. I won't allow my mind to entertain such a disturbing departure from the reality I know and trust. That's what you're doing, Mr. Hartman. The same prejudgment is written all over your face."

Nicholas reached for the dark bottle of Van Der Heyden and poured himself a desperate swig. "We have a saying in the hardware business: *The proof is in the sales*. That's a tangible measurement we can see and believe."

"We also have a saying in the scientific community," countered Professor Broadson. "*The most important components in life are those things you can't see* ... like neutrons, electrons, and those new oscillating particles in string theory. Without the *unseen*, the seen would not exist."

"This is confusing to me," admitted Lola.

"Then, let us simplify," offered Professor Broadson. "Do you believe in a spiritual God, one you cannot see, but you know is there? The Mauertanians did, though they called him by a different name ... *Nous*, meaning Mind. I know because I visited the Mzorz Stonehenge in Morocco many times and studied thousands of hieroglyphic messages carved in granite antiquity. Over thirty six stone etchings refer to the secret of the sacred tree of *Nous*, its power to grant certain wishes and the Mauertanians' obligation to protect it from the outside world."

Lola perked with excitement. "Wishes? You could wish on the tree for anything you wanted?"

"More or less."

"Estupendo!"

"No, Lola. *Extremadamente peligroso,*" replied Professor Broadson, flaunting his mastery of five different languages.

Lola's face soured. "Why you say extremely dangerous?"

"Think about that kind of unlimited wishing power in the hands of someone like Adolf Hitler or Charles Manson or Idi Amin. It could ... no, no ... *WOULD* be devastating, evil receiving the recompense of its dark, murderous convictions. Surely, you can see that?"

Lola dropped her head with disappointment. "I suppose."

"The Mauertanians did indeed see it. So before leaving for the new world, they scraped slithers of memorial bark from the tree and placed the pieces inside a chest ... King Juba's Chest. Then, to make sure the Romans didn't discover the power of the tree, they burned it to the ground."

"So that's what the chips of wood are all about." Nicholas speculated out loud.

The professor's eyes bulged. "My God! Please tell me you haven't opened the chest."

Nicholas and Lola smothered at each other with dumb stares.

The professor gulped the rest of his wine. "You have no idea what you're dealing with here."

"What do you mean?"

"I mean, when you wish on the Juba Chest, people die. That's what I mean."

"I have made no wishes," Lola sternly declared.

"But you will," the professor assured her. "One day human circumstances will seduce you. And in desperation you *will* turn to the chest. And it *will* turn to you. It will slip into the deep hollows of your mind and haunt your dreams ... haunt your very soul. That's why you must give it back to me. So I can hide it like the Mauertanians did ... better than the Mauertanians did."

Nicholas' pale face radiated with doubt. "I'm sorry, Professor. I hear you. I still don't see the evidence."

Professor Broadson retrieved the Juba Chest photo from the table and pointed beneath the African mask to a small black triangle with golden tips. "You see this triangle?"

Lola and Nicholas leaned forward again.

"The etchings on the walls at Mzorz consistently refer to it as "מסע של גאולה". Roughly translated from Hebrew it means the *Journey of Redemption.* The three circular golden tips represent three wishes granted to those who believed."

"And..." Nicholas continued to press.

"When treasure hunter Russell Burrows discovered the hidden cave in rural Illinois containing the King Juba artifacts, the same triangles appeared on the cave walls. Only, those etchings were encircled with the multiple skulls ... a clear symbol of death, Mr. Hartman. These were the many human sacrifices associated with the chest."

Nicholas slowed his mind, chose his words carefully. "Symbols, legends, secret powers. It's an interesting hypothesis. But with all due respect, Professor. You can't be sure, can you?"

"I'm a certified archaeologist, Mr. Hartman, an expert in hieroglyphics. When Mr. Burrows allowed me to examine the photographs of the cave walls, I knew right away."

"Knew what?" asked Lola.

"I knew these were symbols of suffering and death. The Mauertanians were trying to warn us, Lola. They took radical measures to separate the chest from the rest of the artifacts. They sent a wise and trusted elderwoman out to bury it, at which point, she took her own life. This was her final leg on the *Journey of*

Redemption, her ultimate sacrifice, committing her eternal soul to to protecting civilization from the chest and its destructive powers."

A haunting silence enveloped the table.

"So you will bury the chest again?" asked Lola.

"I will put it where no one else can find it. Otherwise, a ruthless new breed of *wishers* will come along and invariably push our society into oblivion."

"How do I know you will not take my chest somewhere and sell it?" asked Lola.

The professor stroked his beard, searching for a convictive reply. "You don't. I guess you'll have to trust me; trust my love for humanity."

Lola thought about it. "I, I don't know."

"Have you ever seen children playing with a brightly colored, delightfully exotic Indian King Cobra?" he asked, not giving her time to answer. "I have. It's a lot of fun until someone gets bitten. At that point the only thing left is to organize the funeral procession. Are you good at that, Lola, organizing funeral processions?"

She dropped her head. "I don't think so."

"Don't worry. The Juba Chest will make you an expert. It trades lifes for wishes. You will get what you want, but so does the chest. The exchange is non-negotiable, don't you see?"

Nicholas intervened. "She needs some time to think about it. That's all she's saying."

The professor looked at his watch, then called for the check. "I left an archeological dig in Central America to come here and reason with you. I need to be back there tomorrow. If you change your mind, and I hope for the precious sake of humanity you do, you can reach me at the Sheraton Hotel. My flight leaves at 8:00 am tomorrow. After that, the blood is on your hands."

A few minutes later, Lola and Nicholas stood outside the restaurant, comparing notes.

"Do you think he's telling us the truth?" she asked.

"I don't know. The long spiel about sacred trees and secret caves and dark powers has my head spinning. I mean, it's hard to believe a little box could possess the power of life and death."

"He could be a phony. I don't want to give it to him," she whined.

"Then, don't. It's your box. You can do whatever you want with it."

That's all she needed, an unwavering show of support from her ... *husband-to-be.*

On Rush Street, just north of the Frank Sinatra Way Crossing, Tiny Johnny walked into Genno's quiet little coffee shop and took a seat at the bar. A sparse crowd of older patrons, mostly men, sat at glass tables that pushed up from the floor like transparent mushrooms. The full-length, iridescent mirror behind the bar reflected the subtle stares of high class hookers, occasionally whirling around on their red bar stools to signal their availability to the next lucky John.

The long-haired bodybuilder bartender finally made his way over to Johnny's end of the bar. "What are you having?"

Johnny slid two hundred-dollar bills in front of him.

The bartender looked both ways, then stuffed the bills into his shirt pocket. "I've got a couple of nice healthy brunettes, maybe one older blonde for this price."

"Keep the toys for now," said Johnny in a low, discrete tone. "What I need is information."

"I'm listening."

"You got a room downstairs, big room, fancy trimmings. It use to be the Lake Casino."

"That was before my time, sir."

"Yeah, but you know about it. Five'll get you ten you've taken a tour of the place, just for history's sake."

"What's your point?"

"Point is, I'd like to take that same tour, tonight, right now, for the sake of history."

"I'm afraid that's impossible. The room has already been reserved."

Johnny reached into his wallet to pull out another crisp hundred dollar bill. "Nothing is impossible these days, not with Ben Franklin in charge."

"I-ahh, I don't know."

Johnny flopped another hundred on the counter but kept his hand over both bills. "If it makes you feel any better, the guy down there is expecting me. You gotta deal here; I gotta deal down there. What you gonna do when a fat payday slaps you in the face?"

The bartender hesitated a long while, his greedy eyes, fixated on the seductive greenbacks. Finally, he whispered four numbers. "Six, two, six, three. That's the code to the freight elevator. That's the only way you get to the room."

****

With nervous flashlight eyes, Johnny stepped through the freight elevator's noisy interlocking iron gates and onto the cold concrete floor. Gripping tightly to the .357 magnum in his leather coat pocket, he navigated the dimly lit hallway to the only open door in sight. Though he had chosen the time and place for their rendezvous, the whole setup had the smell of a turkey shoot, with him as the turkey. Luckily for Johnny, some turkeys could shoot back.

Inside the old ballroom were scattered stacks of broken tables and chairs, their splintered mahogany legs, pushing toward the vaulted ceiling. Storage boxes lined the once exquisite cherry wood wet bar. Some were covered with waves of silky cobwebs crawling up the red velvet walls. The musty smell of mildew and rat droppings lingered in the air, a glib reminder of the many human rats that had frequented the establishment so many years ago.

Johnny finally spotted the back of Stockman's head. He appeared frozen in time, mesmerized by a line of stylized gray and black posters on the wall. Johnny recognized the stark images of Frank Nitti and Al Capone. But most of the other mobsters had faded into the contemptible memories of the past.

With his back still turned, Stockman reminisced out loud. "These were the good old days when the booze and the broads flowed like sewage into the river. I pocketed my first thousand at that table in the corner; watched an undercover informant get an ice pick through the neck behind that bar. Jeanne, the redhead you talked about last night in New York; I met her at the main blackjack table, right there in the middle of the floor."

He finally turned toward Johnny. An older man with streaks of gray, a thin face and straight, immaculate white teeth, he could've easily been mistaken for a senator or head of state.

"I remember a lot of things about this place," he continued in a smooth, settled tone. "But I don't remember you. Could it be you were in the back washing dishes?"

"Could it be I was over at your mama's house, making her scream like a pig? I don't remember either," Johnny fired back.

Stockman smiled, narrowly. "Pretty gutsy move you made in that alleyway. How did you know I was listening?"

"Criminals got an MO. So do dumb ass FBI agents. I just don't understand why you would want to bring attention to this case by getting the cavalry involved."

"There's no cavalry. The gentleman you met is one of my ... associates. I guess you could think of him as a Hollywood double, just in case someone has a nasty inclination toward violence, like you."

Johnny managed a tantalizing grin. "Me, violent? I wouldn't hurt a soul. Of course, I might hurt somebody without one."

"So we finally reach that awkward moment of judgment when one snake in the grass tells the other snake in the grass that he's a moral misfit."

"Me, you know what I am," said Johnny. "I rattle before I bite. You ... you cover yourself up with the sweet smell of justice and duty. And then you strike people from behind your badge."

"I perform a service, Mr.?.?." He looked at Johnny's bulging jacket pocket. "Mr. Big Pistol, for lack of a better name. I perform a service no different from the North Lake Bridge. I link people on one side of the bank with people on the other side of the bank. And I get paid very handsomely, by the way. Isn't that why you're here, Mr. Big Pistol, to pay me very handsomely? And might I add, handsomely doesn't mean the welfare checks you stole out of the mailboxes in your neighborhood before you got here."

Johnny was fuming, but could think of nothing else to say. He reached beneath his bullet proof vest, unstrapped the bulging black money belt and tossed it to Stockman. "Count it."

Stockman waved his hand. "That won't be necessary. One thing I can say about the Jamaicans. They pay for what they want. They may kill us both later. But for now, their money is good."

As Stockman walked toward the door, he couldn't resist one last parting shot. "Isn't it ironic, Mr. Big Pistol? I leave with the money and you leave with ... well ... nothing but my word, the word of a snake in the grass."

"I kind of hope you flip on us. It would give me the excuse I need."

"Now, now, there's that primitive streak of violence again, probably inbred before they brought you savage people over here. I'm not flipping, Mr. Big Pistol. I'm retiring with a cheap gold watch, a pithily ass pension and, oh yeah, two hundred and fifty grand. Other than that, I'll see you in Hell."

For three days Johnny waited in the Omni Hotel on North Michigan Avenue. Finally, he got the call.

"De bwoy is free," Calypso happily informed him. "I will meet you in de lobby in one hour."

Maybe it was fate or bad luck or the Curse of the Billy Goat that had drifted over from the Chicago Cubs locker room. But as Calypso handed Johnny a small brown satchel containing the final $50,000, a familiar face strolled through the hotel lobby. It was Vinnie Meatball's half brother, Raymond Pinzolo, a rising star in Joey the Clown's organization. He glanced over at them a brief second, but kept walking.

Maybe he didn't see us at all, Johnny thought to himself as he drove across the Chicago River, headed back to Litchfield.

Even if he did, there was no way Raymond could trace him. He was Johnny Fountain, an obscure businessman, living out of a P.O Box in Podunk, USA. And to his astonishment, he was not a dead man. In fact, with the money he had in the trunk for the transplant, he was going to live a very long time.

The problem surfaced on Thanksgiving Day.

In four glorious months, Lola and Nicholas had transformed their string of spontaneous rendezvous into a full-blown relationship. Eager to show off his new companion, Nicholas had invited her to accompany him to his parents' house for the traditional turkey day dinner.

Lola had already met Nicholas' mother at the clinic. Seeing her again at the family's elegant Victorian home near Lake Springfield, she seemed even more gracious than before. Nicholas' father, however, a tall, distinguished Illinois Appeals Judge in his late 50's, was not as hospitable. Throughout the meal he peppered her with question after question: "How did you come to America? What do your parents do? What are your goals in life?"

Although his perpetual cross-examination made Lola uncomfortable, she had managed to charm her way through.

Finally, Nicholas rescued her with a rare dissenting remark. "Next time, why don't we bring a stenographer? That way you can review the testimony and make a decision behind closed doors."

After the stinging rebuke, Nicholas' father lost his prying tongue in the roasted turkey and cornbread dressing. Again, her hero had salvaged the day.

The problem was Nicholas' father was right. Although Nicholas had managed to curtail the old judge's awkward intrusion into her personal life, the family fellowship had aroused a sense of inquiry deep in the back of Nicholas' mind.

Throughout their early acquaintance, Lola had been purposely vague about her past. They talked about current attractions such as her classes at Lincoln Land College and his planned ascension up Bishop Hardware's corporate ladder. With fleeting interest, they even discussed the Juba Chest, a seemingly worthless box that, for the time being, rested quietly in a U-Haul storage facility a few miles from her apartment. But for Lola, the past was a bitter pill, a high-risk proposition that could expose her true pedigree and drive him away.

He was a handsome, charming, judge's son, a graduate of Penn State and manager of the city's most popular hardware store. She was an illegal alien with fraudulent papers who had slipped into the country through a back door tunnel outside of San Diego. With her spotted credentials, what were the chances he would take her seriously? Why sabotage their future together with the gritty, unadulterated truth?

She wanted to continue in the safety of her charade, keep the love boat plowing full steam ahead. But after his father's informal inquisition, Nicholas kept turning the rudder, wanting to examine seas they had already crossed.

One night after a candlelight dinner at his apartment, they stood on his frigid balcony, admiring the city's sparkling skyline. He finally offered his assessment.

"I know it's small. But Springfield has a lot of opportunities."

She nodded, tidily.

"Is that why you came here ... opportunities?"

"Came to Springfield?" she tried to clarify.

"No. America. Why did you come to America?"

She wanted to shift into her hyper-analytic, self-induced methodical mode. But her heart kept getting in the way. Although she hadn't shared very much about her past, she hadn't lied about it either. She found herself at a crossroads, a need to choose between a flimsy house of cards that had served her well, and a new house of honesty that might crumble on the spot.

She cleared her throat. "I came to America to stay alive."

It was no secret that with the rise of the Mexican drug cartels, Juárez, the fourth-largest city in Mexico, had become the money-laundering, drug smuggling capital of the Northern hemisphere. But with so many young women being brutally murdered, Juárez had earned another name ... THE CITY OF DEAD GIRLS.

"When I was sixteen they found my baby sister, Amada, wrapped in a blanket, dumped in this muddy field in front of the big plastics plant. My cousin, Maria, was found in a drainage ditch not too far from our house. You know what they do to them? They rape them and burn their faces and cut their breast. That's what they do."

Nicholas draped his arm around her. "I'm so sorry. I didn't know."

"My mother say to me, 'you are next'. I was next in the line of dead girls. It was sure to happen to me. An angel had told her in a dream. That's why she sent me to America."

"It must've been hard leaving your family; trying to get through immigration," he speculated. "I hear processing the paperwork can run two or three years behind."

Lola dropped her head, not saying a word. She wanted to forget the painful details of her ignominious entry into the United States of America. But people kept bringing it up. Even in the privacy of her own subconscious world, her dreams forced her to remember. They crept in from the dark chasms of her mind and fanned the scent of death that lurked beneath the mud and rocks and splintered pieces of wood.

At sixteen years old, Lola had left Juárez with her Uncle Felix, his youngest son, Pedro, and eight Ecuadorean migrants, headed to America. A seasoned farm worker who had crossed the border many times, Felix had developed a keen instinct for the treacherous journey. He knew the desert corridors to travel, the border patrols to avoid and the secret entryways over the mountains, through the swirling river waters and into the drug-smuggling tunnels beneath the shifting dirt and sand. Yet, he had come to understand that each trip was different. There were unforeseen dangers of which he had no control.

To avoid detection and minimize the lethal temperatures of the scorching desert, the group traveled at night. When young Pedro stepped on a rattlesnake, and in his poisoned agony, groaned too loudly, the heartless coyote in charge of the group cured his suffering with a bullet between his eyes.

Felix pulled out a small handgun and shot back, commencing a running gun battle between the two.

The gunfire attracted the Zetas, a ruthless gang of Special Forces defectors who preyed on helpless migrants traveling through the territory.

As Lola explained, "These men kill without mercy. That is what they did to us. They drove up in the pickup trucks and shot the people down."

Nicholas' eyes widened with disbelief. "That's horrible! How did you get away?"

"My uncle was my protector. He took my hand and led me through the bushes to a ravine. Some tree branches covered the smuggler's cave."

Though Lola could feel the familiar sense of nausea

engulfing her consciousness, she couldn't stop ... wouldn't stop. The time had come for him to know everything.

"It was narrow and dark and so hard to breathe inside. It was ... how you say ... *ataúd*, a coffin of death that waited for the living to surrender to it. Sometimes we bent. Sometimes we had to crawl on our knees for hours. To stop me from crying, he flipped on his cigarette lighter every few minutes so I could see in the dark. We did this again and again until we heard the sound."

"What? What sound?"

"I-aahh, I don't know, Nicholas." Her fragile voice cracked. "Maybe big trucks passing over the road. I think we were under the highway or something. All I know is the walls started to cave in."

Lola's uncle was a few feet behind her when some of the wooden braces collapsed, pinning both his legs under a mountain of mud and debris.

"I tried to pull his arms, but he kept snatching them away," said Lola, her eyes now drowning in tears. "He handed me the lighter and told me to go on. I didn't want to leave him but he told me it was wrong for me to disobey. He told me I would bring shame on his name if I didn't get to America safely. And then a piece of timber fell on his head and his eyes went out."

With dirt and debris raining down on her, Lola had found her way through the darkness, only the tiny, flickering lighter flame to guide her. Hours later, she had surfaced in a sewer on the outskirts of San Diego.

After a few nights sleeping in a back alleys on a makeshift cardboard mattress and eating scraps out of a hotel dumpster, she found the safe house her uncle had mentioned.

"The owner was a lesbian woman. She treated us like dogs, the young girls who would not surrender to her. She made us clean these big rich houses for $10.00 a day and then she took back $5.00 for room and board. As soon as I saved $50, I ran away."

"My God, Lola, $50.00?"

"*Si.*"

He cringed. "How were you able to survive on $50.00?"

"In America, living on the street is not so bad. The Christian shelters will take you in at night. There are big hotels that throw full meals into the dumpster cans. This is not bologna they throw away. This is steaks and shrimp and fresh bread. This is what America calls garbage. But this garbage is what kept me alive."

"This is unbelievable, Lola. It, it, it boggles my mind."

She continued. "I met a boyfriend that took me to Texas. He was nice at first. But he was very jealous and started to fight me. So I run away again. I run from the immigration people. I run from the hustlers that want me to trick on the streets. I have spent a lot of time running away."

Nicholas waited a long time. He could see the tears flowing down her cheeks, her body, shivering from the cold. He opened the balcony door and brought her inside where he made her a piping hot cup of chocolate with marshmallows.

Sitting by the fireplace, he finally asked, "Can I tell you a secret?"

She nodded, permissively.

"When I was a kid we used to slip into the old movie theatre downtown. Sometimes, we'd see the same movie we had just watched a few days earlier. It didn't matter. The movie was always better when we slipped through the back door."

Lola began to cry, uncontrollably.

"Okay, why are you crying now?"

"Because I was afraid to tell you, afraid to trust you," she sobbed. There was another reason she was crying, a secret reason.

She walked over to the kitchen counter and unzipped her purse. Searching through the cluttered compartments, she found what she was looking for.

Sitting next to Nicholas, she revealed an old brass flip

lighter with dark scorch marks across its face. Gently, she placed it in the palm of his hand. "This was my uncle's lighter. Since coming to America, it has been my good luck charm. I want you to have it."

"Me?" Nicholas' eyes raditated with surprise. "Are you sure?"

She nodded.

"But why me, I mean, this is so precious, so valuable. Why would you give this to me?"

"Because, I don't need it anymore," she explained. "Don't you see. You are my good luck charm now, *si*?"

He nodded, slowly, acceptingly. "*Si.*"

As their eyes met with a new, poweful, unspoken consent, she started to cry again. It was for the secret reason. For, at that moment, she realized she was in love.

****

When she returned home the next day, she found Johnny stretched out on the sofa. After an hour of languishing in pride, he finally admitted to her he couldn't get up.

When the 911 emergency ambulance took him to the local hospital, the doctor immediately placed him on dialysis. From that day on, Johnny became prisoner to an escalating regiment of dialysis treatments, three times a week.

By early spring, with Johnny's condition deteriorating, the doctor revealed his unsettling prognosis.

"Regrettably, we have reached the point in which dialysis is no longer a viable option. You're going to need a transplant as soon as possible."

On their way home from the hospital, Johnny was livid.

"These quacks are crazy, knowemsayin'. He calls me into his office to tell me I'm dying. I mean, tell me something I don't know."

"He didn't say you're dying, Daddy," she countered.

"Oh, no?" Johnny reached into the back seat to retrieve a stack of pamphlets the doctor had given them. He handed her the one on living in a hospice. "You a college girl. Tell me what that word means."

"It's just a –"

"Death house," he cut her off. "You go to a hospice to die."

"Stop talking that way, Daddy. The doctor is doing the best he can."

"Is he really? I mean, they say I need these treatments. Now they say the treatments ain't working. They say I've gotta have all this money to get a transplant. I go and get the money. Now they can't find a kidney."

"They tell us from the beginning about the waiting list, yes?"

"I ain't seen no waiting list, knowemsayin'? If it is one, I guarantee you ain't nothing but white folks at the top."

"Don't say that, Daddy! You have no right to say that!" She scolded him for the first time ever.

"Ohhhhhhhh, I forgot. You sleeping with a white boy. White folks can do no wrong."

Fighting back the tears, Lola fell into silence. For the rest of the trip she stared blankly at the broken white lines in the middle of the highway, each redundant strip, reminding her of an anonymous white face Johnny had learned to hate. Finally, after what seemed a speechless eternity, she herded the big Cadillac onto the parking lot across the street from the apartment.

Johnny went through his security phone check. "We clear."

Yet, Lola did not move.

"I'm not coming in right now," she informed him, her hands, still gripping tightly to the steering wheel.

He opened his door to get out, then stopped. "Listen, I shouldna' said that about your boyfriend. I was out of line."

"But it is how you feel, yes?"

"I don't know how I feel these days. Maybe a little weak, a little helpless, a little pissed off because these white folks are playing games with me. Nothing personal against your boyfriend."

"But don't you see, Daddy. It is personal. Whenever they say Latinos are only good for working the fields and digging a hole and having the babies, that is personal to me. You lump Nicholas into the *white folks* group you don't like; that is personal to me too."

"I'm sure he's a nice fellow, Babygirl."

"How can you be sure since you don't meet him? I ask you many times, but you still don't meet him."

He dropped his head, momentarily glancing at his swollen ankles "I want to, I really do. But not like this."

"You say you love me, yes?"

"More than anything or anyone."

"Then you will give me a good gift for my birthday next month, yes?"

"Just name it," he declared.

"On my birthday, you will meet the man I love. That will be my gift, yes?"

Johnny hesitated a long time.

"Yes?" she continued to press.

"Babygirl, you're a tricky little irresistible bitch, just like your mother."

She smiled. "You told me she is the only woman you ever loved. So tricky is good, yes?"

"I guess."

"You teach me about the streets and about life. But now I teach you something."

"What's that, Babygirl?"
"I teach you how a woman always gets her way."

On a beautiful spring day in March, two weeks before her birthday, Lola pulled up in front of Bishop Hardware Store with a bright smile on her face. She was too excited to wait until they saw each other that night at his apartment. She had something she needed to tell Nicholas right away.

Her English professor had finished grading the hardest test of the semester. Lola had made an A. It was her first A ever, and unbelievably, in her most difficult subject. The accomplishment was well worth an impromptu celebration. Lola had driven to Springfield to take him to lunch.

Once inside the store, however, her smile quickly dampened. She spotted Nicholas standing next to the checkout counter, whispering in an employee's ear. She wasn't just any employee. She was a tall, slender, blonde with high cheekbones and sculptured hips, the model type you'd expect to see on the cover of a fashion magazine. As she turned to walk toward Lola, they both finished off a curious smile. Her name tag simply read TERRI. But in

Lola's heart, it read *DIABLO* ... demon bitch in disguise.

Nicholas offered an innocent grin. "What are you doing here?"

Lola was so shaken she almost forgot why she had come. "I-I-ahh, I wanted to tell you something, but if you're busy...."

"It's been a crazy morning," he admitted. "Our spring garden inventory has been flying off the shelf, especially the insecticides."

She glanced at the nearby sales display, wondering if any of the cans of insecticides, pesticides and herbicides could be used to control an infestation of unwanted *diablos*.

At that moment, a voice came over the store intercom. "Nicholas ... line one. Call for Nicholas Hartman on line one."

"Excuse me, baby. I'll be right back."

Nicholas stepped over to the desk to answer the phone. It was precisely the time Lola needed to pull herself together. She was acting like an obsessed, love-crazed psycho. Except for her heart, fighting to burst out of her chest, there was no reason to go off the deep end.

Nicholas returned with a proud smirk on his face. "That was my regional manager who, by the way, is coming here today."

"Is it a surprise visit?"

"Not really. I kind of expected it after headquarters had a chance to sift through last year's sales figures. We're having dinner at that exclusive seafood restaurant downtown. She wants to go over some things with me."

"Sheee?" Lola's tongue stuck to the top of her mouth.

"Yes. One thing I can say about this company. They're not sexist or racist or anything like that. They promote the most qualified person."

"I see," Lola acknowledged with secret consternation.

"Anyway, use your key. I'll be home as soon as possible."

That night, waiting for Nicholas to come back to the

apartment, Lola was absolutely certain something was wrong with the clocks. Time moved so slowly, like clumps of sand stuck in an hour glass. Even her cell phone with its instant GPS satellite connection became a cruel, conspiring agent of torture. What was so fascinating about year old sales figures? What was taking him so long to come home?

At 9:20 pm, Nicholas finally walked through the door.

"What happened?" She immediately confronted him. "Did something go wrong?"

"Oh no," he cheerfully replied. "Everything went right."

Nicholas explained that over the past year, his store's performance had been exceptional. The complex metrics used to analyze sales, inventory control, turnover, customer retention and other strategic categories had placed his store at number one in the region and five in the nation.

"Can you believe that? Only four other stores had better numbers. One was in a boom market down in San Antonio, Texas. Another was in Atlanta where they did heavy promotions. If I had gotten those promotional dollars, there's really no telling where I'd be."

He took a deep breath then pulled off his Carhartt jacket. "There's more. She's submitting my name to her boss for a bigger store in Kansas City. At least three regional managers and one vice president have come out of the Kansas City store."

"Would you have to move there?"

"Is that a gag question?" he chided her. "Of course, I would. There's no way I could manage a store in Kansas City, living in Springfield."

She tried to look happy, fighting back the terrifying thought he might pick up and leave her behind. "So when will you know these things for sure?"

"Maybe a month or two. I really don't have a handle on

their timetable."

"I'm very happy for you," she said in a soft voice.

"There's more," he revealed, fixing them two cups of hot chocolate and marshmallows. "Come sit with me on the sofa."

He took a loud, excited slurp from his cup, then pulled a brown envelope from his shirt pocket. He set an oversized check and multi-colored coupon on the coffee table. "You won't believe this part. That's a bonus check for $5000. It's all ours, over and above my salary."

Ours, he said our, she thought to herself.

"That other little piece of cardboard is nothing less than a free Caribbean cruise for two. The company is paying for the whole thing."

"For two?" Lola wanted to confirm.

"That's right," he boasted. "I wanted to do something special for your birthday. And now, here it is. You'll go with me, won't you?"

She smiled widely. "Is that a gag question or what?"

Soon they were hugging, kissing and making tender love right there on the sofa in front of the fireplace. Every dark thought and splinter of doubt was swallowed up in a surreal evening of inflamed passion. The clock began to march forward again, stealing back the precious moments in which it had languished on hold. The logs surrendered to the sweltering flames, serenading their ears with tiny explosions of joy.

Where was the laziness of time when you really needed it? She thought. *Why didn't it reassert its meddlesome repression and stretch the night into eternity?*

Just before they fell asleep, Nicholas raised up from his pillow. "You had something to tell me?"

Exhausted, and floating in her own enchantment dream world, Lola tried to focus. "Huh?"

"You came to the store today to tell me something. What was it?"

"It wasn't important."

"Are you sure?" he persisted.

Lola thought about how small her test score seemed in the scheme of things. "I'm sure."

"Okay. But remember, if you need to talk to me about anything, I'm always here."

Indeed, he was ... *right here*.

She snuggled in his arms and fell asleep.

Two white-coated doctors stood outside of room 424 at Litchfield's St. Francis Hospital, whispering beneath their breath. Though Lola could hear them from her seat in the waiting room, she couldn't understand what they were saying. They were using big words like *Ischemia*, *pulmonary embolism*, *creatinine*, and *hyperphosphatemi*; words that were unfair to an illegal immigrant who had slipped into the country through the back door.

Two days, two hours and twenty minutes before Lola's birthday cruise, Johnny had called her at the college. He was experiencing severe nausea, and vomiting, and couldn't keep his balance. By the time she drove him to the hospital, he had suffered a seizure and couldn't talk. Now, six hours later, the doctors stood in the hallway speaking in terms that only aliens from *Planet Galactica* could comprehend.

They finally approached her in the waiting room.

"I understand you're the next of kin?" The one with the thick gray mustache spoke first.

"*Sí*, I mean, yes." Between the community college classes, home translation tapes and Nicholas' constant encouragement, Lola's English had gotten so much better. She wanted to keep it that way.

"Do you understand what's going on here?" The older doctor, short, with a muscular build, chimed in.

"I know my father is very sick."

"He's experiencing acute renal failure due to a severe infection. He had a seizure and a mild stroke. His prognosis doesn't look good."

"Is there anything you can do? You must do something."

At that moment, the older doctor's pager went off. "I'm going to leave you in the hands of Dr. Campbell, here. He will explain the procedure."

The older doctor hurried down the hallway.

Dr. Campbell glanced at the chart and then tucked it under his arm. "I always try to be honest with my patients and their families. I'm going to do the same with you."

She took a deep breath, desperately trying to slip into her hyper-analytic, self-induced methodical mode. "I'm listening."

"Your father has reached the final stages of kidney failure. We already know that dialysis is no longer an option. There are medications that will help to make him comfortable. But unless he has a transplant in the next few days, he's not going to make it."

"Where is he on the waiting list?" she inquired.

The doctor stroked his thick mustache, trying to find the most appropriate answer. "The list, as you called it, is very deceiving. Even if your father was at the top, it doesn't mean the available donor kidney would be compatible to his molecular makeup. It might be a year or two before a precise match becomes available."

"So what do I do, doctor? Am I supposed to just sit back and wait for him to die?"

"I've been asked that question many times before. I always find myself giving the same answer, the only thing you can do."

"What is that, doctor?"

He looked into her sad eyes, seemingly sharing her pain. "Pray for a miracle. At this point, that's about all you can do."

For a long while Lola sat by Johnny's bedside, watching the pitiful brigade of tubes and wires and monitors, fighting their losing battle, pumping and hissing to an inevitable defeat. Overwhelmed by the relentless sounds of war, she stepped into the hallway and pressed her cell phone against her ear.

All day long she had tried to reach Nicholas. He wasn't at the store, and to her dismay, his cell phone had been disconnected.

He finally called her from his parents' house just after 8:00 pm.

"This has been a horrible day. Some murdering psychopath escaped from the state penitentiary. He was supposedly headed to Springfield to kill my father, our family, jury members and anyone else that had a hand in sending him to prison. The FBI grabbed me from the store and wouldn't let us contact anyone. They locked down all of our communications."

"Are you okay?" she asked, struggling to suppress her own family drama.

"We are now. They caught the guy just outside the city limits, loaded down with weapons and ammo. Guess he meant what he said."

"That's very frightening."

"I was really worried about our trip," he continued. "I didn't want to disappoint you."

"You know I would've understood," she purred.

"Yes, but I don't know if the company would've."

"What do you mean?"

"Well, I've requested for the time off. They're paying for the trip. I wouldn't look very organized to them if I just suddenly cancelled. I mean, do I have control of my life or not? That's important when they consider candidates for upper management."

"Sounds like you sometimes worry about the company more than me," she pressed.

"The thing is we don't have to worry about it at all now. We're set for Friday morning and that's that."

"What if it's no simple that way?" Her voice trembled as her bad English seeped in . "I have a life too, you know."

"What are you saying?" he probed.

"I'll talk to you in the morning." Lola hung up the phone.

****

Back at her apartment, her cell phone kept chiming and vibrating. It was Nicholas, calling from Springfield. She didn't know what to tell him. Too much was still up in the air.

She finally turned off her phone and went to bed.

That night, tossing and turning through one bad scenario after another, she finally came to terms with what she *couldn't* do. Although the cruise was important, there was no way she was going to leave her father on his death bed.

When she called Nicholas early the next morning to explain, he was just going into a sales meeting. When she called him back at lunch, he was tied up with vendors. He finally called her back at 3:00 pm. "Sorry, baby. It's been a hectic day, trying to tie up all these loose ends before the trip. How are you coming on your end?"

"I don't think I'll be able to go." She forced the words out of her mouth.

"I know I didn't hear you right. What are you saying?"

"My father is in the hospital. They don't know if he's going to make it."

He paused. "I'm sorry to hear that. Is there anything you need me to do?"

"I'm headed back to the hospital in a few minutes. Maybe you could meet me over there after work, yes?"

He paused even longer. "I ... I don't know about that."

"I know you wanted to meet him before," she reminded him. "But he wasn't ready. But this week he promised. He promised he would meet you."

"I do want to meet him, but...."

"But what, Nicholas?"

"I don't know if I'll have time. There's so much I still have to do before the cruise."

The CRUISE! He's still going on the cruise, she thought to herself.

She exploded. "Is that all you care to think about?!"

"Lola. Baby. We talked about this last night. This company watches everything. There's a lot at stake here."

"What about my stake?! My father is dying! Did you hear me tell you that part?"

"I said I was sorry, didn't I?"

"Yes, and I'm sorry too, about a lot of things."

She hung up the phone.

That evening, sitting next to Johnny's hospital bed, listening to the incessant beep of a thousand monitors, she had a lot of time to think. She had expected Nicholas to care as much about her father as she did. And yet, when he told her his father had almost been killed by an escaped prisoner, she could've cared less. She had justified her lack of concern by the way the old judge had treated her. But in reality, Johnny had treated Nicholas just as badly.

There was another reality that wormed its way out of the deep crevices of her mind. Nicholas had more than a job. He had a career. He was going places. And if she read him correctly, he planned to take her with him. His references were always *we* and *us* and *our*. The bonus check, which he had earned all by himself, was ... all *ours*.

Deeply enthralled in her complicated thoughts, she suddenly heard a familiar but groggy voice. "Is it your birthday yet?"

Johnny had briefly awakened from his medication.

With her hyper-analytic, self-imposed calmness in place, she peered at the time on her red Blackberry. "Four more hours, but who's counting?"

"DDDDDid your white boy come? I'm ready to kick his ass, just to let him know what to expect if he ever gives you a problem."

"No," she replied, despondently. "He couldn't make it."

"Probably at some Neeooo-Nazi, Ke-ke-ke-Klan meeting," he razzed her.

Or just trying to protect our future, she rationalized within.

She placed her hand across his forehead. "How are you feeling?"

"Like I reallllly need that hospice info."

"Don't say that, Daddy. You will be fine."

"Mayyyyybe, if I'm at the top of the listsss." His words continued to slur as he drifted off again. "Am I at the top of the listsss, Babygirl?"

She pondered a long time, trying to find the words to say. It was too late to explain the system to him. He had already drifted back into a dark, consuming sleep.

****

The next morning was overcast and gloomy. An unseasonable spring/winter storm was moving in from Canada with temperatures in the twenties. It was a great morning to be leaving Litchfield, headed for some tropical beach in the Caribbean. But there she was, stuck in heavy traffic at the Ferdon Street railroad crossing, watching two freight trains creep by.

All night long her thoughts had volleyed back and forth between Johnny and Nicholas, the two men she so desperately loved. It was as though life was forcing her to declare her loyalty, to make one relationship bow down to the other.

In her Cousin Maria's Sunday school class back in Mexico, the Priest would often read from the Bible. One of his favorite verses said: *No one can serve two masters. Either he will hate the one and love the other, or he will be devoted to the one and despise the other.*

But what did the Priest know? He read the Bible on Sunday, but stayed drunk in the Tequila bottle the rest of the week. He had his two masters and so did she. Both of them provided purpose and meaning in her life and were inseparable to her happiness. If life thought it could make her choose between them, then life had another thought coming.

The last freight train had just cleared the crossing when Nicholas' name popped up on her caller ID. There was so much static and background noise, she could barely hear his voice.

"I know I'm not your favorite person right now," he acknowledged. "But I couldn't let this day pass without wishing you a happy birthday. How does it feel to be an old woman?"

She giggled. "Fine. As long as I'm your old woman, yes?"

"You better believe it," he reassured her.

"What is all the noise?" she inquired.

"Lots of people. Lots of luggage. I'm in the baggage claim area at the Fort Lauderdale Airport. Just waiting for the shuttle from the cruise liner to get here."

Lola sighed, deeply. "I am sorry about last night. I was being a real *mocosa malcriada* ... how you say ... spoiled brat. I know you are doing what's best for us."

"No, I want to apologize too," he added. "It was very insensitive of me not to find time for your father. How is he doing by the way?"

"About the same."

"I want to meet him. You know I do."

"I know."

"Three days is not that long. We'll make it happen as soon as I get back," he promised.

With Johnny's deteriorating condition, three days was an eternity. But there was no need to burden Nicholas with the details. Instead, she offered a selfless cheer. "I hope you have a good time for both of us."

"It's a dirty job. But somebody's got to do it. That's what I told my vice president at the home office. He called me, you know, just to wish me a pleasant bon voyage."

"A big vice president called you?"

"Yes, I told you they keep up with everything, especially if they've got plans for you."

"I have plans for you." But he didn't hear her. Someone in the background was making an announcement about buses and lanes.

"Listen. The shuttle is here. We've got to go. I'll call you from the ship."

Lola's heart stopped for a brief moment, as she pressed her cell phone tightly to her ear. "*We*.... Did you say *we*?"

"Yes. I didn't want to waste the other ticket. So I gave it to another employee."

"Who did you give it to?" Lola demanded.

"I don't think you've met-"

"WHO did you give my ticket to?!!!" She roared.

"Her name is Terri. I had planned to talk to you about her. She's my..."

"Little whore, just like me." Lola finished the sentence for him. And then she slung her Blackberry out of the window, into a slime-infested ditch.

When Lola finally reached the hospital, her eyes were blood red from crying. She had barely avoided running down a group of pedestrians along the way. At the last minute she had swerved onto the sidewalk and sent a line of aluminum garbage cans sailing through the air. Only a street full of trash had prevented an off duty Litchfield patrol officer from chasing her down.

Stepping off the fourth floor elevator, she noticed several medical carts parked next to Johnny's room. A black nurse with broad shoulders and manly features beckoned her over to the nurse's station.

"Where have you been?" she reprimanded her. "They've been trying to reach you for hours."

"Caught in traffic." *And learning what a fool I've been,* she thought to herself.

"The doctor wanted to talk to you about your father."

"Is he alright?"

"He had an episode. Have a seat in the waiting room. They'll explain everything."

A few minutes later, Dr. Campbell walked over to her. "I'm sorry to have to tell you this. Your father is in a comma. We're hopeful he'll come out of it. But even so, these are the last stages."

Lola wanted to cry, but had no tears left. "You promised to be honest with me, doctor."

"Yes."

"How much time does he have?"

For a few ponderous seconds, he stood there, motionless,

sucking in the frigid hospital air, forcing his words to line up in a truthful, uncorrupted flow. "Without a new kidney, maybe forty-eight hours."

"Can I see him?" she asked.

"Sure. But only for a few minutes. He needs as much rest as he can get."

Lola stood over Johnny's bed a long while, clutching his huge, lifeless hand. Remembering his recent trip to New York, she whispered softly, defiantly, in his ear. "You are not a dead man. You have forty-eight hours left."

****

Lola stormed out of the hospital, angry ... angry at Nicholas for his heartless betrayal; angry at her father for not being able to throw his protective arms around her and shield her from the treacherous storms of life; angry because there was no one else to point her toward the morning sun and declare a glorious new day of hope, just over the orange horizon.

Hours earlier, she had two masters. It appeared, in less than forty-eight hours, she would have none. If ever there was a time to be a timid crybaby whiner, that time was now.

It took the billboard of a lion's head to bring her to her senses.

Among the many brilliantly colored outdoor signs that cluttered Interstate-55 was a particularly opulent display announcing the re-opening of the Springfield Henson Robinson City Zoo. A new crop of exotic lions and tigers had been brought in from Africa. The Serengeti lion, plastered on the big sixty foot board, looked just like the one she had dreamed about many months earlier; the same one on the Juba Chest.

The little chest had turned out to be a big disappointment.

The antique collectors and pawn shop owners she contacted had all but laughed in her face. Still, the prophetic words of Professor Broadson had never really left her mind ... *worthless to some; priceless to others.* If the chest was worth something to the Mauertanians, maybe it was worth something to her too.

She pulled into the U-Haul driveway. An old frosty headed man that reminded her of a beardless Santa Claus sat at the office desk. After looking up her name on a list, he handed her a plastic access card. "We changed the security system. You'll need this to get in."

She took the card and started out of the door.

He cleared his throat. "I notice you have bin #70?"

She turned back. "Yes."

"Just a reminder. No animals allowed."

"Why do you say that to me?"

"One of the attendants thought he heard something; probably that marijuana and meth combo rolling around in his head. But I figured I'd mention it to you, just in case."

Lola didn't respond. She went to the bin, retrieved the chest and headed back to her apartment.

That night, in the solitude of her bedroom, she gazed into the chest at the harmless chips of wood. The professor's words kept coming back to her: *One day circumstances will seduce you. And, in desperation, you WILL turn to the chest.*

That was exactly what she was doing, without any reluctance or hesitation. Life had a way of stirring up the pot so all the hard choices rose to the top. But for her, there were no other choices. Death was on the march, heading straight for Johnny's room. If the chest held the power of life and death, maybe, just maybe, it would grant him a fighting chance.

She reached into the chest and grabbed the largest piece of

bark she could find. She placed it under her pillow and closed her eyes. Her wish was simple: a kidney for her father, the one miracle that could save his life.

Everyone dreaded the miserable traffic jams in Litchfield. Most of them were caused by the two remaining national rail carriers: Norfolk Southern Railway and Burlington Northern Santa Fe Railroad. Like two iron belts buckled around a bulging hour glass, their parallel tracks split the city in half. To get to Litchfield's industrial east side, you had to cross the tracks. To get to the commercial west side, you had to cross the tracks.

There were always trains coming out of Chicago or going into New York ... long, slow box cars or fast-moving passenger trains that seemed to be driven by ex-racecar drivers escaping prison. Rail transport was a big business in America. People would just have to wait.

Over the years, firefighters and EMS ambulance drivers had gone before City officials, pleading for a remedy. These requests usually came after a fatal house fire or when an accident or heart attack victim died in the back of an EMS vehicle while waiting to get across the track.

Though everyone agreed something needed to be done, underpasses and overpasses cost tons of money, money the small city didn't have. The State had promised to help. The federal government had promised to help. But the money never came.

Tucker "Loverboy" Hoskins was well aware of the traffic problems in Litchfield. At thirty-nine years old, tall and farm-boy strong, he had spent half his life driving gasoline tankers for one big oil company or another. A third of the Fast Stop gas stations to which he delivered were located in the Springfield/Litchfield area. During the summer price spikes, he might deliver as far as East St. Louis.

Although, he loved the smell of diesel and the wide open road, the most rewarding part of his job was the freedom it gave him to drop in on his many lady friends along the way. Though the names and addresses often changed, his standard list of three steadies and one alternate stayed the same.

There hadn't been a problem until the new supervisor for distribution came on board. He was the one always number crunching on his fancy computer, snooping through the records and messing with the schedules. He was the one pressuring Loverboy to change his wild and wooly ways.

"One more late delivery and your services are no longer needed," he had threatened. That's why Loverboy was barreling down Ferdon Street that morning, virtually out of control.

The Canadian cold front had dumped a thin coat of ice and snow on the roadways, the worst conditions to test the agility of a thirty foot tanker truck filled with gasoline. But if Loverboy didn't beat the 9:20 am Burlington Northern passenger train coming out of Chicago, he would find himself stuck at the crossing, a dead giveaway of his unauthorized breakfast-in-bed rendezvous with his main, big breasted sweetie, number one on the list.

Three blocks from the Ferdon Street crossing, Loverboy

observed the red signal lights starting to blink. He had sixty seconds before the double wooden crossing arms came down. He had time. He could make it ... except ... an old woman in a beat-up green Buick had already slammed on her brakes.

Unbelievable! The jittery old hen was literally waiting for the crossing arms to come down.

Loverboy laid on his loud, one hundred and fifty decibels Wolo horn, trying to urge her across. But she just sat there like an old stubborn green turtle, ushering his illustrious truck-driving career to a shameful end.

Loverboy never slowed down. He swerved the big rig into the opposite lane and headed for the tracks.

To his delight, the big tanker clawed through the ice with surprising grit and authority. It was as though the truck knew exactly what was at stake.

All systems were go for his mad dash across the railing. That's when he saw the white bakery truck coming at him with the same mad dash in mind.

Loverboy slammed on his brakes, sending the rig careening up the incline and onto the tracks. When the massive load of industrial steel and high octane fuel finally came to a halt, its extended cab rested perpendicular to the tacks ... a perfect T to represent the horrendous TRAGEDY that was about to occur.

The old diesel engine had sputtered to a grinding halt. He tried to restart it, over and over, again. He pulled the choke, flooded the injectors, stomped on the accelerator.

Nothing. When the wooden crossing arms crashed onto the back of the tanker, Loverboy knew his time had run out. He jumped from the cab and scrambled down the hill.

Unlike the many freight trains that poked along like rickety iron caskets, the Burlington Northern was the fastest train of all. It blistered passengers through the little town at fifty miles an hour, mostly, unofficially faster than that, relegating an *emergency* stop to a ridiculous, laughable ten minute ordeal.

Loverboy knew the train couldn't stop in time. What he didn't know was whether his scramble down the slippery incline would provide him with enough distance to save his life. The more he ran, the more he fell down. His genuine Stetson cowboy boots were no match for the treacherous ice sheets that blanketed the steep slope.

The train's engineer finally spotted the danger.

Frantically, he began blowing his whistle. Car tires squealed in a unified backward motion over the slushy streets. A woman in the distance screamed hysterically; the kind of scream a delirious concert groupie would bellow before the star performers came out on stage. There were no star performers, however, just a lethal locomotive bearing down on a tanker truck filled with gasoline.

Everyone within a ten mile radius of the explosion felt the aftershock. It was like the deafening sound of a giant kettle drum, reverberating too loudly and too long. A huge orange and black mushroom cloud rose up from the crossing. An old timer at the nearby Veteran Affairs Office later reported that it reminded him of the bomb they had dropped on Japan.

When the shock wave from the explosion rocked her apartment complex, Lola was in another world.

She was dreaming about her mother in a beautiful purple dress, clutching a huge bouquet of red roses and smiling, brightly. The setting was unfamiliar, yet warm and festive, with Mexican music playing in the background. Lola found it curious that she and her mother appeared to be wearing the same purplish attire. And who was the stranger ... a tall Mexican Matador, wearing a red satin cape, trimmed in gold ... standing over their shoulder?

Lola awakened to the hard acoustic thump, followed by the delayed shrill of a thousand sirens. A few minutes later, someone in the parking lot began to cry. Perhaps, it was the old African woman with the skull necklace who apparently showed up whenever the

Juba Chest was nearby.

When Lola looked out of her window, she saw a familiar black couple from an adjacent complex, consoling an older woman in a flowered dress. She cried hyterically, both hands, beating the frostbitten air. They finally managed to load her into a pickup truck and then sped away.

Something big was going on. Lola could feel it in her bones. She walked into the front room and turned on the television.

A solemn-faced news anchor from Channel 55 stood a few miles from the Ferdon Street crossing. She clutched a silver microphone, tightly, in her hand:

"IF YOU'RE JUST JOINING US, THERE'S BEEN A CATASTROPHIC EXPLOSION HERE IN LITCHFIELD AT THE FERDON STREET CROSSING. UNOFFICIAL REPORTS ARE CLAIMING MULTIPLE CASUALTIES AS A RESULT OF A COLLISION BETWEEN A GASOLINE TRUCK AND A BURLINGTON NORTHERN PASSENGER TRAIN. IN THE DISTANCE, YOU CAN SEE THE LINE OF FIRE TRUCKS STILL BATTLING THE FLAMES. WE WERE TOLD - AGAIN, THIS IS STRICTLY UNOFFICIAL - BOTH OF THE ENGINEERS WERE KILLED AS WELL AS AN UNDETERMINED NUMBER OF PASSENGERS RIDING IN THE FIRST FEW PASSENGER CARS."

An assistant rushed up to whisper something in her ear. She then continued:

"CITY OFFICIALS ARE ASKING ALL AVAILABLE MEDICAL PERSONNEL AND EMS ATTENDANTS FROM LITCHFIELD AND SURROUNDING CITIES TO REPORT TO ST. FRANCIS HOSPITAL IMMEDIATELY. WITH LIMITED RESOURCES, THEY'RE GOING TO NEED ALL THE HELP

THEY CAN GET.....AGAIN, TRAGEDY HAS STRUCK LITCHFIELD IN AN UNPRECEDENTED MANNER, THE LIKES OF WHICH WE HAVE NEVER SEEN. MANY LIVES HAVE BEEN LOST HERE TODAY. NO ONE SEEMS TO KNOW HOW OR WHY?"

A cold chill slithered down Lola's spine. She threw on some jeans and a heavy suede jacket and barreled out of the door.

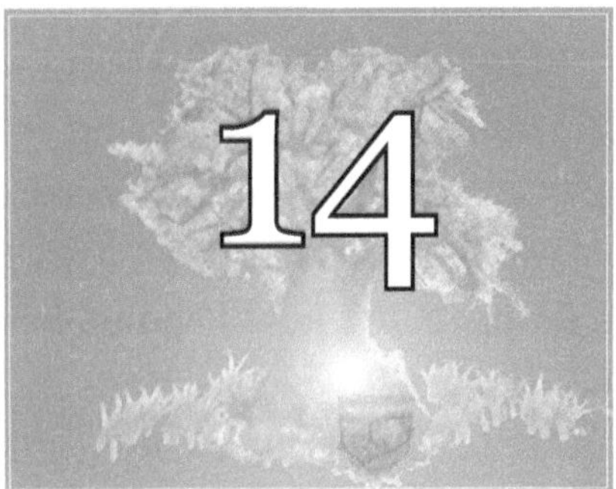

Crisscrossing several back roads she had discovered while working at various Allen Brothers' construction sites, it still took Lola two hours in stop-and-start traffic to reach the hospital.

Inside, everyone appeared wedded in foggish, lockstep pandemonium. Nurses and doctors ran in all directions, shouting conflicting orders. Distraught family members screamed, incoherently, searching the lobby for loved ones last seen at the explosion site; all of this chaos amidst a gruesome backdrop of black body bags, rolling in through the emergency room, one after another.

Reaching the fourth floor, she found the control desk abandoned. One Philippine nurse scurried from room to room, trying to manage the entire wing.

Lola felt relieved to find Johnny in his room sound asleep. She sat by his bedside for hours before Dr. Campbell finally came in.

She tried to give him a piece of her mind for leaving her father unattended. Instead, he interrupted her with some remarkable news.

"I don't want to get your hopes up. But I believe we have a donor."

Her eyes radiated with disbelief. "For my daddy?"

"Yes. We're running tests right now."

"How did you find..."

"We have twenty-six fatalities downstairs, and counting. One was a truck driver with your father's blood type and antigen profile."

Her head dropped. "I guess I should be sorry that this truck driver died. But..."

"What you're feeling is a normal, healthy contradiction. As a part of humanity, you don't want to see a person die. On the other hand, you want your father to live."

"Yes. That is the thing exactly."

He looked at his clipboard. Tucker Hoskin's name was underlined in red. "If it makes you feel any better, they're saying this man's recklessness caused the accident. Of course, that's uncorroborated."

Not knowing what *uncorroborated* meant, she remained silent.

He beckoned her away from the bed and over by the door. "I still want to be honest with you. Even if the tests are favorable, there's always the possibility the new kidney will thrombose or leak or your father's body will reject the new organ, altogether. That could put us back to square one."

"He won't reject it, doctor. I promise you."

Admiring her unrelenting optimism, he managed a narrow smile. "Very well, then. The nurse will bring you the appropriate papers to sign. Also, without insurance, you'll need to deal with someone in the financial office immediately. We're waiting on some final cross-matching results to come back. If all goes well, we'll operate within the next twenty-four hours."

The next day a team of surgeons operated on Johnny for

six hours. Late that afternoon, as she sat by his bedside, he slowly regained consciousness. His dark pupils searched the sterile recovery room, trying to recognize his new surroundings. Seeing Lola's familiar face, he attempted to raise his head. The excruciating pain, however, drove him back into his pillow.

"No, no. Do not move," she ordered. "Just rest now."

He lay there for a long while, occasionally grimacing from the constant throbbing in his abdomen. Finally, he spoke in a low, throaty voice. "Did we beat the white folks to a kidney?"

She smiled, warmly. "Yes, yes we did."

"Keep the hog running," he said, referring to his prize Deville. "Just in case they try to take it back."

****

Most people thought the rudiments of timing came from heaven. But they were wrong. Some timing came straight from hell. At that very hour back in Chicago, Johnny's blue Cadillac Deville was the subject of a more diabolic discussion between Vinnie Meatball's half brother, Raymond, and a shady private investigator named Joe DeLeon.

Raymond had indeed recognized Johnny, completing his transaction with Calypso in the lobby of the Omni Hotel. A clerk at the front desk who had once lived in Vinnie's old neighborhood gladly supplied Raymond with Johnny's credit card information. From there, DeLeon had tracked Johnny to a P.O. Box in Litchfield.

The problem for DeLeon was that Johnny never came to the P.O. Box in Litchfield. There was no way DeLeon could know, as an added precaution, Johnny had his mail forwarded to another P.O. Box in Springfield.

DeLeon's first break had come when a national database

for private investigators showed the same credit card being used to pay for an emergency ambulance ride to St Francis Hospital. Although hospital officials would not release any patient information, DeLeon had tracked down one of the ambulance drivers that delivered Johnny to the emergency room. A $500 contribution to his home liquor cabinet had been enough to get the semi-alcoholic driver to spill the beans.

"I'm close," DeLeon had told Raymond months earlier at a private New Years Eve party at the old LaPietra mob mansion on West 30th. But the very next day, a top Southside boss had pulled DeLeon off of Johnny's case to find a missing insurance executive. The man owed a large sum of money to Jack Tocco and the Detroit organization. It was bad business to let an indiscretion of that magnitude fall through the cracks.

It had taken DeLeon two months to find the missing executive in Buenos Aries. It had taken another two weeks for Argentine officials to fish his body from the Salado River in Roque Pérez. By then, DeLeon was back in Litchfield, hot on Johnny's trail.

"I've got his alias, his address, and his noisy '99 blue Deville, all registered under the fake name of Johnny Fountain," DeLeon reported to Raymond on his trip back to Chicago. "What I don't have is Johnny Fountain. Some young Mexican chick is driving his car. But he's nowhere to be found."

DeLeon had decided to give it a few weeks. He surmised by then, disruptions caused by the big train explosion would subside and Litchfield's simple minded, podunk dwellers would again settle into their normal, small-town routines.

"Sooner or later the tar baby is going to come out to play," DeLeon had predicted. "That's when we bring in the cavalry."

****

Johnny was nowhere near coming out to play. It had taken him a full week to emerge from his tangled web of intravenous drips and electronic monitors.

He sat erectly against his pillow, slurping a spoonful of tasteless chicken soup. "How are your classes coming, Babygirl?"

"They are fine."

He pointed to the bathroom door. "Can you open that door a minute?"

She walked over and opened it. "You need to go?"

"No. I'm trying to see if your professors are in there, cause they damn sure ain't in here, knowemsayin'?"

She dropped her head.

"You've been cooped up in here with me for the last five or six days. When have you gone to class?"

"I didn't want to leave you, Daddy."

"That's why I'm paying all these high-priced doctors," he reminded her. "They can handle their business. You need to handle yours."

She sat there in silence, trying to fight back the tears.

Johnny's voice softened a bit. "You know what's kept me going all this time?"

She shook her head, obliviously.

"I've been clawing and kicking to stay around, just so I could see you graduate from college. You got two months left, Babygirl. Don't blow it now."

"I won't. I promise."

I want you to do more than promise. I want you to get on the phone right now. Call all your professors and find out how far you're behind."

"I-aahh, I no have a phone," she shamefully admitted.

"When I bought you that expensive top-of-the-line Blackberry, I told you to guard it with your life. What happened to it?"

Seeing she couldn't answer, he continued. "You know what, just forget about that phone. You know where my money is?"

"Behind the refrigerator," she whimpered.

"Get yourself another phone. From what I hear, Blackberries are on their way out anyway. My tech guy says these little crappy iphones are the next big thing. But first I want you to go over to that school and get your business straight, knowemsayin'? Get it straight today!"

As she got up to leave, a news reporter came on the television. His cameras focused on the Ferdon Street crossing:

"AFTER THIRTY-ONE DEATHS, MILLIONS IN PROPERTY DAMAGES AND A WEEK OF CLEAN UP AND CONSTRUCTION DELAYS, THE FERDON STREET CROSSING HAS JUST REOPENED. CONSIDERED BY MOST REGIONAL DISASTER EXPERTS AS THE WORST CATASTROPHE IN THE CITY'S HISTORY, MANY PEOPLE ARE WONDERING HOW DID THIS HAPPEN AND COULD IT HAPPEN AGAIN."

Johnny used his remote control to mute the sound. Then he looked at Lola with deep contemplation. "Ever wonder about things like that, Babygirl? I mean, why here, why now?"

Festering in the back of her mind was a horrible possibility, one that made his question too difficult to answer. She wasn't going to answer. She grabbed her jacket and stormed out of the door.

Nicholas' mother knew something was wrong. Somehow, mothers always know.

When he stopped by his parents' house a few weeks after the cruise, his mother immediately noticed his bugged red eyes and skinny frame. She pulled him into her sewing room and began her maternal inquiry.

"What's going on, Nicholas?"

He paused a long while. "I-aahh, I'm moving to Kansas City. I wanted you and dad to be the first to know."

She took a deep breath, hoping to conceal the sudden rush of anxiety, the innate hollowness all mothers feel when their children decide to go away. "Kansas City? I've never heard you talk about Kansas City. What brought this on?"

"It's all job related, part of the organization's master plan."

"Are you happy about it?"

"Yeah, sure, why wouldn't I be? More money, more

responsibility, a chance to move up the corporate ladder."

"Then, why don't you look happy, Nicholas?"

"I'm tired, Mom. Just tired, that's all. There's a huge amount of work and preparation involved in transitioning to another location."

"Usually, tired people can't wait to go to sleep. They're exhausted. They go home and crash out."

"What's that supposed to mean?" he snapped.

"Someone at the clinic told me you came by trying to get a prescription. Something to help you sleep?"

"My God! Do those people know anything about patient confidentiality?"

"They know about family and how we need to look out for each other. Why do you think I've been going there for twenty years?"

"Okay, okay, so it's been stressful. I've had trouble sleeping. Is that a crime?"

She reached out to curl her soft fingers around his thin face. "No. But not trusting your mother enough to tell her the truth is worse than a crime."

Nicholas pulled away from her. Without saying a word he flopped in a nearby armchair and stared at the floor.

She continued. "You know who you remind me of?"

"No."

"Me ... the hopeless, confused, self-pitying me that had found out your father had cheated with another woman and fathered a child. I couldn't eat, couldn't sleep and had the same red eyes. Is that what it is, Nicholas? Has Lola been with someone else?"

"I don't know who she's been with," he bellowed. "It's not my business anymore."

"It is your business if you love her. Do you love her?"

Nicholas fell into silence again.

"I'll take that as a yes," she surmised. "So look at it this way. You have a wise old woman who just happens to be your mother and who loves you and who knows how women think. Tell me everything that happened and let's sort through this whole thing together."

Nicholas spent the next hour explaining the circumstances. When he had finished, she asked, "Did you tell her that Terri is-"

"I tried, Mom. I really did. But she hung up the phone."

"Lola is afraid," she explained in a methodical tone.

"Of what?"

"Of losing you. That's why she's pushing you away."

He shook his head with bewilderment. "I graduated near the top of my class at Penn State. But what you just said is totally over my head."

"Trust me. It's a woman's thing."

"Okay. But what should I do now?"

"Find her. Let her know you love her and just how committed you are to her. Everything else will fall into place."

It didn't take Nicholas long to discover everything wasn't going to fall into place.

Back at his apartment, he rummaged through beautiful Hallmark cards expressing her affection, funny notes she had left in his briefcase, old college textbooks she had used during the winter semester, the empty jelly bean wrappers in the pockets of her designer jeans and a folder containing the Crystal Creek photo of her perfect hole. These were the surviving witnesses to a love affair now gone bad.

Yet, none of the witnesses would speak to him; none would relinquish a single clue to lead him to his backdoor princess whose dark eyes, sweet smell and bright smile clawed relentlessly at his heart.

Her cell phone was disconnected. The hospital couldn't confirm whether her father was still a patient because Nicholas didn't know Johnny's last name. Lincoln Land College was out on Spring Break leaving only a dumb recorder in the administration building to answer the phone.

Meanwhile, his Bishop Hardware clock was ticking with callous precision. He needed to get the back office files in order, train a new manager and move to Kansas City, all in the span of two weeks. At least, he thought he had two weeks.

On Monday, he received an unexpected call from his regional manager. "I need to ask you a big favor. The manager at the Kansas City store was in a horrible car accident. They don't know if he's going to live. Can you move your schedule up a week? We need you over there as soon as possible."

"Up a week?" Nicholas tried to clarify.

"Yes. I need you there next Monday."

"But I haven't finished-"

"I know," she interrupted. "We'll take care of all of that. The company's going to send packers over to your apartment, move your stuff and put you up in a hotel until you can find a place. I'll finish training your new manager."

Nicholas barely had time to tell his mother and father goodbye.

That Sunday night on his way to the Springfield airport, he thought he saw a blue 1999 Coupe Deville go cruising by ... or maybe it was a green one ... or maybe it wasn't a Coupe Deville at all. The ghosts from his past were playing tricks on his mind. A love-sick heart was distorting his proverbial sense of reality. And yet, there he was, the stupid gung ho company man, heading to a distant runway, fleeing from any possibility of relief.

One of his Penn State professors had once said, "Men are

from Venus and woman are from Mars." But Nicholas wasn't from either place. He was from the dumb side of Springfield where corporate-driven workaholics allowed love to slip through their boney fingers and forever pass them by.

****

Fifty miles away, at St Francis Hospital in Litchfield, Lola stood over a sterile white toilet, throwing up her guts. Since her breakup with Nicholas, she could barely keep down her food. The invisible lump in her throat felt as though it was part rock, part razor, slicing each breath into a million needles of air. Intermittent chills caused her hands to tremble. They reminded her of the severe case of pneumonia she had endured as a child.

The painful emotional roller coaster ride had reduced her pudgy waistline and brought her down a full dress size to a very tight ten.

Still, who was going to help her celebrate the unintended, flab-trouncing victory? There were no hordes of love-starved bachelors roaming around outside her window; no desperate male suitors, combing the Want Ads, seeking an attractive, newly-reconfigured psychological wreck? Misery didn't have any company. All it had was an echo in the back of her brain reminding her that even on this side of the Rio Grande, she was still a loser.

When Lola finally returned to Johnny's room, she found him sitting in a flimsy wooden chair next to his bed. Standing nearby, scanning his clipboard with guarded approval and stroking his thick mustache, Dr. Campbell began to smile. "So there you are, the distinguished soon-to-be graduate of Lincoln Land College. A certain proud father has been telling me all about you."

She smiled, nervously, but didn't say a word. She was still searching for the courage to tell Johnny she might not graduate at all.

Nothing was working out.

She had gone over to the college earlier in the week, trying to get her academic life back in order. The two professors who allowed her to take makeup exams had expressed utter disappointment at her dreadful results.

One of them, Professor Gusemano, a legal immigrant from El Salvador, had called her into his office.

"I've watched your remarkable progress this past year. I even took the liberty of sharing your strong will and sticktoitiveness with some of the younger students facing the same insurmountable obstacles. But now you're skipping class and flunking exams. What's going on? Did I misjudge you?"

"I have a lot of family problems," she tried to explain.

"You do know you are hurting more than yourself?"

"What do you mean?"

"Conservative politicians, that's a nice name for mine-and-not-yours, hate our guts. They do it for a living. They get elected based on how loudly they can scream *illegal* and *crime-ridden* and *worthless* and a *drain on society*. By doing this you are playing right into their hands."

"I told you. I have many problems."

"Problems are guaranteed," he warned her. "Graduation is not. Don't expect any more recommendations like the one I gave to Allen Brothers construction company. And don't expect any more breaks in this class, especially if you're not going to take advantage of them. People hate us without a reason. They don't need your help."

All week long, she had thought about all of the people she was going to disappoint ... her professors who had come to respect her; Johnny who had invested his money, heart and soul into her; her mother and Aunt Conchita back in Mexico who had spread the word of her pending success; even Goodboy, the trailer trash white man who had taken her under his wing and tried to protect her from the Allen brother's daily barrage of racist slurs and scornful attacks. Now the doctor had added himself to the list.

Johnny continued to dial up the pressure. "I told her, Doc. The thought of her walking across that stage in cap and gown with that piece of paper in her hand was the only thing that kept me going."

Dr. Campbell concurred. "I do understand. My wife and I don't have children, but we reared our niece, a somewhat troubled child. She got her start at Lincoln Land, then went on to the University of Illinois for her Bachelor's and Master's. She's a vice president now at Penn State University."

When the doctor said Penn State, something exploded in Lola's head. She flopped down on Johnny's bed and began to sob.

The doctor was visibly baffled. "I'm sorry. Did I say something-"

"Don't sweat it, Doc," Johnny explained. "She's been this way since her and that whiii ... well, Caucasian boy broke up. If you say Penn State or hardware store or Caribbean cruise, she'll flood the whole room."

Dr. Campbell walked over and put his arm around her. "I'm sorry. I didn't know."

"It's okay."

"Your first heartbreak?"

She nodded.

"Don't worry. There'll be plenty more."

She bellowed even louder.

"All I'm saying is life is full of ups and downs, heartbreaks and disappointments. But somehow, as members of the unstoppable human race, our resilience takes over and we survive. You're going to work through this. You have to believe that."

"But it is very hard. And nothing is guaranteed," she reflected on her professor's warning.

"But don't you see. That's the whole point of it. Nothing *is* guaranteed. The whole world is completely open to you."

Johnny chimed in. "That's right, Babygirl. You can be

anything you want to be, go anywhere you want to go."

"What's your major over there?" inquired Dr. Campbell.

"Construction Management," she replied.

"Have you had any hands-on experience in your field?"

She thought about her Allen Brothers' fiasco. "Nothing to be proud of."

He pondered for a long while. Finally, he pulled out a small pad from his coat pocket and began to write. "I sit on a community board with this lady. She owns the Redfish Construction Company in Springfield. I believe she would be open to furthering your career."

"But what if I don't graduate on time?"

"You're going to graduate," he reassured her. "But don't wait until then. I want you to go see her right away. I'll put in a good word."

"You see, Babygirl. You don't even have that piece of paper in your hands yet and things are already rolling your way."

She began to smile, the first smile she had mustered in three long weeks. "How can I thank you?"

Well, since you mentioned it..." He chuckled, deviously. "I want you to help me sell your father on something that will help us all."

"What is it, Doctor? You tell me and I will whip him into shape."

Dr. Campbell unveiled the details of a new clinical study comparing different doses of Cellcept in combination with Tacrolimus in new kidney transplant recipients.

"CellCept is one of the three immunosuppressant drugs patients take after kidney transplants," he explained. "This study will measure the amount of CellCept in his blood to determine the benefits of certain levels of usage."

"How long will this measuring take?" asked Johnny. "I mean, no disrespect to the fine treatment I've been getting. But three weeks in the sick house? I'm ready to blow this joint."

"Actually, I've scheduled you to be discharged tomorrow. Your renal enzymes look good and the organ is showing no significant signs of rejection."

Johnny grinned with satisfaction. "Now that's what I'm talking 'bout."

"So will he come back here for the study?" asked Lola.

"Not here," replied Dr. Campbell. "The study is in Chicago."

Johnny and Lola glared at each other, but didn't say a word.

"Is there a problem with Chicago?"

"Yes," said Lola.

"No, not really," Johnny replied at the same time.

The doctor paused. "I do hope you understand the importance of this study. Many lives will be saved or lost, based on our findings."

"Is this an in-and-out kind of deal?" Johnny asked.

"I'm afraid not. You'll be required to spend a full week undergoing extensive physical examinations, stress level protocols and blood and urine testing. After that you'll have to report to the clinic once a month for three months to be evaluated."

"I grew up in the streets, Doc. So I have to ask a very important question."

"Yes?"

"What's in it for me?" Johnny pressed him. "I mean, all that time spent, running back and forth to Chicago. I still have a life, you know."

Dr. Campbell thought about it for a long time. "I didn't grow up in the streets. But I have a very important question for you."

"Yeah, what's that?"

"Why do you still have a life?"

Johnny frowned. "I don't follow you."

"Let's be frank, Mr. Fountain. For all practical purposes, you shouldn't be here. The odds of a donor kidney becoming available at such a crucial time in your treatment are astronomical. Furthermore, the donor had already signed a gift of life commitment to make his organs available. The statistical probability for both events occurring in conjunction with each other is simply off the chart."

"What's your point, Doc?"

"My point is someone had to give in order for you to live. It wouldn't be a bad idea if you considered giving back. We have no African-Americans in the study. So you'd be helping physicians all over the world develop specific protocols for patients of your heritage."

Johnny smiled. "Are you playing the race card on me, Doc?"

"I am ... and the money card too. The $50,000 for maintenance you'll pay for the next twelve months will be underwritten by the study. In other words, for the next twelve months, all of your medical costs associated with the transplant will be covered by our grant."

"Doc, you drive a hard bargain. How can I say no?"

"You can say no because it is Chicago," Lola intervened.

Dr. Campbell studied her worried face. "I take it there are some misgivings about the Windy City. If it helps, the actual study will be at a clinic just outside of Chicago in a suburb called Oak Lawn."

"I know exactly where it is, near the Midway Airport."

"It is still Chicago," Lola fired back.

"Listen. I'm generally not here on Sunday nights. But the paperwork for this study has to be completed and faxed in by noon tomorrow. I'll give you two a chance to talk this over. But I need to know something by tomorrow morning."

"I understand, Doc. Time is of the essence."

The doctor reached into a large envelope beneath his clipboard. "Here's the form. I've highlighted the places you need to sign. If you decide to participate, just sign the form and tell the nurse at the night station to put it in my box."

"Let's say I get on this guinea pig train. When does it pull out of the station?" asked Johnny.

"You'll need to check into the Oak Lawn clinic next Sunday night. I'll provide you with all the details."

When Dr. Campbell left the room, Lola turned to Johnny. "You are not going to do this. Tell me you will not go through with this foolish plan."

"You heard the man, Babygirl. I've got a chance to give back."

"Give what back, your life?"

He got up from his chair and sat beside her on the bed. He stroked her silky black hair as though she were a small child whose kitten had run away.

"Listen. I don't talk about God much. But I know that every once in a blue moon he stops what he's doing to reach into my old sad sack life and stir up the pot. He sent a crazy truck driver across an icy train track, just so I could live again. You think he's going to let some Mafia wise guy screw that up?"

"But what if God didn't send the driver across the track?" she speculated.

He shook his head. "You got me there, Babygirl, knowemsayin'. Because if he didn't, then who did?"

When Johnny's blue hog was running smoothly, it reminded Lola of a gigantic luxury liner, gliding, effortlessly, across a tranquil sea. But seldom did it run smoothly. There were always problems with the exhaust system and overheating heads and electrical sensors. The Landmark Cadillac Dealership in Springfield was so familiar with servicing the '99 Deville, they provided Johnny with a loaner car for free.

A few days after Johnny's release from the hospital, with explicit instructions from Dr. Campbell not to drive, he sent Lola over to the dealership to get his luxurious troublemaker repaired.

"Ask for John-John," he had told her that morning as she left the apartment. "Just tell him that raggedy ass junkyard sensor he put in the last time played out again."

With no classes that day, Lola had planned to spend time familiarizing herself with Johnny's bizarre assortment of medications and trying her hand at some low-sugar, low-fat, protein-rich meals. But understanding the importance of his request, she quickly adjusted her plans.

Being on the run from the mob deprived Johnny of many of life's ordinary pleasures. Understanding his disdain for Johnny's line of work and fearing the mob might place a private wiretap on his phone, Johnny never talked to his brother, ArchieV. And although he occasionally played poker with a few close acquaintances, Solomon Burke, Jr and BottomsUp, Johnny made it a point to have no friends. The mob's deep pockets had a way of turning friends into snitches, and the snitched-upon, into corpses. Besides reacquainting himself with a daughter he had never known, the Cadillac was his only semblance of self-gratification and reward.

Under a pale blue sky, with windows down, music blasting and a crisp March headwind nipping at her face, Lola headed down Interstate-55 to Springfield.

Perhaps, it was Johnny's repeated warnings about safety protocols, or the tragic death of her younger sister back in Mexico. Whatever the reason, Lola kept a mindset of constant vigilance. As she approached the Cadillac dealership in Springfield, she noticed a gray Ford Taurus following her a few cars back. When she turned into the dealership parking lot, the Taurus did the same. The driver parked the car at the edge of the lot, but never got out.

A tall white man with a wide smile met her in the service lane. "Good morning! It's a great day at Landmark Cadillac. How can we help you?"

"I'm looking for John-John," said Lola.

The man placed two fingers in his mouth and whistled, loudly. "Hey John-John. This beautiful little lady is asking for you."

A chubby black man with a round face, wearing blue coveralls and carrying a clipboard, lumbered to the back of the service isle. He glanced at the Deville and smiled. "I don't know you, but I certainly know this vehicle. What has Mr. Fountain done to screw it up this time?"

"He says you screwed it up."

"Yeah, ycah, it's always our fault." He handed her the clipboard. "Sign the bottom line and date it. We're pretty backed up right now. But we'll pull a full diagnostic on it in the morning."

"Tomorrow?"

"Don't look so worried, little lady. You can spend the night at my house, or I can get you a courtesy car for free."

She pretended to ponder her options. "I think I'll take the courtesy car."

"That's probably the best choice. My wife is just so finicky about me bringing strange women home."

John-John led Lola into the showroom. "Just wait here. I'll get you a loaner from the back."

Lola slipped into her hyper-analytic, self-induced methodical mode. "You say the car is in the back?"

"Yes, ma'am. Right across from the body shop."

"Then I will follow you to the back. It will be easier that way."

When Lola drove the new burgundy STS around front, she kept her head low and turned away. She followed the street exit furthest from the Taurus. In her rear view mirror, she could still see the driver sitting there, waiting for her to come out.

Johnny had a system in place. But with the explosion, kidney operation and extended weeks away from the apartment, no one had been using it. Lola had a new phone and a new number. But neither she nor Johnny had bothered to call the security company to make her number accessible to the system.

She kept thinking, *What if the mob had followed her from the apartment? What if they knew Johnny was there all alone?*

She dialed Johnny's number. There was no answer. Maybe, he was asleep or in the bathroom or gagging on one of his baseball-size pills. Or maybe, he was lying on the floor, a bloody gunshot wound to the back of the head.

She turned down one street and then another, trying to avoid passing the dealership, working her way back to Interstate-55. Finally, her phone rang.

"You called me, Babygirl?"

Don't excite him. Don't drive his blood pressure up, she told herself.

"I'm checking on you, Daddy," she calmly announced. "I wanted to make sure you're alright."

"I'm fine. How did you come out at the dealership?"

"I talked to your friend, John-John. He will let us know something tomorrow."

"What are you driving? Did he try to give you one of them little cramped-up, go-cart compacts?"

"No. This car is very roomy, very nice," she reported.

"Then you won't mind making another stop while you're over there?"

"I was headed back home. But if you need something..."

"I do. I need you to look up that construction lady the doctor told you about."

"Maybe later, Daddy. Right now I need to see about you."

"You see? That's what you've been doing the whole week, worrying too much about me and not about yourself. I thought we got a clear understanding at the hospital."

"I'm not missing any classes. This is my day off."

"You're not missing classes, Babygirl. You're missing opportunity. You're missing open doors that were never open to me."

"I don't miss it. I just put it off until you go to Chicago. That way I know you are in good hands at the clinic."

"If I remember correctly, Doc said ASAP. You know what that means?"

"Yes, but-"

"But what?" he growled. "You're already over there in Springfield. Go handle your business. Let 'em know you a new breed of Mexican with a degree on the way."

****

RedFish Construction Company was located in an abandoned Kmart strip center on South Veterans Parkway, a few miles from the Springfield Capital Airport.

Pulling into the parking lot, Lola was overwhelmed by the endless clusters of dump trucks, excavators, asphalt trailers and bulldozers, swallowing up the gray stucco warehouse on all sides. Huge stockpiles of drywall, aluminum siding and prefabricated building supplies lined the sidewalks. Hundreds of racks of patio doors and window screens cluttered the intermittent crates and makeshift storage bins.

Even more mind-boggling was the hectic pace at which everyone moved. It was as though they were on roller skates, zipping, precariously, past each other like frantic travelers from another world. Most of the workers donned white hardhats with a giant RedFish logo on the front. Others wore red coverall uniforms with the same logo across their backs. The only person not sporting the Redfish insignia was a military-looking, black security guard, neatly dressed in a starched blue uniform with a pistol on his waist. He stood in the doorway of a small guard shack, just behind the chain-link fence.

"May I help you?" he queried as she came through the gate.

She stared, nervously, at his stern, ruddy face, then handed him the paper on which Dr. Campbell had written the address. "I'm here to see Mrs. RedFish."

"There is no Mrs. RedFish," he scolded her. "Do you mean Mrs. Cutler? That's the name on this paper."

"*Si*, I mean, yes," she stumbled. "I am here to see Mrs. Cutler."

"Do you have any appointment?"

"No, Dr. Campbell just told me to come."

"What's the nature of your business?" he pressed her.

"I'm hoping she can help me with my career."

He smiled, pitifully. "Listen. There are a thousand people out there who would like to talk to her about their career, their company, their products, their pet project for sponsorship. But without an appointment, it just ain't gonna happen."

At that moment, a white pickup truck pulled away from the building and headed toward the exit gate. A smallish, freckled faced redhead with bony shoulders and a deep tan ran behind it.

An older man with dark owl eyes and a pot belly finally stopped the truck and got out.

She beckoned him to the back. "Tell me, Benny. What's wrong with this picture?"

He surveyed the stack of custom doors and strips of plywood, weighing down the extended truck bed. "I-ah, I probably should've tied it down."

"Probably?" She smiled with thin razor lips.

"I know," he sadly confessed. "I just figured the site was only a few miles away."

"It's 7.2 miles away, Benny. Do you know what can happen in 7.2 miles?" She continued without allowing him to answer. "Same thing that happened last year when that sheet metal slid off your truck and caused a major accident on US-66. Do you remember that, Benny? My insurance company certainly does."

He nodded, shamefully.

"What did we agree to after that?"

"Safety first."

She pointed to the stack of doors, already leaning to one side. "Does this look like safety first to you?"

He dropped his head, saying nothing.

She paused for a long while. "I should fire you right here and now, Benny. But I'm not going to. You know why?"

He shook his head with cautious relief. "No, ma'am."

"Because, you've been with me from the very start. You always clock in early, miss your lunch if you have to, do the grunt work that nobody else wants to do. I know that deep down inside you have the best interest of this company at heart." She smiled again, this time, placing her thin hand on his shoulder. "I also know your daughter has one more year at ... Xavier, isn't it?"

"Xavier University, yes, ma'am," he confirmed.

"So here's what we're going to do. I want you to clock out. The rest of the day will be without pay. Tomorrow, I don't want you to come. The next day, I don't want you to come. That will be without pay as well. Take the weekend to think about how you're putting us all in jeopardy, including your daughter who's counting on you to keep your job and see her through. I want you to come back Monday with a whole new attitude toward safety. And rest assured, if this ever happens again..."

"It won't, Ms K. I can promise you that." He hurried toward the warehouse before she changed her mind.

The lady waved at a young Mexican laborer, gathering tools from a metal cabinet. "Raúl, can I trouble you a moment?"

Immediately, he trotted over. "Yes, ma'am?"

"I'm sure you're very busy. But can you strap this load down and take it to the job site on North Grand?"

"No *hay problema.*" He was already in the truck, backing it up to the building.

She finally noticed Lola at the guard shack. As she approached, the guard began speaking. "Ms K, I tried to explain to this young lady that she needs an appointment to see you."

For a long while, the lady stared at the note. She gradually eyeballed Lola with growing disdain. "What makes you think you can barge in here to see me without an appointment?"

Lola cringed. "I-I-I didn't know-"

"Wrong answer!" She exploded.

The guard's muscular chest protruded, knowing he had done his job.

And then she continued, "You should've said, 'Because Dr. Campbell sent me.' And you should've said it with authority." She smiled again, a different, consoling smile.

Lola's eyes brightened with relief. "Yes, yes, of course he did."

"I'm Kristy Cutler, Ms K for short." She extended her hand.

Lola hesitated. Her mother had taught her, when greeting other females, to extend an affectionate pat on the right forearm or shoulder.

But that is in Mexico, she reasoned to herself. *This is America.*

Lola reached out her hand, slowly, precariously. She was visibly stunned by Ms K's firm grip.

"Come with me," she ordered.

Kristy Cutler led Lola down the noisy concrete sidewalk, past assembly crews with nail guns and power saws and buzzing drills, away from the slow-rolling concrete mixers and sand mounds, toward the front door. From the corner of her steel blue eyes, she observed Lola's bewildered face. "You're wondering why these people don't slow down, aren't you?"

"Yes. They go like there is no tomorrow."

"They go because there is in fact a tomorrow," said Kristy. "A tomorrow they hope to reserve completely for themselves."

She went on to explain that the entire company operated on an hourly-plus-bonus compensation system. Based on historical estimates, each project required a designated number of hours. If teams were able to complete the job prior to the required hours, all saved hours were placed into a pool and shared by employees.

"If a job requires 3000 hours and they complete it in 2000 hours, that's a 1000 hours into the bonus pool. If their cumulative bonus hours surpass last year's figures, they get to take off the entire month of December with pay."

"What about the operation?"

"In December, I shut down the entire company. All those days belong to my employees and their families."

"This arrangement works for you, yes?"

"Right now, we have the highest productivity and lowest turnover rate in the nation."

"I would love to come here," yearned Lola. "It seems you are one big happy family."

"Like all happy families, there is a downside." Kristy, however, never mentioned what the downside was.

Inside the giant warehouse were blocks of glassed-in cubicles. Lola recognized the CAD, Administrative and Sales departments by the computers used and the type of people that use them.

The CAD department, Computer Aided Design, featured large-screen computers with young techies, crunching out colorful room dimensions, columns and stairwells. The Administrative department was disproportionately populated by overweight female number crunchers and accounts receivable collectors, all brandishing unfriendly scowls on their faces. The Sales department consisted of middle-aged white men with raspy, smoke-infested voices. Their wrinkled faces were buried behind sales charts and stacks of job orders.

There was, however, a fourth area her Lincoln Land professors had not profiled. A small work space, shrouded in dark tinted glass and occupied by blurred, ghostly figures. The door was plastered with signs that read:

RESTRICTED AREA. DO NOT ENTER.

"What is that department?" asked Lola.

Kristy smiled, cattily. "It's the future, Lola. That's really all I can say for now."

Kristy's modest first floor office was located at the back corner of the building, near an exit door. Her small wooden desk was crammed with stacks of estimates and invoices and equipment brochures. On the far wall, a bank of eight video screens captured the frenzied activity throughout the warehouse and outer grounds. The miniature model of a new housing development sat on a flat glass table in the middle of the floor.

"Have a seat." She pointed Lola to a leather armchair in front of her desk. "Can I offer you something to drink ... water, soda, juice?"

"No thank you," Lola declined.

Kristy buzzed her secretary out front. "Two waters please."

Maybe she didn't hear me, Lola thought to herself.

"When presented with multiple offers, always try to choose at least one," she instructed Lola. "It brings a level of comfort to the person extending the offering and reinforces the idea that you are accustomed to being accommodated."

"I will remember," Lola promised.

Once the secretary left, Kristy took a long swig from her Ozarka bottle. Lola observed and did the same.

"Now here's how things are going to go," Kristy explained. "You're here because Dr. Campbell recommended you. You're on his dime right now. Luckily for you, I owe him a favor or two. But that little prescription pad with his name on it is not enough to keep you here. You understand?"

"I ... I think so."

"I have some calls to make. When I finish, I'm going to give you a few minutes to convince me why I should waste my time on you or even allow you to set foot on these premises. At that point, you're on your own dime."

Lola waited outside her office on a wooden bench next to the secretary's desk. It didn't help her mental preparation that the little pointed-nosed secretary looked like a younger carbon copy of the she-devil Nicholas had taken with him on the cruise.

Lola couldn't concentrate. All too soon, she found herself back in front of Kristy's desk, facing a blistering interrogation.

"May I see your resume?"

Lola's heart stopped. I-aahh, I don't have it with me right now. But I can bring it back."

"You have any degrees or certificates?"

"I should have my degree from Lincoln Land in two months."

"Should?" she probed.

Lola regurgitated her professor's warning. "In life, nothing is guaranteed."

"What is your area of specialization?"

"Construction Management."

"How do you rank in your class?"

Lola pondered a long while, trying to gauge the impact her only A had had on her mediocre grade point average. "I don't really know my rank. But I'm passing everything."

"Is that how you plan to go through life, just passing?"

The tears began to well up in her eyes. Lola dropped her head.

Still, Kristy continued. "Are you proficient in CAD?"

"No."

"Have you ever attended any MAGIC functions?"

Lola frowned. "Magic?"

"Yes, *Mentoring A Girl In Construction*. They have camps all the time to help young construction professionals get a handle on the industry."

"I know nothing about these camps."

"Do you have any references at all?"

Lola thought about Professor Gusemano who had recommended her for the job with the Allen brothers. Only a few days earlier, he had scolded her and told her not to expect any more breaks. There was no way he was going to recommend her again.

"I'm sure I could bring one back with the resume."

With growing frustration, Kristy stood up. "Look, we're drowning here. I don't want to waste your time. And I certainly don't want you to waste mine."

It's not a waste," Lola pleaded. "I am a very quick learner and very dedicated. I just need a chance, that's all."

Kristy wasn't listening. She was staring at one of the video monitors on the wall. Lola turned to see two brawny employees with bugged eyes and sweaty faces, yelling at each other.

Kristy grabbed her hard hat. "You'll have to excuse me a moment." She scurried out of the door. Lola grabbed a spare hardhat off the glass table and ran behind her.

Just outside the exit door, small yellow flags marked a staging area used to assemble large modular panels. Two men wearing hard hats with the front brims pointing backwards, stood a few feet from each other, cursing like sailors.

Kristy quickly intervened. "What's going on, here?! Hank, Greg, have you two lost your minds?"

Hank was the taller one. "This idiot is going to get everybody killed around here."

"What's the problem?" she demanded.

Hank pointed to the hydraulic nail gun in Greg's hand. "He's using that bounce trigger in rapid fire mode. We're all having to dodge his ricochets and rejects. Hell, it's like Vietnam out here. Bobby took one in the back of his boot this morning."

Everyone in the construction industry knew about nail guns. They were indispensable productivity boosters that cut the fastening process in half. They were also dangerous, low velocity weapons that fired a nail at an average free flight speed of two hundred mph. Over twenty percent of all construction injuries were caused by nail guns. A stray nail to the eye or heart or spine could be fatal to the victim.

Greg chimed in. "First of all he needs to understand he ain't my supervisor. If he wants to boss somebody, he needs to go home to his wife and kids. Secondly, he can't have it both ways."

"What do you mean, both ways?" asked Kristy.

"He's spreading lies, telling people in our group that I'm dragging ass and killing our bonus. I work just as hard as the next man. But if you want speed, I can give you speed."

"You see, Ms K. He knows what he's doing," declared Hank. "He's just trying to prove a point. Now give it to me!"

Hank stepped forward to yank the gun from Greg's strong, weather-beaten hands. As both men struggled for control of the weapon, a wild wrestling match ensued. Greg's leg tangled in the hydraulic hose and tightened the pressure on his trigger finger. That's when the nails started to fly.

Lola had already slipped into her self-induced, methodical mode. Back in Juárez, when neighborhood guns started firing, her mother had taught one thing. "Hit the floor!"

She tackled Kristy around the waist and shoved her to the ground. On the way down, a single nail ripped through Kristy's white silk blouse and grazed her shoulder. The other five or six nails landed in a plywood board just behind them.

Someone inside the building had already summoned the security guard. He ran up to them like an NFL linebacker and knocked both men to the ground. Raúl, who was just returning from his deliver, jumped out of the truck and turned off the hydraulic power. And even though Hank had come to his senses, the security guard prodded both of them with an electrical device he carried on his belt.

Later, inside her office, an EMS ambulance attendant bandaged up Kristy's wound.

"It's just a minor scratch," he reported. "But I'd let my doctors see it, just to be on the safe side."

"Nonsense," Kristy shrugged with an artificial toughness. "The hit I took from Lola hurts worse than that."

Lola stood next to the glass table, watching, waiting, hoping for a chance to resume her disastrous interview from hell. In just a few hours, she had learned more at RedFish than she had during her sixteen months at Lincoln Land College. This was the place she wanted to be ... no ... needed to be.

But what could she say to make it happen? She had nothing to offer to RedFish. She couldn't even muster a reference or resume. She wasn't a new breed of Mexican. She was the same old border scum watching the American dream pass her by.

The security guard marched into Kristy's office. "How you hangin', Ms K?"

She glanced at her arm from which they had cut away the bloody sleeve. "I'm trying to remember that thing about taking a lickin' and keep on tickin'. But this combat fatigue won't let me think straight."

He chuckled, loudly, then dumped a large envelope on her desk. "I got their badges and keys and escorted them off the premises. You need anything else."

"Yes. Tell HR to pull the video, write the whole thing up and send it over to the attorneys. I don't want this thing coming back to bite us."

"Will do, Ms K."

The security guard left the room.

She turned to Lola with a grim face. "Why are you still here?"

She dropped her head. "I was hoping..."

"Hoping?" Kristy mocked her. "What in the world could you be hoping for?"

"Maybe a chance to-"

"You don't need to be here." Kristy interrupted her.

As Lola fought back the tears, Kristy continued. "You need to be in HR, filling out your paperwork and taking a mug shot for your badge."

If Joe DeLeon had learned anything while carrying out his many assignments for the mob, it was that life was short, especially for those poor bastards he helped to track down. If a man intended to squeeze any pleasure out of a perilous existence in the La Costra Nostra fast lane, he'd better do it quickly and often, with no inclination toward holding back for tomorrow. Most likely, tomorrow would never come.

Las Vegas was an ideal place to squeeze some pleasure out of life. He arrived on a cool Friday afternoon and checked into the luxurious Forum Tower in Caesars Palace on the Strip. After a luscious steak dinner and a subterranean magic show in the Celestial Court, he retired to his extravagantly designed glass and marble suite for the business at hand.

That night, the business at hand was two custom-order, longed-legged blond showgirls in skimpy attire. The high-priced escort service had come to know his exquisite taste. They even sent over his favorite music, *Day By Day* and *Five Minutes More,* from an old Frank Sinatra CD.

In his younger days, DeLeon would've kept the duo climbing the walls for the full three hour for which he had paid. But now, at almost fifty years old, a half hour of their wild acrobatics was all he could take. He didn't remember the two girls leaving, just the discrete tapping on the door after they had gone.

Slipping into his red silk Playboy robe and black leather house shoes, he peeped over the safety chain and through the small crack in the door. It was just enough room for the blue steel barrel of a Browning automatic to slide through.

"This can go easy or it can go hard. Your choice, Joe." A husky baritone voice growled from the hallway.

DeLeon had been around long enough to know he didn't have a choice. He opened the door and let them in.

Two burly Italian giants lumbered through the door. One, DeLeon recognized as a hit man they called Lofingers. The name was derived from the three missing fingers an angry meat cleverer had claimed. His thick-necked companion with the droopy eye was unfamiliar to DeLeon. Yet, he needed no introduction concerning the task he was there to perform.

As the thick-necked man surveyed the room for unexpected occupants, Lofingers marched DeLeon over to a table and forced him to sit down. That's when Vinnie Meatball's brother, Raymond, entered the room.

He locked the door slowly, methodically, then slid the chain across the latch. He stood there for a moment, admiring the exquisite décor. "Nice, very nice. I wonder who's paying for all of this?"

DeLeon tried to get up from the table, but Lofingers pressed the barrel of the gun against his puffy ear lobe, forbidding him to move.

"Come on, Raymond. What's this all about?" DeLeon tried not to sound too demanding.

"It's about questions. Questions that need to be answered."

Raymond grabbed a bottle of champagne and a long stem wineglass from the mahogany bar and poured DeLeon a drink. He placed it on the table in front of him. "Indulge yourself, Joe."

"I-aahh, I'm not really thirsty." DeLeon trembled out a cautious decline.

"I believe the man offered you a drink." Lofingers emphasized the order by pressing the gun barrel deeper into DeLeon's huge cauliflower ear.

DeLeon gulped a small sizzle from the glass.

"My first question is of a scientific nature, Joe. I'm wondering when he blows a hole in your little peanut head whether that expensive champagne will run out of the hole going in, or the hole coming out. Do you know, Joe?"

DeLeon was shaking too much to respond.

"Is that something we need to investigate? I mean, you are a freakin' investigator, right, Joe?"

DeLeon nodded, reluctantly, a single bead of sweat, trickling from his receding hairline.

"The problem is, from where I'm standing, you don't look like no investigator. You look like a freakin' con man living high on somebody else's dime." Raymond hurled the champagne bottle across the room, shattering it against the brick fireplace. "Is it my dime, Joe?"

When he tried to answer, Lofingers slugged him with the butt of his pistol, sending DeLeon, helplessly, to the floor.

Raymond immediately stood over him. "I'm paying you $15,000 a month to find one blackass murdering cockroach and all I'm getting is excuses. But you got time for this, right?" Raymond tossed a pair of yellow bikini panties into his face.

"I'm really close, Raymond. You, you got to believe that."

"The only reason Lofingers ain't pulled the trigger is

because I ain't told him to. The only reason I ain't told him to is the people over me said they liked your work in Buenos Aries. They said give you a break. I'm giving you a break, Joe. You got thirty days to deliver. After that, I suggest you find a deep hole to crawl in. Might save everybody some time if you brought a freakin' casket with you."

Raymond and the two gorillas stormed out of the room.

When DeLeon finally gathered his wits, he picked up the phone to call the airline. "I need to change my return flight. I want the first thing out of here tomorrow morning. You got that?!! First thing!"

On Saturday morning, twenty-four hours before his scheduled departure to the Oak Lawn Clinic in Chicago, Johnny woke up in a rage. Lola couldn't tell whether it was the side effects of his multiple medications, or a growing sense of anxiety about his vulnerability in Chicago.

Entering into the kitchen to prepare his breakfast, she listened as he completed an irate phone call. At the end of the conversation, he tossed his cell phone on the table. "These fools must be losing their ever-loving minds!"

Lola continued reading the recipe for a low-cholesterol turkey omelet. "Who do you speak of, Daddy?"

"The security company. I asked them to do three simple things: Fix the cameras, give dial-in access to your new iPhone and send me the archives. You think they heard me?"

Since the Canadian ice storm, the security cameras on which Johnny so desperately depended had gone on the blink.

Sometimes they worked, and sometimes they didn't. Though a technician had come out to repair the system, Johnny wanted video from the previous weeks in which he had been in the hospital.

"They've got a backup system with all the old clips before the storm. I told them to get the clips to me on CD, DVD, tape or something. I need to see that stuff before I leave you here by yourself."

"Don't worry, Daddy. It's going to be alright."

"Yeah, that's what General Custer told his men before the Indians gave him a haircut."

She paused. "I do not know this Custer."

"Just know he's dead because he didn't have video."

Lola's face brightened. "Ms K has video."

"Good. Sounds like they're trying to kill her too."

"But I saved her, Daddy, like I saved you."

Johnny stared, curiously. "What do you mean?"

A cold chill came over her as she realized what she had said. "I-aahh, I just mean I was there for you."

"And I appreciate it, Babygirl. I'm trying to do the same. But I need you to make me a promise."

"What should I promise?"

"That you'll help me tighten up our game. With all these doctors and hospitals and taking this medicine, we've gotten shownuff sloppy. Sloppy is a one-way ticket to hell."

She thought about the gray Taurus that had followed her to the dealership. "You think they are still after you?"

"That's the whole thing about these people, Babygirl. You never know until it's too late."

"What do you want me to do?" she asked.

"I want you to get back to the routine. Don't come in here unless you check things out first. Use your phone, use the cameras, keep your eyes open."

"I will, Daddy."

"One more piece of business," he added. "First thing Monday, I need you to go by that security company in Springfield and get those old clips. Send them to me at the clinic."

She mulled over her busy schedule. "I have classes until noon. Then I go to see Ms K."

"It's easier to see Ms K when the inside of a casket top ain't blocking your view, knowemsayin'? Do what you gotta do. But FedEx them clips to me on Monday."

****

In Kansas City, Nicholas had his own rendezvous with FedEx, a stunning young delivery driver with arched cheekbones, California freckles and pearly white teeth. After weeks of moping around, Nicholas had decided to start over. What better way to expel the love sick demons from his sleepless nights than to replace the precious memories on which they feasted. A new girl, a new beginning, a new parade of memories. That was his formula for recovery.

From the outdoor terrace of an exclusive French Bistro in the Parkville district, Nicholas enjoyed an intimate view of the well-manicured greenery and sparkling lake. He had never seen the young driver outside her purple FedEx uniform. Her low-cut black silk dress and spiked heels made her even more alluring than he had imagined.

"Mattrice? Am I pronouncing that correctly?" he queried.

She smiled. "Close enough."

"It's such an unusual name."

"My mother's oldest sister was named Mattie; Her younger sister, Patrice. In California, we've mastered the art of compromise."

Nicholas chuckled, politely. "So how did you end up in Kansas City?"

"I followed my ex-fiancé out here. Somehow he convinced me my dancing career had a better chance in Kansas City than LA."

"Did it?" Nicholas naively inquired.

"When I pull the truck up to your store and roll in those boxes, does it look like I'm dancing?"

Nicholas retreated to his small glass of red wine. "I'm sorry, I didn't mean to-"

"No, I'm sorry," she reciprocated. "I'm told I have a sharp tongue. I'm sure you're thinking now, all the reports are brutally accurate."

"I'm thinking it's too early in the evening to come to any harsh conclusions. Why don't we enjoy another glass of wine, an exquisite meal and see where the evening goes?"

It didn't take long for both of them to realize the evening was going nowhere. After a remarkably scant serving of braised Halibut at $65 per plate and a clumsy attempt at dancing with a professional dancer, Nicholas ran out of words to say.

Sitting at the table, mulling over their next awkward plunge into triviality, Mattrice finally asked, "Who is she?"

Nicholas almost choked on his wine. "Huh?"

"When you look at me, you see someone else. Who is she?"

He dropped his head with embarrassment. "I didn't think it was that obvious."

"I know the look. Been there, done that," she confessed. "That's why I'm working at FedEx."

He frowned. "I don't follow you."

"I had someone who loved me. But I went with the fast car, devilish blue eyes and a slick conversation. That's how I got to Kansas City. I could call him, the one who loves me. He'd send me the money to get back to LA. But I made this mess on my own. I want to clean it up on my own. Does that make sense?"

"Perfect sense," he acknowledged.

"What about you? Are you trying to get back to her?"

"I-Iah, I don't know how to find her," he stammered.

"That's bull!" And then she suddenly laughed at herself. "Okay, I admit it. The reports were accurate."

"Really, Mattrice. I don't know where she is or how to get in touch with her."

She looked at him with the most serious face of the evening. "Listen to me. If you were around her long enough to fall in love with her, then you know how to find her. Nothing's going to be right until you do."

He spent the whole weekend in his new apartment, rummaging through packed boxes. He took everything that Lola had left behind and spread it out on the living room floor. He walked around it and across it and stared at it from a distance.

Nothing.......

Late Sunday evening, just before midnight, something exploded in his subconscious, something he had overlooked all along. Not ALL of her possessons were in front of him. The most precious, irreplaceable item she owned had been separated out, entrusted to a new owner, an owner that was more precious to her than the item, itself.

"Because, I don't need it anymore. Don't you see. You are my good luck charm now, si?"

He dashed into his bedroom, found an old velvet jewery box that housed his most sentimental possessions ... his first tooth, his Eagle Scout metals, his Penn State graduation ring. He removed Lola's old scorched brass lighter and returned to the pile on his living room floor.

He flipped open the top and slammed his thumb across

the old flint wheel. Ten times he did it ... first a hiss, then a spark, finally a weak flickering orange flame.

Staring into the flame gave him time to realize how foolish he had been. What did he expect? Was the lighter going to hold a conversation with him? Was it going to call out Lola's name?

As the brass exterior heated up to an unbearable temperature, the analytical side of his brain ordered him to close the lid, to extinguish the flame, to retreate from the pain of a foolish experiment gone awry. But the love sick part of his brain told him to hold on ... hold on until he felt her struggle, her pain, her dubious resurection from a black coffin of death.

Like a powerful spark, leaping from the indelible flame to the deep crevices of his mind, it hit him. He closed the lid and started to weep.

He didn't know where she was. But he knew where she would be. And now, no matter what, when the time came, he would be there too.

When Lola arrived at RedFish Construction on Monday afternoon, she was exhausted. Her frantic marathon had begun Sunday morning with a last minute dash to the Springfield Airport to get Johnny aboard a noonday flight to Chicago. Lola's shiny new STS loaner car wouldn't start, and by the time they summoned a local wrecker to boost the battery, two and a half precious hours had gone by.

At the airport Johnny's last words were unmistakable. "Tell John-John to have my hog ready when I get back or I will personally pistol whip his big sorry ass."

Leaving the airport, Lola headed over to the White Oaks Mall to buy some new outfits for her new job. The old ones were too baggy and college-girl casual for her new position at RedFish. To her amusement, she had no idea what her new position was, just that a woman needed to look her best no matter what she was doing.

She bought a book on business etiquette. Gobbling a

hot-peppered sub sandwich on a terrace outside the mall, she plowed through a third of its intriguing content. That's when someone called her name. "Lola? Right?"

She looked up to find the curator she and Nicholas had met on their original visit to the King Juba Exhibition. Dressed in knee length Hawaiian shorts and a museum t-shirt, he stood in front of her table.

"Yes." She finally replied.

"You probably don't remember me-"

"I do. From the museum."

"Yes, yes," he acknowledged. "So how have you been?"

Horrible and alone, she thought to herself, but answered, "Fine."

"The chest. Did you ever determine its worth?"

"Somewhat," she cautiously responded.

"I remember Professor Broadson being pretty excited about it when I contacted him. In fact, he called me from Cuba not too long ago."

"Heee-He did?"

"Yes. Just after the Ferdon Street explosion." He paused a long moment. "Quite an unusual tragedy, wasn't it?"

"What did he say?"

"He asked a few questions. In fact, he asked if I had an alternative number for your ... significant other? Seems he's no longer at the hardware store."

"He's not?" Her dark eyes bulged.

The curator studied her surprised expression. "I take it you're not in contact with him?"

"We kinda ... parted ways," she sadly reported.

"Sorry to hear. If the professor calls again, would it be possible to give him your number?"

"I don't think so." She gathered her book and tossed the

remaining sandwich in a nearby trash can. "It was nice seeing you."

She hurried away.

In the car, she began to cry. At least, this time she was able to hold down her food. Though, she hadn't admitted it to herself, she took some comfort in knowing Nicholas was still close by. There was always the possibility they might run into each other and maybe he would beg her back. But now he was out of sight, probably at some fancy office in Atlanta or New York. And she was out of mind. Just an old fashioned love song that he would never sing again.

And then there was the song she hoped no one would ever sing again: *The Death March at Ferdon Street Crossing.*

At her Cousin Maria's church back in Juárez, the Priest used to talk about a great cloud of witnesses, looking down on our every move. She wondered. How did murderers look to the Mother Mary and the rest of the heavenly host? Did they all appear as wild-eyed maniacs like the Charles Mason clan in California, or a burly hard-faced women wrestler like *Mataviejitas,* the brutal killer of old ladies in Mexico City? Or did some images reach heaven as a young, innocent college girl, sleeping on a piece of wood?

She spent most of the afternoon crying, swallowing back the part rock, part razor in her throat. Finally, her phone rang.

It was her mother calling from Mexico. She spoke in her thick Andalusian Spanish. "My Lolita, I must tell you. Your Papa Jose is dead."

Although he was not Lola's real father, he had treated all of the children the same. He was a good father when he wasn't in prison, and yet, prison seemed more his home. That's where the Sinaloa Cartel had finally gotten to him and slit his throat, in prison.

Lola cried a different cry over the phone, a consoling

cry to comfort her mother as a long, bittersweet era came to an end. As long as Jose stayed in prison and kept his mouth closed, a modest cash stipend arrived at the house each month. Now that he was dead, the money would no longer come.

Her Aunt Conchita grabbed the phone. "Your mother is very depressed. She needs to get away for a while."

That's when the idea of her mother coming to the graduation took flight.

Lola had distant relatives in Houston, the snobbish, upper class type that spent most of their time at Hispanic Chamber of Commerce luncheons and LULAC Celebrations. She didn't care much for them. But they had connections, connections she needed to get her mother to the graduation.

She spent the rest of her Sunday afternoon tracking down her cousin, Carlos Zedillo, the prosperous owner of a downtown janitorial service. He knew the ropes. He knew how to get her mother to Litchfield.

The first thing out of his mouth was *money*.

"*Mucho la lana*, my little *mestizo*. But it can be done."

With Johnny's duffel bag of cash, hidden in the wall behind the refrigerator, that's all she needed to know.

Monday morning she had gone to class, then to her counselor's office, then to the security company in Springfield. After a quick stop at the FedEx office, she had headed straight for the Cadillac dealership.

"You tell Mr. Fountain I've got a bazooka at the house. So his little pistol don't worry me one bit," John-John joked. "And if he'll close the doors tightly on this STS loaner so the interior lights go off, the battery won't run down."

The main thing Lola needed to hear was that Johnny's Deville would be ready before he came back on Friday afternoon.

"We have a couple of minor tweaks we need to make on

the catalytic converter. But Friday is no problem. I'll have the blue goose ready."

****

At RedFish Construction, Lola sat outside Kristy's office, patiently waiting for her to come out of a staff meeting down the hall. The pointed-nosed secretary finally offered her some water, to which she responded, "Orange juice would be fine, if you have it." Lola already knew she did.

When Kristy finally came out of the meeting, Lola stood erectly and extended her hand. "How is your day going?" The book said ask a simple question that could lead to a positive response.

"Horrible," she replied. "We've got a union organizer at the Woodgrove site and a truck in a ditch on Highway 66."

"Nothing we can't handle," Lola reassured her. The book said to align yourself with the challenges and/or objectives of the client.

Kristy smiled. "Sounds like you brought your *A* game."

Lola pulled the crisp white folder from beneath her arm and handed it to Kristy. After perusing her updated resume and letter of recommendation from her counselor, Kristy commented, "You might be RedFish material after all."

"I'll vouch for that." A familiar voice boomed over her shoulder.

Lola turned to see Goodboy, the trailer-trash white man she had met at Allen Brothers Construction. He was clean shaven, well-manicured and all dressed up in a white shirt and red tie.

He grinned, widely. "I knew you liked me. But I didn't think you'd become a stalker and follow me over here."

She embraced him with a generous hug.

"Henry recognized you in the yard last Friday and brought me up to date," said Kristy.

"You work here now?" asked Lola.

"For almost eight years," he revealed. "What you saw over there was my incognito undercover side. I guess my counter intelligence background in the Navy got the best of me."

Fighting back the tears, Lola turned to Kristy. "Many days he was my protector. I will never forget."

He blushed. "Nonsense. With her swinging that big Caterpillar crane around, she didn't need a protector."

"They were mad at me, yes?"

"I wish you could've been there to see their faces. They wanted to sue, but only had a P.O. Box for your address."

"I gave my real address here," she assured them. "Ms K can sue me anytime."

They all laughed again.

Soon Henry disappeared behind the doors marked RESTRICTED AREA.

"No Caterpillar cranes today," Kristy notified her. "Please come with me."

Lola followed Kristy to a nearby glassed-enclosed area with brightly colored blue and gray cubicles. The adjacent shelves were filled with reference books and technical manuals. A lone stenographer with stringy black hair and cat-eyed glasses sat in the back.

Kristy pointed to an empty cubical with a new computer and cushy black leather chair. "This is your space now. Handle it with care."

Lola's heart raced. She wanted to flop down in her new chair and spin around like a deliriously happy child on a carnival carousel. But the book said to be professional at all times and allows the client to maintain control.

"May I?"

Kristy nodded.

The moment she sat down, she observed an envelope at the edge of the desk with her name on it. "For me?"

"Open it."

Lola opened the envelope to find a $200 check.

Kristy explained, "On my first real job I had to wait two weeks to get paid. You can't imagine how nerve wracking that is with no money in the bank. People want to go to lunch and get to know you. You need gas money to get back and forth. Sometimes they want you to take a client out to lunch. I said if I ever became an owner, my employees would never suffer that indignity. This money will be taken out of your second payroll check."

Lola didn't need the money. Johnny saw to that. But Kristy had already schooled her on how to handle such offers. Thus, Lola smiled graciously, "Thank you, Ms K. I will make good use of this."

"Always take care of the people that take care of you, Lola. You'll find, in the long run, it always pays off."

"Yes, ma'am. I will remember."

Kristy paused for a while. "I've given some thought to how I want to utilize your unique skills. I have a project just for you."

Kristy went on to talk about the achilles heel that plagued her operation. "Safety is our biggest problem. I want you to find ways to make us operate with more security for our workers. You think you can do that?"

Lola shook her head, affirmatively. "I can do it."

Kristy walked over to a large cabinet and pulled out a nail gun. With a deliberate sense of precaution, she placed it on Lola's desk. "I want you to start with this, the thing that almost killed us last week. Don't limit yourself to those manuals on the shelf. Go out into the field. Use your bilingual skills. Ask questions, make phone calls, find solutions. In the end, I want you to tell me what to do."

At that moment Kristy's cell phone rang. "Yes. Are they ready? Okay, I'm on my way."

She stared at Lola, silently reviewing all that she had said. "One more thing. For now, you answer directly to me. But I'm not always here. If you have questions or problems, go to Henry. You can trust him completely."

Lola smiled. "Yes, I know."

"Did you also know I just told you something else?"

Lola frowned. "What did you tell me?"

"That everyone here cannot be trusted completely."

Kristy turned and walked away.

With only thirty days left before Raymond terminated the use of his services, DeLeon felt a growing sense of desperation setting in. It wasn't that DeLeon had never lost a client before. But with the mob, termination of services took on a whole new meaning.

To improve his odds, DeLeon hired a young country-bumpkin private eye wanna-be from Nashville named Silas Penrow. DeLeon had met the tall, loudmouth farm boy at the crap table during one of his many trips to Las Vegas. He subcontracted him from time to time to handle low end projects such as insurance fraud and divorce cases.

If there was one thing DeLeon liked about Penrow, it was his persistence. If there was one thing DeLeon hated about Penrow, it was his persistence. Once he honed in on a target, there was no calling him off. He was like a bloodhound on a dead-end trail. Even when the scent faded, Penrow never took his nose off the ground.

Though Penrow had carried out a few low-level hits for the old Marcello bosses in New Orleans, for him there was more prestige in being a smooth-talking, quick-thinking private investigator. Back in the thickets of Tennessee where he had grown up, any dumbass local yokel could pull the trigger on a big whitetail buck. It took a real pro, however, to harness the skill and expertise necessary to first track the beast down.

Young Penrow also understood the importance of technology. He was always buying new detective gadgets on Ebay and Amazon. It was Penrow who had convinced DeLeon to upgrade to a Premium Gold membership with the national database co-op for private investigators. That gave DeLeon the ability to instantly plug in a license plate or drivers license or credit card. Thus, every time there was activity on that particular card, DeLeon received an alert.

Late Sunday night, a fax came in alerting him that Johnny's credit card had been used to purchase a ticket to Chicago. The bad news sent DeLeon though a half bottle of Chivas Regal. The sheer size of the city made Johnny that much harder to find.

On Monday morning, Penrow landed at the Springfield Airport and immediately planted his long nose on Lola's trail. He was certain the young Mexican girl DeLeon had talked about would eventually lead him to Tiny Johnny. Nabbing the big black Chicago street hood that nobody else could find would be his one-way ticket to stardom. After this, clients harboring an appreciation for the clever detective work of Peter Gunn and Magnum P.I. would know Silas Penrow was the real deal.

****

Chicago never changed, always drab, cold and musky. And though Johnny's brief taxi ride from Midway Airport to the Oak Lawn Clinic was quiet and uneventful, he didn't like what he found.

The clinic was located in a red brick business plaza on the busiest end of West 93rd with no security gate or security guard or concealment from the office complex and shopping center across the street. Wondering eyes from the street, the freeway or the elevated crosswalk leading to the shopping center could easily spot visitors shuffling in and out of the clinic's revolving glass doors.

Inside, the building was cold and dim and reeked of pungent chemicals. Johnny wondered if there was an undertaker in the back of the building cooking up a smelly batch of formaldehyde.

To add to his chagrin, the man in charge of the study wasn't even a doctor, but rather, some kind of scientific research administrator. A short, stocky former Marine Sergeant, he seemed to take pleasure in ordering people around.

"We expect to have access to you from 6:00 am to 6:00 pm. You're going to be pricked and prodded and examined from head to toe. The less you complain, the more expeditiously we can proceed. Remember, people, this is for the furtherance of science, not to mention the $60,000 to $70,000 medical burden we're removing from your plate."

Johnny considered another way to further science ... by removing his .357 magnum from his suitcase and documenting how many times the little loudmouth punk could take a lick to his balding skull before kissing the floor goodnight.

But as the Sergeant had said, there was $60,000 to $70,000 riding on the deal. Besides, Johnny didn't want to disappoint Dr. Campbell who had worked so hard to save his life.

After 6:00 pm, members of the oddball fifteen patient brigade were allowed to do their own thing. They could return to their private rooms equipped with computers, phones and satellite TV, go into the dining hall for a dietary regimen of low-sodium, low-cholesterol meals or venture out to the nearby shopping center in a collective, supervised group.

The group shopping spree was designed to add a touch of vacation to their otherwise dreary, needle-plagued stay. But this was Chicago. Johnny had no plans of venturing out. Each day after his grueling guinea pig run, he'd gulp down the surprisingly tasty food in the dining hall, then headed back to his room. There, he took in the sports channels or watched an old western on the satellite TV.

The one exception was the second night when an old motorcycle gang leader from San Diego coaxed Johnny into the basement, flipped out a newfangled tablet device and cranked up a porn flick. He seemed personable and had a few good stories to tell. But with no girls and no whiskey and having to view the movie in a cold, dark theater with a clanking furnace and leaking sewer pipes, their boyish exploits quickly became a burden. They finally traded in their date with *Nympho Nina* for the warmth and comfort of their own rooms.

On the third evening, a lady at the reception desk stopped Johnny in the lobby. "Mr. Fountain, a package came for you yesterday. Sorry for the delay in informing you."

She handed him the FedEx package from Lola. With hundreds of still shots and video clips to review, he shrugged with disappointment.

So much for the big fight on ESPN, he told himself, just so the sports-loving kid in his brain could hear. *I gotta tighten my own game and get on these clips tonight.*

****

After working as a private dick for over twenty years, DeLeon had come to understand that breaks were like shooting stars. They came when you least expected them.

With Raymond and his goons bringing so much pressure to bear, DeLeon had decided to use some of his old fashioned remedies to flush Johnny from his impenetrable hole in the ground. He had called every street thug, petty crook and panhandler he knew to place a bounty on Johnny's head. "Five grand to any lowdown, larcenous, enterprising bastard that can show the way."

The call finally came in around midnight Wednesday. A cook named Leroy Brown, short on money and long on revenge, decided to spill the beans.

"I know the lowlife you lookin' for. Been seeing his ugly mug all week."

"Sure you got the right lowlife?" DeLeon grilled. "I don't pay for look-alikes."

As it turned out, Leroy Brown harbored a lifelong grudge against Johnny. Twenty-six years earlier, in a callous and embarrassing breakup, Peaches, the psychotic hairdresser that had thrown Baby Lola's photos into the fireplace, had dumped fiancé Leroy Brown. Leroy blamed Johnny for his perpetual drinking problems and eternally broken heart.

As Oak Lawn Clinic's head cook, Leroy got an up-close and personal look at each patient coming through the line. From the very first day, he had recognized Johnny, the no-good, womanizing, wife-stealing bastard, now hobbling on a cane. He had prayed for a day of recompense, a day when the pendulum of hurt and suffering would swing the other way. Now that day was here.

Leroy Brown offered DeLeon an ominous warning. "If you want your shot at this low-down cripple, you better get that snitch money in my hands damn quick. Otherwise, I got a mind to poison all of these organ snatchers just to get to him."

The next morning, DeLeon dressed up as a medical supply

salesman and rolled a dolly of sample pumps and syringes into the main lobby. Taking a seat on the sofa next to the dining hall, he waited, inconspicuously, for the patients to break for lunch.

With nervous fingers, he reached into his pocket to glance at the only photo he had of Johnny, a group shot taken at a party featuring a much younger Johnny, standing shoulder-to-shoulder with Vinnie "Meatball" DiVarco and several mob lieutenants. They were all smiles, celebrating a daring Brinks truck heist at the World Trade Center.

When the side door swung open, a ragtag group of medical misfits filed out. DeLeon recognized Johnny right away. Dressed in a blue pajama uniform and sterile plastic shoes, he leaned, intermittently, on a black wooden cane. He was still a huge man, strong in stature with shifting, ever-observant eyes. DeLeon began reorganizing the products on his dolly, trying not to give himself away.

When the group finally emptied into the dining hall, the receptionist turned to him. "Sir, have you been helped? Seems you've been waiting a long time."

DeLeon thought about all of the countless hours he had spent trying to track down Tiny Johnny. "A long time, Lady. I've been waiting a very long time."

****

In Springfield, Lola stood in the lumber yard in back of RedFish's main warehouse, observing a group of workers assemble a stack of prefab modular windows. The rapid fire of their nail guns reminded her of Juárez on a Saturday night.

As she jotted a continuous string of notes on her clipboard, a tall, ruddy-faced man wearing a bandage over his right eye walked up to her. He had a disapproving scowl on his face. "If you gonna be the boss' snitch, you need to do it from a window or from behind a truck. You standing out here in the open is causing a distraction."

Lola smiled, nervously. "Oh no. I am no snitch. I am here to help."

"I've seen help and I've seen snitches. Do I have to tell you which one you look like?"

The book said break down barriers and build trust by operating with unexpected transparency. She handed him the clipboard, allowing him to read her notes.

They began: THE MEN ARE WELL-TRAINED AND OPERATE WITH GREAT SKILL. BUT NO MATTER HOW CAREFUL THEY TRY, THE QUICK FIRE GUNS END UP POINTING IN BAD DIRECTIONS LEADING TO THE CO-WORKER BEING HURT SOONER OR LATER....

He paused. "You got good eyes, even though your English ain't worth a damn. Where were you last week when a ricochet almost blinded me?" He lifted his patch to reveal the deep scar directly beneath his eye.

She sighed with compassion. "I was still trying to get hired."

His chapped lips parted a bit as he warmed up to her. "Okay, you're here. How do you plan to help?"

"I must learn everything first. Then I know how to help."

"What's there to learn?" he asked. "These guns ship from the manufacturer with two triggers. There's your contact trigger where you lock into repeat mode and fire at will. There's your sequential trigger that spits out one nail at a time. When the pressure is on and you're trying to hit your bonus, which one would you use?"

"I have read the repeating guns cause three times more accidents."

"You can figure, on most job sites, about twenty-five percent of all accidents are somehow tied to nail guns; mostly hands and fingers, but sometimes, eyes, spinal cords, even punctures to the brain."

"Ms K is pushing for safety first."

"Yeah, but Ms K ain't paying for safety first. She's paying us to get the job done. And from what I hear, it needs to get done now more than ever."

Lola frowned. "I do not follow you."

"Look. It's no secret that everything about this company ain't peaches and cream. We lost the Landmark Senior Development job to that Allen Brothers outfit. We lost the Walgreen's warehousing job and the Cutter Custom Homes job to those sleaze balls at Tripppple-Saw Construction. You can't stay in business that way."

Lola willed the growing sense of panic from her face. "Are you saying Ms K's company is in trouble?"

He paused. "What I'm saying is we're in the bottom of the ninth. The next time she comes to the plate, she'd better hit a home run."

Back inside the office, Lola spotted Goodboy in the hallway. "Where is Ms K?"

He looked at his watch. "Hopefully, on a plane back to Springfield."

"Where did she go?"

He smiled, coyly. "Now that's a question she'll have to answer. Why do you ask?"

"I-ah, I wanted to give her an update." Lola glanced at her clipboard.

"If it's a report, just pass it on to her secretary. Most everything goes through her anyway."

"I have another question," Lola added.

"Yes?"

"I never knew your real name."

He chuckled, loudly. "It's Henry Mason. But I like the way

you say *Goodboy*, with the ring of Spanish aristocracy. If it's all the same, you can continue calling me that."

"I will."

She headed down the hallway to Kristy's office. As she opened the door, the secretary turned abruptly from the top file cabinet draw. "Yessss?"

Lola was thinking. *It's not her fault the little marbled-eyed, blond-haired she-devil looks like that Bishop Hardware whore. Try to be nice for a change.*

"Sorry to disturb you. I have an update for Ms K."

"Just leave it on my desk." She continued in a surprisingly snippy tone. "And in the future, it would be a good idea to knock before you come into Ms K's office."

The book said intermediaries hold far more power than their titles indicate. Try not to offend them.

Lola dropped her head. "I am sorry. It will not happen again."

Lola went to the Human Resources department to retrieve a three-year accident report. She had just returned to her cubical when her cell phone started to vibrate.

"This is John-John at the Cadillac dealership. I have some good news and some bad news. Which do you want first?"

Lola opted for the good news.

"Your Deville is ready. I know Mr. Fountain will be back tomorrow and neither one of us wants to hear his mouth."

"What is your bad news?" she inquired.

"We had to send it out to an electronics shop across town. The guy won't deliver it until after 8:00 pm."

"That late," she whined. "I'll be back in Litchfield."

"Precisely. That's why I'm calling, to see if you need me to bring it to you."

In the back of John-John's mind lingered an intriguing possibility. If a hot little Mexican señorita had a sweet tooth for older black men, with Johnny out of town, maybe her lusty Chicano cravings would open her up to a convenient substitute like him.

Lola pondered, briefly. “I wouldn’t want to be a bother.”

“It’s not a bother,” he assured her. “We’re open until 9:00 pm and this happens to be my late night. Once we close, I can head your way.”

“It would probably be too much trouble. You wouldn’t know how to find me.”

“1150 South Van Buren Street.” John-John rattled off the apartment’s address.

Lola’s mouth flopped open. “How did you know-?”

“GPS tells it all, sweetheart. When we loan out a $40,000 vehicle, we need to know where it is.”

Lola could hear Johnny’s voice in the back of her mind. *Don’t take any chances. Keep your eyes open. Sloppiness is a one way ticket to hell.*

But how was John-John’s simple delivery an exercise in sloppiness? Johnny knew John-John well. He had dealt with him many times before. And since he already had the address, what was there to hide?

She finally acquiesced. “I guess it will be okay.”

“No problem, sweetheart. Call you when I’m on my way.”

John-John pondered for a long moment, reflecting on the restlessness he had seen in her dark, seductive eyes. It was nothing the ole Cadillac stud horse couldn’t cure. He went to his locker in the back and pulled out his fancy diamond earring and genuine alligator loafers. He could feel it. The stars were lining up. It was going to be a good night in Cadillac country... yes, a good night, indeed.

Raymond didn't want the hit to be too extravagant, not like the two Chinatown stoolies he had tortured and dangled from meat hooks outside a Wentworth Avenue storefront. Too much publicity meant additional heat from The Chicago Crime Commission which didn't seem to have the good sense to be intimidated or bought off. He just wanted Tiny Johnny dead, maybe a few initial slugs to the zipper and kneecaps to exacerbate the pain.

By late Thursday afternoon, all the logistics were in place. Lofingers and his thick-neck associate were going to go into the clinic after hours, create a commotion, and in the process, blow Tiny Johnny's face off. The plan seemed simple enough.

Under normal circumstances, DeLeon stayed as far away from the hit as possible. He felt that once he led the dogs to the rabbit, there was no need to stick around to watch them tear the meat off the bone. This hit, however, was different. Tiny Johnny's elusiveness had put DeLeon's neck on the chopping block. He wanted to see the recompense up close and personal, at least, from the shopping center parking lot across the street.

Sitting in his gray Lincoln Town Car, gnawing on a smoked pastrami sandwich on rye and listening to *Over The Rainbow* on his favorite *Frank Sinatra* CD, DeLeon watched the 5:00 pm business crowd filing out of the adjacent office buildings, headed for their cars. They were like rats, fleeing a sinking ship, zombies whose individualism had been stripped away by their company's standing mandate to surrender all.

These were the moments DeLeon cherished his decision to pursue his own fortune in life. Pissing in a cup during all-night surveillances, digging through nasty garbage cans and videotaping cheating husbands coming out of sleazy motels were not the most glamorous tasks in the world. But they were his tasks, in a career he controlled. Only another private investigator could truly appreciate the self-gratifying intangibles of the business. That's when he thought about Silas Penrow.

Over in Litchfield, Penrow had waited off and on for three days for Johnny's young Mexican girlfriend to drive through the gate. The closest match had been a young Indian/Pakistani girl in a burgundy STS. But that wasn't the '99 Coupe Deville to which Penrow had been alerted.

There was no doubt in DeLeon's mind Penrow was still there in Litchfield, bird-dogging the property like a real estate broker in heat. But with the hit already set in motion, there was no need for his continued vigilance. The least DeLeon could do was extend a professional courtesy so the young wanna-be could head back home.

When Penrow's cell went off, he was sitting outside the apartment gate in his white Impala rental, longing for the roomy comfort of his big black Lincoln Navigator back in Tennessee. He immediately recognized DeLeon's raspy voice. "What do you want, old man?"

"You caught the big tar baby yet?" DeLeon teased.

"Ain't seen hide nor hair of him."

"That's because he's up here in Chicago."

"You got him?" asked Penrow.

"Damn right, I do."

"Under surveillance or under the ground?"

"In a few hours, under the ground," DeLeon confidently declared. "We've got a little party planned for him later tonight."

"You sure you got him? I mean, a deer in the woods ain't the same as a deer on the wall."

"What are you saying?"

"I'm just saying this guy's been pretty careful. I don't see him waltzing up to Chicago and leading the Thanksgiving parade."

"Trust me, it's him, a big black over-the-hill, slow-walking drum major. In a few hours, the parade will be over."

Penrow could feel his chance for stardom slowly slipping away. "Maybe I should hang around here, just in case-"

DeLeon snapped. "Look, I'm paying you out of my pocket, no problem. But after this conversation, you're on your own dime. Got it?"

"Got it." Penrow hung up the phone.

DeLeon didn't remember falling asleep. But when he awakened, it was pitch dark. The parking lot had cleared and the energy-efficient pole lights had gone off. His phosphorescent green watch face read 7:55 pm. His heart began to pound.

At 8:05 pm, he watched the lights in the clinic lobby go dim. A lone receptionist climbed into her Saturn and sped away. By 8:30 pm the traffic in the lobby had diminished to an occasional straggler in blue pajamas, passing the large glass window, headed for the darkened wing of private suites.

At 8:50 pm a white City of Oak Lawn maintenance van pulled up in the driveway. No one got out. An eerie silence choked the night air as the whole universe fell into darkness. Then, suddenly, at 9:15 pm, Tiny Johnny's party began.

Two hulking figures carrying black duffel bags jumped out of the van. Even in baggy overalls with military gas masks strapped over their faces, DeLeon recognized them as Lofingers and his iron-neck associate. Lofingers bashed in the front glass doors with a steel crowbar and bolted inside.

With a flick of the wrist, they hurled smoking canisters throughout the lobby and down the dark hallway. Lofingers' associate walked over to a lighted box on the wall and pulled the fire alarm.

The incessant ringing reminded DeLeon of his early days back in grade school. It sounded like old keys jingling inside a glass jar; the same irritating bell that rang when it was time for DeLeon and his other little musty tagmates to come in from recess. Tonight, however, the bell tolled for one student and one student only. Tiny Johnny would be coming in from the playground and never going out again.

Lofingers and his associate hid behind the receptionist counter and watched with mutual intrigue as the stampede began. One, then two, then five panic-stricken cripples emerged from the white smoke, coughing and screaming and hobbling toward the door. Finally, fourteen weary eyed residents and an elderly night attendant stood on the sidewalk adjacent to the driveway. Lofingers quickly realized that patient fifteen wasn't coming out at all.

With only a few minutes before the fire trucks arrived, Lofingers and company assaulted the dimly lighted hallway in a room-by-room death search. Half way down the wing they reached the room bearing the name plate: JOHNNY FOUNTAIN.

With Browning automatics drawn and a mindset to shoot anything that moved, Lofingers kicked in the door. There was nothing moving, no one inside.

Lofingers' thick-neck associate checked the other rooms,

inside the closets, under the beds and behind the bathroom shower curtains. There was no sign of Tiny Johnny.

With police and fire truck sirens screaming in the distance, the puzzled duo made a last-minute dash past the dazed crowd and into the maintenance van. They squealed out of the driveway, onto the busy freeway and faded into the night.

With headlights off, shrouded in inconspicuous darkness, DeLeon glided down a back street in the opposite direction of the approaching cavalry. He was ten minutes away from the clinic when his cell phone rang.

"Tell me something, Joe. Tell me I'm dreaming and I'm going to wake up very soon." Raymond spoke in a slow, deliberate tone.

"DDDDDDid they get him?" DeLeon's voice trembled far worse than it had in Las Vegas.

"They woulda got him. But he wasn't there to be got," said Raymond. "The thing is, you told me he was there. I didn't see him with my own eyes. But I believed you, Joe. I went to a lot of time and expense based on what you told me."

"I swear to you, Raymond. He was there. I saw him with my own two eyes."

"Sure, Joe. Sure you did."

DeLeon could feel the collar of desperation, tightening around his neck. He prided himself at being a professional. He didn't like lying to his clients, no matter what. But realizing the naked, incompetent truth was about to get him killed, he knew it was time to break his own rules.

"Listen, I didn't want to tell you this. But I have a backup plan. I'm sure I can whack this scumbag before the night is gone."

Raymond's voice perked up. "Sing me a song, Joe. Make sure it doesn't have any sour notes."

"If he's not at the clinic, then I know where he's headed. I've got a man waiting for him right now."

Raymond pondered a while. "Go on."

"I just need you to say it's okay for my man to take him out."

Raymond pondered a while longer. "It's not the way I planned it."

"I know. I know. But this might be our best chance. You're tired of this dragging on and so am I."

"You're right, Joe. I am tired. Vinnie's been dead a long time. And nobody's paid the piper. You tell your man he's got a green light. Call me when it's done."

DeLeon could already feel the sweat pouring down his brow. He had made thousands of bets in Las Vegas. But none of them compared to this one. He was betting that Penrow was too stubborn to go home, that Johnny just might show up in Litchfield and that the young Nashville wanna-be, who had killed before, could finish the job.

When DeLeon reached Penrow, it was 9:45 pm. "Tell me you're the same old rock-headed Nashville hick who doesn't do as he's told. Tell me you're still there in Litchfield, bird-dogging that apartment gate."

"I'm packing it in right now, Bossman. You were right. Ain't nothing shakin' but the leaves on the trees."

"How far away are you?" DeLeon squeezed.

"Maybe five minutes."

"Go back!"

"Huh?"

"Get back to that apartment," ordered DeLeon. "You got the hot hand."

Penrow swerved his big Impala around in the middle of the highway. It was a two-wheel nail biter in front of an angry dump truck; a mind-boggling maneuver not even Magnum PI could've pulled off.

He picked up the phone again and pressed it to his ear.

"Okay, Bossman. I need the whole skinny right now."

"We threw the party, but the tar baby didn't come. I'm pretty sure he's headed your way."

"What makes you so sure?"

Because if he's not, I'm a dead man, DeLeon thought to himself.

Instead, he answered like a professional. "I've got a hunch. I always play my hunches."

"Let's say your hunch is right, then what?"

"You need to take him out," said DeLeon.

"Hold on. That's not what-"

"Forget about the old agreement! I'm offering you a new deal ... twenty grand to make this bastard hug the ground."

"What about the boys in Chicago?"

"I told them about you. They're kosher with everything."

Penrow's head started to swell. "You told this Raymond guy and the other about me?"

"I told them you're the best in the business, well, next to me. I hope you don't let us down."

Penrow parked his Impala outside the gate. "Just so they understand. If this guy doesn't show..."

There was a long pause in Penrow's voice. Finally, he came back on the line. "I see your tar baby right now."

And then he hung up the phone.

****

When John-John pulled up to the apartment gate on South Van Buren Street, he felt like a celebrity. Sporting his baggy designer slacks, alligator loafers and single diamond earring, he bobbed his head to an old CD. Sitting in the middle of Johnny's $5,000 speaker system, *Night Time Is The Right Time* by Ray Charles had never sounded so good.

There was something classy about those old Devilles, a soothing sensation deep inside the gut that the new space age STS's and Escalades couldn't reproduce. Had he not been acutely aware of the extraordinary cost of maintenance and the oddity of sensors and gadgets that seemed to always go on the blink, he would've gotten his own hog. That surely would've driven the ladies up the wall.

This night, however, was not for the other ladies. It was for Johnny's sweet little neglected Mexican *princesa*. John-John had boned up on a few Spanish words just in case.

He called her from outside the gate. "I'm here. I need the code to get in."

After a long day at RedFish, Lola had taken a soothing bath and slipped into her comfortable blue silk gown. Sitting on the sofa waiting for John-John's call, she had decided to forego her favorite CSI crime shows and use her time more wisely. That's what the book said to do.

Spread out on the coffee table in front of her were several manuals and diagrams of the most popular nail guns in the industry. Parked at the very edge of the table like a loaded pistol was the actual silver and black gun that Kristy had supplied.

I want you to start with this, the thing that almost killed us last week. Don't limit yourself to those manuals on the shelf....

Still, Lola was reluctant to examine the gun too closely. A sample packet of long black nails had already been loaded into the gun's interior. A fresh battery pack dangled from a single cord, just below the handle. And although the safety appeared to be on, she couldn't tell whether the current setting pointed to the dangerous repeating trigger or the sequential trigger that spat out one nail at a time. Both triggers looked the same. For now, studying the manuals and diagrams was a safe, no-risk bet. That's where Lola's hyper-analytic brain cells needed to reside.

John-John had arrived much later than she had expected. A fifty mile drive from Springfield shouldn't have taken that long. But what right did she have to complain? After all, he was doing her and Johnny a favor.

"Press #555#," she finally instructed him. "Drive all the way to the back."

She threw on a long white cotton robe over her gown, grabbed the keys to the loaner car and headed outside, down the narrow wooden stairway and under the aluminum parking shed. By the time John-John pulled up, she was standing next to the burgundy STS.

He smiled, broadly, taking his time getting out. He was delighted to see she didn't plan to waste time with that tired cliché: *Excuse me, while I slip into something more comfortable.* She was already there.

"You look gorgeous, sweetheart. All that's missing is a hot oil massage."

Nicholas had given her several exquisite massages. The thought of his long, firm fingers, caressing her stiff neck made her cringe. "I suppose it would be nice."

"Maybe I can help you."

She laughed at his playful antics, wondering if he would be as bold with his wife around.

"I don't think so." She handed him the key to the STS.

He pulled out a couple of sheets of paper. "I just need you to sign a few forms. Maybe it would be better if we did it inside where there's plenty of light."

She took the gold pen from his hand. "I have very good eyes. Show me where to sign."

He took a deep breath, signaling his frustration. "Are we going to play these games all night?"

She paused. “I do not understand.”

“Come on, baby. We want the same thing. I can see it all over your face.”

It was at that moment Lola’s cultural naivety evaporated into the thin night air. The book said many sexual harassment confrontations could be avoided by the skillful use of deflection. But it was late at night and she was alone with a strange man. And she had no clue what deflection meant.

The hell with the book. She grabbed the papers. “Please show me where to sign.”

He pointed to the lines with the X’s.

She handed them back. “I need the keys, please.”

He surrendered the keys to the Deville, a shameful expression on his face. “Look. Maybe I overstepped my bounds. I thought-”

“Daddy considers you a friend. He does not have many friends, so I will not hurt him with this. But do not look my way again. If you do, I can promise you Daddy won’t be the only one getting hurt.”

“Don’t worry. I get it. I get the whole thing.”

Lola had already reached the top of the stairs when she discovered John-John’s expensive pen still in her hand. People were quick to label Mexicans as thieves. She was not a thief. John-John and the rest of the world needed to know. She hurried back down the stairs to return his pen.

Rounding the corner leading to the shed, she heard four muffled thuds. She watched as John-John grimaced with pain, then tumbled to the pavement in front of the STS. A tall man stood behind him, then over him, pointing at his head. Another round of thuds, orchestrated by his high end Trident silencer, cracked the night air.

Slowly, methodically, he fixed his eyes on her. They were

cold, red eyes, the kind of eyes that death would borrow if for some reason, he misplaced his own. His pale white face narrowed with a gloomy realization of the impending task. He was already reloading his gun *and* his mind for phase two. Lola, the stupid eyewitness, was phase two.

The wooden steps seemed steeper and longer, stretching upward toward an elusive eternity. By the time she reached the top, the killer was only a few feet away. Unlike the horror movies in which the victim nervously fumbled with the key until the monster caught up, Lola rammed her key into the lock the very first time.

She bolted through the door and slammed it behind her. Only, it didn't slam. His steel toed country boots wedged into the open space, preventing the door from closing.

She thrust her fragile body against the door, desperately trying to hold him out. But one gigantic surge from his hardened shoulder sent her careening over the sofa and onto the floor.

For a brief moment, he lost sight of her, long enough for Lola to grab the nail gun and come up firing.

Like steel bolts of lightning, five nails blistered out toward him. Two lodged in his shoulder, a third in his cheek. He stumbled back a few steps, the dark red blood trickling down his jaw. With one sacrificial jerk, he removed a bloody tooth from his mouth. Working his finger around his tongue, he pushed the protruding nail from his jaw.

Finally, he smiled ... a long, painful, sadistic smile. Lola had no way of knowing Penrow was thinking about an old farm mule that had kicked him in the face. If a thousand pounds of pressure from a mule's shoe couldn't stop him, what did she think a nail was going to do?

She tried to fire again, but the repeating trigger jammed. For a split second her distraught mind soared outward, searching for a way to update her report to Ms K. These cheap unpredictable nail guns were going to get somebody killed. Seeing Penrow raise his nickel plated .45 Remington toward her face, she realized that somebody was her.

That's when she heard it ... powh, powh ... two reverberating explosions, like a couple of huge black cat cherry bombs on New Year's Eve. Penrow's pale face turned flush red. His body contorted and plunged to the floor. Like a mountain behind a mountain, Johnny stood in the doorway, his .357 magnum drawn.

With no wheelchair and no walking cane, he looked weak and unstable. His eyes were bloodshot. His shooting hand trembled. Lola rushed over to him with a smothering hug, a timely display of affection that helped to prop him up.

Her eyes welled up with tears. "Daddy, I'm so glad to see you. Where did you come from? How did you know-"

"Shuuuush," He placed his long index finger across her lips. "I know you got questions. But this ain't the time. We got to get out of here."

She peered through the door. "You think more of them are coming?"

He shook his head with certainty. "Eventually."

"What do you want me to do?"

"Pack whatever you can pack in thirty minutes. Load it in the hog. Don't leave anything with your name on it, nothing that can be traced back to you."

"What about him?" She pointed to Penrow's body, a trail of dark blood, oozing from beneath his arm.

"My guess is, he's got some kind of false ID. Let the locals figure him out. Don't touch him. This new advanced DNA testing picks everything up. Just leave him be."

"He killed John-John."

Johnny shook his head. "John-John, the poor bastard. Now that's a different story. I've got to go downstairs and clean up that mess."

By clean up, Johnny meant removing his wallet, wrist

watch and earring so it would look like a robbery. It would also delay the amount of time it took police to identify John-John and his place of employment, the very dealership at which Johnny's Cadillac had been serviced.

Still weak and staggering, Johnny took down all of the video cameras and loaded them into his trunk. He pushed back the refrigerator and grabbed his large black duffel bag from the hole in the wall.

Thirty minutes later, Johnny and Lola were cruising out of the gate.

Reminiscently, he looked through his rearview mirror. "It's been a good nest. But it's time to fly away."

"You think the apartment manager will tell them anything?"

"Yes." Johnny reached into his pocket and pulled out another false ID, the one he had used to rent the apartment. "He'll tell them what he knows ... that Johnny Wexler III always paid his rent in cash and on time."

Penrow never called DeLeon back. He didn't have to. A Friday morning newscaster from Channel 7's WLS-TV said it all:

"IN OTHER NEWS, LITCHFIELD POLICE ARE TRYING TO UNRAVEL THE DETAILS OF A BRUTAL HOMICIDE THAT OCCURRED SOMETIMES LAST NIGHT OUTSIDE A SMALL APARTMENT COMPLEX ON SOUTH VAN BUREN. THE VICTIM, AN AFRICAN-AMERICAN MALE, IN HIS LATE FORTIES, WHO WAS SHOT SIX TIMES, EXECUTION STYLE BY UNKNOWN ASSAILANTS, WAS PRONOUNCED DEAD AT THE SCENE. POLICE CONSIDER ROBBERY A POSSIBLE MOTIVE, BUT ARE PURSUING ALL ANGLES. THE VICTIM'S IDENTITY HAS STILL NOT BEEN DETERMINED...."

Well, whatta you know? DeLeon grabbed his Chivas Regal bottle and poured a full shot of celebration. To his amazement, the Nashville wanna-be had pulled it off. What were the odds that all the stars in the universe would line up to cover an outrageous, Las Vegas style, chips-all-in debacle? With luck like that, even a young wanna-be had a promising future in the PI business.

DeLeon poured himself a second shot.

A few minutes later, his office phone rang.

Raymond's crusty voice came on the line. "Was that our tar baby?"

"In living color," boasted an emboldened DeLeon. "Except, I guess you would take the living part out."

"Good job, Joe. I always knew you had it in you."

"Let's face it, Raymond. Who in their right mind wants to let you down?"

He chuckled. "Listen. I want you to be my guest at the party Saturday night. The guys are throwing a little something for Zizzo's birthday."

Realizing those kinds of events were traditionally reserved for the elite outfit bosses, DeLeon stammered. "Ummmmm-me?"

"Sure. After all your hard work, you deserve it. Me and the boys'll pick you up around eight."

"Thanks, Raymond. I won't forget it."

DeLeon spent most of Saturday morning shopping for a new suit. If he was going to rub shoulders with La Cosa Nostra's upper echelon, he needed to look his best. In the back of his mind, he still wondered why Penrow hadn't called him. But with a $20,000 payday coming, he knew it was only a matter of time.

Raymond was a notorious tipper. With Tiny Johnny out of the way, DeLeon suspected his final retainer might grow exponentially, perhaps, enough to put a dent in the $20,000 he owed Penrow. But if not, it really didn't matter. Raymond's personal introduction to some of the mob's most elite movers-and-shakers was going to be worth a lot more than a bloated gratuity.

An underboss from the Lucchese family in the Bronx had once promised DeLeon some work. But it never panned out. Maybe he'd be there so they could reconnect. If not, the Lombardo people who got along very well with Zizzo and his outfit would surely be there. They were known to pay top dollar for services rendered. One word from Raymond, and DeLeon would be swamped with assignments. He could already see himself hiring an entire PI crew, maybe his own personal secretary who didn't mind giving the boss a little massage every now and then.

DeLeon's office was located over a bakery shop on Taylor Street in Little Sicily. Rather than have Raymond come up, DeLeon stood in front of the bakery, waiting for them to arrive.

About 8:15 pm, a long black limo pulled up to the curb. Raymond lowered the tinted window in the back seat.

"Nice, very nice, Joe," Raymond immediately acknowledged DeLeon's spiffy navy blue suit and white shirt. Lofingers left his seat up front, next to the driver, came around and opened the back door.

Get in, Joe." Raymond slid over. DeLeon climbed into the back seat. Lofingers climbed in behind him.

DeLeon immediately reached into his coat pocket to pull out a small white box. "I've never met Mr. Zizzo. Do you think he would appreciate this small birthday token?" His nervous fingers fumbled the lid off the box to expose an exquisite set of diamond cufflinks.

"I'm sure he'll be very pleased," said Raymond. "Here, let me present them for you."

As Raymond set the box in a tray on his side of the limo door, DeLeon noticed a Chicago Sun-Times, folded neatly across Raymond's lap.

After a few miles of awkward silence, DeLeon tried to make conversation. "So where is this party?"

"The Hilton Suites on Delaware Place. It's just up the street."

There was something about Raymond's short answers and

Lofingers' continuous stare that DeLeon didn't like. But mob clients were quirky like that. One moment they'd be laughing at you, and next, stabbing you with an ice pick. DeLeon had learned to go with the flow. Everything eventually worked itself out.

A few blocks from the Hilton, Raymond turned to him in an upbeat tone. "Joe, have you had a chance to read the paper today?"

"No, not today."

"You should. In fact, I have one right here." Raymond placed the Sun-Times on DeLeon's lap.

Assorted headlines blanketed the front page ... The President's visit to Chicago, the Blackhawks' latest acquisition, Michael Jordan's new line of footwear, a one-hundred year old building scheduled to be demolished. There was nothing that DeLeon found significant or personal.

As the limo pulled up in front of the Hilton, Raymond gave DeLeon a pitiful stare. "Turn to page seven."

DeLeon flipped the flimsy pages, a methodical rhythm to conceal his trembling hands. Finally he saw it, a follow-up story to the murder in Litchfield.

The headline read: LITCHFIELD HOMICIDE VICTIM IDENTIFIED. His name was John J. Spencer, affectionately known as John-John, a long-time customer service rep for the Landmark Cadillac Dealership in Springfield.

"That's your tar baby, Joe."

Raymond never looked at DeLeon again. It was as though he was no longer visible, his shameful existence erased from the annals of time.

Stepping out of the limo onto the sidewalk, Raymond removed the cufflink box from the tray and stuffed it into his coat pocket. "Don't worry, Joe. I'll give Zizzo your best regards."

The limousine pulled away from the curb, quietly, reverently, like the funeral hearse of a great dignitary, carrying the family to the gravesite. But DeLeon was no dignitary. He was just a washed-up PI whose pink slip had been signed in blood.

In the back of his mind, he could hear a song playing. It was Frank Sinatra singing *Over The Rainbow*. That's where he told himself he was going ... over the rainbow to a land in a lullaby, where all the dark clouds were behind him and the skies were pretty blue.

The next morning, a feisty reporter from the Chicago Tribune stood on a sidewalk in front of a Taylor Street bakery, shouting last minute instructions to her rookie photographer. "Get a left side front before they take him down."

Him was a bloody corpse in a navy blue suit and white shirt, dangling from a meat hook, roped to the second floor window.

The scene was all too familiar to the white-haired detective in charge, a long-time veteran of the Organized Crime Task Force. The Tribune reporter observed the detective circling the suspended body, scribbling a few notes in his small brown notebook.

"So what's the story on this one, Bill? And don't give me that official *blah-blah preliminary too early to tell* BS," she warned.

He finally smiled with familiarity. "Pretty obvious, Peggy. Don't you think? The man tried to use a meat hook to commit suicide. When that didn't work, he shot himself two times in the head."

Perhaps, she was too busy crying to remember the details of their frantic midnight exodus from their Litchfield apartment. For Lola, the harrowing journey down Interstate-55 had been blurred by tears of self-pity and repressed fear. Posttraumatic Stress Disorder was what her history professor had called it when he talked about the delayed reaction of troops returning from Iraq. But what name did he give to the growing suspicion that, no matter what she did, the syndrome of violence and poverty and uncertainty would follow her to her grave?

Back in Mexico, the priest had talked about the curse of the devil, swallowing up families, even whole generations. That night, fleeing from the carnage and disillusionment of living underground, Lola longed for a sacred mirror, some reliable means by which she could look deep inside her existence to make sure 666 had not been imprinted upon her immortal soul.

Though the tears blurred her vision, she could still see the somber look on Johnny's face. It was a stone face, the cold stare of reality, reflecting his undeniable status as a marked man. All hope of reconciliation with his former employees had dissipated. His mind churned with a single thought: *survival*. That's all that mattered now.

An hour down the highway, somewhere between Peoria and Springfield, Johnny turned onto an old gravel road that snaked deep into the forest. Ghostly trees and ravenous underbrush blotted out the moonlight, leaving the Deville's powerful high beams as the only refuge from the stranglehold of darkness.

Their creepy stealth-like advance through the shadowy thickets finally came to a disquieting halt in front of an old wooden cabin surrounded by an iron rail fence. Though she could not see it, the suspended billows of fog and perpetual cry of bull frogs signaled a large body of water nearby.

"Wait here," Johnny instructed.

She watched him follow the light beams through the gate and into the house. A few minutes later, the glow of a small orange lantern illuminated the two front windows.

When he returned, she inquired with growing anxiety, "What is this place?"

"My place ... well, our place now," he corrected himself. "It's our best bet until things cool down."

"How did you-"

With rekindled amusement he explained, "I won it in a poker game when I first came to town. A crazy rich white boy wanted my hog. I pulled a diamond flush over three aces and ended up with this lake house. I kept the place under wraps. Figured it might come in handy one day."

Following in lockstep closely behind him, fully aware of the water snakes that slithered along the ponds and river banks at night, she approached the gloomy two-story structure like a reluctant trick-or-treater on Halloween night. On the porch, she noticed a broken down rusty sign, tacked up against the front door post. Its faded white lettering read: HOME SWEET HOME.

The words said it. But all of her instinctive senses disagreed. With crickets chirping and snakes lurking and angry frogs, bellowing in the distance, this home didn't seem sweet at all. And yet, she was too incredibly drained to argue with a sign. She followed Johnny inside, found the nearest sofa, and with one eye partially open, slowly drifted off to sleep.

Late the next morning, she awakened to a buzz of activity. Suitcases, boxes and jumbled clothing that had cluttered the trunk and back seat of the Deville now resided in small piles across the hardwood floor. Ten bags of groceries lined the kitchen counters. Four buckets of house paint, tape, brushes and rollers formed a chaotic stack near the living room door.

Johnny stood in the kitchen, fumbling with the latch on a new box of tools. He finally looked up to greet her. "Rise and shine, Babygirl. We got thangs to do."

Lola rubbed her sleepy eyes. "What's all of this stuff?"

"I figure it should be different the time. I mean, I ain't no Paul Bunyan wilderness type. But if this is gonna be our home, we might as well make it look the part, knowemsayin'?"

Lola and Johnny embarked upon a remodeling marathon, cleaning, restoring and replacing everything according to their own mutual preferences. Johnny tackled broken windows and missing planks in the walls. Lola scrubbed, sterilized and polished each piece of furniture to a dazzling shine. A battery of door locks and window guards were softened by cans of glitter and psychedelic paint. The security cameras, mounted on the roof's sun deck, were camouflaged by twin bird houses and a bright red wind fan.

Finally, to enhance security, Johnny removed the wooden planks that led from their back door to the small private boat dock along the Sangamon River. They didn't own a boat, and didn't want anyone who did, slipping in from the backside of the house to give them a La Cosa Nostra joy ride.

By Sunday afternoon, the old log cabin was brimming with new life: a fresh coat of paint in the spacious living and dining area downstairs, varnished kitchen cabinets, a new microwave and mini-fridge, a big screen television near the fireplace and two large Mexican throw rugs, covering the freshly polished hardwood floors.

Lola silently longed for one of her mother's beautiful paintings to match the color scheme in the red, orange and brown throw rugs. But it was only wishful thinking. There was no way her mother was going to chance one of her precious paintings with the international postal service. And there was no way Johnny was going to give FedEx or UPS or anybody else his new address.

For a long while, Johnny stood at the top of the stairs, admiring their finished handiwork. "I think we did it, Babygirl. We totally pimped this place out."

She smiled, approvingly, from the kitchen, never taking her eyes off the simmering skewers of beef and shrimp shish kabobs. "Look at these colors. This is why your people are not welcome to the neighborhood."

"If they couldn't put George Jefferson and Weezie out, they better not mess with me."

She paused a moment. "I do not know this Weezie."

"Just know she didn't have a .357 magnum and I do."

Johnny's tough guy response was a sure sign he was feeling better. So was she. Remodeling the lake house had been a wonderful therapeutic agent, purging their recent memories of blood and death and fear.

A few minutes later, sitting at the dining room table, enjoying a delicious platter of shish kabobs over rice and Mexican steamed cauliflower and broccoli, Lola felt it was time to fill in the blanks.

"You never told me why you came back to the apartment that night."

"Because you took care of business, Babygirl. You sent those video clips just like you were supposed to do. Otherwise, we'd both be six feet under."

Johnny went on to explain his critical discovery. The DVD's contained hundreds of still shots from previous weeks. Scanning though the first batch on Wednesday night, he had found nothing unusual.

"Three patients threw up from a nasty guinea pig dye solution, so they let us out early Thursday afternoon. I wasn't hungry, so I went back to the room and started looking at the second DVD. That's when I saw him."

"Saw who?" Lola's eyes widened.

"The man with the big ears. In the video, he was snooping around our apartment complex. Not one day, but two or three days. I couldn't figure out why he looked so familiar. And then it hit me. I had just seen him in the lobby that same morning."

"At the clinic?"

"Yeah. He was sitting on the sofa checking me out. I knew then what was about to go down."

"So how did you get back to Litchfield?"

"When I was down in the basement with this crazy motorcycle fool, I noticed a door leading to the sewer. So Thursday night I snapped the lock and followed the sewer under the street to the shopping mall. From there I took a cab to the Avis Rent-A-Car place. From there, I headed straight to you."

"You knew I was in trouble, yes?"

"I knew I had to get you out of that apartment. If trouble hadn't found you, it was just a matter of time."

She flashed an analytical frown. "How did they know where to find you ... us?"

"It's hard to say. These people are good at what they do. I don't know, maybe, it's an Italian bloodline thing. But the mob takes pride in hunting you down and whacking you in your tracks."

She made a passing glance at the front door. "Will we be safe here?"

"For a while, as long as we're careful," he declared. "I've already switched to a new ID and credit cards. I'm going to East St Louis tomorrow to have the hog repainted or maybe trade it in and get a whole new car and new tags. Hell, I don't know. We just gotta switch things up."

"What about the Avis car?"

"Friday morning, I called it in as stolen. They'll find it at the apartment, sooner or later."

She stared at him, proudly. "At this, you have become a *perfeccionista*?"

He stared back with saddened eyes. "Nothing lasts forever, Babygirl. At some point Humpty-Dumpty, the wall, all the king's horses and all the king's men will come crashing down."

"Don't say that, Daddy."

"It's true. That's why it's so important you march across that stage in three weeks. I don't want you to end up like me, a hoodlum on the run. Better a cheap gold watch and pithily ass pension than a gang of killers on your trail."

"You're a good person, Daddy."

He smiled, credulously. "You watched me kill a man a few nights ago in cold blood. Shot him in the back. Was that the mark of a good person?"

"You were trying to protect me. You did what you had to do."

"Say I was a doctor or lawyer or airline pilot. You think killing him would've been on my *to-do* list?"

Lola didn't want to answer. The silence answered for her.

He continued. "It's about the life you chose and the fallout that comes with it."

Her eyes watered with compassion. "You must tell me. What is your biggest regret? Living in the fast lane? Having to hide from the authorities and the *Mafioso*?"

He thought about it for a long time. "My biggest regret, Babygirl, is not bringing your mother back to America with me."

"Mama." Lola could see the lingering pain in his eyes. "You still love her, don't you?"

He didn't answer, excusing himself to a mouth full of beef.

"I talk to her on the phone every month. But you never ask to talk to her. You stay away from her."

"Because the horses have already circled the track."

"I do not follow you."

"I'm saying, I had my chance, fair and square. But now, it's too late. No need to rehash and speculate and talk about what coulda been. She's got your Papa Jose and the older kids and I've got you. That's a pretty sweet deal if you ask me."

Lola was thinking about an even sweeter deal.

Later that night, after Johnny had fallen asleep, she called her cousin, Carlos Zedillo, in Houston. "Have you made the arrangements?"

"Have you sent the money?" He fired back.

"You were to call me with a figure."

"Five thousand. That's your figure my little *mestiza*."

"Why so much? This is *madre*, mama, your Aunt Ruby. Remember?"

"I do remember. That's why it is not seventy-five hundred."

She sighed, deeply.

"Listen," he continued. "Things are different from when you came over. They got ten times the border patrols, electric fences, cameras and planes. They even got these patriotic rednecks on motorcycles with binocular, pistols and baseball bats, trying to keep the maids and ditch-diggers and lawn-boys and toilet cleaners from coming in stealing jobs away. Everything is checked and double checked. People gotta be paid to get the job stealers across. People gotta be paid big time."

"Mama is too old for the desert and the fences and the baseball bats."

"Don't worry," he reassured her. "I'm bringing her in another way. You just make sure I get the money this week. Otherwise, don't waste my time."

On Sunday morning, a black nurse named Nellie with bad arches, varicose veins and an attitude to match, roamed the hallways inside St. Francis' emergency care unit, searching for her missing patient. A man with a southern drawl and fancy cowboy boots had stumbled in early Friday morning with a badly bruised rib cage and bloody black nails, protruding from his chest.

He had attributed his injuries to a freak accident at home. But with a Tennessee drivers license, why was he being treated in Litchfield? His story had too many holes for Nellie. But when she mentioned it to the usual cut-and-shoot weekend police brigade, none of them seemed to care.

Now he was gone. A bill for services rendered would be mailed to his address. Of course, he wouldn't pay. And sooner or later somebody was going to piss her off with a sad story about the high cost of health care and the difficulty with giving her a raise.

Silas Penrow wasn't dead. The experimental super Kevlar

vest he had bought on eBay from some quack inventor out in California had actually worked, had actually sheilded him from the deadly .357 slugs. Now it was just a matter of lying low until he could recuperate from his injuries. Then, he would find the low-life that shot him in the back.

He thought it odd DeLeon hadn't answered his phone, that is, until Monday night when he stumbled across a USA Today in the Holiday Inn Express hotel lobby. There DeLeon was on the front page, hanging from a meat hook in front of his office. A local radio station, recapping the Litchfield apartment homicide, kept referring to the dead man as John-John. And none of the stories mentioned law enforcement's possible interest in the Mexican girlfriend or the '99 Deville.

By week's end, Penrow realized he had killed the wrong man. Even more agonizing was the inescapable fact that DeLeon was too dead to pay him.

He thought to himself, *What would Peter Gunn do in a tight spot like this?*

The answer came flying back to him like a pie in the face: Go to the source.

DeLeon had told him enough about Raymond's prominence in Joey the Clown's organization. It was just a matter of finding him in Chicago. If that didn't work, Penrow had a few connections down in New Orleans that could, at least, get him an audience with Raymond, the man paying the bills. If he was going to track down the scumbag tar baby that had shot him in the back, why not get paid for it?

Friday afternoon, he checked out of the Holiday Inn Express in Litchfield and boarded a plane for Chicago.

On a sun-drenched Saturday morning, one week before her scheduled graduation from Lincoln Land Community College, Lola came downstairs. She found Johnny sitting on the sofa watching a Cubs double hitter. He had a grim expression on his face.

"Your team is losing again, yes?" She poured herself a large glass of orange juice.

Begrudgingly, he squeezed the remote, as if choking it for his unknown troubles. Finally, the big 52 inch screen flipped off. "It's not the game, Babygirl. Not the game at all."

"Then why do you look so sad?" she asked.

"I got a problem. Might as well show you. Throw on some clothes. Come go with me."

A few minutes later, they pulled into a small car lot on the outskirts of Springfield. He walked her over to a late model candy apple red Honda Accord Coupe with shiny sports rims and a spoiler on the back.

She gazed at him with a puzzled look on her face. "What is this?"

"My problem," he replied, demurely.

"I do not understand."

He looked back at his new 2000 maroon Deville, the one he had recently traded for in East Saint Louis, then at the Honda. "It's like this. No matter how hard I try, I can't drive them both at the same time. Think you could help me?"

He reached into his pocket and tossed her a set of Honda keys.

She stood there mesmerized, still uncertain about what he was saying.

Finally, he made it clear. "Happy graduation, Babygirl. This one is for you."

She was still standing there afraid to move, afraid the alarm clock would go off and she would awaken back in Mexico, late for her Aunt Conchita's English class.

A couple of salesmen applauded in the distance. The United States flag on the pole above the office flapped, gloriously, in the wind. The manager's lofty voice came over the loudspeaker, calling out her name. "It's not going to bite you, Lola. Take it for a spin."

He didn't have to ask twice. She leaped upon Johnny's neck with a huge bear hug, tears merging into a slobbery kiss. Without the support of his trusty cane, she almost pulled his hulking frame to the ground. The next moment she was spinning out of the driveway, wild-eyed, waving, stopping traffic with her blinding smile.

"Don't forget to put some gas in it," Johnny tried to remind her. But it was too late. She was already on the entrance ramp to some turnpike in the sky.

****

Over in Tamaulipas, Mexico, just across the border from Laredo, Texas, no one was smiling, at least, no one in the noisy, smoke-filled van that had brought Lola's mother from Juárez. The five passengers ... a teenage boy and three other young women ... rode in deathly silence, petrified they might say or do something to cause the two coyote drivers to change plans.

In the illicit underworld of human smuggling, changing plans might mean robbing, murdering or charging their human cargo more money than agreed upon. In the notorious smuggling corridors outside the rape camps in San Diego County, coyotes had a reputation for dragging the young women off into the bushes, then hanging their panties in the trees.

Ruby watched with growing consternation as the two men whispered to each other. They reminded her of the demon voices that had haunted her childhood nightmares long ago. Yet, every bone in her trembling body told her this was far worse than a childhood nightmare. It was the grim reality of entering the promised land through the back door.

She had tried the front door. But long lines wrapped around the American Consulate building like a giant python around an overwhelmed prey. *Mara Salvatrucha* street gangs extorted money from the weary petitioners camped outside in the blistering sun. Crooked Mexican officials demanded kickbacks to get through the door. Those lucky enough to file an application to enter the United States had to wait months for an official interview. And more and more, as the pressure against illegal immigration ratcheted up in America, the answer to the endless requests for temporary visas came back: NO ... Hell NO, with Tea Party signatures written in red.

If Ruby had any chance of making her daughter's graduation, it was with the coyotes, the brutal, unpredictable experts in smuggling human cargo across the river. That's how she had talked herself into the van.

A few miles from the US-Mexico border crossing, they veered off the main street into a dark, abandoned alley. The driver, a ruddy-faced, sunburned man with a pot belly and hollow eyes, got out first. He was soon followed by his partner, a younger, muscular man with a double scar on his jaw and a cream-colored *charro* rodeo hat cocked to the side of his head. He clutched a large brown paper bag in one hand, a smelly cigarette stub in the other.

"*Salgan!*" The driver ordered them out like cattle. He lined them up at the back of the van, the smoky exhaust fumes, choking off their lungs.

"There has been a slight misunderstanding." The driver spoke in a broken Spanish dialect. "Some of you have not paid your fair share."

They all knew better. The total fee had to be paid in advance. Otherwise, the lowly travelers wouldn't have been allowed to board the van.

The young teenage boy accompanied his mother. Shaking, profusely, they both had begun to cry.

The man in the cowboy hat walked over to them first, reached into the bag and handed them documents. "Relax, you are fine."

He turned to Ruby and the other two women. "With you, we have a big problem."

A thin Salvadorian woman in her late twenties with a red bandana handkerchief tied around her brow spoke up. "What is the problem?"

"You three are short 5,000 pesos. That is the problem."

"I'm sure my uncle paid you in full," she reported, a growing sense of desperation in her voice. "I'm sure of that."

"Our records show a different amount. I am sure of that," he quickly rebuked her.

Reluctantly, she reached into the zipped leg pocket of her brown Khaki pants. She counted out the 5,000 pesos with only a few hundred left.

He smiled, fully exposing his crooked teeth. "Now that is the best way to straighten out this confusion." He reached into the bag and handed her several documents.

The driver glared at Ruby. "You! Are you ready to straighten out your confusion?"

Ruby couldn't speak. Her voice was buried under an avalanche of fear. If she could just remember what her nephew, Carlos, had told her to say. And then it dawned on her that she had written it down.

She pulled open the Velcro strip on the small pouch tied around her waist. She handed the driver a wrinkled piece of paper with two words scribbled on the back. The driver looked, then handed it to the man in the rodeo hat, the only one who could read.

The words read: *El Gallo*. In English it meant the Rooster, the legendary Gerardo Salazar, the godfather in international human trafficking. In Houston, Dallas and San Antonio, Salazar and his sons operated a huge network of sleazy *cantinas* and camouflaged brothels. With his army of lieutenants, trolling the small Mexican villages for gullible young teens, Salazar had smuggled thousands of young women into the United States. His reputation for brutality and ruthlessness not only controlled his expanding harem of sex slaves, but sent a deadly warning to other smugglers to leave his precious cargo alone.

The man in the rodeo hat stared at the paper for a long while. Without saying another word, he reached into the bag and handed Ruby the packet. The fake documents included a Mexican driver's license, a Mexican passport and an American Consulate-issued B2 travel visa. They all had been printed in the US and smuggled across the border, precisely for her crossing.

Finally, the coyotes turned their attention to the young girl with the soft eyes, plump cheeks and long flowing black hair. Throughout the ordeal, she had quietly stared at the ground.

"What do you say, little princess? Ready to settle your debt?" The man in the hat queried.

She looked up, slowly. "I do not have the money."

"You are so close to a new life in a new county and you don't have 5,000 pesos?"

She shook her head from side to side.

"What about four? I give you the *Los Dos Laredos* discount."

She shook her head again.

The man in the hat looked at the driver with a knowing, snaggle-toothed grin. And then he said, "Maybe we can work something out."

He set the bag on the ground and placed his arm across her shoulders. "Why don't you come into my office?"

The girl was trembling, trying not to cry.

Ruby's heart was pounding so loudly she didn't hear herself speak. "I, I, I have the money. I will give it for her."

It was the equivalent of four hundred American dollars. If Ruby ended up short on the other side of the border, she was confident Lola would make up the difference.

The man in the hat offered a hard glare, dropping his eyes to the pistol on his belt. "I would advise you to mind your own business. This is between me and the little princess."

They all watched, silently, helplessly, as the little princess and the man in the hat boarded the van and locked the doors. Even with the motor still running, they could hear her intermittent whimpers of humiliation and pain. The old springs on the van began to rock faster and faster. Her soft, innocent whimpers were quickly overtaken by his deep, guttural groans.

After what seemed to be an eternity, the door slid open. The little princess stumbled out, pulling up her jeans, buttoning up her dainty flowered blouse, wiping the spotty liquid from her reddened face. She staggered over to the edge of the alley and threw up a brownish slime.

Clutching a white silk handkerchief to wipe her face, Ruby followed behind her.

"One day you will forget the pain," she told her. "But for now, remember it. Let it be the fire that drives you to a better life."

A few minutes later, Ruby walked across the Gateway to the Americas International Bridge. Still numb from the sleazy, manipulative attack on the little princess, she didn't care about the two border agents that spot checked her baggage and glanced over her documents. Reciprocally, they didn't seem to care about her. They barely looked at her precious credentials before waving her across.

Several blocks away, with a single black suitcase in hand, she boarded the bus for Chicago. It wasn't just any bus. It was the Super Express from Houston, the bus line that Salazar owned. It would take her to Chicago using the back roads late at night, when Immigration and Customs Enforcement agents were sleeping and Highway Patrol officers drank their coffee at local cafés.

If all went well, she was going to see her daughter graduate, the first in her family to get a college degree. And even though she didn't want to admit it, her heart pounded with anticipation at the prospect of seeing an old stranger, the only man she had ever loved.

The boardroom was crowded Wednesday afternoon. Lola saw the endless circle of hunched shoulders through the tinted glass. Since Kristy Cutler's return from her trip a week earlier, she had been distant and nervous and inaccessible. She and Goodboy and a small supporting cast had been working long hours, trying to get ready for some big event. Observing a dozen unfamiliar faces, huddled around the conference table, clad in expensive business suits, frantically punching their Androids like Enron accountants fresh out of prison, she suspected this was the big event.

She walked down the hallway to Kristy's secretary's desk and offered a congenial smile. "Who are all those people?"

"I'm not at liberty to say," she smirked "But trust me, it has nothing to do with you."

"I really need to talk to Ms K?"

"Concerning...?"

"My graduation ceremony is Saturday. I want to take the next two days off to prepare."

"Yes, I believe someone did mention you had made it through. Do you plan to go on to a real college? I understand a number of opportunities are finally opening up for your people, given the right degree."

My people! Did that little pointed-nosed bitch say my people, Lola was thinking to herself. *And what did she mean by a real college*?

The book said if you allowed yourself to be pulled into a frivolous public debate by confrontational coworkers, you were no better than the coworkers initiating the pull.

Why didn't the book offer an alternative, like pistol-whipping that particular coworker with your father's big gun?

Lola gathered her thoughts. "I also wonder about my safety report. Did she receive it?"

"Yes. But don't get your hopes up that she's read it. You can see she's been very busy."

"Yes, I can see," said Lola. "I can see a lot of things." For a fleeting moment, their eyes propelled invisible daggers at each other.

It was well after 5:00 pm when the meeting finally adjourned. Wearing a polite smile, Kristy escorted the visitors out to the parking lot. Afterwards, she went directly into a follow-up meeting with Goodboy and the other RedFish team members. By 8:00 pm, except Kristy and Lola, everyone had gone.

Lola waited a long while before knocking on her door. When no one answered, she stuck her head through a small crack. Kristy sat at her desk, staring at the computer screen, needle tears, streaming down her freckled face.

"Ms K, are you alright?" Lola approached, cautiously.

Kristy took a deep breath, then turned the screen toward Lola. The email was from The Missouri Custom Home Development

Group. The words were cordial, almost apologetic, notifying her of the decision they had made:

THANK YOU FOR YOUR INTEREST IN PROVIDING CONSTRUCTION SERVICES FOR OUR NEW CUSTOM HOME DEVELOPMENT PROJECT ON HUNTER LAKE. WE HOLD THE HIGHEST REGARD FOR YOUR REPUTATION AND CAPABILITIES AND VIEW YOUR ORGANIZATION AS A LEADER IN THE INDUSTRY. UNFORTUNATELY, WE HAVE SELECTED ANOTHER VENDOR FOR THIS PROJECT. IN OUR EFFORT TO MAINTAIN TRANSPARENCY TO ALL BIDDERS, WE HAVE POSTED THE AMOUNT OF THE WINNING BID BELOW.

CONFIRMED BID: $8,499,000

BIDDER: Trippple-Saw Construction

What I'm saying is we're in the bottom of the ninth. The next time she comes to the plate, she damn well better hit a home run.

The toxic warning from her patch-eyed coworker came rushing back to Lola.

Kristy shook her head. "Three in a row. This is unbelievable." Trippple-Saw Construction had underbid her on the last three jobs. "It's like they're reading my mind."

Lola pondered. "You think, maybe, they have your phone bugged?"

"I never discuss bids over the phone. I don't even discuss the final number with RedFish managers. I gather the cost estimates from each department. I trim the fat and submit the bid. Nobody knows but me."

Lola dropped her head. "I ... I don't know."

Kristy's voice softened. "And you shouldn't know. I apologize for dumping on you like this. Here, pull up a seat."

Lola flopped in front of her desk. "I won't be long."

"Tell me what's on your mind." And then like an inspired fortune teller, Kristy continued, "No, let me tell YOU what's on your mind. You're graduating Saturday. You need some time off to get ready?"

Lola smiled, broadly. "How did you know?"

"Hey, we girls know about the hair and nail bit, maybe a facial and new outfit. We've got to look our best, right?"

"Right."

"I want you to know, I'm proud of you. Proud of the progress you've been making at RedFish. I haven't had time to get a card. But I will."

"What did you think of the preliminary safety report?" asked Lola.

Kristy frowned. "Report? I haven't seen one."

That's because that little pointed-nosed slut never gave it to you, Lola was thinking, but replied, "I will send another copy to your email."

"I'll look forward to it."

"One more thing," Lola added. "I looked at my last paycheck. They did not take out the $200 that was given to me in advance."

Kristy gave Lola a long, hard stare, as if looking through her, then sank back in her chair. "I know."

"You do?"

"Yes. We never take it out," she revealed. "In a way, it's a test of character."

"I do not understand."

"About eighty percent of employees never say a word. They're hoping for an administrative error. They're hoping to end up $200 to the good. But twenty percent do say something. These are the people I promote to the top. These are the people I want running the company."

Lola grinned with mischief. "What is my new title, President, CEO?"

Kristy giggled, loudly. "I'm afraid that's my headache right now. But who knows? Keep doing what you're doing and one day it might be yours."

Later that night, driving back to the lake house in her spiffy new Honda, Lola tried to imagine herself as president of a big company. She could see the fat checks rolling in with her name on them, not to mention the bonuses the board of directors would shower upon her for doing such a fabulous job. People would come to her each day for instructions, hanging on to her every insightful word. With each new contract, the newspapers would plaster her name on the front page of the Business Section. Somewhere in the shadows, Nicholas would be kicking himself for the foolish choices he had made.

She had already worked herself up to Chairwoman of the National Association of Home Builders, with the President of the United States on the line, begging her to become Secretary of Commerce. That's when her iPhone chimed.

"Lolita?" A soft, familiar voice crooned through the speaker. It wasn't the President. It was someone far more important, the only person who dared namesake her after their distant cousin, the famous Spanish actress and singer, Lolita Flores.

"*Mama*?" Lola breathed a long sigh of relief. "I was beginning to worry. Where are you?"

"I ... I don't know."

A deep baritone voice immediately came over the phone. "Miss, can you hear me?"

"Yes."

"One of the managers found your mother wandering around in the parking lot. My Spanish is a bit rusty, but she seems to be lost."

"Where are you?"

"The Wal-Mart on North Dirksen Pkwy."

"Please keep her there. I'm on my way."

As it turned out, Salazar's Super Express bus line had taken Ruby as far as Chicago. The bus driver had put her into a van bound for Springfield. Once in Springfield, the driver had dropped her in the Wal-Mart parking lot and sped away.

In the safety of Lola's Honda, headed to the hotel, Ruby began to weep, quietly, uncontrollably. She wept for the humiliating charade in which she had partaken, the indelible moments of uncertainty and fear, the demeaning stares at each small-town restaurant and the harsh criticism from distant onlookers, whispering words of unprovoked hate and condemnation she could not understand. She wept for the little princess and all the other young girls whose coveted bodies earned them a seat on Salazar's Slave Ship Express.

Finally, she wept for her country, tormented by murder and corruption and drugs. The youth were like zombies, marching toward inevitable destruction. Her precious little baby daughter was already dead.

Under the clear, starlit night, with all the luxurious sparkle of America streaming pass her window, Ruby's trembling voice finally emerged from the torrent of tears. "Lolita, I am sorry, so sorry."

"For what, Mama?"

"For sending you away from home so young. How terrible it must have been."

Lola thought about her trip through the scorching desert and the dark walls of the tunnel, closing in on her. The memories were too painful to regurgitate, her life and death decisions, too horrifying to review.

"I do not want to talk about that," she declared. "You did what you thought was best, because you love me, *Si*?"

"With all my heart," Ruby sobbed.

"Then be proud, Mama. Be proud of what your love has done." Lola reached into the back seat to retrieve a plastic packet containing her Lincoln Land cap and gown. She placed it in her mother's lap.

As though it were a new born baby, Ruby caressed the package with loving affection, holding it close to her throbbing heart. Suddenly, she began to cry, all over again.

Staring in the mirror, observing how perfectly his shiny gold cufflinks matched his tan shirt and brown Sansabelt slacks, Johnny cringed at the pinstriped, brown and white snake around his neck.

"This tie is a freakin' deal breaker," he yelled up to Lola's bedroom. "It's got me trapped between an old country preacher and a bait-n-switch undertaker."

"Now, Daddy, you promised you'd wear the tie. This is my special day, remember?"

"What if I replaced your Honda with a little baby Mercedes? Could we lose this tie in the garbage can out back?"

"No! I love my Honda. Besides, the tie makes you look distinguished. You never know who you might run into."

"Usually, the people I run into want to kill me. This tie is just gonna justify their actions."

Lola didn't respond. She was too busy applying her seductive blend of hairspray and makeup and lip liner. When she finally descended the stairway in her rose-colored, V-necked Aussie designer suit, spiked heels and dangling pearl earrings, Johnny's jaw dropped to the floor.

"How do I look?" she asked, already beaming with confidence.

Johnny grabbed his heart. "Babygirl!!! If I was going to try my hand at incest, this would be the day."

She smiled. "I look pretty, yes?"

"No. Beautiful ... just like your mother. I wish she could see you right now."

Lola didn't respond to his wishful thinking. It would be answered soon enough.

On the way to the graduation ceremony, Lola informed Johnny of a last-minute stop at the Hilton Springfield Hotel. "I need to check on the arrangements for our class after-party. It won't take very long."

Johnny parked along the VIP curb in front of the main entrance. He waited ten ... then twenty ... then thirty minutes. Lola still hadn't come out. A few minutes could be the difference between life and death in his world. He was about to lock his car and go inside when Lola finally emerged.

She had someone with her, a middle-aged woman with long-flowing black hair intermingled with elegant streaks of gray. Her auburn face was strikingly beautiful, a natural complement to the sparkling sterling earrings that dangled from her thin lobes. She wore a long purple floral embroidered dress with a matching brown Reboso shawl. Deep, rose-tinted sunglasses concealed her dark eyes.

It wasn't until she removed the glasses that Johnny knew for sure. "Ruby?"

Twenty-seven years earlier, he had called her name for

the first time. Still, the sound of his voice ravaged her heart with uncontrollable surrender.

They embraced for a long, tender moment, saying nothing, allowing the swell of their befuddled emotions to speak in a hidden language that words could not express. Finally, Johnny pulled out a soft white handkerchief and wiped away her tears, then his own.

He turned to Lola. "Why you ... little ... sneaky-"

"Now, now, Daddy. This is my graduation day."

"You'd better be glad," he acquiesced. "Otherwise, I'd pull me a limb off one of those lake house trees and beat your behind."

Ruby fondly remembered his tough-guy antics. She processed enough of the language to offer a fragmented reply. "*Abrázala.*"

Johnny looked at Lola.

"She says if you will get the stick, she will hold me down."

They all began to laugh.

For the first time in her life, Lola felt a strange surge of happiness. A sense of completion swirled around their unique threesome like an invisible wind. She wanted to stay there, observing her family phoenix, rising from the ashes of coyotes and border fences and life on the run. But her fancy Wittnauer watch reminded her that time was marching to a grander drum beat.

She loaded her parents into the back seat of Johnny's Deville and headed for the convention center.

****

Spring Prairie Capital Convention Center was a huge multi-purpose facility in Downtown Springfield. It hosted the city's most prestigious events. There were always concerts, trade shows, rodeos, monster truck races, and other sporting events churning a perpetual crowd of thrill-seekers into the spacious arena. Most of the larger academic institutions held their graduation ceremonies there as well.

Lola found the main arena breathtaking. Colossal walls of blue silk curtains formed a royal backdrop to a thousand strobe lights illuminating the gigantic triangular, wood paneled stage. Dignitaries wearing distinguished, golden tasseled Doctorate tams postured erectly in black king chairs that resembled sacred thrones. They stared with practiced ostentatiousness at the two hundred and fifty eager graduates, desiring to join their elite ranks.

Marching in seemed a surreal journey, the reenactment of triumphant soldiers returning home amidst the jubilant screams and wild applause of relatives and love ones of whom a great enemy invader had tried to devour. Taking her seat on the arena floor, five rows in front of the stage, she realized the great enemy invader was hopelessness, the deep-seated fear that failure would find her no matter on which side of the Rio Grande she resided.

But inundated by the cheers, the pomp and circumstance of the hour and joyful tears streaming down her mother's face, Lola found the courage to breathe a liberating sigh of relief. The great enemy invader was now defeated, its parasitical sting, taken away. A few more minutes and she would march across the stage to collect the official declaration of surrender. She would buy a large frame and hang it, proudly, on her wall.

Lola had no way of knowing all enemy invaders had not surrendered. High atop the west bleachers, with a pair of Ebay military binoculars pressed against his lantern face, Silas Penrow meticulously scanned the crowd. He was looking for a young Mexican girl named Lola Salinas. She was the key to finding the tar baby. A few more days of solid detective work and they both would be dead.

Penrow had flown back to Chicago and made his deal with Raymond. He regretted shifting all of the blame for John-John's untimely demise to DeLeon. But since DeLeon had already paid the ultimate price for the mix-up, it seemed appropriate he should receive the ultimate credit.

The main thing was that Raymond had given Penrow the green light to find Johnny and take him out. If Penrow needed help, Raymond would send it. There was a $10,000 bonus if he could do it alone; just so Raymond was able to verify the kill.

DeLeon had once told Penrow that breaks were like shooting stars. They came when you least expected them. That was precisely what had happened the night Johnny shot him in the back. He had landed on top of one of Lola's college study guides. The name, LOLA SALINAS, had been scribbled across the front of the book and on some of the practice exercises inside.

Posing as an auditor from the U.S. Department of Education and National Student Loan Data Systems, Penrow had sweet-talked a young inexperienced administrative assistant into giving him Lola's information.

"Our records indicate she'll be graduating on Saturday. The ceremony is at the convention center in Springfield."

Now, Penrow waited, patiently. At some point during the ceremony, one of the old crow-eyed professors on stage was going to call her name. That's when he would rev up his old backwoods tracking skills and pounce on the little Mexican girl like a bloodhound on a Texas armadillo.

Sooner or later the tar baby would show up. And when he did, Penrow would slap both their carcasses on the pit.

****

The guest speaker, a boring Academician from the Science Academy in Washington DC, eventually finished his useless spiel.

The music started. Graduates began to flood the ramp. One by one they marched across the stage, brandishing proud smiles, waving to the cheering crowd. Lola's heart pounded louder and louder as she inched her way up the ramp to the edge of the platform.

Finally, it happened. The announcing clerk called her name: LOLA SALINAS. The sound echoed throughout the building, all over America and Mexico too.

Lola walked slowly, deliberately, making certain her stylish spiked heels didn't tangle with some inadvertent crack in the floor. As the president of the college handed her the leather-bound certificate, he smiled, "Congratulations!"

Somewhere in the galaxy, an explosion erupted. A new star was born.

Back at her elementary school in Mexico, a foreign exchange teacher from Dallas, Texas used to play *America the Beautiful* so they could compare the words to the *Mexican National Anthem*. Back then, Lola could only image what the songwriter meant by purple mountains and alabaster cities that gleamed. But at that moment, gliding across the stage in glorious celebration, she understood every word. For the first time, she understood them with her heart.

She had reached the exit ramp and started her descent. That's when she spotted the familiar blond hair, pointed nose and tanned face. Terri, the Bishop Hardware *diablo* that had stolen Nicholas away from her, was standing on the floor next to the handrail. She offered a congratulatory smile, but Lola turned away.

The nerve of her showing up at the graduation. Hadn't she done enough damage? Was it necessary to ruin the most important day in Lola's life?

After the ceremony, most of the graduates and their family members reconvened on the steps outside the convention center. Lola took time to congratulate some of her classmates and confirmed the after party scheduled for that evening. Working her way through the crowd, she eventually found Johnny at the bottom of the steps, holding tightly to Ruby's hand.

She opened the black leather binder to display her Lincoln Land associate degree. "Isn't it beautiful?"

Ruby rubbed her fingers across the embossed lettering. "*Regalo Del Dios.*"

What did she say?' asked Johnny.

"She says this is a gift from God."

"You better believe it. Now, that makes two gifts." Johnny rubbed his hand across his new kidney.

Lola wasn't paying attention. She was staring at the pointed-nosed blond standing a few feet away."

"Excuse me." Lola walked over to Terri, a bitter scowl on her face.

"This is unbelievable," Lola scolded her. "Are you here to try to take my degree too?"

"I came to talk to you," explained Terri.

"We have nothing to talk about. Go talk to your lover man."

"Nicholas is not my lover man," she revealed.

"What happened? He dumped you too?"

"He was never my lover," she declared. "Nicholas is my ... brother."

Lola's dark eyes bulged. "Brother???"

"Half brother," she clarified. "He tried to tell you. But you wouldn't listen."

"Wah-Wah-Why should I fall for such a lie?"

"Because I'm here. Because deep in your heart, you know it's true. Twenty years ago, Nicholas' father met my mother at a law conference in Baltimore. They had an affair and I was born. They tried to keep it a secret, but Nicholas' mother found out. I'm the bastard child that almost ended their marriage."

Lola didn't want to admit it, but as she listened, she could see Terri's stark resemblance to Nicholas.

"Nicholas' father hated me and my mother," she continued. "He felt she had set out to trap herself a prominent lawyer, even though she didn't ask for a dime. But Nicholas' mother made him pay. She made him pay because it was the right thing to do."

Lola dropped her head. "I wish I could believe you."

Terri grabbed her by the arm. "Come with me."

Terri led her back into the building and over to the concession stand. At a small table in the back, Nicholas lifted his head.

"If you don't believe me, maybe you'll believe him. He begged me to talk to you." She paused a while. "He's not well, not since you broke up with him. He loves you, Lola. You need to think about that before you make any harsh decisions."

Terri walked away.

In the dense crowd outside the convention center, Penrow spotted a young teenage slacker with shaggy black hair and wired earphones, protruding from his music player.

Penrow approached with a friendly smile. "I can tell you don't want to be here. Who's graduating, your sister? Brother?"

He nodded, not specifying which.

"Listen, I'm gonna give you a chance to turn this loser event into a worthwhile gig, just for you. Would you like that?"

The young teen nodded again.

Penrow reached into his wallet to pull out a twenty dollar bill. "You see that tall black man standing at the bottom of the steps?"

The teenager peered over a cluster of cackling relatives and flashing cameras to spot Johnny and Ruby on the steps below. "I see him."

I want you to walk up behind him and call his name. It's

Johnny. Can you remember that? *Johnny.*"

He nodded again.

"Tell him an old friend would like to talk to him. I'll be waiting up here."

Penrow handed him the twenty.

He watched as the teen followed his instructions to the letter. A few steps in back of Johnny, the boy paused. In a small voice with noted apprehension, he called out Johnny's name.

Even in the noisy crowd, Johnny's instinct picked up the boy's muted vocals. He turned to see an unfamiliar pubic face, standing behind him. "Do I know you?"

"No. No, sir. But that man says he wants to talk to you." The teenager pointed to the spot where Penrow had been standing. But no one was there.

"What man?" Johnny demanded.

"He was there a minute ago." The youngster insisted.

"How did he look?"

"I, I, I don't know. He was just a man," he stammered. Sensing the growing irritation in Johnny's voice, the teenager began to back up.

Johnny's forceful interrogation was suddenly interrupted by a gentle tap on his shoulder, enough time for the teen to disappear into the crowd. He turned to find Lola and some skinny, bird-faced white boy standing in front of him, hugged-up and smiling.

"Daddy, Mama. There is someone I want you to meet. This is Nicholas," Lola proudly announced."

Nicholas extended his bony fingers in a surprisingly firm handshake, first to Johnny, then to Ruby.

"I'm so pleased to finally meet you," said Nicholas.

Lola was still blushing from ear to ear. "Nicholas came all the way from Kansas City to attend my graduation. He is very thoughtful, yes?" She then looked at her mother. "Kansas City, *fuera del estado.*"

Ruby nodded with vague understanding.

"Nicholas has something he wants to say to you." Lola slammed her elbow into Nicholas' rib cage.

He cleared his throat. "I know this might be a little abrupt and certainly not the best place in the world to talk about something of this nature. But I don't think it can wait. Mr. and Mrs. ahhh ..." Nicholas still didn't know Johnny's last name.

"Wexler, Wexler the III," Lola tried to help him out.

"Mr. and Mrs. Wexler, I am asking for your permission to marry your daughter."

As Ruby glanced behind her, searching for the people named Wexler, Johnny's head swelled up like a big charcoal balloon. "Oh hellllll no!"

Lola was stunned, started to panic. "You cannot mean that, Daddy."

"Isn't this the same Gigolo joker who had you crying all night and throwing up all over the kitchen sink? Does he understand he almost caused you to flunk out of school?"

"It was my fault, Daddy!"

"Your fault because he hit the high seas on a blond booty call and left you here to pick up the pieces?"

"That girl was his sister," she tried to explain.

"And you believe that?"

"I know it, Daddy. I know it in my heart. It's true."

"What? Is this boy some kind of freak, carrying on incessin' with his sister?"

"Nothing like that, sir," Nicholas quickly defended. "I begged Lola to go. But she stayed here. She stayed here because of you."

"So it's my fault now," Johnny surmised.

'No, it's my fault for going anyway. I put Bishop Hardware

before Lola. And since my sister was having such a hard time with the breast cancer, I thought the cruise would do her good."

Johnny quietly reflected on his own near-death experience. "This so-called sister of yours. Is she going to ... make it?"

"The operation went well," Nicholas reported. " She's back at work and they expect a full recovery."

There was another long pause. "Listen, Boy. Do you know how much vomit I had to clean up behind you?"

Lola cleared her throat. "All of it was not behind him, Daddy."

"What do you mean?"

And then came the bombshell, the secret that Lola had harbored for months. "I'm pregnant, Daddy. I'm pregnant for Nicholas. I didn't want to tell you until after the graduation."

Johnny's hand was visibly shaking, his white eyes, slashing back and forth. He pushed down hard on his fancy black cane, desperately trying to stabilize himself. "I need to sit down. And wherever we sit, they better be serving double shots of Johnny Walker Red."

At a crowded Mexican restaurant on South Grand Avenue, the foursome settled into individual platters of tacos, albóndigas, enchiladas and fluffy Mexican rice. Lola and Ruby were on their second round of margaritas when Johnny reconvened his interrogation.

"Okay, I got some questions for you two young fools. You can tell me the honest truth, or I can beat it out of you with my cane."

Seeing the worried look on Nicholas' face as he soaked in Johnny's tough-guy antics, Lola struggled not to laugh. "Go ahead, Daddy. Tell us what you want to know."

"When did this marriage thang come up?"

"Maybe five minutes before we told you."

"No, sir," Nicholas corrected. "It's been on my mind for months. I just couldn't find her."

"When did you ask her to marry you, before or after the pregnant cat jumped out the bag?"

"Before," said Nicholas.

"After," said Lola at the same time.

Johnny tapped Ruby on the shoulder and pointed to the vacant chair. "Okay, pass me that damn cane because I see how this is going to go."

"No, no, you do not understand, Daddy. He asked me to marry him. But I could not accept without telling him about the baby. Once I told him, he asked me to marry him again."

"You felt obligated, didn't you?" Johnny hypothesized.

"No, sir ... special; I felt special because I had found her again. But to hear I had found more than her and the *more* was really me inside of her ... well, it just made me want her even more."

Johnny shook his head, pitifully. "You realize the responsibility you taking on, I mean, diapers and milk and Disney World tickets ain't free, knowemsayin'?"

"This is our future, Mr. Wexler," said Nicholas. "We're willing to do whatever it takes."

"Howard."

Nicholas paused. "Huhh?"

"Howard is my last name, not Wexler," said Johnny. "If you're going to be a part of the family, you need to know my real name."

Lola started to cry.

Johnny turned to Ruby. "Well aren't you going to say something? Maybe, stop these fools from making the biggest mistake of their lives?"

Ruby didn't know what to say. All of the words had been in English. And even though she could pick up bits and pieces, communication in America had been relegated to a series of gestures and voice inflections.

Nicholas waited until Lola and her mother had gone to the restroom. "Mr. Howard, I hope I don't offend you by what I'm about to suggest."

Johnny reached over to the vacant chair and gently slid the walking cane onto his lap. "Go on."

"There may be a way to improve your communications with Lola's mother. It's a new device that translates English to Spanish, and back again."

"You're saying it talks for her?"

"Yes, sir. It operates on an advanace Google algorithm. Does a pretty good job."

Johnny's face brightened. "How do I get it?"

Nicholas thought for a minute. "There's a Radio Shack a few blocks from here. I'm sure they have it."

Johnny reached into his wallet and handed Nicholas one of several credit cards. "Don't sweat the name. I'm still Wexler to the rest of the world."

When Lola and her mother came back to the table, Lola asked, "Where's Nicholas?"

Johnny tried to keep a straight face. "He left with a blonde chick in a convertible Maserati. Said they had to go take care of some personal business."

Lola's face blistered. "Daddy, do not play with me like that."

Johnny grinned, mischievously. "Relax, he'll be back soon."

When Nicholas returned to the table, he and Johnny immediately tore into the little blue box and inserted the batteries. The electronic translator resembled an old walkie-talkie with a small keyboard and digital screen. A large oval speaker protruded from the bottom.

"Say something!" Johnny pushed the translator up to Ruby's mouth.

A bit stunned, she finally unlocked her tongue. "*Hola!*"

The translator fired back in a Cyborg electronic voice: Hello.

Ruby smiled, widely. "*Estoy en America.*"

Translator: I am in America.

Ruby grabbed the translator from Johnny's hand.

Flashing an even wider smile, she bellowed, "*Escucha.*"

Translator: You must listen to what I have to say."

Johnny looked at Nicholas. "What have we done?"

Ruby spoke for a long time, first praising Lola for her accomplishments, then Johnny for his support and unselfishness in taking her in, then Nicholas for his commitment to her and the baby.

"The baby," she emphasized. "That is your future. Each generation must sacrifice so that the next generation will have a better life. This will be the measure of your success."

While Ruby was speaking, the manager, a plump, Americanized Spaniard with a thick black mustache, came over to the table. He was fascinated by the speaking device. After trying his hand at it a few times, he inquired, "What is the occasion today?"

"My daughter just graduated from college," Johnny proudly announced.

"This is magnificent! Say no more." He beckoned for two members of a mariachi band to come over to the table. One clutched a violin, the other, a glittering tambourine. He stepped over to the counter, reached into a glass cabinet to retrieve two large bouquets of red roses.

He handed one to Lola. "This is for being very smart and making good decisions at a young age." Then, he handed the other to Ruby. "This is for giving birth to this special young lady. She is very beautiful, just like you."

Ruby's eyes welled up.

Johnny pointed to Nicholas. "Hey, what about me and him?"

The manager smiled, "Of course. I crown you with *el regalo de la celebración!*"

Johnny grabbed the translator and shouted. "Reggolo something de hell or nother." Unable to make sense of his gibberish, the device remained silent.

"It means the gift of celebration." The manager happily explained. "For the rest of the night, all your drinks are on me."

The two band members began to play *Cielito lindo*, a song of triumph. Ruby thought about all that Lola had been through and released another flood of tears. Johnny ordered another round for everybody, a double for himself.

That's when Nicholas pointed to the two gift boxes at the edge of the table. "When are you going to open them?"

In all of the excitement, Lola hadn't gotten around to opening her only two gifts, at least, the two that had been wrapped, bowed and placed in a box. The other gifts ... the graduation, Nicholas' surprise return, her mother's visit from Mexico, Johnny's acceptance of her future husband ... were all too splendid and overpowering to fit into a box.

Her mother's gift was the size of a laptop, wrapped in shiny silver paper with a blue bow. Lola opened it the way her mother had taught her as a little girl, slowly, with reverence and appreciation, resisting the urge to rip the paper into a thousand shreds.

Inside, she found two gifts. The first was an exquisitely sketched charcoal rendering of Lola's entire family. They were all sitting at the dinner table, smiling. Papa Jose sat at the head of the table. Ruby's only son, Fernando, sat next to his father. Ruby sat on the opposite side, flanked by the oldest sister, Frida, then Lola, and finally, the youngest sister, Amada.

Lola's eyes brightened. " You drew this, Mama?"

She spoke into the translator. "*Sí*, from an old photograph your Aunt Conchita took years ago."

Remembering her love for painting and the arts, Johnny smiled. "You still got the touch, huh?"

"Whenever the time will permit."

"You have a lovely family," Nicholas observed. "Are they all still in Mexico?"

When Ruby dropped her head, Nicholas realized he had asked the wrong question.

"Well, I mean, everyone except Lola," he tried to clean it up.

"Maybe we don't talk about that," Lola intervened.

"No," said Ruby. "He is part of the family now. He needs to know."

"If it's a private matter-"

"Go ahead and tell him," Johnny insisted. "Jose is in prison. And some of those low-down dirty cartel thugs killed the baby girl years ago; sad bastard that would do a thing like that. Wish I had a name."

"Daddy..." Lola tried to curtain the tragic discussion of her younger sister.

"Sorry, sorry about that."

"One correction," added Ruby. "Jose is also dead."

Johnny blinked, but said nothing.

"No way for you to know," she continued. "As far as Fernando. We try very hard, but he seems to set his mind to follow in his father's footsteps. He is now in prison in Chihuahua."

"I'm so sorry to hear that," said Nicholas.

"But my girls have made up for this," she declared with an uplifted spirit. "Frida is a famous dressmaker in Argentina. And my Lola, my favorite one, has graduated from college and has a good job with a *pequeño bebé dulce* on the way."

Lola beamed with satisfaction. "I will name her after you, Mama."

Johnny barged in. "Hold on. You don't know what you're having. Could be a boy. Could be the next star running back for the Chicago Bears. Nobody wants a star running back gallivanting up and down the field named Ruby."

They exploded with laughter.

"What should we name this star, Daddy?" asked Lola, fully aware of his answer.

"*Johnny* has a good strong ring to it, knowemsayn'?"

"I agreed," said Nicholas. "I'd certainly be afraid to tackle a star running back named Johnny."

"Listen to your future husband," Johnny admonished her.

Lola surrendered with a huge smile. "Okay, Johnny it is."

Lola reached into the box for her second gift ... a beautiful brown Reboso shawl, identical to the one Ruby was wearing.

Ruby spoke into the translator. "It is a tradition of our family for the mother to give her daughter three gifts of love that keep mother and daughter together, even when they are apart."

She held out her wrist to display the third gift, an aging 24kt silver bracelet engraved with a bandolier filled with shot shells. "Your great grandmother, who rode with the famous General Pancho Villa, gave my mother this bracelet. She had another just like it, the one I gave to Frida when she left for Argentina. Now I give this one to you."

Lola slipped the bracelet over her wrist, then draped the shawl around her shoulders. "They are beautiful. Thank you, Mama."

"When you were a little girl, I tried to keep you safe and warm. I pray now this shawl and bracelet and family drawing will do the same."

Lola noticed the other side of the shawl was a deep purple. "Is it reversible? Can it be worn either way?"

"Either way," Ruby confirmed. "It is your choice."

Lola pondered. "It is a hard decision. I will think about it."

"Think about it while you open your second gift," Nicholas suggested, impatiently.

Lola reached for the second gift, a box the size of a cell phone, wrapped in green. She opened it to find an even smaller maroon box with a velvety texture. Inside, she found an exquisite diamond solitaire mounted on a single white gold band.

"It's just a starter," Nicholas explained, nervously. "I wasn't sure you would accept it, and well, I figured we could go back and replace it if..."

Lola gently slipped it on her finger, then held it up to the light. "It's perfect. I love it. And I love you."

Johnny intervened. "That mushy talk is why we got a grandson running back on the way."

"Granddaughter." Ruby corrected him.

Everyone looked at Lola for clarification.

"I do not know. I do not care," she informed them.

Johnny shook his head, pitifully. "A mama with no preference. This is how your unisex kids are born."

At that moment, a photographer came over to the table. He was an older man with a stiff neck and balding gray hair. "How about a family photo to capture this special moment?"

"Long as you ain't asking an arm and a leg," specified Johnny.

"I generally charge twelve dollars a shot. But tell you what. Since you're such a beautiful family and the manger seems to be partial to you, I'll do two for twenty or four for thirty-five. I can develop them right there in the back."

"That two for twenty sounds like a winner," said Johnny.

The foursome huddled up together with big smiles and watched the flash go off.

"How about the second one?" inquired the photographer.

Ruby spoke into the translator. "I would like one of just me and Lolita, if it would not offend?"

"Yes, in your beautiful shawls," suggested Nicholas.

Ruby thought about it. "I would like the purple side this time."

Ruby flipped her shawl to the other side. Lola did the same.

"Hold your flowers, ladies, and imagine you just left the

stage at the Academy Awards." Johnny handed them each a bouquet.

The photographer stood them up against the wall by the bar. "This backdrop will give us a bit more pizzazz. Now, get ready, all smiles..."

The blinding flash christened their eyeball.

Back at the table, Lola glanced at her watch. "The after party has already started. I guess we should head that way."

Johnny looked at Ruby and she looked back at him. "I think we're going to pass on the after party. We ole timers will just end up slowing you down."

Lola grinned, precociously. "I think I understand."

Johnny turned to Nicholas. "You take care of my Babygirl, young man. I would hate to see this cane come walking all the way to Kansas City."

"Don't worry, sir. She's in good hands."

Johnny paid the check.

They had gathered up the gift boxes and started for the door, when the photographer came running from the back. "Don't forget your pictures. As you will see, they turned out quite lovely."

It wasn't until she and Nicholas sat in the rear seat of Johnny's Deville, headed back to the convention center, that Lola got a chance to look at the photographs in their immaculate detail. They were surprisingly crisp and bright with perfect contrast; so much more professional than a back room restaurant photographer should've have been able to produce.

The first photograph captured the cheerful couples at the table ... an old tested generation of resilient survivors, sitting across from a new hopeful generation, ready to launch out on its own. It represented a profound moment in time that Lola would never forget.

It was, however, the second photograph that caught Lola's attention. With her arm draped across her mother's shoulder, the two of them were smiling, such genuine, radiant, contagious smiles. They were happy in ways that words could not describe. And yet, something was wrong.

It slowly dawned on her that it was not the exuberant smiles that troubled her, but a nagging sense of familiarity that cast a dark veil over her memorable clip in time.

They had pulled into the convention parking lot next to Nicholas' rental car, when she finally spotted it ... the dark image of a Mexican Matador on the background wall. Drapped in a red satin cape, trimmed in gold, he was the ominous spoiler, the unforgiving culprit that pulled her back into the dream she had had just before the Ferdon Street explosion.

Suddenly, the vivid images from the dream exploded in her head ... the matching purple shawls, the bouquets of red roses, the swashbuckling bullfighter, peering over their shoulders. The professor had warned her, *The chest will slip into the deep hollows of your mind and haunt your dreams ... haunt your very soul.*

The eerie, tell-tale photograph now confirmed every chilling prediction he had made.

Lola expected to be flooded by a renewed sense of guilt and remorse. But seeing her mother and father's hands entwined like rich thread, resting on the console, and the proud expression on Johnny's weathered face, Lola didn't feel guilty at all. If anything, she felt vindicated, like a mother lion, watching her helpless cubs eat a fresh kill.

It was life, itself, that stirred up the pot, forcing all the hard choices to the top. What daughter would've refused the chance to save her own father? What child would've passed up the opportunity to give her parents a second chance?

The old Baobab tree had made its decision. And now, she had made hers too. She was going to stop feeling guilty about the treacherous climb up America's purple mountains. From this day forward, she was going to take the breaks that life handed her and live in the alabaster cities that gleamed.

Two thousand miles away, at an oceanside mansion in Santa Cruz, California, Phillip Barlow parked his black Mercedes in the u-shaped driveway overlooking the blue surf along the Pacific coastline. A handsome, fit, health-conscious executive with gray eyes and silver hair, he found the jaunt up the twelve marble steps leading to the stately wrought iron door mildly exhilarating. It reminded him of the new maxi-twister step machine he had purchased for the combination gym, pool and sauna at his own smaller mansion over in Long Beach.

The familiar stiff-faced butler greeted him at the door, that is, if you wanted to call it a greeting. The old man never said more than *follow me* or *this way* or *he's waiting*, which, coming from the master servant of Bradley Bean, the second richest man in California, was considered a privilege within itself.

Very few people saw the inside of Bean's magnificent palace. The young internet guru had very explicit ideas about the type of people that meshed into his reclusive, idiocentric world. He didn't care for pretense and formal bureaucracy. And yet, he was smart enough to realize he needed both to succeed in a perpetually bureaucratic world.

Thus, to complete his vast army of technicians and programmers, Bean hired *tweeners*; executives who thoroughly understood the technical jargon of apps and WAN's and storage in the cloud, and yet, possessed the skills to navigate a business boardroom and turn a balance sheet upside down. Barlow was Beans' best *tweener*. He paid him $400,000 annually plus bonuses to keep the other dot com competitors from stealing him away.

Bradley Bean was an avid movie buff. He owned a film library that made the average Hollywood distributor drool. That night, Bean sat comfortably in his darkened in-home theatre watching *Apollo 13*.

As Barlow settled gracefully into one of the deep cushioned theatre style viewing chairs, Bean confessed, "Here's the part I don't understand. Why couldn't these dumbasses anticipate the future? They knew this trial and error space exploration crap was dangerous. Why not build some kind of titanium life pod for those astronauts to crawl into, just in case all hell broke loose?"

Not wanting to make his boss appear unreasonable, Barlow chose his response carefully. "Back then, I don't think it was that simple."

"What do you mean?"

"During the Apollo program, the use of titanium was in its infant stages. The Russians knew more about it than we did. Plus, over-exposure to some of those exotic, heat-resistant metals was known to put spots in the lungs that quickly accelerated into cancer."

"You're saying if things didn't work out, those dudes were pretty much toast."

"Pretty much," Barlow confirmed.

Bean's unruly thatch of brown hair flopped over his pointed forehead. He thought about it for a while, then turned off the movie and brightened the lights. "Think I'll stick to this internet game."

The butler brought out a silver tray of Kahlua and cream

and Oreo cookies. Bean dunked a cookie into his glass, then popped it into his mouth.

"Have you seen the Oregon figures?" he mumbled, pointing to a single blue summary sheet with flow charts and diagrams.

Barlow nodded. "Of course. I've been living and breathing the figures every day."

"Talk to me, dude. Tell me why it looks like Stevie Wonder has taken over the cockpit in *Snakes On A Plane*."

"It's a very complex process, Bradley. I tried to explain it a few months back."

"You know I've got ADD Deficit something or other. Why don't you run through it one more time? Start with when you talked me into authorizing $220 million to build a state-of-the-art data storage farm way up in Prineville, Oregon."

Barlow took a deep breath. He knew it was going to be a long night. Not even the sharpest minds in California's Silicon Valley understood all the idiosyncrasies of riding the new technological wave of remote data storage. Microsoft, Google, Yahoo and many other well known internet giants had jumped into the ring, trying to beat the competition to the punch. But like powerful warriors with blindfolds on, much of their swinging was hit and miss.

The main culprit had been the explosive growth of the internet. Every click, every e-mail, every upload to the server had to be stored somewhere. Critical records of each transaction had to be available for government entities, looking for fraud and terrorists and sexual predators. Every megabyte of data had to reside inside the complex partitions of millions of servers throughout the world.

The solution had been large data centers or data farms with massive banks of storage computers. But these centers consumed tremendous amounts of electricity, driving the cost of operations through the roof. Beyond that, their cumulative tendency to overheat from the stress of operating twenty-four hours a day required large, expensive cooling towers with an abundant supply of water nearby.

Competing companies searched for a unique combination of cheap land, cheap labor, low electricity costs, a cool climate and an abundant water supply. They finally found exactly what they were looking for in Oregon.

Hard-hit by the recession, with shrinking timber revenues and declining wages, local officials welcomed the big internet companies and their data centers with open arms. And then everything started to change.

"The first year we did fine, considering the cost of construction and getting the operation set up," Barlow explained. "The second and third year, we began to show a substantial profit."

"I saw that," said Bean. "I remember thinking to myself, *Philip was right. He's always right. That's why I pay him that outrageous salary.*"

"Last year was when all of the problems really surfaced," Barlow recalled. "The environmentalists got involved; said we were contaminating the land and the water supply. Then, the Fish and Wildlife Department got involved; said we were siphoning off water from the local Trout and Sockeye fish hatcheries. We ended up doing a $40 million dollar settlement with them."

Bean's eyes bucked. "Holy Toledo, Batman! Aren't the Republicans supposed to save us from this environmental crap?"

"It gets worse."

"Worse?" Bean flipped out of his chair, onto the floor and grabbed his heart. "I'm coming to join you, Elizabeth. This is the big one. I just can't take any more."

Though Bean's crude imitation of the famous *Sanford and Son* comedian, Redd Foxx, brought a rare smile to Barlow's stern face, he continued his steady descent into their Oregon valley of doom. "We had to use heavy-duty trucks to haul in water from a hundred miles away. That drove up our transportation costs. Plus, the further the trucks had to go out, the more we paid for carbon emissions credits."

"I don't like that look, Phillip, you know the one where your eyes are glazed and your lips are still cocked like a pelican dunking for minnows. It means you've got more bad news."

"Here's the new piece," said Barlow. "It could turn out to be more significant than all the others."

Bean lifted himself up, into a more serious posture.

Barlow continued, "The bottled water companies have joined the hunt. Nestle, Pepsi and Coke are slowly running out of fresh water springs to supply their operations. So they've come in with huge amounts of capital. They want to take all of the available water supply off the table."

Bean slid back into his chair. "We both know as supply dries up, prices are headed for the moon."

"Precisely."

Bean took another hard look at the summary sheet. "I've got this dude from the Joint Chiefs of Staff calling my office every few weeks. They're ready to dump their whole back-end data library onto our secure servers for indefinite comprehensive storage. If they do it, you know the White House and Congress are going to follow. Long term, we could be talking trillions."

"I understand."

Bean shook his head, this time, allowing his hair to completely cover his eyes. "I find this amazing. We're sitting on the verge of a whole new industry. Cloud computing, remote storage and retrieval, secure lockdown, multi-encrypted transmissions in a 100% virus free environment. The new world customer is washing his hands of the technology. He wants to leave all of the housekeeping to us. But we're having to say no because of a primitive, mindless, extraneous, toilet-flushing commodity like water?"

"It's mind-boggling, I know."

Bean looked at Barlow. "Please tell me you have a solution for this. Or should I expect a memo next week recommending we shut it down?"

"No memo, not yet. I took a team out to Springfield earlier this week. What we saw was very promising."

Bean perked up. "Go on."

"A small outfit named RedFish Construction, with a solid reputation in commercial and custom home building, has made some impressive forays into a new technology. They call it Evap-X3."

"Is this Evap-X3 going to save our asses in Oregon?" asked Bean.

Barlow thought about it for a long time. He knew not to make promises he couldn't keep. In the early years before he joined the company, Bean had fired his top engineers for leading him to believe they had written the code to solve the Y2K crisis. It didn't work. When a trade journal revealed the simplicity of the code that did work, Bean tossed the whole department out on the street.

Barlow hedged. "I'll be returning to Springfield in a few weeks. I'll have a better handle on it then."

Bean massaged his cleft chin. "Evap-X3, hummmh. Sounds like something you'd drink and then beat the hell out of Mike Tyson. You think?"

Barlow smiled, but didn't answer. Mike Tyson was small potatoes compared to the colossal heavyweights that had him down for the count. He needed to beat the hell out of Coke and Pepsi and the saber-rattling army of noisy environmentalists. So far, RedFish Construction, an inconsequential dot on the power grid of internet giants, was his only hope.

Barlow finally spoke. "I'll have some answers for you in a couple of weeks. For now, let's stay as far away from Mike as we can."

Johnny and Ruby arrived at the lake house just after dark. With two long stem glasses and a chilled bottle of Kosta Champagne, they climbed the stairway to the roof, slowly clutching hands under the starlit sky. As the distant serenade of frogs and crickets echoed through the tall trees, an occasional breeze fluttered the edges of Ruby's silky black hair. A jealous coyote howled in the distance. The sweet smell of honeysuckles thickened the night air.

Johnny poured them a modest portion of bubbly, then pointed to the red bird house on a pole above their heads. "You hear that?"

"You mean the wild dog?"

"No, listen closely."

Ruby honed in on the quiet chirping.

"As soon as we put that house up, the mama bird moved in and built a nest. She's got three little chicks up there. I call them Meeny, Miny and Moe."

Ruby sniggled, still speaking into the electronic translator.

"I did not know you liked birds."

"It's not so much the birds. It's the lessons they teach me."

"What do they teach you?"

"The power of a mother's love," he revealed. "I mean, the mama bird goes out every day, hustling, scrambling, trying to find food for the little ones. The daddy is nowhere around. But that doesn't stop her."

"She cannot let it stop her. She must take care of her young ones, no matter what."

"I wish I could find the daddy and tell him what a fool he is. These are precious times, watching them grow, teaching them how to fly. But he's off somewhere, doing his own thing."

She waited a long time, allowing the full meaning of his analogy to soak in. "You did not know about Lolita. She told me the letters never got to you."

"But something did. Call it a hunch or feeling or a throbbing in the gut. I knew something had happened between us. But I was afraid to follow up."

"Afraid?"

"Yes, afraid of following my dumb heart; afraid of bringing a wife and three kids across the border and having to be responsible. It would've changed everything."

She gazed at him with understanding eyes. "In America they call it a ready-made family, yes?"

He nodded.

"No one could blame you for avoiding such a trap. Besides, Jose would've told the drug lords to hunt us down. They are very good at killing on both sides of the river."

"Still, I should've done something."

"You did," she reminded him. "Look at Lolita. Look how you have brought her along."

He smiled, congenially. "It's more like she's brought me

along. I have been living for this very day."

Ruby looked up at the birdhouse. "You must know that sooner or later, they all fly away. What will you live for then?"

Johnny gently removed the translator from her hand. He pulled her to him tightly and kissed her hungry red lips. With hearts pounding and resurrected emotions spiraling out of control, they surrendered themselves to a universal language, far more powerful than the walkie-talkie translator on which they had relied.

Johnny thought about a few special amenities the previous owner had installed. He pulled away, unexpectedly, then whispered to her in a soft voice, "Hold on."

He walked over to a metal control box and pressed a switch. Suddenly, reminiscent of a 1970's disco dance floor, colorful lights began to swirl beneath their feet. Several small wall speakers came to life with a slow, pulsating ballet by Barry White. A bubble machine spewed out plumes of clear, circular balls, rising into the night sky.

"Do you remember that crazy night we had, riding the river?"

She searched the deep fissures of her mind, slowly retrieving the distant images of the two of them, dancing under the moonlight on a Rio Grande party boat.

She looked at him with glistening eyes, "Will you dance with me again?"

Soon they were dancing, laughing, caressing, slowly finishing off the last of the champagne. Johnny led her down the stairs to his bedroom and closed the door. They were young lovers alone in the universe, breathing in the thrills and romance of Old Mexico, all over again.

****

At 3:00 am, Lola reached over, trying to feel Nicholas'

warm body next to her. Instead, she clawed into a lump of damp, twisted sheets, left over from their wild lovemaking.

The after party at the Springfield Hilton had quickly fizzled. Nicholas and Lola had gotten a suite high above the drunken revelers, on the 25th floor. Now, as she lifted her head from the huge king size bed to scan the dimly lighted room, she spotted Nicholas, standing next to the window, gazing out at the crystal skyline.

She slipped into one of the hotel's white terry cloth robes, walked over and wrapped her arms around him. Burying her sleepy eyes into his hairy chest, she inquired, "What's wrong?"

"Nothing. I, I couldn't sleep."

"Having second thoughts about getting married?"

"Of course not."

"Then what?" she pressed.

He was quiet for a while. "I told myself if I ever found you again, I'd never leave you. But I am leaving you, tomorrow. I've got to be on a plane back to Kansas City in the morning, unless..."

"Unless what?" she asked.

"Unless you come with me."

"I cannot just walk away from my job. You know that."

"Why not?" he inquired. "I'm up to 90k now. I can take care of me, you and the baby."

"But Ms K gave me a chance. I cannot just walk out on her."

"Lola, baby. You're just a safety coordinator. There's no reason you couldn't find another job in Kansas City."

She pushed him away. "JUST a safety coordinator! Is that how you feel about my job? Is that the same as JUST a maid or JUST a nanny or JUST an old migrant farm worker ready to pick up and leave as soon as the harvest is done?"

"That's not fair, Lola. If I had those kinds of hang ups, would I be asking you to marry me?"

Lola began to sob. "Then why do you belittle my work? Do you know how hard it is to get into this country? Do you know how many times they look down their noses and call me names? What am I today, wetback, border rat, illegal scum? How much damage have I done to the Social Services this year, do you know? Have the totals gone over the bailout for Chrysler and the big banks?"

Nicholas draped his arm over her shoulders, trying to console her. But she pulled away.

"I learn the language, I go to school, I get a job. But even to my husband, the man who loves me, I am JUST a safety coordinator."

Nicholas forced her into his arms. "You're so much more than that to me. You're the woman I love, the mother of my child, the reason I live. You're right. Your job title doesn't mean anything to me. But if it means that much to you, I won't belittle it, ever again. From now on, you are my little safety coordinator, until you become, well, CEO or Chairman of the Board."

She finally nudged out a reluctant smile. "Ms K says it could happen one day."

He rubbed his chin in deep contemplation. "That's fine. Just so you know that CEO salary is going to cut into your welfare payments and food stamps."

"You bastard!" Lola grabbed a large cushion from a nearby chair and started beating him across the head.

****

Ruby got up early Sunday morning to cook Johnny a sizzling breakfast of sausages, eggs and cheese in large corn husk tamale wraps. At the dinner table, after choking down a line of kidney pills, he posed a serious question.

"Now that your children are grown and Jose is ... well ...

out of the picture, what reason do you have to go back to Mexico?"

She picked up the translator. "What reason do I have to stay?"

"I told you last night," he reminded her.

"You did not tell me. Your eyes might have said it, but the words never came from your mouth."

He cleared his throat. "Okay, here goes. I've never met another woman ... I mean, since we first got together twenty some years ago, no one else has really ... I mean, in my heart, I've always known that you ... Oh, what the hell! You need to keep your ass right here in America and be with me."

It was a long time before she stopped laughing. "Is that a proposal? Will you make me your bride?"

"Whatever it takes for you to stop laughing at me," he said.

"Then I accept. I want a pretty ring, just like Lolita."

He shook his head, then mumbled under his breath. "Damn! That white boy is causing problems for everybody."

He got up from the table, went over to the refrigerator and rolled it back from the wall. A crude wooden plate with silver hinges covered a deep hole in the plaster. He reached in, retrieved his black duffel bag and then returned to the table.

"Your daughter's been in this bag, beatin' down my cash. Hope everything else is intact."

He reached into the bag and pulled out a black velvet cloth bulging with jewelry. He poured the expensive gold watches, necklaces, pendants and coins onto the table. Sorting through the pile, he finally found a sparkling diamond and sapphire ring with three half carat stones. "You think you'd like this?"

Ruby was spellbound. Reflecting the light, the crystal laser-sparkle blinded her eyes. "I've never seen anything so beautiful."

"Johnny Howard's Brinks Truck Jewelry Store carries only the best," he boasted, referring to the jewelry the mob had given to him as a bonus. "Try it on. See if it fits. We can always take it in and have it resized."

To their surprise, it was a perfect fit.

"Now! Will that keep you in America?"

She thought about it. "Maybe for a few months. After that, I will need my own maid, cook, chauffeur and young tennis pro, like I see in the American movies."

"You need to understand those movies were made in those white-collar crime neighborhoods on the other side of the track. Over here, all you get is two hot meals a day, the crack dealer's direct number and a ten percent coupon off your bail bondsman fee."

She started laughing again. "In all of the years, you have not changed."

"Now that's where you're wrong," he corrected her. "I'm older, slower, sicker. I got a kidney that could turn on me any time. I've got a bullet wound that used to throb like hell when the weather changed. Now it doesn't wait on the weather. This money bag used to be full. Now I can see the bottom. And if that ain't enough, the people I used to track for, well now, they're tracking me."

"And you're asking me to stay with you?"

"One side of me is ... the selfish side, the side that believes you're the only woman in the world for me. The other side is saying it would be wrong to put you in danger, to get you mixed up in a lifetime of risky decisions and shady deals."

"Which side will you listen to?"

"Both, and neither," he said. "Last night with you in my arms, and this morning, watching your face light up with the ring, I hear my selfish side loud and clear. But tonight when I go to bed with my .357 under the pillow, and tomorrow when I wake up and check my hog to see if it's gonna start or blow up, I hear my sensible side. I guess it comes down to what you want to do."

Ruby rose from the table, slowly, gracefully, her daughter's borrowed silk housecoat, trailing out behind her like embroidered swan feathers. She strolled over to a nearby mirror and began scrutinizing herself from head to toe. A thousand memories from her precarious journey through life flooded her mind.

How quickly the imagery of a beautiful young maiden celebrating the magic of a *quinceañera* had faded into a drooping chin, blurred vision and middle age wrinkles. How thoroughly disobedient her sagging breasts and bloated waistline had become. No matter how much she had pleaded, the mirror remained a heartless companion that told the bitter truth. At that moment, it was telling her that time was relentless and no longer on her side.

She stroked her delicate fingers through her long, silky, peppered-gray hair. "Do you know why hair turns gray?

He shook his head with unawareness.

"Because time whispers to each root and tells it to stop making color. It tells the root that the person is old and useless and nobody cares anymore."

Johnny squinted with intrigue, taking in every word.

Ruby lifted a select clump of gray strands high above her head. "You can see that some of the roots believe what they hear and just give up. But what if a special person told them they were useful and really meant something? Do you think they would give up?"

"I'm not sure what you're saying."

"I am useful to you, yes?"

Johnny nodded. "Yes, yes you are."

"You will whisper it to me every day, yes?"

"Every day," he confirmed.

"Then why should I give up? Why should I go back to Mexico where I am useless and nobody cares?"

"You know it's dangerous here and we'd be living on the lam," he reminded her.

"The stray bullets fly in Juárez day and night. Can you tell me whether a stray feels different from one intended for you or for me?"

Johnny prided himself on not being a crying man. But the tears forced their unwanted presence into the gullies of his huge white eyes. "I'll protect you as best I can."

"That is good. But what matters most is that you love me the best you can. Promise me our last day will be as happy as our first day. You promise, yes?"

"I promise," he nodded again and then, again.

She stretched out both arms. "Then, I accept your two hot meals and the coupon. Come over and kiss your new bride."

When Lola returned to work on Monday morning, she was brimming with excitement. She had graduated from Lincoln Land, Nicholas had proposed marriage, a new baby was on the way and her long separated parents were back together again. If that were not enough, Kristy had called the night before, asking her to come in early.

Entering the building, she ran into Goodboy. "Good morning, Lola. I was about to come looking for you. Kristy is waiting in the conference room."

Lola's heart began to pound. The book said when you fire someone, try to do it before the other workers arrive. And always have another manager present to witness the proceedings.

Lola tried to figure out what she had done that was so terrible. Walking through the conference room door, she realized her unforgivable sin had been ... graduating from college.

In the middle of the table towered a large white Italian

cream cake, striped with green decorations, a leprechaun green to match her cap and gown. A solitary white candle blazed from the cake's crumbly smooth center, a flaming torch of grand celebration. Tasty breakfast tarts and Starbucks cappuccino cups encircled an elegant silver and bronze serving tray. The tube writing on the sweet icing read:

CONGRATULATIONS GRADUATE LOLA!

Kristy broke into a wide smile. "Thought you were in trouble, didn't you?"

Lola nodded with relief.

"Just wanted you to know we're very proud of you. It might be a bit early for cake, but the fat-free pastries are a good start until later in the day. Go ahead, dig in."

"Thank you, Ms K!"

A third man named Hank Stover, short and stocky, with a gray Spitzbart beard, sat at the end of the table. Lola turned to him. "You will join us, yes?"

He hesitated a moment. "Why not?" He grabbed a kolache and a cup of cappuccino.

"Hank is waiting for the rest of the budget committee. We have a meeting this morning," Kristy explained.

"Will you be talking about spending for this year?" inquired Lola.

"This year and next," said Kristy. "We'll most likely have to revisit our original projections."

"I would like to attend," said Lola. "It would answer some of my questions about the money we have for safety."

Goodboy intervened. "I'm afraid that won't be possible right now. I can appreciate your enthusiasm. But most of the information is strictly confidential."

Kristy thought about it. "Why don't we give her a try?"

Goodboy stuttered. "H-Huh?"

"If she thinks this will help her to do a better job, let's empower her with all the information she needs."

It took thirty minutes for the other five participants to arrive: the head accountant, two department managers and two senior procurement officers. They all seemed stiff and a bit uncomfortable.

At first, Lola suspected her presence was causing the quiet anxiety, a gloomy infirmity that smothered the room like an invisible fog. But soon she realized it was the collective sum of bad news that painted the somber expressions on everyone's face.

With an egg-shaped bald head and long, grim face, John Bossley, the head accountant, began the sad eulogy. He reported actual revenue lagged far behind original income projections, almost 50% behind. Outside vendors had begun to complain because he had moved them from a 30-day to 60-day to 90-day payment cycle.

He warned, "Some of our primary vendors have threatened to cut us off at the end of the month if we continue to stall them. Also, the bank called last Friday; said they're not in a position to extend our loan payment for a third time."

One of the old seasoned department managers chimed in, "I told the foreman to place a temporary hold on the job down in Pawnee. The materials from China have been delayed again. I'd cancel the order and buy from somebody else. But the margins are so razor thin, we'd end up taking a loss."

A female senior procurement officer added, "Speaking of a loss, we all know the cost of aluminum siding fluctuates with volume. Thanks to Trippple-Saw, we lost two major projects, which means we're buying less siding and paying more for it. The difference in net profit could be as much as 13%."

Kristy shook her head. "I didn't think it was this bad."

"It didn't have to be this bad," Bossley blared out.

Kristy knew what he was thinking. "Go ahead and say it, John."

"If we hadn't diverted all of our working capital to..." He paused, reminding himself of the people in the room not yet privy to certain decisions Kristy had made. "To, to, to these risky, untested areas, we could weather this storm with no problem. But now, well, I don't know."

"We've just got to tighten our belts and keep believing," said Kristy. "When my husband died and I took over running this company, we were a heartbeat away from bankruptcy. But we came back. We can do it again. Now think, people! Surely you have ideas about how we can save some money and buy a little more time."

To everyone's surprise, Lola's hand went up. It was a knee jerk reaction to the issue that had been simmering in the back of her mind.

"Yes, Lola?" Kristy formally recognized her.

"I know how we can save money," she declared. "By paying our workers more."

Bossley snickered with indignation. "Annnnddd you are who, again?"

"I am Lola Salinas, the safety coordinator."

"Well, Lola, this may come as a surprise to you. But you don't save money by paying more out."

She stared at the table for a while, collecting her thoughts. "In a way, this is what they told Mr. Sam Walton of Walmart. You don't make more money by selling for less."

A hush fell over the room. All eyes were on her.

"Why don't you continue, Lola," Kristy instructed.

She didn't have to say it twice. This was the moment for which Lola had waited, and prepared. She was well into her hyper-analytic, self-induced methodical mode. There was no turning back now.

She knew sooner or later Kristy would ask her to present

her safety findings. She had gone over the words a hundred times in her mind, new, unfamiliar, business words that would help her plead her case. She hadn't expected an expanded audience. But gaining the trust and respect of coworkers would be an added bonus ... if she could pull it off.

She left her seat and walked over to the board. With a blue marks-a-lot in hand, she began her pitch.

"I came to this meeting today to get an accurate reading on how much safety is worth to our company. After listening to all of the figures and noting the absence of any dollars devoted to safety, I have to conclude it has no value."

She paused, allowing her statement to soak in. "I have visited most of our job sites and talked to a lot of workers. They all feel the same way. The company talks to them about safety, but pays them to get the job done. In other words, we preach safety, but we do not..." *Get this word right, Lola,* she was thinking to herself. "...we do not incentify it."

Goodboy's eyes were bloated and glazed, as if he were seeing a ghost, an astounding reincarnation of a little Mexican girl in a rain slicker and mud boots, flagging cars on the highway. He glanced at Kristy with an approving smile.

Lola continued. "The people in HR say in our fast-paced environment, we have, on average, three accidents a week, maybe another two unreported. About 53% percent of these accidents are connected to nail guns. The nail guns are another..." *say it, say it,* she coaxed herself, "...faaa-faaa-formidable challenge in my report, which I hope to cover, maybe in a later meeting."

Kristy nodded, encouragingly. "I'd be more than happy to arrange that meeting. Continue."

Lola proceeded. "Yes, about the accidents. If we use the lower number of three, that is 130 accidents per year. I am not including the month of December because most of the time the workers have earned the right to a long *siesta*. But you will agree,

130 accidents is a lot, yes?"

Most of the people in the room nodded. Bossley remained rigid, like an immovable rock.

"Each accident costs the company in lost man-hours, increased insurance and medical cost and sometimes lawsuits. On the average, each accident costs the company $19,000 per oooh-occurrence. That comes out to $2,470,000 per year.

"What if we could pay the workers not to have accidents? Let's say we gave each work group with zero accidents per year a $10,000 bonus. We have five work groups so at the most, we would pay $50,000. Anything less than five accidents per year would earn a bonus of $5,000. Industry experts and our own HR department estimate we would reduce our accident rate by half. That is a saving of $1,235,000 per year or $103,000 per month. Maybe that could pay the bank loan ... or help with my raise."

They all chuckled, lightly, except Bossley, who interrupted. "I don't know how accurate your figures are. But let's say they're close. That's still not enough to get us out of this hole."

"But it's a start, yes?" Lola inquired in a sincere voice.

Bossley didn't answer, but Hank Stover did. "It *is* a start. I like it. I like her approach of cutting up the elephant into small pieces. We bring the beast down one piece at a time."

Kristy began a round of applause. "Very good, Lola."

One of the department managers looked over at the cake. "Where did you graduate from again, Harvard, Yale, MIT?"

She smiled, bashfully. "I think my government professor has the best answer for that ... Don't ask, don't tell."

They all started laughing again.

In the hallway after the meeting, Goodboy walked up to her. "Excellent job, Lola! I can't tell you how much we needed that spark."

"Still, the accountant says it won't be enough to save us."

"John? He's just an old prune, though, he's probably right."

Her eyes widened. "You think Ms K will have to close the business?"

"Why, heck no. Unless you want to starve to death."

"No, no, I must eat," Lola began rubbing her stomach. "I have a little one on the way."

Goodboy threw his head back and clapped his hands. "Well congratulations for the second time today. Does Kristy know?"

"Not yet. I plan to tell her soon."

"Then I'll keep your secret," he vowed. "I'm good at secrets."

Lola thought about the RESTRICTED AREA with the tinted glass in which he spent most of his time. She still had no idea what went on behind those closed doors.

"Anyway," he continued. "I wanted a copy of your safety report. Is it available?"

"I can email it to you." And then she remembered the extra copies she had printed and left in her car. "Walk with me to the parking lot. You can finish explaining why we will not starve."

Exiting the building, they spotted Kristy's secretary returning from lunch. She drove a black BMW Z4 convertible.

"How's it going, Shannon?" Goodboy offered a polite smile.

"Fine." She barely looked their way.

Once she was safely inside, Goodboy commented, "She's a real piece of work. I'm sure you've noticed."

The book said to avoid slandering coworkers. But Lola couldn't help herself. "I thought it was just me. Why does Ms K keep her around?"

"Because she's good at what she does. She keeps Kristy organized and protects her from a bunch of crap. Doesn't matter she's got the personality of a King Cobra."

Reaching her Honda, Lola retrieved a stack of papers from the passenger's seat. She handed Goodboy the twenty page document, though he didn't seem to pay much attention to it. He was too busy peering through the back window at the multiple suit bags hanging from both hooks.

"Looks like you're going on a trip."

"My parents are doing the traveling. They left this morning for a week's vacation down south."

"How nice."

"Yes. My daddy is taking my mother to a big crawfish festival in Louisiana and then they will go to the *Escaramuzas* Riding competition and the Riverwalk in San Antonio."

"My brother took me to one of those *Escaramuzas* Riding Exhibitions in California many years ago. Beautiful young women dressed in colorful handcrafted costumes, riding at blazing speeds and making their horses dance to the music. It was fascinating."

"I'm not so much into it. But my mother is a big fan. She love the horses, the *Escaramuzas* folk music even more."

"So you plan to join them?" he asked.

"No, I will be at a hotel this week. I don't like staying at the lake house alone; very spooky, you know?"

He laughed. "You remind me so much of my oldest daughter. She was in the Army, handled all types of rifles, bazookas and grenades. But when she came home on leave, she still slept with a light on, the same as when she was a little girl."

"Is she still in the service?"

He lowered his head a bit. "No. We lost her in Iraq some years ago."

"I'm sorry to hear."

He quickly changed the subject. "You asked if we'd have to shut down the business. I don't think so. But I'm not at liberty to say why. All I can tell you is I trust Kristy and the choices she's made for the company. I think in the long run, we'll all benefit. Meanwhile, you keep doing what you're doing and everything will be fine."

Later that afternoon, Lola saw Kristy in the hallway. "Ms K, I need to leave a little early if it's okay with you?"

"Sure, if you have to." She pressed the back of her bony fingers against Lola's forehead. "Not feeling well?"

"No, nothing like that. I have an appointment with a man who fixes nail guns. On the phone he said he might have a way to make our guns safer."

"Now that would be fantastic," she gleamed.

"While I'm over that way, I want to meet the night crew. They're putting in a loft on South MacArthur Blvd."

"I'll say it again. You're doing an outstanding job. Keep up the good work." Kristy started down the hallway then turned back. "Don't forget to take the rest of your cake. If you don't, the cleanup people will just dump it."

The book said show appreciation for special gifts and personal recognition by superiors. Otherwise, they'll have second thoughts the next time around.

Lola bagged up a few slices and headed for the door.

****

The repair shop on Lenox Ave was an old broken down wood-framed shack in the back of the Town & Country Shopping Center, about twenty minutes away. As her front tires inadvertently dropped into a shallow parking lot pothole, Lola apologized to her beloved, little Honda, rolled her eyes at the faded letters on the rusted red sign: MAYBERRY TOOL REPAIR.

With a RedFish nail gun in hand, she stepped onto the cluttered porch, tip-toeing through a graveyard of old generators, cement mixers, and assorted beasts with sharp teeth and metal arms. Inside, she maneuvered her way down the narrow aisles to the cluttered counter.

An old man in blue overalls with curled gray mustache handles and a throaty voice, came out from the back. He clutched some kind of wedge tipped soldering tool in his hand.

"Looks like you got trouble there," he said, his frog eyes, bulging from behind a pair of thick safety goggles. Removing the goggles, he reached out his hand. "Mind if I take a look?"

Lola passed the gun across the counter.

He studied it for a few seconds. "Yep, the old Seeko 2000, pneumatic power, crunch barrel, contact bounce trigger ... trouble from the time it left the factory. I guess you're the one that called?"

"Yes. You said you could possibly make it safer?"

His thin lips crinkled with amusement. "Let me give you the long answer and the short answer and we can go from there. Agreed?"

She nodded. "Agreed."

"Here's the short answer. Stop using these contact triggers. Order yourself some sequential triggers that don't blast nails out like Machine Gun Kelly. The new triggers will require your workers to completely release and lift the nose-piece from the surface before refiring. With sequential, there's no such thing as locking into fire mode."

Lola took a deep breath. "That is your *short* answer?"

"Yep ... and the one that's full of crap," he added. "I was a journeyman for eighteen years. For wood framing and sheathing, this Seeko 2000 was the workhorse of the industry. If we had used those sequential triggers, we never would've gotten a job out on time."

"But the contact triggers are dangerous, yes?"

"Yep, so are those NASA space shuttles. But if you hang around down there in Florida long enough, you'll see another one take off with great pomp and circumstance. In a capitalistic society, people respond to dollars not common sense. That's a lifelong lesson I'll throw in for free."

Lola stood there, quietly soaking it all in.

"What is your long answer?" she finally asked.

"Take a look," he said, waving his wrinkled hand at the many pieces of antiquated equipment, cluttering the shelves. "The long answer is all around you."

Lola's head corkscrewed from shelf to shelf. "Maybe I see it. Maybe I don't."

He walked over, grabbed a dusty Magnavox VCR and set it on the counter. "I fixed this two years ago, but the fellow never came back to pick it up. Just like that hand cassette tape recorder or that lawn edger with the rotating blades. The long answer, young lady, is innovation. Something better comes along and takes something else's place."

"But this Seeko is the best on the market, yes?"

He grinned, coyly. "The best you know about. What if there existed a gun that was faster and safer? Would you buy it?"

"Yes, of course."

"What if it costs four times as much? Would you buy it then?"

"I-aaaaahh..."

"I didn't think so."

"Is there such a gun?" She bubble with intrigue.

The old man lifted his eyes high into the ceiling as if reflecting on the precious years gone by.

"Back in the late '90's, a little Taiwanese fellow came in here looking for a recoil spring made in '78 or '79, but only in America. We got to talking a bit and he went out to his car and brought the gun in. It was a piece of work, alright ... both pneumatic and battery enabled, a condensed barrel for more power, a special retrofitted contact lip that prevented misfires, and get this, a voice-activated microphone that allowed the user to speak rapid fire sequence control."

"Where is this gun, now? Will I be able to get it?"

He chuckled, "Afraid not."

He went on to explain that the Taiwanese inventor had attempted to bring the gun into the United States. But when American companies found out about it, they lobbied Congress to pass a law placing a high import tariff on the gun, making it impractical to buy.

"It's like forcing a candy bar to cost twelve bucks," he compared. "Who's got that kind of sweet tooth?"

"So what happened with the gun?"

"Nothing, as far as I know. Too many complications. Back in his home country, a hit-and-run incident paralyzed the guy for life. Some say the Chinese were behind it. They accused him of being a Western spy."

"You think he is still in Taiwan?"

"I don't have the foggiest. But I'll give you his name." The old man searched through a dusty card file holder and pulled out a yellowing slip of paper. "Okay, it's weird. So I suggest you write it down ... Lo Lee Soong."

She wrote it down. "You have been very helpful. What do I owe you?"

He thought about it. "Let's make this one on the house."

She looked around the house. It seemed to be crumbling down. Like most of his old gadgets and tools, the value of his services was slowly fading away.

In the back of her mind, she could hear Kristy Cutler's voice. *Always take care of the people that take care of you.*

She reached into her purse and pulled out a crisp $100 bill. "You will let me buy your lunch this week. And if everything works out, I will be back with a finder's fee."

"Listen, young lady, you don't have to..."

She couldn't hear the rest. She was already out the door.

She had just pulled out of the driveway, headed for the job site on MacArthur Blvd, when she noticed a black BMW Z4 cruising past her. To her surprise, it was Kristy's pointed nosed secretary. She puffed on a long white cigarette. Her blonde hair whipped in the wind.

A few blocks up the street, she turned onto an asphalt parking lot and followed the winding curb to a discreet spot on the side of a red brick building.

Lola had planned to continue to her appointment with the night crew, that is, until she saw the name on the building. It read: TRIPPPLE SAW CONSTRUCTION.

That couldn't be right, she thought to herself. She lurched over into an adjacent driveway beneath some tall trees and watched as the secretary entered the building.

A thousand possibilities raced through Lola's mind. Maybe, the snobbish little Cobra snake was working undercover like Goodboy. Or maybe, RedFish and Trippple Saw were involved in some secret joint venture that would bail Ms K's company out of the red.

None of the possibilities tempered Lola's mounting suspicions. Her intuitive sense of larceny grew with each moment the secretary remained inside. After thirty minutes or so, Lola moved her car closer, making sure the approaching darkness did not impede her view.

Finally, an hour later, the secretary came out. A tall, athletically built jet-setter type with wavy brown hair strolled out with her, his arm draped around her waist. Lola pointed her iPhone camera toward them, just in time to capture a slobbery kiss. A final affectionate wave and the secretary pulled out of the driveway and melted into the afternoon traffic.

Lola sat there a moment, staring at the pictures on her phone. As she studied the devious smile on the secretary's face, she was reminded of her old job, flagging cars on the highway at the Allen Brothers' construction sites. It was her responsibility to warn unsuspecting drivers of the impending danger ahead. Now, although she had a new job with a new company, her mandate was the same. She would find Ms K and flag her down. She would warn her before it was too late.

The Louisiana Crawfish Festival in St. Bernard Parish was like nothing Ruby had ever seen. Beneath the hundred year old moss-covered oak trees, along the dark waters of the Mississippi River, endless crowds of wild-eyed, juiced-up Cajun revelers danced and screamed and passed out to the best Zydeco and Swamp Pop Music in the world. Unlike the harsh reception she had received riding Salazar's slave bus to Chicago, the Thibodeaux's and Broussard's and Bellefontaine's welcomed her with open arms.

After two days of devouring huge platters of boiled shrimp, crawfish and oysters on the half shell, Johnny's weakened digestive system could take no more. They packed up and headed down Interstate-10, toward Houston.

Johnny was delighted to introduce Ruby to the beautiful, chaotic rhythm and culture of Cajunland and the southern hospitality that lured visitors back again and again. But deep down inside he struggled with a nagging sense of uneasiness. He couldn't shake the feeling that he was being watched.

Over the years he had learned to trust his instincts. But nothing at the Festival corroborated his fears.

Upon leaving town late the next morning, just inside the city limits of Breaux Bridge, a Louisiana patrol car with red flashers on, pulled up behind his Deville. When Johnny didn't stop, the patrolman turned on his siren.

"*Quieres huir, sí*?" Too rattled to use her translator, Ruby wanted to know if Johnny was going to stop.

Johnny didn't answer.

A few miles down the highway, Johnny spotted an exit with a blue emergency hospital sign. He veered off the main highway and followed the street that led to the hospital. Then, he saw another sign that indicated one mile to the BREAUX BRIDGE MUNICIPAL COURTHOUSE. Immediately, he turned down the courthouse street. Finally, he saw what he was looking for, the big sign next to the courthouse that read: BREAUX BRIDGE POLICE STATION. He pulled his Deville right up to the front steps.

Ruby was shaking, ready to hand over her false documents and go to jail. But to her surprise, the patrol car kept going. It turned off its flashers and cruised slowly out of sight.

She turned to him with astonishment, this time, using the translator. "You are not afraid of the police?"

He looked at her with cold, calculating eyes. "There are people out here a whole lot worse than the police."

Johnny remembered the two highly decorated New York City police detectives that carried out hits for the mob. They would pull victims over on a routine stop and then blow them away.

"You think he was a real policeman?" asked Ruby.

"Maybe. It doesn't really matter if his main agenda was to stop us from breathing."

"Or maybe he got another call over the radio that was more important," Ruby speculated.

Johnny flashed a sarcastic smile. "I like that. I'm going to use it to override my better judgment and finish this vacation as planned."

Eight hours later they pulled into the Holiday Inn parking lot on Interstate-45 just south of downtown Houston. The frantic freeway traffic and sparkling skyline of multi-colored glass skyscrapers made Ruby's heart race.

"What will we do here?" she asked.

"Check in first. Then haul ass over to the best soul food place in town. It closes in twenty-five minutes."

When Johnny ushered the big Deville up to the door of *This-Is-It Soul Food Cafe* in the heart of inner city Third Ward, the parking lot was almost empty. The manager had just flipped the sign on the door: CLOSED.

Johnny jumped out of the car and banged on the locked glass door. "Hey, come on, brother. We right here at the door."

The manager, a short, plump man in his early 40's, shook his head. "Sorry, we close at 7:00 pm."

Johnny reached into his wallet and pulled out a twenty. "I think your clock is a little fast."

The man looked back at the big white-faced wall clock behind the counter. It read 7:03 pm. He shook his head again. "Sorry, sir."

Johnny pushed the twenty back into his wallet and pulled out a $100 dollar bill. "That model clock had a lot of defects coming from the factory. Don't you remember?"

The manager slowly turned the key in the lock and swung open the door. "I do remember reading something about a big clock recall."

Johnny smiled, inconspicuously, sliding the bill into the manager's open palm. "A terrible miscarriage of trust for a time-clock conscious society, as I remember."

"Well, don't just stand there and catch a cold," said the manager. "Come on in and enjoy the best soul food cooking in town."

A few minutes later, Johnny and Ruby sat at a table by the window, feasting on oxtails, pork chops, collard greens, cornbread and baked sweet potatoes. There was a full pan of peach cobbler pushed to the side, waiting for its turn to stuff them into full cardiac arrest.

Above his loud smacking, Ruby and the translator could barely decipher Johnny's words. "So what do you think?" *Chop, smack, pop, lick, chop, smack.* "Ready to kick those tacos and hot tamales to the curb?"

Ruby maintained her prim and proper eating etiquette. In a small voice, with her napkin still neatly folded across her lap, she replied, "I do not think so. This food is too greasy. And too many things on this plate make the sound of a pig."

Johnny looked up toward the counter. The manager had just closed out the register and turned off the last heating tray.

"Mr. Manager. Can you come over here a minute?"

The manager walked over to the table. "Is something wrong?"

"You bet it is. This foreign Mexican woman here is insulting the black community and some of the traditions handed down by our forefathers who came to this country in chains, just trying to survive."

The translator took a while to process Johnny's historic cry for justice and emancipation. Immediately, Ruby's face flushed with embarrassment. "Johnny! I can not believe you."

The manger waved her off. "Don't worry, ma'am. I'm pretty sure a beautiful lady like you wouldn't do a thing like that."

Ruby smiled, congenially.

Johnny was still sucking on a pork bone. "Before you take sides, you need to consider who's paying the outrageous cover charge to get in here."

The manager chuckled. "You're not from here, are you?"

"Me and my brother first came through here from his home in Atlanta twenty years ago. Course you were in another location. I came back maybe five years ago, after you had moved." Johnny took a satisfying bite out of his cornbread. "Glad to know nothing has changed except the location."

"Actually, a few things have changed," he admitted. "We have new owners and new hours. Can't stay open late like we used to."

"Why not?" asked Johnny.

"Too many robberies. Jo-Jo's Fresh Fry just got hit two nights ago. Frenchy's Chicken a week or so back. In fact, I wasn't sure whether ya'll had a little some-um-some-um in mind."

"You talking about us? Jackin' the place?"

"Think about it. Two vehicles suddenly pull up on the lot right at closing."

Johnny frowned. "What do you mean ... two?"

When you pulled in, there was another vehicle that pulled in behind you. He stopped over there behind that big sign and killed his lights."

Johnny whirled around and glared outside the window into the darkness.

"He's gone now," said the manager. "But working over here in the hood, we're trained to spot these things."

"What kind of car was it?" pressed Johnny.

"Couldn't see that; some kind of black truck or SUV or something. My guess is he was just lost, getting his bearings."

Silently, Johnny scolded himself for getting caught up in the soul food stampede and letting his guard down.

At that moment, the back door behind the bar swung open. An old black man with thick gray eyelashes, deep facial wrinkles and a wooden cane hobbled out of the office. He had a small brown bag in his hand.

"Is that one of the new owners?" asked Johnny.

The manager smiled. "In a way. He comes over to check the receipts every few days." And then he went on to identify the man as Jerome Biggers, younger brother and only surviving relative to the late, renowned painter/sculptor, John Biggers.

As it turned out, John Biggers had spent a great deal of time at the café during his tenure as an art professor and department head at Texas Southern University.

"He wasn't so in love with the food as much as the people who came in to eat it," explained the manager. "He often sat in the corner, drawing sketches of the different characters from the neighborhood. In fact, that's why old man Jerome came by tonight."

"To draw some sketches?" asked Johnny.

"No, no. Mr. Jerome couldn't draw a stickman on a black-board," said the manager. "We found one of Dr. Biggers' old sketchbooks back in the storeroom. Don't know how it got there. But Mr. Jerome came by tonight to pick it up ... well, count the receipts and pick it up."

"Why is old man Jerome counting *your* receipts?"

"Long story short, when the former owners got into financial trouble, Dr. Biggers extended them a loan. They paid all but $3,000 back. When the new owners took over, with Mr. Jerome over the Biggers estate, they try to pay the balance in full. But the old man wouldn't take it."

Johnny frowned. "Why the hell not?"

The manager shook his head. "It took them a while to figure it out, but the old man had nothing else to do. The bulk of the estate was being managed by a fancy law firm downtown. Collecting this little debt was the only thing to keep him active. So he put them on a payment plan of $100 a month, so long as he could come by and check the books ... and well, you know, protect his investment."

Mr. Jerome had stopped behind the counter to pour himself

a frosty root beer.

Johnny smiled, widely. "You know, that's the way the community used to be; Looking out for each other. In his case, giving the man something to live for."

"Used to ... now that's the key phrase. You won't find this anywhere else."

Ruby's translator was having trouble keeping up.

"So that is the famous John Biggers?" she asked, staring at the old man in awe. "He is spoken of highly in Mexico, like Diego Rivera, Frida Kahlo and José Clemente Orozco."

"No, that's his brother," Johnny corrected, then gave the manager a pitiful glance. "She get's all excited when you talk about art. She's into drawing and painting."

"Well, he's not Dr. Biggers, but the sketchbook is. Would you like to see it?"

"Sketchbook?" Ruby didn't see a sketchbook.

The manager turned toward the counter. "Mr. Jerome, could you spare us a few minutes of your time? These customers would like to meet you."

The old man guzzled his root beer, then hobbled over with slow, measured steps. "I'll tell you now. I've got a list of charities I give to. Not looking for any more."

"No, no, nothing like that, Mr. Jerome. These people are big fans of your brother. They wanted to meet the financial genius that keeps his empire intact." The manager winked at Johnny.

The old man stiffened his shoulders and extended his hand. "Jerome Biggers, Biggers Management and Investment. And you are....?"

"Johnny Wexler III," Johnny responded, cordially. "And this is my beautiful wife and up-and-coming painter/artist Ruby Salinas ... Wexler."

He immediately pointed to the translator. "What is that

contraption? You recording this conversation?"

"No, no, Mr Jerome. That little gizmo helps to bridge the language gap. When she tells me she loves me and will never leave my side, I need to hear it in plain unmistakable English, so she can't take it back."

He thought about his three marriages and the wives that had died or walked out on him in sixty years. "Have you heard it yet? I mean, have the words come out of the machine?"

Johnny shook his head. "Not yet, Mr. Jerome. I keep telling myself it's because the batteries are low."

They all burst into laughter.

"Good luck with that, young man," said Mr. Jerome.

The manager paused. "The lady here is a famous painter from Mexico. She was wondering if she could see Dr. Biggers' sketchbook?"

"Not famous," Ruby corrected him.

Observing her honesty and apparent meekness of spirit, Mr. Jerome reached into the brown bag to remove the sketchbook. It was an odd-shaped 10 x 12 inch off-white tablet with several rough images of black dockworkers, with International Longshoreman's Local 872, scribbled on the front page.

He handed it to Ruby.

She embraced it as if the book were a small delicate child. And then her eyes welled with tears.

Johnny frowned. "What's wrong, baby?"

The old man shook his head, alerting Johnny to hold his tongue and allow her to enjoy the moment.

Finally, she spoke. "I am sorry. This is a great privilege to me, to be so close to a man with such talent. Do you know he won many awards, but could not go to receive them because blacks were not allowed in the building?"

"How did you know that?" asked Johnny.

"My sister, Conchita, read the articles to me."

"You deeper into this art thang than I thought," surmised Johnny.

For a long time, Ruby stared at the drawings, then handed the book back to Mr. Jerome.

Without warning, he handed it back to her. "You keep this one, young lady."

Her mouth flew open. "Whaaa-What?"

"I have at least five more at home. But you have to promise me you'll continue to pursue your craft with great enthusiasm, in a way that would make my brother proud."

"I promise! I do promise! *Con mi corazón.*" she said.

"Then carry on." He took a few feeble steps toward the door, then turned around. "And next time ya'll come a little earlier. Burning these big overhead lights for one table after regular hours is cutting into my profits."

Johnny pointed a condemning finger at the manager. "I told him I thought it was kinda late, Mr. Jerome. But he twisted our arms and made us come in."

****

The next day, they took a tour of the NASA Mission Control Space Center in Clear Lake and the Buffalo Soldier Museum in the Central Museum District. Then, gobbling down street vendor sausages-on-a-stick and slurping giant Cokes, they sat on the hood of Johnny's Deville, watching the colorful 1*912 Our Lady of Guadalupe Church Danza de Matachines Parade* in Little Mexico's Navigation Boulevard Warehouse Sector, go marching by.

Johnny had planned to take Ruby to the Downtown Aquarium and Restaurant to watch the exotic orange spotted fish glide through the blue waters behind the glass. But Ruby had heard about a cartel shootout at an aquarium in Mexico in which bullets had broken the glass. Tons of shark-infested water had roared through the premises and one customer had been eaten alive.

Johnny didn't try to convince her otherwise. There were Chicago sharks trying to eat him too. By early afternoon, they had checked out of the hotel, headed down Interstate-10 to San Antonio.

As they left the contemporary hustle and bustle of Houston, Ruby didn't say much. She was too busy adding images to her new celebrity sketchbook.

About eighty miles outside of town, she pushed a rough pencil rendering in front of his face. "What do you think?"

He gazed, intermittently, between the highway and the book. "What is it?"

"What does it look like?"

"Like Santa Claus has been eating too many sugar cookies."

She dropped her head. "It is supposed to be the space suit at that NASA place."

"Yeah, yeah, that's what I was about to say."

"No, you are right," she admitted. "It looks like nothing. And the others are worse."

"Look, Ruby, I saw that sketch of your family. You got skills. But you gotta draw something that means something, knowemsayn'? Something that means something to you."

She smiled with illumination. "Yes, you are right. The things that touch my heart."

She flipped the page and began to draw again.

"Just so there's no misunderstanding. Most of those pages better have a picture of me," he warned her.

"No worry, my sweet. I have already drawn your picture right here." She flashed the page of the moon suit Santa. And then she added a pork bone to his hand.

The trip was pleasant and uneventful. The ever-changing topography of lush green fields, low-lying mountains and cattle-brown ranch dirt inspired Ruby's creative juices. It added a heightened sense of obligation to invigorate her sketches with variety and detail.

Johnny bobbed his head to the driving beat of James Brown and Otis Redding, never neglecting to scan his rearview mirror for anyone coming up too fast or laying back too far. One pit stop in the small town of Schulenburg interrupted their routine before they entered the busy 410 John Connally inner loop of San Antonio.

It was late that afternoon when they checked into the Crowne Plaza Hotel on the famous Riverwalk. As soon as they were inside the room, Ruby unzipped her suitcase and began laying out clothes for the rodeo.

"It is 3:30 pm now. We must be there by 6:00 pm or there will be no seats," she warned, a nervous twitch in her voice.

Johnny frowned. "I looked at the map. This little podunk horse stable is only thirty minutes away. What's the rush?"

"It is not a podunk stable. It is a first class *charro* arena. And this is the last night of the female *escaramuzas* competition."

With a frantic look on her face, Ruby retreated to the bathroom and turned on the shower. Twenty minutes later she emerged with dripping hair and a large terry cloth towel draped around her body.

She glared at Johnny. With total disregard for her sense of urgency, he sat in a plush armchair in front of the television, taking in a pre-game interview with players from the San Antonio Spurs.

"Why have you not started to get ready?" she snapped. "Do my words mean nothing to you?"

Johnny turned to observe her stern expression. Slowly, he reached for the control and turned off the screen.

He walked over, put his arms around her and sat her down

on the edge of the bed. "I got sense enough to know when I'm missing something. Tell me what's going on."

With uncontrollable hissing and choking, Ruby broke down and started to cry.

Johnny retrieved a handful of Kleenex tissues and sat quietly as she buried her face.

Finally, she composed herself. "Did you know I was once an *escaramuzas* rider?"

He nodded. "When you had Lola checking on all of this rodeo stuff for our vacation, I asked her about it. She said you and your mother used to ride."

"I was just a young girl trying to please. I was never the rider my mother was. She learned it all from her mother who rode under the great revolutionary folk hero, Pancho Villa."

Ruby explained that during the Mexican Revolution of 1912, General Pancho Villa used women on horseback to win many decisive battles. The young female riders, mostly wives and relatives of the train-loads of soldiers, followed closely behind in coordinated groups, bringing up food, water and supplies.

As the battles intensified, these skilled horsewomen distracted enemy soldiers by riding in different directions, cutting their horses back and forth and kicking up miles of dust, luring rival soldiers away from the main fighting and into strategic battlefield traps.

"These women were very brave and well respected," said Ruby. "Stories of their bravery spread throughout the countryside. People used to wait by the road to see them come through, hoping they would make the horses do tricks of magic. This is how the legend of the *escaramuzas* riders began."

Johnny listened, quietly, still not sure how the Mexican Revolution had snuck across the border to put a stranglehold on their vacation.

Ruby continued. "My grandmother, a great leader of the women, was killed during one of the final battles at Chihuahua, but not before she passed down many skills and many secrets to my mother. This is how my mother became famous."

"So your mother was a famous fighter in the war, just like your grandmother?"

"My mother never fought in the war," explained Ruby. "By the time she became of age, the war was over, Pancho Villa had been assassinated and the politicians were back to their same old tricks of bribery, corruption and stealing land from the poor."

"Then what was she famous for?"

"For carrying on the great heritage of our country and spreading hope to our people," Ruby proudly acknowledged. "She used *escaramuzas* riding to remind the young women there was a brighter future ahead."

"You make her sound like some kind of female Martin Luther King."

"Her name was Estrella Villarreal. But she was known throughout the countryside as *Estrella Reina de la silla de montar lateral* ... Queen of the side saddle."

"So when you break everything down, we're still talking about horseback riding, right?"

Ruby took her time, trying to choose the right words to overcome Johnny's simplistic view of her country's profound history.

"You must understand. *Escaramuzas* riding was more than a scheme on the battlefield. It was a show of great skills and techniques carried out by women ... women who were told they could do nothing but cook the food and have the babies. If *escaramuzas* died with the war, then so would the hopes of millions of young girls who knew they were worth more; knew they could do more. But my mother wouldn't let it die. She went from town to town, teaching young girls, not only how to ride and rope and make the horses dance, but how to care for their bodies and their minds, how to believe in themselves when nobody else did. She took *escaramuzas* riding beyond history and made it a living art. Maybe this is why art is in my blood today."

"Okay, so your grandmother was a hero. Your mother was a hero. Why are you so upset about this exhibition tonight?" asked Johnny.

She paused a while longer. "Just before my mother passed away, the Mexican Charreadas Association decided to honor all of the old horsewomen of Mexico that had made *escaramuzas* a living history throughout the country. My mother, well into her sixties, was the main attraction. The event was held in a big arena outside of Monterrey. I promised her I would be there."

Johnny cocked his head. "You didn't go?"

"I tried. But at that time I had very young children and Jose was in jail and I missed the first bus and the second bus overheated on the road. By the time I reached Monterrey, the ceremony was over. That's when they told me."

"Told you what?"

"Mama Estrella was dead." Ruby started to cry again.

Johnny stroked her damp, frizzy hair. "I'm sorry, baby. What happened?"

Ruby sniffled a bit more. "For a week or so, she had not been feeling well, you know, with the headaches and all. The village doctor gave her some pills. But what pills can you take for a tumor on the brain?"

"Did she know-"

"I don't know," snapped Ruby. "She never told me. She never told anyone. What I do know is she willed herself to the ceremony. She took her last ride and found a way to smile and wave to the crowd. Then, she went to the dressing room, collapsed and died."

"Baby, it's not your fault."

"No, Johnny. I should've been there. I should've left with her the day before or started out early trying to find a babysitter and trying to get on the bus. But I waited. I waited and then it was too late."

Suddenly, Johnny understood her obsession with the time and their getting an early start. She was reliving the ghostly decisions she had made long ago. Voices of guilt convinced her that procrastination, not a tumor, had taken her mother away.

Johnny looked into her eyes, longing to confiscate her many years of pain. "I need to give you a warning and I need to give it to you right now."

Ruby frowned. "Warning? What is your warning?"

"If you ain't ready to go to that horse arena in thirty minutes and see priceless history in the making, I'm going to have to leave your slow, uncultured, tv-watching ass behind."

The famous San Antonio *Charro* Ranch was located on Padre Drive near the tall trees, quiet lakes and exquisite greenery of Mission County Park. By the time the masses of eager spectators rolled in, Johnny and Ruby were comfortably seated in the front row bleachers, munching on salty corn nuts.

At 6 pm, the opening procession began.

Johnny was amazed at the hundreds of horsemen and horsewomen that galloped through the main gate into the huge dirt arena. Adorned in brilliantly colored costumes with silver and gold accents hanging from every conceivable part of their body, the group seemed part of a colossal dress rehearsal for a big budget Hollywood movie.

High atop the bleachers, from the glass announcing booth, the master of ceremonies shouted something in Spanish. Then, as a courtesy to the many non-Spanish speaking Anglos in the crowd, he quickly translated the phrase: LET THE COMPETITION BEGIN!

And began, it did.

For the next two hours, riders, ropers, horse jugglers, singers and dancers mesmerized the crowd. Rugged sharp-spurred *charro* bull riders and calf ropers, leaping into the air and rolling in the red dust, offered the perfect contrast to the flurry of beautiful young *escaramuza* riders who raced into the arena at blazing speeds, performing precision, daredevil maneuvers in a fast-moving ballet.

With wide excited eyes, often standing to her feet, Ruby shouted, *"Espere su turno! Manténgase en línea! Usted está desplazando! No tan cerca!"*

Johnny didn't need the translator to understand the meaning of her words. He already knew the meaning. Ruby was happy again. And that's all that mattered to him.

During the brief intermission, Johnny got up. "I'm going to make a run to the little boy's room. You need anything?"

Ruby looked over at the box of buttered popcorn they had scarcely touched. "No, I'm fine."

"Okay, be right back."

The restrooms were down the ramp, beneath the bleachers. But for some odd reason, Johnny headed up to the announcing booth.

Ruby watched as he talked to the master of ceremonies, his face, stern and inhospitable. Finally, Johnny shook his hand and left the booth.

When he returned from the restroom, Ruby inquired, "What did you tell the announcer, Johnny?"

"That those speakers are killing my ears. I mean, I know the music has to be loud for the dancing horses. But there's no reason for him yelling into the microphone like that."

"Johnny!"

"Hey, it's done now. The guy understood and life goes on."

Ruby wanted to chastise him more. But the performances

started up again and the cheering crowd drowned her out.

Toward the end of the ceremony, the announcer's voice came over the microphone. "We have a special presentation tonight. For those of us who have come to this country from Mexico, we are fully aware of the lasting influence *escaramuza* riding has had on our country, our families and our individual lives. Many of the brave old horsewomen of Mexico were responsible for preserving this great heritage. But none was greater than the legendary Estrella Villarreal, known to most of us as *Estrella Reina de la silla de montar lateral.*

The crowd had already begun to applaud.

The announcer continued. "Tonight, I am told her daughter is with us. As a tribute to her mother and all of the beautiful young girls she helped, her daughter, Ruby, will ride our prized Andalusian stallion and stable mascot, *Viaje*, around the arena to greet one and all."

Ruby's mouth flew open. "What?!!!"

Johnny kept a pan face. "If I heard the man right, they want you to ride some kind of fancy horse."

Ruby was still having trouble getting her words out. "You did this, Johnny!"

Johnny leaned over with his hand cocked behind his ear. "Can you speak up. I can't hear you."

It was a legitimate request. The chant of the crowd was growing with each passing second. *Ruby! Ruby! Ruby!* Finally, the whole arena erupted as a lone *escaramuza* rider in a bright red and white dress led a beautiful tan stallion into the arena and over to their seats.

A security guard opened the small entry gate and beckoned for Ruby to come down.

Ruby's face was filled with panic. "I have not ridden for years."

Johnny grinned. "You know what they say. Once you've

learned to ride a bike, you never forget. Only this bike got legs."

The chants grew louder. *Ruby! Ruby! Ruby!*

There was nowhere to hide. Ruby descended the steps onto the arena floor and mounted the stallion with side saddle perfection. The young girl handed her a pole with two small flags: one representing the United States of America, the other, Mexico.

Without the slightest coercion, as if fully aware of the occasion, the horse took off in a slow, show-pony trot. With the flags waving, the crowd cheering and the gentle night breeze, rippling through Ruby's hair, time disintegrated. The annals of the past merged with seamless perfection into the blurred faces and rambunctious applause and ethereal flashes of light from the present. She was no longer Ruby Salinas. She was *Estrella Reina de la silla de montar lateral,* making her farewell ride in Monterrey.

She circled the arena once ... then again ... then again. The third time was at a graceful gallop, allowing her to bring the horse to a breathtaking stop in front of their seats, exactly the way her mother had taught her.

The audience went wild.

For a brief eternity, long after the deafening cheers had subsided, she sat next to Johnny, smelling the bouquet of red roses they had given her, holding on to his shoulder, crying her eyes out.

Finally, she spoke. "Thank you Johnny. I love you." She said it in English without the help of the low-battery machine, a heartfelt declaration that would've made old man Biggers proud.

He shrugged his shoulders. "I didn't do anything."

In his mind Ben Franklin deserved most of the credit. For, it had been the $1000 cash handshake with the announcer that sealed Ruby's *escaramuza* fate.

They left the little podunk horse stable with the past resuscitated and the future unbounded. In the kernel of their private thoughts, possibility raged ... the possibility that, long before they unraveled their twisted, irrational destinies, they were, indeed, meant for each other, that old wounds could be healed and that life on the run did not have the authority to leave happiness behind.

Back in the Crowne Plaza Hotel parking lot, a block from the Riverwalk, Ruby noticed the crowd of onlookers along the narrow canal bank, gawking at something in the water.

She stopped a young Latina girl passing by. "*Qué está pasando?*"

She responded, quickly, not wanting to be delayed. *"El caucho carrera anual de pato para obras de caridad. Muchos premios para usted."*

Ruby turned to Johnny, this time with the translator. "It is some kind of duck race. Please, let us join the fun."

Amidst the festive atmosphere of open-air restaurants, crowded bars, sparkling waterfalls and mariachi street bands, Johnny and Ruby pushed into the bustling crowd to watch a thousand rubber ducks race down the river. Like a slow-moving mini armada, the white, green, red and blue plastic bobbers cruised along the rippling waters.

Because the event benefited a homeless shelter in Highland Park, Ruby didn't care whether her duck won or lost. But Johnny did. He walked along the banks of the river, rooting for his personal $20 Go-green bobber all the way ... that is, until a huge three hundred pound drunkard in a red clown suit, accompanied by his apparent family, blocked Johnny's path.

"Excuse me?" Johnny politely asked, trying to get around him. But the man continued to lumber and stagger and hog the sidewalk. After the second or third time trying to get the man's attention, Johnny finally forced his large frame against the big green-nose, freight train stumbler, almost pushing him into the river.

The man started to say something, then turned red-faced,

grabbed his heart and fell to his knees.

The woman next to him shout, "*Oh Dios, su corazón!*" ... which Ruby explained later, was her suspicion of a heart attack.

With so many San Antonio police officers in plain sight, Johnny Howard Fountain Wexler III didn't need any trouble. He continued moving forward, slowly fading into the crowd.

At the end of the race, Johnny didn't know whether his duck had won or lost.

Further up the Riverwalk, he saw a rickety old wooden flower stand that resembled the one Ruby had used in Mexico. As a sentimental gesture, he wanted to buy her a handmade floral bouquet to wear in her hair.

"How much for that clip of white hair flowers?" he asked the old lady behind the cart.

She smiled, a bit embarrassed, then looked at Ruby. "*Por favor, propietario se ha ido fuera.*"

"She's just standing in for the owner," explained Ruby. "She can't really-"

"Speak English," Johnny finished her statement. "Come on. I'm hungry. Let's go."

Not wanting to move his car from the parking garage, Johnny flagged a passing cab. He intended to locate a famous barbecue restaurant named TexMex County Line. But the cab driver, a recent transplant from El Paso, didn't really understand his non-Spanish request. When they eventually found it an hour later, the hostess showed them to a table near the kitchen where noisy pots and pans clanked, loudly, through the automatic washer.

"You got a better sitting area?" asked Johnny.

The young girl frowned.

"*Una mesa tranquila,*" Ruby clarified.

Before she could answer, the manager came over the public address system, announcing the winner of an earlier pot luck drawing. Of course, he announced it in Spanish.

Johnny was fuming.

He grabbed the translator and stood up next to his table. "What's wrong with you people?!!! Don't you know you're in the United States of America? We speak English here. Ebonics is also acceptable. Even ghetto slang with ho's and bro's and baby mama's. You ain't in Mexico no more. You understand that?"

Ruby grabbed the translator. "Johnny, please sit down. These people have done nothing to you."

"Nothing but try to make me feel like a fool! Come on, forget the barbecue. We'll order something in the room."

Back at the hotel, Ruby waited, patiently, for Johnny to calm down. She kept staring at him until he finally looked her in the eyes. Then she began to laugh.

"What's so damn funny?" he growled.

"Seeing you go through what we go through when we come to your county."

"You said it: *my* country. Now that's the key. These people are trying to turn it into their county."

Ruby tried to muster a serious face. "They should be shot or beat up or put in jail. Maybe the military should drop a bomb on San Antonio, yes?"

"Something to bring these fools to their senses."

Ruby thought about it. "There is a place in Mexico called *Ajijic*. Most of the people there speak English. Should not the Mexican military drop a bomb on them too? Stop them from turning Mexico into their county?"

"What's your point because I'm about ready to snitch out you and this whole town to the immigration people? Maybe they'll give me a big reward and make me feel better."

"My point, Johnny, is this is a great country of freedom, a

melting pot for all to come. There is none other like it in the world."

"Right, right. That's why we can't let it get messed up, knowemsayin'?"

She walked over and stood in front of him, massaging his slick skull. "You're not listening."

He took a deep breath. "Okay, I'm listening."

"Your country is a melting pot. But its beauty and strength comes from freedom, the freedom not to melt. I can make a choice to become Americanized like my Lolita, or if I am too frightened of all of the changes and requirements, I can hide in the shadows of the old ways. I have seen pictures of your American Indians. Do you think they have melted? Should we drop a bomb on them too?"

Johnny didn't like the sick feeling in his stomach. It reminded him of when, as a boy, he had broken into a neighbor's house and stolen her good silverware and expensive clock. He thought nothing of the intrusion since he and the other kids had pegged the old spinster to be a witch.

A few days later on Christmas day, that same old lady had shown up at his house with a new bicycle.

He had overheard her telling his mother, "Sometimes, being a single mom for two boys is a struggle. I was blessed to work some extra hours and thought this would help you. It's one bike. I hope they don't mind sharing."

It had taken him three weeks of selling newspapers, shoveling snow and taking out trash to buy the items back from the pawn shop. But the day he rang her doorbell and returned her possessions ... that was when the sick feeling went away.

Johnny offered a begrudging stare. "You know, I had this immigration thang all figured out until you came along. Now, you're making me feel like a black Rush Limbaugh."

Sounding exactly like Lola, she responded, "I do not know this Rush Limbaugh."

"Just know he's a closed-minded jerk who needs someone like you to straighten him out."

"I am useful to you, yes?" she purred.

He shook his head in amazement. "In ways you'll never know."

She pecked his forehead with a warm kiss.

At that moment, someone knocked on the door. "Room service."

Johnny opened the door, cautiously, his .357 behind his back. A young Hispanic girl in a hotel uniform stood next to a cart, holding a silver tray.

She smiled. "You ordered the glazed chicken dinners and wine?"

Johnny reached over to grab the wine, then signed the check. "You can go ahead and charge us for everything, but take it back. We've ... well ... come to our senses on some things, knowemsayin'?"

The girl appeared a bit confused.

Johnny cleared his throat. "Do you *comprenedi* the words that's coming out of my mouth?"

Ruby's head snapped. "Huuh?"

The young girl surrendered a respectful nod. "*Si.*"

Johnny searched his pocket to pull out a crisp $20 bill. "Oh by the way, *senoreta,* a few pesos for your troubles." He passed the money to her and closed the door.

Ruby frowned. "That was our dinner, yes?"

"No," he said. "We wanted barbecue, and barbecue it's gonna be. Now change into your dancing shoes, fire up that translator so it recognizes a heavy dose of Ebonics and accompany the legendary black Spanish hustler, *Señor Gringo Johnny Wexler III,* back to the all night TexMex County Line."

Lola waited until the secretary went to lunch, then knocked on Kristy's door.

"Come in!" She barked with an agitated voice. Kristy was neck-deep in paperwork and barely made eye contact.

"May I speak with you, Ms K?"

"Lola, Lola, Lola," Kristy sang her name like a nursery rhyme. "This is a very bad time. Can it wait until Thursday when I get back in town?"

"No, ma'am, it cannot wait," Lola replied in an uncharacteristically firm voice.

Kristy's head popped up from her paper stack. Seeing the stressful look on Lola's face, she invited her to sit down.

"You will forgive me for asking. But is Shannon on a secret assignment?"

Kristy squinted. "I don't understand your question."

"Goodboy, I mean, Henry, was on assignment with the

Allen brothers. I do not understand all of the details, but this is something you wanted him to do, yes?"

She nodded, cautiously.

"I am asking if Shannon is on assignment for you at another place."

"No. Why would you think she was?"

Lola removed her phone from the top pocket of her blouse and handed it to Kristy. "Because of this."

Kristy stared at the photo a long time. Finally, she regurgitated the name. "Paul Grinner."

"You know him, yes?"

"Yes, there's Patrick, Peter and Paul. He's the third P in Trippple Saw. When was this taken?"

"Yesterday."

Kristy stroked her chin with budding discovery. "She left early for a doctor's appointment. I guess Paul is her new gynecologist."

"You think she told him about your bids?"

"It's the only scenario that makes sense. She had exclusive access to my personal files and apparently a very strong motive to share them with her ... doctor."

"You will call the police and arrest her, yes?"

Kristy chuckled at Lola's naivety. "It doesn't quite work that way. I mean, yes, corporate espionage is a crime, punishable by law. But the most she'd get would be a slap on the wrist. It's not worth it. And to be honest, Lola, we're all doing it."

Lola appeared bewildered. "They never mentioned this at the college."

"And I hope they never do. It's nothing we should be proud of. Frankly, it's the worst part of my job."

"But necessary, yes?"

Kristy paused, briefly, trying to determine how far she should go. Something told her Lola was ready to become a member of the club, the tainted old sour-bellies who understood how the sleazy side of capitalism really worked.

Somewhere in the world, a Toyota executive was reading the confidential plans of a new car design by Ford Motor Company; A Procter & Gamble manager was listening to a recording of a planned Johnson & Johnson product launch. A FedEx driver was spilling his guts to interested parties at UPS about competitive pricing for the coming year.

Kristy decided. "I'm going to contaminate your beautiful young mind with a little history. Stop me when you've had enough."

Kristy began with her first exploits into the corporate espionage arena.

"The security guard spotted a man on our premises, confiscating the trash. When we ran the license plate, it turned out the guy was from Ace Custom Builders over in Litchfield. Of course, they've gone under since that time. But they made us aware of how the game was being played."

"So you've decided to play the game too?"

"Not at first, not until we found that our switchboard had been bugged. Henry had one of his old friends from Navy intelligence to reverse track the transmission. Turned out the information was being collected by a local private investigator hired by Tripppple Saw. That's when we put together our own trash detail and hit all of our competitors."

Kristy sniggled, reminiscently. "You would think, since they were monitoring our trash, they'd be more careful with their own. Dahh! It was incredible the amount of information we found."

Kristy went on to explain that their biggest break had come when her daughter's computer-nerd boyfriend had hacked into the Allen brothers' main server. The emails and confidential documents revealed an impressive system of cronyism and kickbacks that kept the company afloat.

"Allen Brothers Construction is just a front for their Uncle

Abner Allen in Texas. He's chummy with a powerful US Senator and gets a lot of no-bid contracts from the government." Kristy explained with a growing sense of intrigue. "Now, here's the important thing you need to understand. This Uncle Abner is quite clever. He has a nose for money and a history of closing some extraordinary deals. When we heard he was working on something big, we had no choice but to sit up and pay attention. That's why Henry went undercover for twelve months."

Lola thought about the short, loudmouth, swan-faced man in the white cowboy hat. "I saw this Uncle Abner a few times at the job site. I did not like him."

"Our feelings about him don't really matter. Uncle Abner is popular with the movers-and-shakers in Washington. He knows how to spin a web."

"Did you find out what he was working on?" asked Lola.

Kristy smiled, coyly. "Come with me."

She led Lola down the hallway to THE ROOM ... the one, shrouded in secrecy with RESTRICTED AREA, DO NOT ENTER plastered across the front. She punched a long series of numbers into the security access pad, then opened the door.

Lola was amazed to find a giant glass bubble room with sterile white floors, stretching out forty to fifty feet in length. Goodboy and a small accompaniment of technicians in heavy white lab coats, stirred like frantic ants around a huge generator in the center of the floor. The generator, the size of a work van, reminded Lola of a spinning top on steroids, ablaze with red, blue and orange lights.

Translucent tubes flowed out of the top thermal connectors into three large water coolers, sturdy tanks that stood like bloated soda machines against the glass wall. A series of stainless steel refrigeration coils spiraled out of the back side into an electrical compression box. Mounted atop the box were twin turbine blowers with razor thin blades.

Lola took a deep breath. "What is all of this?"

"It's the future," explained Kristy, pulling two lab coats off the rack. "And, an excellent place to catch a cold. Here, put this on."

Lola had noticed the frigid temperature and slight smell of algae in the room. Shc suspected it came from the three snakelike nozzles above the turbines that spewed a fine mist of grayish vapors into the air.

Kristy allowed Lola a few minutes to observe the secret laboratory, then revealed, "This is what John Bossley, our friendly accountant, is upset about. This is where all of our money has gone. The US patents alone cost two million dollars, not to mention the scientific technological experts we've paid to come through that door. When a small company like ours puts out millions of dollars, you hope and pray it pays off. But so far, we don't know."

Lola was still confused. "What is it supposed to do?"

Kristy laughed. "I'm so sorry. I left you back at the Allen brothers, shaking hands with Uncle Abner."

As it turned out, Uncle Abner had stumbled onto some inside information about the government's desperate need to expand its data collection and storage capabilities. With the requirement of so many new laws, forms and electronic documentation, the government was running out of safe, internal, hacker-proof systems to store the information. A high level decision had been made to outsource the storage function. But not even the technological giants like Microsoft and Google were equipped to take on the massive overload.

"Uncle Abner figured out the main problem was the high cost of operating a storage data center," said Kristy. "Specifically, the cost of keeping thousand of servers from overheating and losing the critical information. He hired enough consultants to tell him the future was evaporative cooling. He almost got a federal grant to do the research for free, except Microsoft's lobbyists pulled the plug on that. In the end, he concluded it was going to cost way too much to pull this whole cooling thing off."

Lola shook her head. "I do not understand this evaporative cooling."

"Frankly, I don't either, not completely" Kristy admitted. "But it's been around a long time and it works. The main thing to remember is that it takes heat out of an environment and replaces it with cool air."

She waved at Goodboy, signaling him to come over.

He finished writing something on a clipboard, then stepped over to them. "I see we have a new recruit."

"Believe me, she's earned it. I'll share some very enlightening discoveries with you later. Right now, we're calling on your extensive engineering training in the Navy. Explain to us in a paragraph how this process works."

"One paragraph, huh? So long as you don't deduct points for the paragraph being a couple hundred volumes long."

Kristy smiled. "I'll let you slide this time."

Goodboy composed his thoughts. "An evaporative cooling system is a diabatic process that cools air through the simple evaporation of water. Unlike the standard refrigeration process used in most homes, evaporative cooling uses a vapor-compression principal. Think about the human body, cooling itself by sweating. It's brilliant. Heat is drawn out of the body as those little sweat droplets evaporate into the air."

Lola thought for a minute. "If it is that simple, I don't understand why Uncle Abner quit."

"Oh, it's far from simple, especially when you're trying to cool down a thousand servers in one humongous complex. You've got humidification problems, condensation problems, liquification problems, cryogenic and cryostatic problems. Maintenance can be a nightmare replacing cooling pads, trying to keep fan blades from corroding and sealing pressurized leaks."

"So was Uncle Abner right?" she asked.

"Yes, about his design. But this is a new generation, state of the art design that no one has seen before," declared Kristy. "We call it Evap-X3 because it's three times more efficient than the old machines."

"And it works fine, yes?"

A quiet apprehension smothered Kristy's face. "We're down to one last problem. We have a few weeks to work it out."

"That's why I'd better get back to my post, ladies." Goodboy returned to the generator.

Back in the office, Kristy asked to see the iphone picture again. As she studied it, Lola inquired, "Do you plan to fire her?"

"Yes, but not right away. I'm thinking about a more ... shall we say ... useful deployment of her services. But I'm going to need your help."

At that moment, Shannon returned from lunch and stuck her head in the door.

Kristy immediately went into a mini-tirade. "Lola, this is unacceptable. If you can't do your job, there's no place for you at RedFish."

Lola instinctively followed Kristy's lead and shamefully dropped her head.

With a tight smile of approval, Shannon did her best to remain businesslike. "I-ah, I just wanted to let you know I'm back."

"Okay. But hold my calls. I'm going to be here for a while," Kristy instructed.

When Shannon closed the door, Kristy looked up into the ceiling. "That *unacceptable* line is from a movie, but I can't remember which one. Anyway, so much for our Hollywood debut. Let's get down to business."

Kristy pulled out an RFP from The Springfield Airport Authority. Capitol Airport had solicited bids to construct two

40,000 square foot T-Hanger buildings for private airplane storage.

"I need you to put together this bid for me, Lola."

"Me?!" Lola cringed.

"Yes. I started on it, but ran out of time." And then she paused, abruptly. "No, that's not right. Let me be honest with you. I ran out of courage. After losing three bids in a row, I just couldn't take another slap in the face. You ever felt that way?"

Lola tried to say something, but Kristy's pending assignment had barricaded all of her words, deep inside her throat.

Kristy continued. "Normally, I wouldn't waste my time on a job like this. These kinds of projects take years to materialize. But the Springfield Authority is under pressure to get this job completed. Time has run out on the capital improvement plan and they could lose the 50% matching federal funds if they experience any more delays. Besides, we need the revenue, maybe four or five million if we win the thing."

"Ms K. I have never done a bid before," Lola confessed.

She smiled, calmly. "My question is ... are you willing to try?"

Lola tried to stop her heart from racing long enough to remember what the book had said. *When presented with an opportunity to abstain or fail....*

Lola couldn't remember the rest. What she could remember was Kristy Cutler taking her in and giving her a chance and shining a bright light of discovery along the way. If Kristy was asking for help, she was going to give it to her, even at the price of failure.

"I will do my best."

Kristy pulled out an old bid submitted by her husband for construction he had done on the Decatur Airport in Macon County. "We'll use this as a template. Get everything set up and I'll give you the numbers to drop in."

Lola pulled her seat up to a computer in the corner. Kristy continued to work on her paper stack for the Oregon trip. Except for the homogeneous clicks of the computer keyboards at both desks, the room fell into a strange electric silence.

It was two hours before Lola realized she was actually making progress; three hours before she was irrational enough to believe she might actually pull it off. The fourth hour, she turned to Kristy. "I think I'm ready for the numbers."

Kristy bellowed from behind her depleted mini-stack of documents. "That Decatur job was seven years ago. Increase all the numbers by 40%. We've got to add rolling curtain doors, super skylights and ridge vents to this one. Add another $100,000 for an impact study. Add another $125,000 for soil testing. Add another $155,000 for legal fees."

Lola was amused. "Lot of lawyers, yes?"

"Really, just one. The mayor's son owns a hotshot legal firm downtown. If we get him on board with us, it will help our chances if this thing comes down to a backroom political vote."

When Lola completed the bid, she printed it out and took it over to Kristy. They checked it for errors and slid it into a fancy RedFish portfolio.

Kristy announced, "This is our *real* bid. We'll call it package one. I'll be out of town, so I want you to hand-deliver it over to the Authority on Thursday."

"Three days from now," Lola confirmed.

"Correct. Now here's the fun part," said Kristy. "I want to create a second bid. We'll call it package two. I want you to increase all the numbers by another 50%, but take out the legal fees so they don't get wind of our political strategy. I want an electronic copy of package two on my computer and a hard copy on my desk. While I'm out of the office, there's no telling who might come snooping around."

Like a little girl with a school yard secret, Lola placed her hand over her mouth. "You think she will see it?"

“Yes, and hopefully take it back to her doctor for a second opinion.”

Lola followed Kristy’s instructions to the letter. When she had finished, Lola walked over and gave her a big hug. “Thank you for having confidence in me.”

“No. Thank you, Lola, for being everything I hoped you’d be. There’s a bright future for you here, if we can just work our way out of this hole.”

“We will, Ms K. I know we will.”

As Lola left Kristy’s office and passed the secretary’s desk, she dropped her head in scorn. She wore the face of an employee on her last leg, disgraced and reprimanded.

Shannon eyed her with a false sense of compassion. “You were in there a long time. Are you alright?”

Lola looked up, pitifully. “Ms K has all of these high goals and expectations. She does not understand the limitations of my people, not like you do.”

And then Lola broke out with an old slavery song that Johnny often employed to keep her from nagging him: “NOBODY KNOWS THE TROUBLE IZZ SEEN, NOBODY KNOWS BUT JESUS....”

On their way back from San Antonio, a few miles outside of Oklahoma City, Johnny thought he spotted a black SUV following them from a distance. However, with the thick gray overcast and intermittent rain, he couldn't be sure.

Not wanting to alarm Ruby, he pointed to a brightly colored billboard on the side of the road. It read: RIVERWIND CASINO, Owned and Operated by the Chickasaw Nation.

"How good are you at the slots?" he queried.

"I have never played," she replied.

Johnny veered off Interstate-35 onto the Goldsby, Oklahoma exit. "Why don't we give it a shot? I hear this Riverwind Casino pays out some big pots."

"And I hear these places take your money."

"Not if you're a pro like me," he boasted, subtly watching his rearview mirror to see if the SUV was still following them. Observing the black Navigator continue down the Interstate, Johnny breathed a sigh of relief.

Ruby eyed him, coyly. "So you are good at this?"

"Expert level, knowemsayin'? My best advice to a rookie like you is to watch and learn. See how we pros do it. Then, when you feel comfortable, I'll give you a few coins to feed to the wolves."

Inside the casino was like a dark, smoky barn, haunted by a thousand noisy boxes of blinking lights. The low-level chatter and electronic game music was sporadically interrupted by distant screams of celebration. A deep throated announcer continually invited customers to try the new ten-coin victory slots located on the far side of the food buffet.

Johnny bought $200 in coins and located a remote section of the building where the older one-armed bandits had not yet been replaced by electronic push button machines. He selected a three-level progressive slot in the very center of the row and pulled up two deep-cushioned stools.

He popped his knuckles like a great pianist preparing to play at Carnegie Hall. "Have a seat for your first lesson. The objective is to line that big screen up with all cherries. Pay attention because I'm subject to hit on the first coin."

Two hours later, after too many drinks and too many trips to the counter to replenish his empty bucket, Ruby could no longer restrain herself. Her whole body shook with laughter. She stood up behind him, draped her arms over his shoulders and whispered, "With the lessons I have learned so far, I think it would be better to rob a bank."

"Very funny," he said. "What you don't understand is this is like fishing. It takes patience to catch the big one."

She looked at the few coins left in his bucket. "Do you always feed the fish four or five hundred worms before they bite?"

He reached into the bucket and pulled out a hand full of coins. "Since you know so much, why don't you try?"

"I will. As soon as I get back from the ladies room."

She headed down the aisle.

Johnny stood up as if to stretch his weary arms. It was a technique he used to survey the room to see who might be watching him. Most of the gamblers were older retiree types, just passing the time away. No one appeared ready to pull out a gun and start shooting Italian bullets at him.

An elderly black couple, sitting a few seats away, got up and started for the door. Wearing casual baggy jeans and white-sole arthritic shoes, they appeared to be in their late sixties. They limped along like broken down old soldiers, and yet, managed the strength to hold each other's hand. The man smiled and gave his wife a kiss. "Don't worry. You'll get 'em next time."

Realizing they had caught him staring, Johnny offered a cordial smile. "Have any luck?"

The woman looked a bit teary-eyed. "Not at all. Of course, he tried to warn me."

The old man whispered, "When you've been married forty years, you're in it together, win or lose. She wanted to try, so we did. Ain't no pointing fingers. We got window fans. We can make it another few months."

Johnny frowned. "What do you mean, make it?"

"Our air conditioning went out back at the house. I don't have to tell you how hot it gits around here this time of year. On a fixed income, we gonna have to wait a long time to give them people what they asking to fix it. Mary thought we could take our social security checks and maybe git lucky."

Johnny paused a long while, trying to pick up any indication of a scam. "What was your goal? What were you trying to win?"

"We had $600. We just needed $1300 more," she revealed.

Johnny leaned over to them, whispering as the old man had done. "Don't you know these places are rigged for the House to win 90% of the time?"

"My cousin said she won a $1000 here just last month," the old woman reported.

"Yeah, and you and me and a thousand other people just paid it back."

She dropped her head. "Yes, sir, you right. Just like my husband told me."

Johnny reached into his pocket. "I'm going to help you, but on one condition."

The woman eyed him warily but said nothing.

Johnny took $2000 in cash from his back pocket and handed it to the man. "I want you to promise me that you'll never come in here again."

The man smiled. "This is really our first time. Can't you tell?"

"Then make it your last. Unless they strike oil on your property and you're in here for a little recreation, this ain't the game for you."

Stunned by his generosity, the old woman fought back the tears. "If you give us your address, we can send you payments."

"Just seeing you old timers holding hands and sticking together after forty years is payment enough for me."

"Thank you. God bless you. Thank you so much." They both said it at the same time.

As they stood there talking, someone opened the front door. The wail of a distant horn echoed through the building.

"What's that sound?" asked Johnny.

"It's the tornado siren," she warned. "We'd best get back to the house because something is surely coming our way."

They hobbled toward the entrance and out of the door.

When Ruby returned from the restroom, Johnny sat in front of the machine like a zombie, staring into the screen. She could tell his mind was in another place.

"What's wrong, Johnny?"

"I just saw something, something we ain't got yet. But we're going to get it."

"What are you talking about? You are making no sense."

He was still thinking. "Do you have your ring?"

She stuck out her hand, proudly.

"Okay, take it off and give it to me.

"What?"

"I'll give it back to you at the ceremony."

"What ceremony?"

"Our wedding ceremony. We're going to get married right now." He grabbed her by the hand.

"Wait. Wait," she protested. "You said I could try one slot."

He shrugged with impatience. "Come on, Ruby, before I change my mind."

"Just one," she whined.

He reached into the bucket and handed her one of the Susan B Anthony Dollars. She dropped it into the machine and pulled the lever.

At first nothing registered, as though the machine was broken. Then one cherry came up, then another, then another and another. Suddenly, there were six cherries across the screen. The machine started to rock and smoke and make Pac-man noises. Finally, the coins began to roll out.

Ruby grabbed the bucket, though still unable to catch them all. Immediately, a young security guard with a long ponytail and weightlifter's chest, came over and handed her a drawstring cotton sack. "I'm just here to secure the area, ma'am. Take your time and collect your winnings."

She handed the sack to Johnny. "I will let my husband-to-be do the honors. He taught me good lessons on fishing and what NOT to do."

Begrudgingly, Johnny loaded the sack. "Beginner's luck, that's all it is."

She winked at the security guard. "I wonder. Did someone tell the machine I was a beginner?"

Amused by her quick wit and adept use of the little translator box, he inquired, "Where are you from?"

"Mexico," she proudly announced.

"Beautiful place. My dad took me there once to visit an Aztec burial ground. They are somehow part of our ancestry."

"Mine too," she revealed. "I'm told our relatives are buried under the pyramids in Tenochtitlan."

Having loaded all of the coins into the sack, Johnny intervened. "Look. You want to get married? Or do you want to stay here, digging up your dead kinfolks?"

The security guard chuckled. "You two will make a swell couple. When is the wedding?"

"Today. Right now if I can separate her from this stupid machine."

She laid her hand against Johnny's shoulder and cuddled close to him. "Please forgive me for this delay." She took a quick look at the screen. "This $5,000 delay."

Johnny couldn't help but smile. "I'll let it slide this one time. But only because it's your wedding day."

The security guard was still laughing at them. "Where will you hold the ceremony?"

"I don't have a clue," Johnny admitted. "Figured if there's a casino around, there's got to be a wedding chapel too."

He thought about it. "There's Ivory Garden Chapel in Norman. But you don't want to go over there right now."

"Why not?" asked Ruby.

"The news people say there's a mile-wide tornado coming from that direction. I'd be surprised if we didn't shut this whole casino down in the next thirty minutes or so."

"Come on, there's got to be another joint around here we can tie the knot."

The security guard pondered a bit longer. "Chief Danny might marry you."

"Who?"

"Danny Suke, Chief of the Kickapoo Tribe. He's a little strange, mind you. But he's also a very powerful medicine man. Ain't scared of nothing ... tornadoes, blizzards, scorpions, snakes."

"Is he authorized by the State to marry people?"

"Oh yeah. Any tribal Chief can perform a legal marriage."

"Then, Chief Danny it is."

They wrote down the address, cashed in the coins and headed out the door.

The clouds were darker now, swirling slowly like giant mixers in the sky. The angry wind whipped the tree limbs and blew trash across the highway. Even with the windows up and the local weather report blasting over the radio, they could still hear the storm sirens, baying in the distance.

Ruby was visibly shaken. "You think we should find a safe place to ride it out?"

"If it's a mile wide, there probably ain't no safe place. I mean, it's just a crap shoot as to which side of town it's going to hit. We pick the wrong side and..."

She gazed at him with affectionate eyes. "I want you to know I love you, Johnny. This is the happiest I've been in my life. If we don't make it, you must know I am your bride, even without the wedding ceremony."

"Baby, I know that. But I'm pushing because I saw something today that was pure and real. These old people had a commitment to one another in a stupid, old fashioned, never-say-die kind of way. Marriage forever was like a big neon sign on their backs. You couldn't miss it, you knowemsayin'?"

She sat quietly, soaking in every word. Finally, she asked, "This neon sign. Was it more for them, or the rest of the world?"

"I don't know. This is all new territory for me. What I do know is you could still see the happiness in their faces, even after losing their last $600 bucks. It was like they were saying, '*we in this together, no matter what.*' I want that for us, Ruby. I want it right now."

They followed a long, winding highway past the David Perry Regional Airport along Adkins Hill Road to a gravel fork at North Main Street. Along the right side of the highway, behind a row of white camper trucks, stood a two-story converted garage apartment. The big sign out front read: KICKAPOO NATION SOUVENIR SHOP.

They scampered up the rocky sidewalk, lined with war-painted human skulls. The hollow heads whistled and trembled like nervous dead men in the wind.

The front of the building bore tattered murals of buffalo herds, wild horses and Indians in full dress. The entrance was crowned with dried rattlesnake hides, their venomous fangs still protruding from their flattened heads.

Inside, the shelves were cluttered with aging bone necklaces and bird feathers and endless jars of mystical roots and herbs. A stuffed mountain lion sat on the front counter, with vicious teeth, ready to devour.

The room was dim. The building cracked from the howling breeze. An eerie wind chime crashed against a small back window.

Finally, a deep, crusty voice boomed out from a room in the rear.

"How dare you enter the sacred grounds of our great Kickapoo ancestors, buried beneath the floor! They are now angry and much disturbed! They will wait until the dead of night and hunt you down like dogs and cut out your tongues and feed your scalps to desert coyotes. There is no atonement for this great sin of intrusion. You are cursed! ... cursed I say, until your bones rot in hell!"

And then he let out a blood-curdling laugh.

Ruby pulled Johnny closer to her. "I do not like this place."

"Relax. They said the man was strange. He'll probably just come out with an old Tommy-hawk and ask for your little finger."

Despite his kidding around, Johnny kept his hand on his .357 holster in the back of his belt.

Eventually, the Chief appeared from the back room. He was a short man with a long auburn face and thick glasses. His black ponytail was draped in colorful bands, matching his checkered blue shirt.

He stared at them with obvious disappointment. "Awh, no kids to wet in their pants? I like it when the children hear my voice and start to boohoo. It's just a little payback for what the white man did to our families when they took our land. Know what I'm saying, brother?"

Johnny smiled in collaboration. "I do. And just for the record, your opening spiel wasn't a complete waste." He nodded his head at Ruby who was still wide-eyed and holding him, tightly.

"You need something to calm your nerves, young woman. I've got just the thing." He reached under the counter and pulled out a jar of dried purple berries. "This is my best seller. It's grown from a rare Jalto bush found only on the reservation, and blended in a secret formula. It'll calm your nerves, give you stamina and strengthen your inner being."

Ruby shook her head. "I do not want it."

Johnny interceded. "How much is it?"

"Regular $50.00 American dollars; But for you on a beautiful day like today ... half price."

Johnny pulled out a $20 bill. “I’ll give you twenty bucks if you throw in a package of your best beef jerky.”

“Sold!” The Chief stuffed the jar and jerky into a brown bag. “Will there be anything else?”

“Yes,” said Johnny. “We want you to marry us. And we need to do it before this tornado comes and wipes us off the face of the earth.”

Johnny pulled out his cellphone and showed the Chief a Google weather map on the screen. A large orange and red disturbance crept across the grids like an advancing army platoon. “The national weather people are tracking this thing. As best I can tell, we’ve got about a half hour before it’s in your house.”

He waved his hand, nonchalantly. “Not to worry, my friends. I have talked to the Great Spirits who live in the clouds. We are not in danger here.”

“Still, if you can get us out of here, I’d appreciate it.”

The Chief disappeared into the back room again.

Ruby looked at Johnny. “I do not like it so much here.”

“Is it because the guy is different? Maybe, he hasn’t melted into the big pot enough for you?”

She dropped head in silence.

Johnny took a deep breath. “You gave me this long lecture about people having the right to be different. You said they could choose not to melt. Now you’re having trouble with your own rule.”

“I feel he is hiding something,” she rationalized.

“Have you looked at my drivers license and credit cards lately? Or maybe that passport that got you into this country? Do you think he’s hiding as much as we are?”

Ruby fell into silence again.

“Look. If you’re getting vibes this guy is some kind of serial killer or something, then we need to get the hell on up out of here. But, if it’s because he’s not wearing a sombrero and speaking

Spanish, you need to come to terms with your own fears, like I did."

For a long time she didn't speak. Finally, she reached into the bag and pulled out the jar of berries. "You think it will calm my nerves and strengthen my inner being?"

Johnny grinned. "It's probably so loaded with whiskey. It'll do most anything you need it to do."

They were still talking when the Chief came back out in a fringed tan leather jumpsuit, woolen moccasins, white war paint and a full feathered headdress. He had a small suitcase in his hand.

He opened the case and pulled out some candles, casters of oil, small shot glasses, official documents and a thick brown Bible. "Do you already have your marriage license from the courthouse?"

"No," said Johnny. "Is that a problem?"

"Not to worry. I'll handle everything right here." He pulled out his calculator.

Watching the Chief in full dress, banging on his calculator, made Ruby sniggle.

"Yeah," said the Chief with an insightful expression. "I get that all the time in these threads. People think my hands should be gripping a hunting knife or throwing wood on a campfire. I'm going to charge you an extra fifty dollars for that racist thought."

And then they all broke into laughter.

"Okay, filing the license with the court, performing the official ceremony and providing you with a framed marriage certificate on the spot is going to be $450."

Johnny flopped $500 on the counter. "There's an extra $50 if you beat this hellacious wind."

"Ohhhhhhhhhhhhh humbeka, soloka, getakka foeh..." The Chief immediately broke out in a Native American chant. He was still singing as he marched them over to his makeshift wooden podium. He reached behind the podium to a small goblet of whiskey and poured himself a drink. Guzzling it down, he threw up both hands. "Let the ceremony begin!"

He was still chanting when he placed a big bowl of water in front of them.

"Water is the symbol of purification and cleansing. Wash your souls of any past evils and lingering thoughts of past lovers."

While they were washing their hands, he stepped over and put on a musical CD. It sounded like a full blown choir, chanting and singing, accompanied by endless drums and rattles. He reached over to drape a white veil with dangling pearls across Ruby's face. He cloaked them both in colored ribbons: white for the east, blue for the south, yellow for the west, and black for the north. Finally, he tied a silver sash around Johnny's waist to ward off evil spirits.

"Is there anybody here who objects to these two joining in holy matrimony?" He paused with searching eyes. "Let the record in heaven show that no one came forward that we could see.

"You must understand that your marriage is a hearth, from whence cometh peace, harmony and warmth. Warm your loved one's body with your healing touch. Remember that as babies can die from the lack of touching, so can marriages from the lack of intimacy.

"Bind yourselves in love and trust. Throw out suspicion and doubt. Show yourselves to each other as you really are. Remember that each of you is an individual, born of flesh and blood, entitled to your own opinions with each having equal weight."

As the Chief went on, the winds grew stronger. Johnny reached into his pocket and took a quick peek at his cellphone. The tornado was bearing down on them.

He whispered to Ruby. "Be ready to blow this joint as soon as we say I do."

"Do you have the ring?" asked the Chief.

Johnny removed it from his pocket.

"Then place it on her finger," he ordered.

Johnny slid the ring on Ruby's finger.

The Chief anointed their foreheads with oil and lit the candles. "May this sacred oil protect you and keep you from all hurt, harm and danger."

Mostly from this killer tornado that's about to blow us to hell, Johnny was thinking to himself.

Finally, the Chief poured what looked to be dirty water into the shot glasses. "Drink from the sacred springs of our ancestors."

Ruby looked at Johnny to see if it was okay. With time running out, they both guzzled down the liquid. To their surprise, it tasted sweet with a bit of a fizz. They didn't want to know what was in it.

As a huge tree limb crashed against the back of the building, the Chief uttered the words for which they had been waiting. "Johnny Howard, do you take this woman to be your lawfully wedded wife, to love and protect her for the rest of your life?"

"I do, I do."

"And Ruby Salinas, do you take this man to be your lawfully wedded husband, to love and obey him for the rest of your life?"

"Yes I do, for the rest of my life," she promised through the translator.

"Then, by the power vested in me by the Great Spirits above and the state of Oklahoma, I pronounce you man and wife. You may kiss the bride."

Johnny lifted the veil from her face and plastered a long, passionate kiss on her awaiting lips. When they opened their eyes, the Chief was gone. A few minutes later, he returned from the back with their marriage certificate in a beautiful rosewood frame.

"I'll mail your license to the PO Box you left."

"Thank you, Chief." Johnny handed him the ribbons, veil and sash and grabbed their bag of berries. "We're out of here. You're welcome to come too."

He shook his head, calmly. "No need."

The building was trembling, furiously. Small nuggets of hail had begun to thrash the roof. As soon as they opened the door, they spotted it in the distance ... a huge black funnel cloud with an ominous tail, angrily whipping the ground. It sounded like a train. The invisible tracks guided it directly into their path.

As they squealed out of the driveway and onto the main highway, Johnny caught a glimpse of Chief Danny, standing on the second floor balcony. He was still in his Chieftain regalia with arms, stretched out to the sky.

"You see that fool?! He's going to get himself killed!"

Ruby looked back. "Can we go back and get him?"

"It's too late." Johnny was already up to 70 mph, fleeing in the opposite direction.

They watched with growing horror as the edge of the funnel moved in on him. The furious winds picked up two camper trucks and slammed them to the ground. And then, without the slightest warning, the black funnel darted upward, high into the gray skies. The hail suddenly stopped and the wind slowly mellowed into a cool country breeze.

Ruby's jaw dropped. She turned to Johnny, the look of bewilderment and awe, plastered on her face.

"Don't ask me a damn thang," he said, his white eyes thrashing back and forth. "And don't eat up all those purple berries. Whatever he put in that jar, I want some too."

Because of a critical, in-store product promotion, Nicholas was unable to fly out of Kansas City until late Friday night. When Lola picked him up at the Springfield Airport, it was almost midnight.

As they whizzed down Interstate-55 in her spiffy red Honda, Nicholas complained, "I hate flying Carter Blue Airlines. The service is lousy, they lose your luggage and they never get you there on time."

Lola consoled him with a heedful smile. "The main thing is you're here with me ... well, us." She placed his open hand across her pooched stomach.

"Is the appointment still set for tomorrow?"

"Yes, 10:00 am. My doctor can't wait to meet you."

"What did you tell her about me?"

"That you had broken my heart."

"What?"

"And put it back together again," Lola added.

"So when I see her tomorrow, will I be a hero or a goat?"

"A little of both. She blames your cruelty on the disgusting condition of the male species."

"Well, thanks a lot for the warm introduction."

"There is something else I should warn you about."

"Let me guess. There's a trap door somewhere in her office where disgusting males fall in and never comes out."

"No, Dr. Fox is really nice. My daddy's kidney doctor recommended her. But she's somewhat of a religious, born-again ... how you say ... crusader? She'll want to know when you plan to marry me."

"Did you tell her I've been asking that same question? Or was I the villain on that one too?"

Lola grinned, mischievously. "My book says a scapegoat is someone who is not around to defend himself."

He pinched her hard on her shoulder. "So I was the villain?"

"Ouch! You are assaulting a pregnant woman. I must report this to Dr. Fox as well."

"Just answer the question, pregnant woman. Me and the doctor need to know."

"Okay, since you've been asking, I will tell you my choice. I want to get married next month in Oklahoma."

"Oklahoma?!"

"Yes. That's where Mama and Daddy got married this week. They came back from vacation last night with these wild stories. They told me about this Indian Chief who has great powers. If he marries us, we will stay together forever and ever."

"Lola," he spoke in a more serious tone. "It doesn't matter who officiates the wedding. I'm never going to leave you."

"Us," she corrected him.

"Yes, us. I'll have to get used to that."

"Dr. Fox says a lot will change between us once the baby is here. Some good and some not so good."

"I think I know the good," he said. "What's the bad, besides dirty diapers, sleepless nights and bigger, more expense tennis shoes each year?"

"She says we will have to work hard to keep our relationship going, like doing the things we like to do, just me and you. We'll have to find the time."

"I've got it," he perked up. "We could put the baby on a plane, let him stay at my apartment in Kansas City while we paint the town here in Springfield, just me and you."

Lola's face saddened. "At work, Ms K calls it the white elephant in the room."

"Living in separate places is a big musky dinosaur. And it's not going away until we do something about it."

"I know we have to make some hard decisions. But I love you and you love me, and I promise you, we will work things out."

The next morning, just after 10:00 am, in a small clinic off East Dodge Street, Nicholas and Lola sat in a sterile examination room, waiting for the doctor to come.

"Why is it so cold in here?" asked Nicholas.

"I'm the one that should be complaining." Lola reached behind her neck and closed the opening in her flimsy blue gown.

When the door swung open, a tall, blonde woman with drooping shoulders and a long crane face stepped inside. She removed her fashionable red rimmed glasses and held them up to the light.

"The more I wear these, the less I can see," she declared to herself, as if concluding a debate with another side of her brain. She tucked the red pair into the pocket of her white smock, then pulled out a second black clunky pair that seemed more appropriate for an old spinster. Once she had fitted them on the brim of her pencil nose, her eyes bulged like shiny blue marbles.

"I suppose my guest appearance as the glamorous Dr. Fox, on *All My Children,* will just have to wait?"

Nicholas and Lola chuckled, politely.

She walked over to Nicholas and stretched out her hand. "I'm Dr. Fox. And you must be the Springfield Heartbreaker."

Nicholas blushed, profusely. "Why did I know that was coming?"

"Actually, I've decided to take it easy on you. Lola seems to think you have some redeeming qualities."

"That's the very reason I'm trying to marry her, Doctor," he declared. "She's a wonderful judge of character."

Dr. Fox looked at Lola. "Ah! He's a good looker and a smooth talker. He's definitely got half my vote."

Nicholas frowned. "Half?"

"Yes. The other half will remain in escrow until you've answered these questions."

Reading from her clipboard, the doctor led Nicholas through a litany of medical questions: *Any chronic illnesses; any major surgeries; any current addictions, medications or supplements; any excessive smoking, drinking or use of recreational drugs? What about your parent's health? What did your grandparents die from?*

When the doctor finished with him, he wondered if he was actually carrying the baby, and Lola's expanded stomach was just a decoy.

The doctor left for a few minutes, allowing a nurse to take blood, urine and skin samples. She quickly returned with a huge needle, the size of a miniature jackhammer.

She stood in front of Lola. "Results from your previous

exams have come back flawless; praise God from whom all blessing flow. Blood pressure, sodium content, probiotic intake, folic acid and glucose levels, and fetal growth were all superb. But in this second trimester, we have to dig a bit deeper."

Lola stared at the gigantic needle with bloated eyes. "Deeper?"

"At this stage there are certain precautions we must take to detect any serious irregularities or deformities in the fetus. Besides today's pap and pelvic exams, we're going to perform an amniotic fluid test or AFT. This will help us detect any genetic abnormalities associated with certain rare diseases such as Down Syndrome, sickle cell and the general effects of GAGS."

Lola still gawked at the needle. "It looks like it should go into a person that is strong and brave, maybe, the father?"

Dr. Fox chuckled. "I'm afraid dad gets a free ride on this one. But don't stress yourself out. It's not as bad as it looks. We'll apply a local anesthetic to the abdominal wall to relieve the pain."

Nicholas rose from his chair. "I-aahh, I don't know if I really need to see this."

She winked at Lola. "Awh, daddy doesn't want to see the wall of the uterus penetrated and bloody fluids drawn from the amniotic sac?"

Nicholas was staring at the needle, swallowing hard, trying not to choke. Finally, he made a mad dash out of the door to the nearest restroom.

Lola shook her head. "The disgusting male species."

Dr. Fox hunched her shoulders. "What's a girl to do?"

****

At the lake house, an ever-widening glimmer of sunlight cut through the stout forest greenery and into Johnny's bedroom window. It not only spoiled his lazy morning siesta, but forced him into an unwanted level of consciousness that exposed the throbbing pain in his side.

Being the practical man that he was, Johnny had relegated the growing agony to his lousy pill regimen and spicy food binge during their vacation. But somewhere in the back of his mind, a deeper suspicion lingered.

The doctor had warned him of certain symptoms: kidney pains, flu-like fever and chills, and an unexpected gain in weight. These were the telltale signs of a kidney trying to run away from home. These were also normal responses from a broken down, ole-school gangster who had eaten too much Cajun, gotten soaked in a tornado and neglected to take his pills.

Johnny chose *normal* as the culprit. Now that he was the happiest man in the whole world, kidney rejection was just not an option. There was no way an unruly piece of slab was going to deprive him from embracing the few granules of enjoyment still left in his lifelong hour glass.

After a hot shower, a hot breakfast and a thousand kidney pills, Johnny sat on the sofa next to Ruby, flipping though the security camera images on his phone. Most of the shots had been taken while they were on vacation.

"You see that boat?" He pointed out a small brown fishing boat trolling up the Sangamon River behind the lake house. A few frames later, the boat came back the opposite way. "Seems pretty innocent, doesn't it?"

She nodded.

He fast forwarded to the images time-stamped a few hours later. "Okay, here's the same boat going back up the river."

She appeared puzzled. "What does it mean?"

"Probably nothing. Could be some fisherman that forgot his tackle box, or just decided to check several different spots up and down the river. Can't really see the guy's face, thanks to those freakin' bird droppings all over the camera lens."

She shook her head. "I still don't see you with those birds. What kind are they again?"

"Red robins, I believe. We put up that bird house and feeder next to the cameras, never thinking they'd spray the freakin' lenses every time they flew by. Those three little chicks should be flying away any time now. I'll probably just take the whole thing down."

"You are a mean *dueño*," she chastened him without the translator.

"Hey, those birds are messing with our lives. This boat guy, running up frequent miles behind our house, could easily be trying to set us up. I tore down the boat dock the other owner had built, just so nobody could come in here from the river. But it doesn't mean they can't cruise by and check us out."

"What will you do if the boat comes back?" she asked.

"What I always do. Shoot first and ask questions later."

****

Silas Penrow had made up his mind. The hell with the $10,000 bonus Raymond was willing to pay for a solo hit on the big tar baby. Penrow's country boy instincts told him he was going to need all the help he could get.

To his amazement and frustration, Johnny seemed to have the luck of Bolo Ash, a legendary whitetail buck from the Nashville thickets that required the collaboration of an entire army of hunters to bring him down. The deer had gotten its name from the unusual ash color of its coat and the hunter, Jake Bolo, who, after getting too close, died at the hospital from a hoof in the neck.

With the help of the young slacker at the graduation ceremony, Penrow had made a positive identification on both, Johnny and Lola. Both had seen him at the Litchfield apartment complex. Both needed to die.

Penrow still hadn't completely identified Lola's handsome young Caucasian boyfriend. But if he got in the way, he would die too.

It hadn't been easy following Johnny and his Mexican girlfriend across the country, especially with Johnny's apparent awareness of the slightest irregularity, creeping into his cautious, calculated existence.

At an early morning breakfast stop at an IHOP in Little Rock, Penrow had placed a small GPS tracking device under Johnny's Deville. It was a technique he had learned from the surveillance pros in the movies. The high tech receiver in Penrow's black Navigator allowed him to follow at a safe distance without being detected.

On a distant knoll above the Louisiana Crawfish Festival, using a high powered rifle and scope, Penrow had tried several times to take Johnny out. But too many local swamp head coonasses kept getting in the way.

The inadvertent interference by the drunken, crawfish-crazed crowd had forced Penrow to call in an old favor.

Bobby Charbonneau, a psychopathic misfit removed from the Lafayette Police Department for bribery and extortion, had also done a few jobs for the New Orleans mob. One of his most memorable victims had been a popular horse jockey he beat to death with a tire tool for refusing to throw an important race at Evangeline Downs. Using a stolen patrol car he kept in his barn, he had pulled the young jockey over on a lonely highway and issued him a moving violation all the way to the grave.

Penrow had hoped Bobby Charbonneau could do the same for Tiny Johnny. But for whatever reason, the tar baby had refused to pull over. The nerve of Johnny, using police headquarters to protect himself from the police, well ... former police. Inside his twisted reasoning, Penrow felt it was dirty pool, a lowlife taking advantage of the good services of the law.

In San Antonio, Penrow had set up his rifle and scope in a late night ambush on the Riverwalk. But at the last second, some fat ass clown had jumped in the way.

Penrow didn't mean to kill an innocent bystander. But such was the nature of the business. Not even the well-trained, well-intentioned US military could avoid civilian casualties of war. And hearing the people yell heart attack, Penrow reasoned the overweight creep was on his way out, anyway.

Oklahoma was the last straw. An approaching tornado had almost blown his Navigator off the road and damaged his GPS receiver to the extent that he could no longer track the big Deville. He had lost Johnny in the hail and rain somewhere outside of Norman on Interstate-35.

Penrow ended up coming back to Springfield early.

Reluctant to drive down the narrow, bush-infested entrance road like a sitting duck, he had rented a small fishing boat to see if he could invade the lake house from the rear. As it turned out, the river was too far away and the boat dock had been removed.

There were too many dead end streets leading to Johnny's funeral. Like Bolo Ash, it was going to take an army of trained professionals to finish the job. What Penrow needed now was a foolproof plan. A few more days of watching and following and executing good old solid detective work, and he'd have enough information to put the whole thing into place. Then, he would call on Raymond's army to come in and bring the big tar baby down.

When Lola arrived at work on Monday morning, she observed head account John Bossley and Goodboy huddled up in Kristy's office. Later that day when she saw Kristy in the hallway, she inquired, "How did the Oregon meeting go?"

"Quite well," said Kristy. "And thanks again for freeing me up for the trip. We should hear something on our little airport project in a few days."

Kristy still appeared uneasy. Lola had been around her long enough to notice the tightness in her face.

"Ms K, is there something else I can help you with?" she offered.

Kristy displayed a dubious half-smile. "Not unless you have a key to the US Mint."

And then she sauntered down the hallway.

At that moment, Lola's cell phone went off. Nicholas was on the other end. "Okay, listen to this. A German guy just came in the store. I recognized him from the fitness center downtown. He's some kind of research scientist from Dow Chemical. He says their safety coordinator just got transferred to St. Louis, which means they'll be looking for *someone* pretty soon. He thinks with a good word from him, that *someone* could be you."

A sharp pain spiraled down the back of Lola's neck. She was so thankful to have a fiancé intent on bringing them together. But the thought of leaving RedFish made her want to cry.

The book said a perceived lack of appreciation could turn an advocate into an enemy. Nicholas was advocating the new position, not only for her well being, but for the well being of their future family. How could she disagree with that?

She paused a long while, much too long. Nicholas shouted into the phone. "Hello. Are you still there?"

"Yeass, I-aahh was in the middle of something, and well, you caught me off guard." She stumbled out a reply.

"So what do you think?"

"It is a very interesting possibility, but nothing I could discuss, well..."

"While you're on your job," Nicholas finished her sentence.

"Yes, privacy," she confirmed.

"I'm sorry. I wasn't thinking. Just call me tonight. Let's talk about this before the door closes."

"I will call you tonight. I love you." She hung up the phone.

Turning around, she noticed Goodboy coming toward her. He was dressed in a dark blue suit and carrying a briefcase. There was a stern look on his face.

Lola mustered a cheerful grin. "Good morning. How was your weekend?"

"A lot better than today." He barely slowed down as he headed for the door.

Something had everyone on edge. But Lola didn't have time to figure it out. She had her own job to do, which included interviewing employees involved in a work related accident. A piece of sheet metal had slid off a stack and cut a deep gash into an employee's leg. In one hour, she was scheduled to talk to Raúl Hernandez to find out how it happened.

There was a storage room two flights up the stairs at the very top of the building. It was a graveyard for dusty old files and records. Broken down tables, chairs, office equipment and safety signs also found a quiet resting place there in the attic.

In search of old nail guns, Lola had visited the room before. She had observed the many rows of file cabinets and storage boxes. For someone researching the company's past, the room was a rich treasure trove of knowledge.

A woman in Human Resources had informed her of several files that documented the safety record associated with each sheet-metal vendor. RedFish no longer used certain vendors because their packaging and shipping methods proved to be unsafe.

Lola decided to visit the room before her interview with Raúl.

She opened the door. Wading through the darkened mounds of clutter, searching for the light switch, she noticed a dim glow, coming from a small desk lamp in the far corner. Someone was crying. It was a familiar cry.

Kristy sat behind an old desk, wiping her eyes, a glass of water in her hand. She looked up at Lola, dejectedly. "I think I've figured out who you really are."

Thinking of the false documents Johnny had given her to establish her American identity, Lola's heart pounded. Social security numbers, birth certificates and credit cards were bought and sold on the internet like hotcakes at breakfast time. Lola's social security number pointed to a ninety-nine year old woman, already in the grave.

Living a lie had its built-in vulnerabilities. There was no reason to believe Kristy wouldn't eventually find out.

"Who am I?" Lola tried to remain cool.

"You're my guardian angel," she replied. "Every time I'm in trouble, you're always there."

"What trouble do you speak about, Ms K?"

Kristy waved her hand toward a spare armchair. "Pull up a seat. The bar is open. This was once my husband's hideaway, so we've only got Vodka and Scotch."

"Do you have water?" Lola inquired. "My boss insists we stay sober until the end of the shift."

Kristy chuckled and passed her an Ozarka. "That's the first laugh I've had all day."

"What's wrong? What happened?"

Kristy told her the whole story.

The accountant had brought in the certified letter early that morning. The bank had officially called in RedFish's loan, demanding payment in full within thirty days. The sobering effect of the bank's decision was obvious to everyone involved. Without operating capital, the company would have to shut down.

"From a selfish standpoint, I don't have to worry. My husband left me with enough to get by. But you know what I worry about, Lola? All of these people who depend on this company for their livelihood. What are they going to do?"

Lola observed the sadness in her eyes. "Do you have a plan, Ms K? You always have a plan."

"Henry just left. He has a banker friend that might pick up the loan. But it's doubtful, considering our recent payment history."

"What about Evap-X3? That will be millions of dollars, yes?"

Kristy snapped her neck back with another shot of Vodka. "Last week, when I met with Phillip Barlow at the data center in Oregon, the first thing he asked was, 'Have you resolved the problem'. All I could say is we're working on it. They'll be back here next week for the final evaluation. Time is running out."

"What is this big problem?" asked Lola.

Kristy shook her head. "Even I can't explain all of the details. The technology is too complex. But think about it like this. We've developed one hell of a system. It cools down a room at 85% capacity of a big expensive refrigeration unit. But the cost of operating our unit is less than a third of what it would cost to run the refrigeration unit."

"That's fantastic!"

"Yes, but here's where the problem comes in. Remember the example Henry gave us about cooling down the body by allowing it to sweat?"

"Yes."

"Think about it. Where does sweat go? Some of the perspiration drops might fall on your clothing. But for the most part, the drops end up on the floor. That's fine, unless you have a thousand computers underneath you. Everybody knows computers and water just don't mix."

Lola thought about it. "So why not cover the computers up so they don't get wet?"

"In the winter when you're cold, you cover yourself with a blanket to keep the heat in, right?"

"Right."

"Any protective covering would make those servers run twice as hot, which completely defeats the purpose. Remember, we're trying to cool them down."

Lola dropped her head. "I'm sorry, Ms K. I don't know what to do."

"I don't either, Lola. In fact there's an entire room of technicians downstairs that don't know either. Of course, I'm in a lot better position than they are."

"Why do you say that, Ms K?"

Kristy held up her glass. "Because I have the Vodka and they don't."

****

At 3:00 pm, Lola was downstairs in her cubicle, waiting for Raúl Hernandez to arrive. Fifteen minutes later he strolled in, fashionably late, in baggy pants, brandishing a charming smile. "Sorry, baby. They had me all tied up."

The longer he slouched in front of her desk, the more Lola smelled the stench of marijuana in his clothing. His eyes were glassy, his speech, slurred and out of sync. He kept referring to her as *baby* and *Miss Sweet*. Most alarming was the tattoo on his upper arm. It pegged him as a member of the violent *Mara Salvatrucha Gang* better known as MS-13.

Lola had come across the desert with cut throat coyotes. Her first boyfriend had been an abusive drug dealer. Her father was a bag man for the mafia. She had shot a hit man in the face with nails. To her, Raúl's suave indignities and subtle intimidation were child's play.

She smiled, politely. "Why don't we take a stroll?"

He grinned, widely, then followed her into the lumber yard. In his mind, they could've easily been heading to the back seat of her Honda.

She found a wooden bench next to the fence where employees often took their smoke breaks. She glared at him with stone cold eyes. Her trance-like, hyper-analytic, self-induced methodical mode had already kicked in.

"Do you know why I asked you to come outside?"

He was still grinning, his lustful eyes, undressing her in advance. "Because I'm irresistible, baby, you know, like a play toy thing that can rock your world?"

"No. Because you were stinking up the office with cheap *chafa* dope and talking like a piss head *naco* not used to being in a professional environment. Ms K thinks you're a hard worker. She has no idea you're just another Mexican *lacra mojado* headed to jail."

He exploded with anger. "Who you talkin' to, bitch?!"

"Awh, what are you going to do? Interrupt your little gay gang bangers from *acariciando a sí mismos* on the toilet seat. I see that cheap tattoo on your arm. Just so you know, I've got friends out of Chicago that will wrap your little buddies in pizza dough and eat them for lunch, then puke them back up so they can eat them again for dinner."

He stood up. "I don't have to listen to this *mierda* from some *lambiche*!"

She smiled, coolly. "Yes you do. You know why? Because I have to write a report that will tell Ms K who was careless and who needs to turn in their badge and be escorted to the gate. Right now, your name is all over the gate report like chili beans on a dirty plate."

"It wasn't my fault!" he defended.

"Okay, here is our agreement. You sit down and we will talk about it. You do not disrespect me and I do not disrespect you, yes?"

He sat down, slowly, reluctantly. "I was just trying to help."

"It doesn't surprise me. My first day on the property I saw how Ms K trusted you. And I remember it was you who disconnected the power cord during the nail gun fight. Why don't you tell me the whole story?"

Raúl explained that Mike, the other employee, had gotten a forklift, loaded with sheet metal, stuck in a pot hole. When Mike couldn't get it out, he asked Raúl to help. Raúl gunned the engine to rock the forklift back and forth. When the sheet metal started to slide, Mike ran over and tried to keep the stack from falling.

"When he saw he couldn't hold it, he tried to get up out of the scene, but it was too late. A piece of metal caught him in the back of the leg."

Lola waited for him to finish. "I will let Ms K know you were only trying to help and it was the other employee's idea to try to keep the stack from falling."

He breathed a sigh of relief. "Can I go now?"

"Not yet. I have a question for you."

"What now?"

"How old are you?" She had already looked at his personnel file.

"Twenty-two."

"You have a family?"

He glanced at the tattoo on his arm. "Yeah."

"No, I mean a real family."

"You writing a book? Why all the questions?"

She took a deep breath. "I have seen Ms K send you out to work with the carpenters. The next day she sends you out with the electricians. The next day it's the welders and fitters."

"So?"

"So that tells me you are smart and a quick learner. Why would you waste it on gang banging and being locked up in jail?"

"It's the streets. I don't make the rules. It is what it is."

"What if you could come out of the streets?"

"And do what?"

"And go to college."

He started laughing. "Now I see you been smoking that *Carrujo* too."

"You could not handle it, no?" she taunted.

"I could handle my business. But you talking fantasy land. You got to have the right papers, a high school diploma and big time *feria* green.

"What if I could get you the papers, help you with your

GED and find you a *patrocinador* to pay for your college enrollment?"

"You up in the big house with Ms K and the soft seats and cool air blowing. Why would you want to help me?"

She displayed a willful smile. "I see potential in you. But until you can see it in yourself, let's just call my offer a Mexican *thang*."

He was silent for a long time. "I don't know."

"Okay, if you decide, this is how you will let me know. You will remove that MS-13 tattoo and you will never ever get high again, at least, not on this job."

He roared back with superficial indignation. "What if I don't want your help?"

"Then I will keep my eyes peeled for your WANTED picture on the post office wall."

****

Later that evening, when Lola arrived back at the lake house, there was smoke coming from the roof. Inside, she discovered that Johnny had fired up a grill on the balcony and was roasting jumbo beef hot dogs over an open flame. As she reached the top of the stairs, she almost tripped. Johnny had set up a small oscillating fan to blow smoke away from the house, into the night sky.

"Hey, Babygirl! Feel like some hot dogs? I have to remind your mother every so often that she's not the only one that can cook."

Ruby stood a few feet away, listening to *escaramuzas* horse dancing music and painting on a small linen canvas.

She shook her head at his nonsense. "*Ese idiota*. He believes burning a hot dog is cooking."

"I mean, it's not as good as BIG EASY Burgers with their secret New Orleans receipts. But when I add these onions, radishes and chili, these babies can hold their own."

"Have you taken Mama to the BIG EASY?" asked Lola.

"No. They're closed for remodeling. But in a few weeks, I'll treat her to the best burger she never had."

As he spoke, a gust of wind caught the flames and blazed the fire dangerously high. Johnny grabbed a nearby pot of water and doused the flames. A large plume of gray steam and ashes bolted into the dark sky.

"When you're a pro like me, you have to be ready for every possibility," he bragged.

Ruby laughed, then grabbed her translator. "He is also a pro at the slot machines. But somehow, they keep eating up his worms."

Lola chuckled at their antics, marveling at how quickly their relationship had grown. She couldn't help thinking about Johnny on his death bed and how much happiness he would've missed.

She decided to place her order. "I'll take two dogs. The baby says hold the onions, radishes and chili."

"You gonna let a little stomach baby push you around?" Johnny prodded.

"Yes, just as your kidney should be pushing you around," replied Lola.

Johnny immediately recognized her nagging tone and began to sing: NOBODY KNOWS THE TROUBLE IZZ SEEN, NOBODY KNOWS BUT JESUS....

After an hour or so on the balcony with her family, Lola retired to her room. She had to call Nicholas. She dreaded the conversation, dreaded how he would respond to her insistence on staying at RedFish.

Knowing the company might shut down any day was all the more reason to listen to his proposition. But her emotional ties to Ms K and Goodboy and maybe even young gang-banger, Raúl, kept getting in the way.

Nicholas was a wonderful husband-to-be. He deserved the truth. As painful as it might be, she would give him just that ... the truth.

He came on the line with a sad voice. "I've given the offer some thought. I don't believe it's going to work out."

"Wha-why not?" she stuttered.

"Do you know what kind of chemicals our child might be exposed to at that job site? I mean, this is Dow Chemical. These are the guys that made Napalm for Viet Nam. It's too dangerous for both of you."

Lola tried to hold back her tears. "I ... I don't deserve you."

He laughed. "Just so you remember that when the lights are low and the soft music is playing."

"In two weeks, I will visit you in Kansas City. I will remember it like never before."

"One more thing," he added. "I told the guy you would call him to get a feel for the position. Just out of courtesy, would you give him a call tomorrow? Here's the number."

Lola jotted it down. "Good night, baby. I love you."

Lola knew there were no earthquakes in Springfield. It must've been the power of the idea that shook her bed.

At 5:00 am, she sat straight up with a resounding glow on her face. Sometimes during the twilight of morning, her brain had conceived an extraordinary child of its own.

By 8:01 am, she had showered and dressed and was on the phone with Kristy Cutler. "I will be late coming in this morning. I hope you don't mind."

Kristy responded with an accommodating voice. "No problem." Thinking Lola had already begun her search for a new job, she added, "I will give you an excellent reference."

"I'm afraid you can't get rid of me that easily, Ms K. I'm your guardian angel, remember?"

At 8:30 am, Lola called the Dow research scientist. The questions in the back of her mind had nothing to do with being a safety coordinator. Her imagination had seen something her eyes had overlooked. It had taken half the night for the visual to invade her consciousness.

When Johnny had thrown the water onto the raging pit, the swirling cloud of smoke, steam and ashes had soared upward, not because it wanted to, but because the little oscillating fan had forced it to. The fan had forced the steam away from the floor. If a group of computers had been on the floor...

The Dow research scientist came on the line. "This is Hans. How can I be of assistance?"

"My name is Lola Salinas. You spoke with my fiancé on yesterday about the safety coordinator's position."

"Yes, yes. Your fiancé spoke very highly of your natural skills and problem-solving abilities. If you're only half of what he reported to me, it would be my privilege to recommend you."

"I do appreciate your willingness to help. But after we looked at how our new baby would fit in, we agreed this is not the time for a change."

"He didn't mention the baby. Congratulations!"

"Thank you. This will be our first and we are nervous about a lot of things."

"That's to be expected. My wife and I have three and we still get nervous, he confessed."

"You have been with your company a long time, yes?"

"Almost eleven years."

"Then maybe you can tell me. Is there a way to make steam go up without blowing it with a fan?"

He paused. "Perhaps. Why do you ask?"

"It's just a little home experiment I'm trying to do."

"Well, if you're using a simple heating process, you will notice that, because vaporized water is lighter than air, steam rises quite naturally without external intervention. In other words, you don't need a fan."

"Does the steam keep going up?"

"Relatively speaking, until it reaches its dew point or point of condensation at which time molecular clusters become heavier and transform into liquids again."

"Do these liquids keep going up?"

He laughed with amusement. "I'm afraid not. Eventually, the joyride ends and all the accomplices come crashing back to earth, usually in the form of rain, sleet or snow."

"I have one more question for you and then I will let you go."

"I'm listening."

"Is there a way to keep the joyride going?"

"You mean, keep the liquid from coming back to earth?"

"Yes," she confirmed.

"This must be an extraordinary experiment you have going?"

Lola remained silent.

He thought about it. "What you're asking the liquid to do is defy the laws of gravity. Now that does require external intervention."

"Like a fan, yes?"

"Yes. Or creating some kind of ionic charge on the droplets so they respond to another apparatus in an elevated zone."

"I-ah, I do not follow you," she confessed.

"Unfortunately, I have to go into a meeting, so I can't get into the details. I would recommend you do some reading on electromagnetic suspension systems and proceed from there."

"Thank you so much, Hans."

"Oh yes, tell your fiancée I do see what he's talking about. If you decide to pursue a position with our company at a later date, please feel free to call me."

"I will," she promised.

At 10:30 am, Lola walked into the administration building of Lincoln Land College, her old Alma Mater in Litchfield. The curriculum had forced her to take biology, which she almost failed.

At the time, it seemed ridiculous to force a construction management major to fire up Bunsen burners and cut open frogs. But the experience had exposed her to a bright young science professor whose published papers on a variety of disciplines was turning the scientific community upside down.

She found him in his office, rummaging through his cluttered credenza, searching for a pamphlet he had lost. When he turned to find her standing in the doorway, there wasn't the least bit of familiarity in his expression. If anything, he appeared perplexed and annoyed.

"May I help you?" He asked in a whiny voice. His Albino-ish eyebrows twitched when he spoke.

"You probably don't remember me. I was one of your students last year."

"You are correct. I don't remember."

"My name is Lola Salinas."

"I still don't remember."

"That is not important. I just need to ask you a question."

"Make it quick. I have a class in ten minutes and I can't seem to find a shred of evidence that suggests I'm the instructor." He continued his frantic search for the pamphlets and lecture notes.

"Do you know anything about electromagnetic suspension systems?"

Fascinated by her question, he finally turned to face her. "Perhaps. What do you need to know?"

"Is it possible to keep water droplets that used to be steam from falling back to the ground?"

"Yes, of course, depending on the extraneous variables that might contaminate the environment. There are scenarios that would allow the temporary or even permanent suspension of liquids."

"How would it be done?" she pressed.

He squeezed his bony chin. "You could employ colloidal mixtures of ferrofluids, or magnetic particles irradiated by lasers, or organic solvents with an electrical charge, or..." He rummaged through his desk drawer to pull out a wrinkled newsletter. As he re-familiarized himself with the content, a distant buzzer went off.

"Yes, yes. This is it. This is the cutting edge stuff." He handed it to her. "Make a copy and put it back on my desk, no, no, in that big leather chair in the corner so I'll know where to find it."

Lola glanced at the chair and saw another pamphlet. "What class will you teach this morning?"

He thought for a moment. "Physics 101."

She walked over to the chair, picked up the Physics pamphlet and notes and handed them to him. "This will help, yes?"

He nodded, gratefully. "Thank you, Miss Sagoness." He ran out of the door.

Lola glanced at the newsletter. The symbols and formulas were way over her head.

At RedFish, she sat down at her cubicle with two dictionaries, a science almanac, an online English translator, a physics terminology website and a series of electromagnetic suspension articles. The most she could decipher was the bottom line: New high-powered laser etchings on the surface of silicon strips could make liquids flow upward, literally defying the pull of gravity.

With time running out, the bottom line would have to do. She walked down the hallway to Kristy's office with the newsletter in hand. The pointed nose secretary greeted her with a spiteful stare.

"Is Ms K in?" Lola inquired.

"Yes, but she's unavailable right now."

"Do you think you could buzz her and just let her know I would like to see her as soon as possible? It's very important."

"Perhaps, you weren't listening," Shannon scolded her. "Mrs. Cutler is not available."

Lola's face hardened. "Either you will buzz her now and let her know I'm out here, or I'm going to walk through the door with very high hopes that you will try to stop me."

"Fine. It's your funeral." The secretary slammed the intercom button as though it were a bug needing to be squashed.

Kristy's voice bellowed. "Yes!"

"Mrs. Cutler, Lola is out here demanding to see you. I explained to her that you were in a meeting but-"

"Send her in."

Hearing the irritation in Kristy's voice, Shannon reprimanded Lola, "It seems you haven't learned your lesson from the other day. Maybe this time, what she says to you will be *permanent*."

Lola made her eyes look big and full of worry. "Oh Great Lady of Guadalupe! What have I done?"

Inside the office, Lola was pleasantly surprised to see Goodboy sitting in front of Kristy's desk. It appeared they had been going over financial projections.

"I'm sorry to disturb you, Ms K. You know I wouldn't unless it was very important."

She smiled, then pointed her finger through the door at Shannon's desk. "We're still trying for that Hollywood debut, remember?"

Lola took a seat. "I believe I know a way to solve our problem."

"Which problem? Number five or number five thousand?"

Lola remained serious. "The problem with Evap-X3."

Goodboy slowly straightened up in his chair. Kristy pushed the financials aside.

Lola continued. "As I understand it, the water vapor that

cools the computers will cause a problem if it falls back down into the computers, yes?"

Goodboy intervened. "Technically, it's not just water. We have a three-tank system that uses a mixture of water and other chemicals to cycle the heat from the room. But yes, you are correct. If the liquids get into the servers, they will create all kinds of corrosion and circuitry problems."

"What if the liquids never get to the servers? What if they rise up and never come down?"

"That would be great, except we have a little problem called gravity. It pulls the vaporized liquid back to the floor."

"What if we could defy gravity itself?"

Kristy chuckled. "I think only Superman can do that."

Lola handed the newsletter to Goodboy. "You are now Superman."

A hush fell over the room as Goodboy read the article.

"What is it?" Kristy anxiously inquired.

Goodboy appeared zombie-like, finally passing it over to her. Kristy then read it once, twice. "I still don't understand."

Goodboy was still trying to digest the new knowledge. "The article is saying, as the moisture rises, we can suspend it at the top of the room using these laser etchings on silicon strips; Maybe even recycle it back into the system to gain efficiencies."

"Can that really work?" quizzed Kristy.

He didn't answer. His mind was spinning in another universe.

"Henry? Henry!"

"Yes, I'm sorry. What did you say?"

"Can this technique work?"

"I don't know. It's all cutting edge stuff," he admitted. "What I do know is it gives us a hell of a fighting chance ... lot more than what we had ten minutes ago."

She looked at Lola. "How did you come up with this?"

She smiled credulously. "I went to a wiener roast."

Phillip Barlow sat in his spacious, ultra modern green glass San Mateo office on the 20th floor, overlooking the luscious redwood trees in Silicon Valley. He was waiting on an important phone call. Bradley Bean, his eccentric billionaire boss, was finishing up a conference in London and had scheduled a three-way from Big Brother, one of the company's two private jets.

Finally, Barlow's executive secretary buzzed him. "Mr. Bean is on the line."

On speaker, high above the North Atlantic Ocean, Bean sounded as though he was inside a box. "Hey, Phillip, I've got Walter Pritchett on the line with us. You should remember him from our IPO historical performance meetings in New York. The son-of-a-bitch has made so much money off our company, I'm tempted to start calling him Sir Walter."

Bean's comments touched off a landslide of laughter.

"Hello, Philip." A second, throaty voice came on the line. "Great to talk to you again. How's this penny-pinching bastard been treating you?"

"If I say good, Bradley will take that to mean I don't have enough to do. So I'll just say about the same." Phillip Barlow's response ushered in another round of laughter.

"Okay, here's the deal," said Bean. "We've got this annual stockholders meeting coming up in a week or so in San Francisco. From what Walter is telling me, it could result in a substantial boost in our stock price. Or, it could send us tumbling down Brokeback Mountain."

Walter Pritchett explained. "We're vulnerable, not necessarily because of a lack of performance by our company, but because of flashier performances by our competitors."

"These bug-eyed consumers are drooling over iPhones and iPads and wireless Kindles and Google boogle doggle crap which doesn't hold a candle to our advanced internet protocol architecture and world class warp drive business servers. But the innovation buzz is going to those clowns," Bean complained.

"Stock price has a lot to do with perception," added Pritchett. "Which companies are moving forward, which are staying home. If investors perceive a company is getting left behind, they assign it a lower value. Of course, I'm not telling you anything you don't already know."

"Walter feels we need to make a big announcement at the meeting," said Bean. "I told him you're sitting on the biggest announcement we've got. At least, I hope like hell you are."

Phillip could feel the pressure ratcheting up on him and his prized Data Storage Center division. "Things are looking very promising. But I don't know if we'll have all of the kinks out by next week."

Bean paused. "Here's our dilemma, Phillip. If we don't time this thing out for San Francisco, our market cap could drop by billions. You don't want that to happen, do you?"

"Of course not, Bradley."

"Then, let's save Private Ryan one more time. I'm giving you carte blanche on everything. Take one of the jets over to Springfield and stay with those corn-fed yokels until they get it right. Just make sure you're back in San Francisco next Friday morning, ready to inform our stockholders of what an innovative bunch we are. We need to tell our story." And then Bean changed his voice to sound like Muhammad Ali. "We need to shock the wuuurld!!!"

****

In Springfield, Goodboy stood by the front door, anxiously watching two delivery men struggle with a heavy wooden crate. It was marked in dangerous, forbidden red letters: FRAGILE! BREAKABLE! HANDLE WITH EXTREME CARE.

Three days earlier, he had flown out to a high tech semiconductor manufacturer in Albuquerque, New Mexico to have the silicon strips digitized, laser-etched and express shipped back to Springfield. The hefty manufacturing fee, paid in advance for a pipe-dream experiment that might easily crash and burn, drove accountant, John Bossley, up the wall. Kristy, however, overruled his superior financial judgment, essentially signing the company's death certificate if the new electromagnetic suspension process failed.

With only a weekend and a day before Phillip and his inspectors returned, no one was planning to go home. Kristy called the three white coated technicians into her office to explain that she was unable to pay them for the weekend work ahead. In the back of her mind, she wondered if she would be able to pay them at all.

The three technicians, Ali, Jeff the joker and Fat Pat, didn't care about the extra money.

"You've been good to us, Ms K." They all agreed. "Pay us when you can."

Goodboy stayed on the phone most of Friday afternoon, jotting down last minute tips from one of his high-tech Navy Intelligence contacts. Lola ordered pizzas and soda for the anticipated all-nighter.

Shannon, Kristy's fire-breathing secretary, watched with consternation at the heightening activity. No one was telling her anything. No one was asking her to do anything. She finally strolled into Kristy's office to find Lola, standing over Kristy's shoulder, evaluating a supplemental request sent to the three finalists for the Capital Airport project.

"May I speak with you a moment?" she requested.

"Sure, Shannon. What is it?" responded Kristy.

She glanced at Lola with disdain. "I'd prefer to speak alone."

Kristy paused a moment. "Actually, it might be better if Lola remained."

"What do you mean?"

"I guess with so many changes during the last few weeks, I've really been remiss in sharing our new structure with you."

She squinted. "New structure?"

"Yes. Given our new budget constraints, we're trying to redirect our human capital in ways that will allow us to operate more efficiently. You know, save a buck wherever we can."

"I understand," she nodded.

"Lola has come up with a way the company can save money by improving our safety numbers. In heading up that effort, she's going to need a lot of help. So I'm going to be moving you over to become her assistant."

Shannon's eyes bulged. "HER assistant?"

"Yes." She pointed to Lola over her shoulder. "This will be your new boss."

"Uh, well, I-I-I-I'm not sure that would be acceptable," she stuttered.

"Well, think about it. In a way it gives you a chance to

expand your knowledge and collaborate with your fellow employees," said Kristy. "You do like knowing things and collaborating with others, don't you?"

"Uh, I suppose."

"Then, you guys should do just fine." Kristy waited a few seconds. "Of course, she's a bit stricter than I am. But I'm sure you'll get used to her way of doing things."

Careful not to reveal her total ignorance of the new arrangement, Lola instinctively chimed in, "*Ola!* Welcome aboard."

Shannon left the room. A few minutes later, she returned with her letter of resignation, sealed neatly in a white envelope. "If things change, you know how to reach me." She flipped her badge and keys on the desk and walked out the door.

Kristy turned to Lola. "I don't know whether it's your personality or management style. But you simply must do a better job of holding on to your staff."

On Monday morning just after dawn, Phillip Barlow and two of his most competent technicians boarded the company jet in San Jose, California, headed for Springfield. *Little Brother* was the name given to their metallic gold, midsize Cessna Sovereign, an appropriate antithesis to *Big Brother*, the luxurious Citation X that Bradley Bean reserved for his numerous junkets around the world.

Though Bean's plane was larger, with an extended non-stop flying range, Barlow preferred the Sovereign because of its lightning speed, aerodynamic handling and spacious double-club cabin. The jet provided comfortable, ergonomic seating for nine, with a stand-up dressing room, a private lavatory with a flushing toilet and a vanity sink that ran hot and cold water. Barlow was especially fond of the convenient refreshment center which carried snacks, a liquor bar, ice-cold drinks and a hot beverage tank.

Cruising over the treacherous terrain of Death Valley, Herman "Birdman" Johnson, the young, black, handsome electronics circuitry technician who hated to fly, looked out of his window. "Even if you survived a crash down there, which is highly unlikely, the wolves would eat you alive."

Barlow was fully aware of Birdman's disdain for flying, the reason his co-workers had pinned him with his contradictory middle name. His great uncle had died when an Air Force bomber went down over the Pacific. But nobody expected tech eggheads to be that sensitive and connect the dots.

Barlow looked up from his notes on water distribution in the Northwest, then, smiled, prerogatively. "We don't use that word up here."

"Wolves?"

"No, *crash*," Barlow clarified. "On this jet, positive thinking is what keeps the engines going."

The other computer tech, Otis Redden, a chubby, long-haired nerd in his mid-thirties, chuckled to himself. He had heard Barlow's spiel before. It seemed only natural that a dude with a Master's from Caltech, a long-legged blond wife, a half-million-dollar salary and mini mansion hanging off an oceanside mountain would talk about positive thinking. *Positive* was all he knew.

Though there was a recent chink in his armor, the rumor that his blond wife had run off with a German weight lifter, the personal stuff had nothing to do with his stellar, almost legendary performance at the Bean Systems, Inc. He had a reputation for making solid decisions and choosing the right technology horse at just the right time.

That's why, when Barlow said he had a potential solution to a trillion dollar technological nightmare germinating in the offices of a no-name, low-tech custom home builder in dust-bowl Midwest Missouri, Otis took him at his word. He had asked Barlow serious, drill-down questions about the project, did his own painstaking research and ran his own cooling simulations. In the end, he and Barlow were the only two in the department that still believed Evap-X3 was the right system. That's why he was on the plane.

Before they landed in Springfield, Barlow made his speech

short and sweet. "You have one objective: to leave here with a system that works. We all know the consequences of selling Bradley a bill of goods. He'll pay now. But we'll end up paying later. This is our career, gentlemen. Unless you want to stay here in Springfield and pursue an alternative career as a grain farmer, let's bring Private Ryan home in one piece."

****

At 2:00 pm, Kristy received a call on her cell from the security guard. "The people from California are here at the gate."

"Send them through." She headed to the front door to greet them. She wanted to appear fresh and vibrant in her ruffled white blouse and blue business suit. Only she and the other members of the team realized the only thing keeping her eyes open were the three heart-palpitating cans of caffeine enriched energy drinks.

For three days straight, the team had worked at a feverish pitch, trying to assemble the final components to their pie-in-the-sky, make-or-break technological wonder. Only, because they had begun to smell like rank chimpanzees and getting on each other's nerves, did the technicians finally go home Sunday afternoon for some personal hygiene and much needed sleep. By midnight, however, they were back at it again, trying to force all the pieces to their complex, gravity defying puzzle to fall into place.

They had encountered one disaster after another.

The back side of the silicon strips didn't want to stick to the makeshift ceiling over the laboratory floor. One of the two test computer servers went on the blink because, in adjusting the nozzle calibration to the new ceiling strips, some of the vapor went directly into the server and shorted out the circuit board.

The initial vapor that flowed upward to the ceiling did

in fact stick to the strips and not come down. However, as the moisture began to accumulate on the strips, the ensuing droplets bounced off the watery surface and plunged onto the floor.

Goodboy's Navy contact talked him through a series of *Apollo 13* makeshift fixes which included stringing a parallel line of Christmas lights with varying wattage that adhered to several mind-boggling equations, cleverly altering the temperature along the silicon strips. When Goodboy wrote M L2 / T2 divided by T = M L 2 / T 3 on the board, Fat Pat warned him it was against the law to build an atomic bomb.

Nevertheless, the wildcard remedy from Santa's sack of goodies forced the water along the strips into a recycling duct that fed back into the tanks. Goodboy's ambitious vision of recycling efficiencies was slowly becoming a reality, and the bazaar system of water flowing magically along crevasses in the ceiling was falling into place.

When Kristy led Barlow and his two technicians into the frosty chamber, Goodboy and his team hadn't had time to run a final test. Whatever grim realities lurked inside the hodgepodge of generators and tanks and turbine blowers would be viewed in simultaneous horror, a suicide pill for all to consume.

Lola stood, quietly, in the corner, wearing her pristine white smock, pleading with her raging emotions, trying not to have her baby right there on the spot. It was she who had led them down this last minute, panic-stricken path of uncertainty. The blood of RedFish's final cash reserves was on her hands.

People weren't going to remember her good intentions. Life wasn't a fluffy ball of twine that unraveled with good wishes and heartfelt thanks. No, what they were going to remember was the ridiculous, delusional, pie-in-the-sky newsletter she had single-handedly, and without solicitation, introduced to the people that trusted her. She had convinced them that water could flow along the ceiling upside down.

Watching Goodboy press the huge red power button to jump-start the system was like watching an executioner fire up the electric chair. There was a very good chance someone's precious career was about to be fried.

They all gazed with growing anxiety as the red, blue and orange lights whizzed around the oversized spinning-top generator. The tanks began to bubble. The refrigeration coils trembled and groaned. The twin turbines turned faster and faster as the three snake-like nozzles spewed out their precious dew.

All eyes were on the ceiling as the vapor rose like the morning fog and rode the electromagnetic currents along the grooved black strips and into the recycling duct. They watched in silence for almost five minutes before Fat Pat and Jeff the joker began a slow, cautious round of applause.

Before long, the whole room was filled with thunderous clapping and wild screams of celebration. Everyone was giving everyone else high fives, that is, everyone except Birdman Johnson, the young circuitry technician who hated to fly. His narrow eyes focused on the temperature gages next to the two servers. He didn't like what he saw.

With his own weird-looking meter in hand, he walked over to the servers and stuck the double forked thermometer gadget directly between the servers. Using his extensive background in chemistry and quantum mechanics, he reported, "We've got problems. The LMTD is too low."

Kristy looked at Goodboy. "What is he saying?"

"The Log Mean Temperature Difference or rate of heat transfer. He's saying it's too low."

All of the smiles disappeared.

"What's causing that, Herman? Can you tell?" asked Barlow.

He studied it a moment. "We have a hot flux on the lower extremities because the electromagnetic drag is not allowing the cooling process to reach the critical heat zones."

Goodboy again interrupted, “The vapor stream is going up and out. It never gets down to the actual servers.”

“Why don’t we just point the nozzles directly at the servers and increase the output?” suggested Fat Pat.

“That would be fine if we had only two servers to point at,” said Goodboy. “But we’ll have thousands.”

There was a long silence. Finally, Otis Redden chimed in. “I think I have a solution. But we won’t know if it works until in the morning when the sun comes out.”

The perpetually positive Barlow gritted his teeth with concern. “What if it doesn’t work?”

Otis shook his head. “Then I guess we might as well find ourselves a good Midwestern tractor and start harvesting grain.”

Carter Blue Airlines had a reputation for getting the most out of its pilots. Steve Swanson, a self-assured Midwesterner with a pale face and bulging brown eyes, knew that when he joined the company six months earlier.

Sitting in his supervisor's office in New York with a sixteen-hour, seven-takeoff flight day ahead of him, he was concerned the regional flight scheduler had gone too far.

Twenty years earlier, The National Transportation Safety Board had recommended the FAA update pilot flight duty time rules, especially after statistics continually pointed to pilot fatigue as a major contributor to many modern-day crashes. Federal law, however, required the FAA prove that the cost to the airline industry of implementing new rules was actually justified by potential lives saved.

It was a laughable law, one designed to protect the major airlines from costly changes in their flight procedures. Ironically, no one was laughing at the disproportionate surge in regional airplanes falling from the sky.

Steve Swanson knew how difficult it was to move up the food chain to the real money the experienced pilots raked in. He didn't want to ruffle any feathers on his way up the ladder. But a sixteen-hour schedule, combined with the high stress of so many takeoffs, was a dangerous scenario to even the best of flyers. There were too many lives at stake to simply look the other way.

His bronze-faced, ex-Navy pilot supervisor sat behind his desk, simultaneously studying the flight log and Swanson's record. "I see here you've now been with the company six months?"

"Yes, sir," Swanson confirmed, shifting his slightly pudgy frame from one side of the chair to the other.

"Then it's probably time you received a more comprehensive understanding of how this thing works. Back in the day, I was on a 440-yard high school relay team that won the state championship. Are you familiar with relay track?"

Swanson nodded. "I believe so."

"You have four members of a team with one objective: Move that little baton around the track as quickly as possible, without interruption. You would think the key to the race is speed, but it's not. The key is the handoff. The smoother the handoff, the better chance you have of winning the race. You follow me so far?"

Swanson nodded again.

He continued, "The larger airlines book these flights between cities, but they lose money if they actually fly them. With their big planes and overhead, it's just not economically feasible. So they hand their customers off to us. We take responsibility for moving the baton. But if we don't fly, we don't get paid. So we've got to fly, Swanson. We got to fly long hours in bad weather and flop up and down like grasshoppers in a wheat field. That's the only way we stay in the race. That's the only way we keep the Harvard accountants at the home office from marking a big red X across our company mug-shot."

Swanson tried to choose his words carefully. "I don't mean to sound unsympathetic. But isn't there a point where safety overrides getting paid?"

The supervisor looked around his office as if trying to make sure the ghost of management didn't suddenly materialize out of thin air. "I like you, Swanson. You remind me of me a long time ago. Except, with five months left to retirement, I can't be the crusader I once was, the one that you are now. So I say this off the record and hope it helps with your future career decisions. Carter Blue and safety have never been more than distant cousins. Before I got here and twisted some arms, the two weren't even speaking. But even with the changes, the motto in the cockpit is still the same ...*fly till you die.*"

Swanson sat there, thinking about his wife and new baby and the impact of walking out right then and there.

The supervisor continued, "I can scratch you off this schedule. I've never sent a man on a mission who didn't want to go. But there are two or three hotshots, sleeping in the crew lounge right now. They'll gobble up this payday and never look back. So you tell me. What do you want to do?"

Tuesday morning, just before 8:00 am, the RedFish development team, Phillip Barlow and his two technicians, and two carpenters stood outside in the lumber yard, facing the rising sun. They were waiting for Otis Redden to finish his final calculations concerning the position and angle of the three silicon solar panels Goodboy had special ordered the previous afternoon.

Using a compass, a map and some other exotic metering device to compensate for the sun's summer bias in the northern hemisphere, Otis finally shook his head with satisfaction. "Okay Springfield is at Latitude: 39.7817213. So we want the panels here, facing solar south at this angle." He held his hand out about four feet from the ground.

The carpenters immediately swung into action, bracing the panels with a series of makeshift support walls. Otis and Goodboy hooked a set of large heavy duty cables from the solar panels to a digital charge controller. When Otis saw the high quality of the controller Goodboy had ordered, he winked his eye. "Smart move. This baby will block any reverse currents and prevent battery overcharge."

Kristy turned to Barlow with a futile expression. "I feel so useless just standing here. Is there anything we can do?"

"I think at this point, the techies rule the world," said Barlow. "All we can do now is give them every overpriced miracle gadget they ask for, and hope they can heal the land."

As Fat Pat and Jeff ran a second set of cables from the digital controller to a platform of three massive high voltage batteries, Jeff chuckled, loudly. "Hey, when we finish with these monstrosities, we can take them down to NASA and sell them to mission control to launch the next Shuttle."

Everyone welcomed a reason to let off steam.

A few minutes later, Goodboy and Otis pulled the entire group together for an official update.

Otis explained, "Here's where we are. The panels will feed solar energy into the digital controller, which will regulate the precise flow of energy into those batteries. The battery will provide DC voltage to the inverter inside the chamber. The inverter will then convert the DC voltage to common 120 volt AC power, which is what we need to run the fans without creating a negative impact on EROEI."

Kristy cocked her head to the side. "EROEI?"

"Yes, energy returned on energy invested," he explained. "You'll see when we get inside. The main thing to remember is to harness enough of the sun's power for minimum amp capacity, these panels need at least four hours of peak sunlight."

"That means at 12 noon we can throw the switch," added Goodboy. "But not a minute before."

"So we just stand around and wait?" asked Kristy in an anxious tone.

"I wish," said Otis. "We need, at least, that much time to set up the fans. Why don't we go inside?"

When the group reassembled inside the chamber, Goodboy pointed to a stack of cardboard boxes against the wall. "We have ten small oscillating fans ready for assembly. We just need Otis to tell us where they go."

Everyone looked at Otis, who displayed a sheepish grin.

"What's so funny?" asked Barlow.

"I was just thinking. I really could use a Twix Bar right now. Maybe that would buy me some time to come up with an answer."

Lola needed a Twix Bar too. She was in Kristy's office on the phone with a Midland, Texas wheeler-dealer who was eating her lunch.

Earlier that morning, Kristy had pulled her away from the group with another critical assignment.

"There's no way we're going to meet payroll this Friday without additional revenue," Kristy had confided. "I want you to go through this list of company assets and find everything we own free and clear. Get the current market value and see if we can find a buyer within the next forty-eight hours."

There was another crucial sticking point. Whatever Lola sold could not inhibit current operations. All jobs currently in progress could not be stripped of the critical equipment necessary to finish the job on time.

In the end, Lola needed to identify $85,000 in disposable net assets without having workers find out why stuff was disappearing.

Lola had identified two cement mixers, a night generator, some left over copper tubing, steel rebar and a pickup truck. If she could get sixty cents on the dollar, she would be able to reach her goal. But Billy-Bob, or whatever his name was, had been an equipment broker for twenty years. He knew every price by heart.

"Little darling, I'm offering top dollar for them cement trucks. But that's only if you do the deal right now. If you've gotta get off the phone and go ask your supervisor, well, that's tying up more of my time. And we all know time is money."

Lola was trying to fight her way out of an unfamiliar maze. "You know these are not my trucks. I feel you are trying to get me in trouble with my boss."

"Or get you a promotion, once he sees what a fine job you've done."

"He is a she," Lola corrected.

"Even better. I mean, you're a woman. Who knows a woman boss better than another woman? Unless, of course, you're not that close to her."

"We are very close," Lola defended.

"Then, you ought to know how she feels about a good deal."

"But this is not a good deal."

"The hell it ain't," he countered. "You got a '05 Peterbilt 357 with only 350 horsepower and a whopping 88,500 miles on it. Your best hope is $40,000. I'm offering $37,000. And no offense, but the other one is a joke. An '03 International Single Axle Kimble Mixer with 101,000 miles. If you get $27,000, you need to go to church on Sunday and dance all up and down the aisle."

While the broker was talking, Lola noticed something on her cost sheet. Whether it was a dirt spec or smudged whiteout or a miracle from heaven, she had incorrectly read the mileage on the Peterbilt truck. It wasn't 88,500, but rather, 38,500.

She took a deep breath. "You drive a hard bargain."

"Well, darling, tell me what it's gonna be? I got an auction to go to in Dallas. If you won't take my money, those hungry bone-pickers certainly will."

"I need the money. So I guess I will have to sell you one of our low mileage trucks. It is probably the best one we have."

"What kind?"

"It is also a top of the line Peterbilt, but with only 38,000 miles on it."

"How much you asking?" The urgency rose in his voice.

"With the low mileage, my boss would have to get $70,000."

He paused a while. "I'll give you $67,500 depending on what my inspector says when he looks it over."

She paused, hoping to make him sweat as much as she had. "I will agree to that. But you have to give me a better price on the International Single Axle."

"Alright, tell you what. I'll give you $67,500 on the Peterbilt and $28,500 on the International. That's the best I can do."

"On a giveaway like this, I will need a 10% deposit to hold it. It must be wired to our account today."

"Deal, Little Darling. Fax me a contract, VIN numbers and your banking information. Understand, my inspector's gonna run a background on those VINs to see if they're stolen or wrecked. If things check out, I'll wire you the funds today."

Lola got off the phone and grabbed the calculator. The total was $96,000. She needed only $85,000. The company was going to meet payroll with a little to spare.

At that moment the phone rang. With Sharron gone, Lola had been answering Kristy's line all morning. It was the foreman on the Gates Lakewood Development project. "We've got problems. I need to speak with Ms K."

As it turned out, the company's only dual hopper all-fiber attic-blowing machine had gone on the blink.

"We've got nine attics we need to insulate today," he report. "Otherwise, we're going to miss our deadline and have these revenue penalties kick in. I'm talking $30,000 to $40,000."

Lola thought for a moment. And then she remembered the man in the little cluttered shop who had helped her with the nail gun. "There's a shop on Lenox Ave called Mayberry Tool Repair. The guy can fix anything. Tell him I sent you. And tell him to send an invoice back so we can pay him right away."

Lola called the law firm, trying to get them to draw up a sales contract on the trucks. But without Kristy's approval, Monte "Gate Mouth" Fields, the cantankerous old attorney that handled all of RedFish's legal matters, refused. When she asked the accountant to give her the banking information, he also refused. Who was she to be making deals and requesting proprietary information? It quickly became apparent to Lola she had gone as far as she could go.

It was 11:45 am when Lola walked into the chamber with a stack of documents for Kristy to review. The room was a beehive of activity ... fan motors blowing, hand drills whining, white coats dashing from one side of the room to the other. If the NASCAR pit crews were ever in need of a training film, that day in the chamber would've been the ideal place to stage it.

When Lola saw the floor-level configuration of oscillating fans beneath the servers, she started to smile. She could already hear Johnny threatening to sue her for stealing his idea. Even more amusing was the way the ragtag assembly of anomalous components had come together. They reminded Lola of a huge junkyard of failed experiments, something she would expect to see in front of Einstein's house just before the garbage truck arrived.

Kristy, who had been standing next to Barlow observing the team's final adjustments, walked over to Lola. "How's it going on your end?"

Lola showed her the inventory list with all the items still intact, except for the two cement mixer trucks.

She whispered, "We have enough for payroll with maybe $10,000 over. But I will need your help with the lawyers and the accountant to close the transaction."

"Outstanding job, Lola!" Kristy whispered back, her voice,

filled with approval. "Just tell me what you need."

After a brief consultation, Kristy stepped out of the chamber and got on her cell phone. When she returned, she nodded at Lola. "You won't have any more problems."

Lola was about to return to her duties when she heard Otis announce, "We're ready."

Kristy grabbed Lola by the arm. "Don't leave. You're a part of this."

Lola turned to face Einstein's junkyard.

As Goodboy pushed the power button and started the sequence, a brittle hush fell over the room. Everything preceded as before, except this time, the oscillating fans, positioned face up about twelve inches from the floor, started to hum. The circulating air, combined with the incessant blasts of moisture from the nozzles, felt like a cool wintry breeze, streaming through Lola's hair.

Kristy turned to Barlow. "Is everything working according to plan?"

Barlow kept watching Otis. "We'll know in a minute."

"Shut it down," shouted Otis after taking a few measurements. "The cooling threshold is still too high."

Goodboy looked at the nozzles atop the generator, then looked at Otis. "You thinking what I'm thinking?"

Otis pondered for a moment. "Let's do it."

They climbed atop the generator and detached the nozzles. They removed the long extensions and placed the two primary emitters face up on wooden blocks, right next to the fans.

"Fire it up again," ordered Otis. "And this time, turn the nozzles to maximum output."

Soon, the wind stream from the fans lifted the misty vapors directly over the servers and onto the ceiling. The moisture collected on the silicon strips until the variance in temperature, created by the Christmas lights, moved the miniature river along the ceiling and into the tank ducts.

With a grim, doomsday face, Birdman Johnson took repeated temperature readings directly over the servers, then on either side. He showed the results to Otis who pulled out a second meter and walked all around the server taking more measurements.

Finally, he threw up his hand with a loud roar. “Yeaaaaaah! Nerds rule the world!”

Einstein’s junkyard was working perfectly. Everyone shouted for joy. Kristy gave Lola a big squeeze, then turned to Barlow’s awaiting arms. She was smiling and hugging him and dancing around. And then it hit her. She was no longer thinking about the machine, but rather, how wonderful it felt being in his strong arms.

Since her husband’s untimely heart attack eight years earlier, she had tried her hand at a few awkward encounters, only to discover that at thirty-eight, a dashing knight in shining armor was impossible to find. Phillip Barlow reminded her of everything she had been looking for. But like so many other potential suitors, some dimwitted cheerleader type had already placed him under wraps.

There was an invisible line drawn in the sand that business cohorts weren’t supposed to cross. This was certainly not the time to ignore decorum and allow her personal feeling to sabotage the opportunity of a lifetime.

Still smiling, she pushed away in an awkward release and refocused on the job at hand.

Hand....

Kristy wondered why Barlow was still clinging to hers. He finally whispered just above the noisy celebration. “We’ve got to get back to California.”

His words saddened her, slowly chiseling away at her robotic smile. “Of course you do. How soon will you leave?”

“No, no WE need to get back,” he clarified. “I want you to

come with me."

"Beg pardon?"

"This project is going to be the centerpiece of our stockholders' meeting on Friday. I want to introduce you to our investors, and maybe, have you talk about the innovation behind this thing."

She studied his bronze face, trying to gauge the seriousness of his proposal. "You want me to speak to thousands of Bean Systems' precious stockholders?"

"Yes, why wouldn't I."

"Henry is really the technical mind behind this project. Wouldn't he be more appropriate?"

"Perhaps. But who do you think they'd be more receptive to? A beautiful young woman entrepreneur with an extraordinary vision, or an old tech guy who understands the nuts and bolts of the backend?"

He thinks I'm beautiful. She struggled not to blush.

She paused for a long time. "How quickly do you plan to leave?"

"How quickly can you pack a bag?"

Kristy pulled Goodboy and Lola outside of the chamber. "I have to go to California. I'm leaving you two in charge."

Lola's mouth was still open like a stunned grouper fish when Kristy said, "Sorry, Lola. I'm firing you as safety coordinator."

Lola frowned. "You are?"

"Yes. You are now Operations Manager answering to Henry here, our new Executive Vice President. I'll deal with salaries and stock options when I get back. Meanwhile, we can't let anything get in the way. Do whatever you have to do to keep this company afloat."

Nicholas was surprised when his regional manager called on Monday morning to say she would fly into Kansas City on Tuesday to meet with him. His store numbers were decent, if not exceptional. And as far as he knew, there were no major complaints. In the back of his mind, he wondered whether they intended to offer him an even larger store.

Sitting in a small meeting room upstairs, overlooking the retail floor, Nicholas and his manager went over some preliminary sales projections. Eventually, she laid her expensive company ink pen on the table. "I might as well tell you the real reason I'm here."

Nicholas had never seen her crimson, Queen-of-England face harbor such an intense expression.

She continued. "A recently hired employee filed a substantial medical claim with our human resources department.

Her name is Terri Farnsworth. You may remember her from your previous store. She was battling with breast cancer?"

Nicholas nodded. "Yes, I remember."

"Before HR approves a claim of that magnitude, they do an extensive background check, you know, the usual stuff: social security verification, criminal background, pre-existing conditions and claims. It's nothing personal. It's just what they do."

Nicholas's heart had started to race. "Nothing personal. I understand."

"Anyway. I have no idea how this happened, but one of the records that came back indicated you and Miss Farnsworth had the same father, which would make her your sister?" She waited for his answer.

"Half sister," he finally confirmed.

She paused again. "Do you know what nepotism is?"

"Yes. It's favoritism or partiality shown to relatives in a business environment."

"At Bishop Hardware, it goes a bit further. It's the actual hiring of relatives without supervisory approval. It's all spelled out in your performance contract with the company. Violation of the nepotism policy can lead to dismissal."

"Are you firing me?" asked Nicholas, not wanting to drag it out.

"My superiors tell me I should. But I'm not. You've done so well with this company. I believe you'll go far. But policy is policy."

"So what's the final verdict?"

"A six-month suspension without pay," she reluctantly announced. "That's the best I can do."

"And when I come back?"

"You'll be on probation for a year. After that, we wipe the whole thing from your file. It'll be like it never happened."

She pulled out a stack of papers from her briefcase. "If you agree to the terms, you'll have to sign these documents."

"And if I don't agree..."

She shook her head. "I don't want to even think about that possibility, Nicholas. You've made a mistake. Swallow your medicine and move on."

Little Brother lifted off from the Springfield Capital Airport in clear blue afternoon skies. Kristy found the sheer power of the Cessna's smooth ascent into the heavens remarkable, compared to the slow, clunky rise of most commercial airliners. The cabin was surprisingly spacious, and the seats, fit for a queen. However, her favorite attraction quickly became the refreshment bar, especially when Barlow poured each of them a cool velvety glass of Napa Valley Cabernet Sauvignon.

"To magnificent teamwork," he proudly toasted.

After a quick sip, Herman Johnson, sitting near the front, looked back at Barlow with a sarcastic grin. "How does Mr. Bean feel about us drinking on the job?"

Barlow smiled, naughtily. "Bradley admires a drunk that compensates for his problem by turning a bigger profit for the company."

Herman raised his glass high. "Then, here's to bigger

profits." They all laughed, then chugged another round.

An hour into the flight, Kristy turned to Barlow. "So how is it, working for the infamous Bradley Bean? Is he the shrewd, heartless tycoon that tramples his competition into the dust? Or is he the boyish, soft-spoken philanthropist that gives millions to the hopeless and downtrodden around the world?"

"A little bit of both, I would have to say. He's a very complex individual with multiple drivers. And he seldom takes no for an answer."

"I suppose responding to all those drivers keeps you busy, away from your family?" Kristy carefully inched her way into his personal life.

Barlow felt awkward, explaining he didn't have a family anymore. It didn't seem flattering to tell people his wife had grown weary of his being away all the time, and decided to cash out. So he just gave the usual answer. "You try to stay focused and do what you have to do."

Kristy retreated to a more pressing issue. "So what will all of this mean to your career?"

He beamed with anticipation. "Are you kidding? We're on the verge of launching a trillion dollar data storage industry and we have the only game in town." He paused. "Well, you have the only game in town. But you're on my plane. That has to count for something."

"We've been so preoccupied the last year, trying to make this project work, I haven't given much thought to what would happen once it did," she admitted.

"I can tell you what will happen. Bradley will want to own the thing one hundred percent. He'll make you an offer and you'll refuse. And then he'll make you an offer you can't refuse. Bean Systems will end up owning 90% and you'll own 10% and your 10% will be worth more than all of the money you could ever dream of making in the construction business."

Kristy smiled. "I just love happy endings."

At that moment, an unexpected blast of air turbulence rocked the Cessna from side to side. The interior lights flickered off, then back on.

Herman Johnson's head popped up from his laptop.

The pilot's voice came over the small intercom. "I'm being told we have some inclement weather over the Utah-Nevada area. Might get a little bumpy, but nothing to worry about."

Hoping to stir Herman's squeamish nerves, Otis Redden made a scary face. "There's trouble in them Utah mountains, trouble I say."

The pilot continued, "Might be a good idea to make your way to the lavatory ... that's if you have to go."

Kristy unbuckled her seat belt. "Ladies first. I don't know if I can trust you gentlemen to let down the toilet seat."

"Don't worry," said Otis. "If you fall in, we have some silicon strips to pull you back up to the ceiling."

****

Back in Springfield, Lola enjoyed the last sweet sip from her plastic party cup. Goodboy had gone out and gotten a bottle of champagne for the Evap-X3 team's private celebration. After sharing their mutual respect and admiration speeches, fatigue had begun to sap their enthusiasm.

Goodboy locked the chamber. Everyone headed home early to catch up on some much needed rest.

Lola had planned to stay behind to help Goodboy with several unfinished company matters. That's when he pulled official rank.

"Absolutely not, Chief Warrant Officer Salinas. No tired, overworked pregnant officers allowed on-board, at least, not until in the morning. Go home and take care of yourself." And then he confided that early in their marriage, his wife had lost a baby from stress and over extending herself.

Reluctantly, Lola grabbed her purse and headed for the door.

In the parking lot, she spotted Raúl standing next to her car. Not knowing whether he was friend or foe, she gripped the mace sprayer on her key chain.

She offered a cordial nod. "Hello, Raúl."

He didn't smile back. Instead, he lifted his shirt sleeve to show his MS-13 gang tattoo had been removed.

There was also a black bruise under his eye.

He pointed to the spot where the tattoo had been and then the blackened slit under his eyelid. "Does this qualify?"

Lola's eyes started to water. "It sure does."

"So what's next?"

"A hug," she said. "But don't push too hard, I'm pregnant."

He pulled her in with a respectful embrace. "Damn, that shoulda been my baby."

She glanced at his eye again. "And that shoulda been my lick."

They both laughed.

She pulled out some paper and a pen. "Give me all your information: real name, social, date of birth. If we're going to remake you, we'll need to get the proper papers."

He wrote everything down. "It's that easy, huh?"

"No, it's not easy at all. And this part is not right. So if you're ever picked up and deported, remember, it wasn't right in the first place."

"But we're going to tell this big lie anyway, right?"

"Yes, same as when Americans born in this country lie about their taxes or lie about their income to get a new home, or about their work experience to get a new job. You know Mr. Henry in there? I call him Goodboy."

"Yeah, everybody likes Mr. Henry. He's a cool dude."

"He lied about his age to get into the Navy. He was an outstanding Navy man. But his career started off with a lie."

"I understand."

"No, Raúl, you do not understand. According to them, your lie, or should I say our lie, is different. Our lie is not legitimate like their lie. We don't deserve the privilege to lie because we shouldn't be herc in this country in the first place."

"That's wacked!" he complained.

"But it is reality, yes? And it does not change until we prove their opinion of us is a bigger lie than the lie we told to get here."

"How can you prove that to these racist gringos who already have their minds made up?" he asked.

"By working twice as hard; by achieving more with less; by playing the game better than the people that created it. Even then, some will tune into Fox News to find a single illegal immigrant murder. There may be ten murders that week, maybe an old white blue blooded American serial killer with twenty young girls , buried in his backyard. But the murderer from Mexico that slipped over the border is the one they will talk about at the family barbeque."

"That's double wacked!" His voice rose in frustration.

"But reality, yes. Our hope is, slowly, there will be more people like Ms K, and less like the gringos that ride the borders with bats and guns, looking to kill, looking to satisfy the rage in their own hearts. Love is good. But hard work is better. It is a blinding light to even the most hateful of enemies."

"This is what you do inside the office, blind them?"

She smiled, then nodded. "*Si.*"

"Then get me the papers and I will blind them too."

****

Two hours into the flight, Herman Johnson's worst nightmare had come true. Swirling billows of dark gray clouds had engulfed the little Cessna, tossing it around like a ping-pong ball at a weekend tournament. Bullets of rain pounded the tiny windows. Angry bolts of lightning flickered past the wings like jagged daggers of fire.

A morbid silence spread over the cabin as the pilot's voice bellowed through the intercom. "We've encountered significant turbulence in this storm sector. But hang in there. In a moment, I'll be climbing to 42,000 feet. We can avoid some of the rough stuff."

As the plane nosed upward, Barlow glanced at Herman, sitting, quietly, in his seat. "You okay, Herman?"

He was slow to answer. "I guess I could lie. But what good would that do?"

At 42,000 feet, the plane leveled off. The turbulence seemed less volatile, and on occasion, intermittent rays of sunlight peaked though the broken cloud cover.

"This is better," declared Kristy.

She had no way of knowing how strongly the pilot disagreed. He could see them coming directly at him like a thousand snowballs on a cold winter's day. It was far too late for evasive maneuvers. Their huge sixteen pound bodies had already begun to pelt the wings.

"What was that?" asked Herman.

From the ground, the answer would've been utter admiration for the magnificent flock of American White Pelicans. They soared upward with grace and beauty from their natural habitat in the Utah marshes. But from the pilot's vantage point, it was utter chaos. A dozen of the hulking creatures had wedged their plump bodies into the core of the jet engines.

The Pratt & Whitney turbofan engines were an engineering marvel. But they were no match for the relentless assault of huge bills, flapping pouches and webbed feet. A white feather trail slowly littered the skies. Both engines grounded to an inevitable halt.

As the plane began its steep descent, the pilot engaged the drift down procedure, trying desperately at precise intervals to restart the engines.

Finally, he radioed the local tower with the ominous news.

"Have failure in both engines. Cannot restart. We are going down. I repeat ... we are going down."

When Lola drove back to the lake house that afternoon, she found Johnny sitting on the sofa, skimming through the newspaper.

"Here it is," he announced with boyish excitement. "BIG EASY Burgers is reopening this week. I already made reservations for that Mongolian Restaurant on Friday. But next Friday I'm taking you to Litchfield's hamburger joint extraordinaire."

Ruby stood in front of her most recent painting, a magnificent black *escaramuza* stallion with front hoofs, lifted to the sky.

Johnny lowered his paper. "Are you listening to me or drooling over that damn dancing horse?"

Ruby's eyes watered with admiration. She turned down her Mexican folk music CD so he could hear her. "His name was *Bailador*. He was the first horse my mother let me ride."

"I'm talking priceless burgers, here, knowemsayn'? Tell her, Babygirl."

Lola nodded. "Yes, they are good."

Johnny gawked at Lola's tired face. "You look whipped down. Them white folks making the safety coordinator pick cotton too?"

She tried to maintain a sad face. "I am no longer the safety coordinator."

He looked at Ruby. "You see. I told you. These young people don't understand their purpose. Now they done busted her down, just like they did my brother, ArchieV."

Ruby stepped away from her easel and brushes. "Is that true, Lolita? Have they busted you down?"

"No Mama, they have busted me up." She released a wide smile. "I have been promoted to Operations Manager."

Johnny looked at Ruby. "I told you that girl was going places." He stretched out his arms to Lola. "Come give Daddy a big hug."

"Don't even think about it."

"Okay. But you're going to need ole Johnny before ole Johnny needs you."

She remembered her promise to Raúl. "Okay, a hug for a favor."

"What favor? I mean, how do I know this is going to be an even exchange?"

"I'll make up the difference for her," promised Ruby.

He rubbed his chin in deep contemplation. "Huumh. The difference might call for that little pink nighty with the black straps and-"

"Please!" Lola interrupted. "That is too much information."

"Have a seat," he said. "Let me hear your request."

Lola told him about Raúl and her promise to get him into college.

"But he's going to need new ID, just like you got for me."

Johnny pondered a while. "That might be a problem."

He went on to explain that the FBI's cybercrime division had shut down the internet's biggest one-stop supermarket for stolen credit cards and passport forgeries.

"There are some others out there. But with so much heat, they're gonna to cost an arm and a leg."

"How much?" asked Lola.

"For the total package, maybe three grand."

"Then, I need to make a loan from you," Lola concluded.

"Oh hellll no! How did this good Samaritan venture start digging into my pocket?"

"Please, Daddy. He's trying to turn his life around."

"Yeah, and put me in the poor house at the same time."

"I will be making a good salary. I will pay you back."

"And if she has trouble, I will pay you back with my casino winnings," offered Ruby.

"This is the very reason we didn't want ya'll in this country in the first place," said Johnny. "We knew sooner or later you'd rise up against the black race."

"*Viva Mexico!*" Lola walked over and gave her mother a high five.

Johnny frowned in defeat. "All I know is I'd better be seeing a pink negligee around here real soon."

****

The next morning, Lola awakened to a loud commotion on the roof, followed by a series of gunshots. She scurried from her bedroom to find Johnny, standing on the balcony, peering up toward the bird feeder. He held his .357 in one hand and a flapping baby chick in the other. A trail of bloody feathers draped the railing.

"What happened?" asked Lola.

He pointed to a huge, spotted red-shouldered hawk he had

blown to pieces. "That big bird came in here, killed the mother and started eating the chicks. This is the only one still alive."

Johnny's hand was still shaking.

Lola found an old shoe box filled with bolts and screws. She dumped the contents, place some strips of paper in the bottom, and gently set the chick inside the box.

Johnny looked off into space, no doubt, concocting a plan to enter the forest and shoot all of the red-shouldered hawks in the vicinity. "You see that, Babygirl? You see how quickly death can come in on you?"

"You did your best, Daddy. You must not look at the lives that were lost. You must look at the life you saved."

She handed him the box.

He stared at the little red chick, flopping around in the box. "You think the little runt will survive with its family gone?"

"We'll bring it inside, give it some seeds and worms. You'll see. In a few days it will be strong enough to fly away and start its own family."

Johnny glanced at Lola's pertruding stomach, and how strong and mature she had become. There was a fleeting sadness in his eyes. For, they both knew soon, she too would fly away.

****

Upon entering the building at RedFish, she noticed a large group of workers, crowded around a television in the employee lounge, watching the national cable news. Their faces were somber. A few women from the human resources department were crying.

Goodboy observed her coming in the door, and stepped out into the hallway. "Good morning, Lola. Can you please come with me?"

He led her into Kristy's office. He pointed to the two chairs in front of Kristy's desk. "Let's talk for a moment."

Lola's heart raced. "What's going on? Why are all those people in there?"

"I'll explain. But first I need to remind you of something very important. You have a baby on the way. God has entrusted you with a special gift. So it's your responsibility to keep a level head and not get overly excited. You understand what I'm saying?"

She offered an appeasing nod.

He paused a few seconds longer. "Kristy's plane went down late yesterday afternoon. The weather is still so bad in Utah, they haven't been able to search for the wreckage."

Lola could feel her whole body trembling. Her tears were like unruly prisoners, forcing their way out of their watery cells. The baby kicked against the lining of her stomach, as if in retaliation for allowing the horrible news to enter her psyche.

Goodboy handed her a box of Kleenex, then sat quietly, giving her time to regain her composure.

"Do they know if anyone survived?" The words finally pushed out of her throat.

"Frankly, they don't know anything right now, just that the plane went down. Overcast skies are hampering rescue operations. Search and rescue teams are being dispatched as we speak. We just have to stay hopeful."

She took a deep breath. "What do you need me to do?"

"First and foremost, take care of yourself. Secondly, we need to do what Kristy asked us to do ... hold this company together."

"How do we do that?"

"The word has gotten around that we are the go-to guys. Employees will be looking at us, feeding on our strengths and weaknesses, believing in the future we show them. We have to go back out there and show them stability and hope and give them a reason to continue doing their jobs. Otherwise, we might as well shut down right now."

"I'll give my best."

He smiled. "From what I've seen, that's pretty darn good. Let's get back out there and keep this ship afloat."

In the dark, rugged mountains, battered by torrents of wind and rain, the Cessna's fiery crash looked like a log from a blazing campfire, kicked into a watery grave.

The sparks from the initial impact with the rocky terrain set the jet's fuel tank ablaze. But as the plane's momentum carried it through a gully of rainwater and mud, the fire reluctantly choked out, leaving only white billows of thick smoke riding the wingless fuselage down the mountainside.

For what seemed an eternity, the Cessna rolled and tumbled and fractured on every side. Toward the end of their deadly roller-coaster ride, Kristy watched in horror as a jagged rock formation sliced into the nose of the plane, ripping away the entire forward cabin and sending the cockpit, the pilot and Herman Johnson's row of seats into the darkness below.

In the end, the fuselage was nothing more than a scorched cigar, wedged between two rocks, overlooking the dark, rainy abyss. Twisted in such a severe downward angle, the only thing standing between Kristy and a fatal free-fall through the open mouth of the plane was her seat belt; a precarious strip of Nylon that cut into her breathing and made her want to throw up.

As she vacillated in and out of consciousness, she heard muted groans coming from the smoke-filled section of seats directly in front of her. In a waning moment of clarity, the repeated flashes of lightning illuminated the cabin just enough to expose the blood, gushing from the back of Otis Redden's head. Fragments from one of the broken champagne bottles had lodged in his neck.

"Otis!" She tried to cry out. But the words were too bitter, tainted by the twisted metal in her mouth. She spat the blood-soaked splinters into her lap until the painful purging drove her back into unconsciousness.

Her last thought was of Phillip Barlow. He had been sitting in a seat just across the aisle from her. Now, the whole seat was gone and Phillip was nowhere to be found.

It was early morning when she heard the loud rumbling, coming from the rear of the plane. With the dark gray clouds still hovering over the wreckage and the clear, watery droplets seeping through cracks in the roof, Kristy assumed the noise was thunder. That's when she spotted the huge piece of metal sliding down the aisle past her chair. Like a square cannon ball, the octagonal clump of fiberglass and steel cabling soared out of the Cessna's mouth, over the 3,000 foot cliff and onto the slippery rocks below.

She turned just in time to see Phillip, still strapped in his seat, sliding toward the same dreadful destination.

As it turned out, he had been pinned under the smashed metal all night. Once he managed to push free, he discovered the metal had been the only thing keeping him from plunging out of the plane to a certain death below.

Kristy observed his frantic struggle to unlatch his seat belt. As he slid pass her chair, she stuck out both legs. The same legs her husband had once caressed and cherished as soft and curvy and sexy were now giraffe-like, blood-splattered, wreckage-scarred poles.

The momentary delay was precisely what Barlow needed. He wrestled the belt from his waist and grabbed the bottom support pedestal on one of the remaining seats a few feet from the opening. His doomed chair continued its dreadful plunge. But Barlow managed to hold on.

With quiet determination, he muscled his sleek body up the slippery sliding board, finally coming to rest in a seat directly behind Kristy. He pulled and grunted and fumbled until he had safely strapped himself in.

He leaned over the back of her chair, gently wiping the glazed soot from her pale face. "I thought I'd never see you again. Are you alright?"

There was something new in his voice, a sense of caring she hadn't heard before.

"Yes ... no." Reluctantly, she allowed the truth to prevail.

"Don't worry. I'll get you out of here. I'll get all of us out of here."

She stared at Otis, his collar soaked in blood. "He's not breathing anymore."

Barlow unbuckled his belt. "I need to check on him."

"No, Phillip. Please don't move again. I think it's ... too late."

"Otis! Stay with us, okay? Just hang in there," Barlow's voice carried down the darkened aisle. There was no response. They both knew he was dead. So was the pilot. So was Herman Birdman Johnson.

So were both of their cell phones. Barlow quickly discovered there was no tower reception in the mountains.

"What are we going to do?" asked Kristy.

Not knowing exactly where they were or how long the inclement weather would last, he made another of his calculated decisions.

"We'll stay here for now. It's not the Ritz Carlton, but we have water and snack food. That should hold us for a day or so."

"A day or so?!" Her panic-stricken voice harmonized with the distant thunder. "You think it'll take that long to find us?"

"In this unforgiving terrain, it's hard to say. The emergency transmitter probably went with the cockpit, wherever that is. And with this thick cloud cover, they wouldn't dare try to fly blind in these mountains. They'll have to wait until it clears."

Kristy managed an awkward smile. "Thanks for the wonderful news. I bet your wife is always complimenting you on how you find ways to brighten her day."

He didn't smile back. "I-eeh, I guess it's time I told you. My wife and I are not together. My attorney says to expect the divorce papers any day."

"I'm sorry to hear," said Kristy.

That made him smile. "No you're not. I mean, I know there's something going on between us. But I didn't want to..."

"Cross the line," she completed his thought.

He slowly scanned the battered cabin, the gloomy images of death and devastation. "They say behind every dark cloud there's a silver lining. You think, maybe getting a chance to really know each other is our silver lining?"

"That depends."

"On what?" he asked.

"On whether or not we get a chance to act on it."

He leaned over, softly kissing her blistered lips. "I'm acting on it right now."

He was still staring into her teary blue eyes when they both felt it. The weight of the plane shifted forward a few inches and stopped. Something or someone was walking on top of the fuselage.

Barlow unbuckled his belt and climbed across the rear seat to investigate. As soon as he peeped through one of the cracks in the ceiling, he heard a loud growl. Three gray wolves were sniffing and scratching, trying to find a way in. They smelled the blood inside the cabin. Their frantic squirming had jarred the plane's sleek exterior away from the grip of the rocks, nudging it closer to the edge.

Barlow spotted a small fire extinguisher on the back wall. He grabbed it and sprayed a hefty plume through the largest cracks. It was enough to drive the hungry trio off the plane and into the underbrush.

The secret the wolves had exposed, however, was much worse than their ravenous hunger. What was left of the scorched cigar had become a time bomb, slowing creeping toward the jagged edge of death. Their pressing decision was painfully simple. Find a way out of the plane and become wolf bait, or stay inside and go over the edge.

It didn't make sense to stay at the office all night long. Lola had a television at home. She could've monitored the search from the comfort of her bed. But she was too afraid she'd miss the phone call from the National Transportation Safety Board or FAA or National Guard search and rescue helicopters reporting they'd found the wreckage and everyone had survived.

Knowing he wouldn't be able to sleep, Goodboy had also spent the night at the office. Together, with a small skeleton crew, Goodboy and Lola had guzzled down a hundred pots of coffee and monitored every available media source in the universe.

Just after midnight, a teenager's Facebook posting from Utah claimed a nearby farmer had stumbled across eight dead Pelicans near the probable crash area, their bodies ripped to shreds by what appeared to be some kind of mysterious monster. However, none of the information could be verified. Authorities reminded Goodboy that reports of bizarre sightings and odd discoveries just after a crash were par for the course.

To add to her frustration, Lola had received a call from Nicholas. He had, unexpectedly, arrived in town and needed to see her right away. She had agreed to meet him for lunch, only because Goodboy made her promise to eat. It didn't matter to him that she wasn't hungry.

Besides Nicholas' call and the twenty or so local and national news inquirers, clamoring for an update on Kristy's fate, Lola also received a call from her doctor, Johnny's doctor, Ruby, the owner of Mayberry Tool Repair and the bid manager at The Springfield Airport Authority. On her way to meet Nicholas for lunch, she listened to each message.

HER DOCTOR: "Hello, this is Dr. Fox. Lola, I need you to call me as soon as possible. I know you're not scheduled to come in for another week, but we may need to alter that schedule. Okay, talk to you soon and may God bless."

JOHNNY'S DOCTOR: "Hello. This is Dr. Campbell. I hear you're doing well over there at RedFish. I just wanted to remind you that you still owe me big time; which means I need you to strong-arm your father in here for his checkup. He's critically overdue but refuses to call my nurse back to set an appointment. Please contact me as soon as possible."

RUBY: "Lolita? *Ola*. This is Mama. You need to talk to your father because he is stubborn like a goat. He was in great pain last night, but won't go to the doctor. I believe he will listen to you. Can you call him? *... por favor, hacer esto rápido*."

THE OWNER OF MAYBERRY TOOL REPAIR: "Hello Ms Salinas. This is Harry over at Mayberry Tool Repair. First of all I wanted to thank you for your business. I was able to fix that little attic-blowing machine. And I felt like I gave you a good price.

Anyway, I just got this letter from your accountant saying the purchase was unauthorized. Do you know anything about that? It's only $401 including parts. Is there anything you can do? Call me."

THE BID MANAGER AT THE SPRINGFIELD AIRPORT AUTHORITY: "Hello, this call is for Lola Salinas. My name is Jay Potter, Logistics Manager with The Springfield Airport Authority. I've been trying to reach Kristy on her cell phone because her direct line at the office is going to voicemail. Your number was given as an alternate number to call. Anyway, someone from RedFish needs to be down here tomorrow at 2:00 pm. Your company and one other bidder have been selected as finalists. The revenue people have some additional questions. Just tell her to come to the main desk and ask for Potter. She knows me. I'll see you guys then."

Nicholas was waiting at a small health food sandwich shop across from Lincoln Park. In sporty jeans and a Penn State T-shirt, he appeared casual. The expression on his face, however, was quite intense.

"I've been suspended from Bishop Hardware." He came straight out with the bad news. "It'll be six months before I can go back."

She kept thinking about Goodboy's advice to keep a level head.

"What happened?"

"When I hired my sister, I violated the nepotism rule."

"What is this nepotism?" she asked.

"It has to do with favoritism to relatives," he explained.

She manufactured a hard expression. "So when I become CEO of RedFish, I will not only lose my welfare payments and food stamps, but because you are a family member, I will not be able to hire you to come by and strip out of your clothes during my lunch hour, like the Allen brothers' pole dancers did?"

"No, blood relatives are..." He was about to explain the technicalities of nepotism when he realized she was only kidding. She wasn't panic-stricken or upset as he had expected. In fact, she appeared almost relieved.

And then he realized she was relieved. The dilemma they faced in living in two separate cities had magically disappeared, at least for six months. By then, the baby would be born and their long-term family planning could begin in earnest.

"So I take it you're okay with this ... getting married and having a baby for a man who doesn't have a job?"

"I am not okay with it, but only because of the stress I see on your face. As far as the job thing, you are forgetting. I didn't have a job when you met me and we still fell in love."

"But a man is supposed to provide for his family," he declared. "That's the way it is. That's the way it's always been."

"And you will," she assured him. "But for now we can make it on an Operations Manager's salary."

He frowned. "Operations Manager?"

"I've been promoted," she announced with a big smile.

"That's the pits!" he complained. "I get suspended and you get promoted."

"It's the American way. I suppose you will have to beat me just so I remember you're still wearing the *pantalones*."

"Gladly!" he vowed. "Especially, if you're making more than I am."

Her face suddenly saddened. "I don't know how much I'm making. Ms K didn't get a chance to..."

"What?"

She finally decided to break the news. "The private plane that went down in Utah?"

"Yes, I heard it on the news."

"Ms K was on that plane."

"My God, Lola, why didn't you tell me?"

Her eyes began to water. "I didn't want you to worry. About her. About me."

"Was she ... I mean, are there any survivors?"

"They don't know yet," And then she looked at him with a strange certainty. "But I know, Nicholas. I know she's still alive."

At that moment, her phone went off. Goodboy was on the other end. "How long before you get back?"

"I can come now. Why do you ask?"

"Nothing urgent. It's just that, well, courtesy of a little arm twisting from one of my old Navy contacts, the FAA is sending the satellite photos over in a few minutes. I figured you'd want to see them."

"I'm on my way." She hung up the phone and turned to Nicholas. "Where will you be staying?"

"With my parents for the next few days. After that, I'm moving into my grandmother's house in Woodside Township. Since she died a few years ago, the house has just been sitting there. My mother felt I could save money until this suspension thing blows over."

"Will you be accepting company from pregnant women?" she queried.

He pondered a while. "I don't know. A deadbeat with no job, living with his parents ... I guess I'll have to take what I can get."

"Then I will see you this weekend," she promised. "But for now, I have to be there for Ms K. We must do everything we can to bring her home."

****

When Lola arrived back at the RedFish complex, she immediately went to Goodboy's office on the second floor. There, she found Fat Pat in the corner, sitting in front of a big-screen computer, waiting for the satellite transmissions to come in.

Standing over her shoulder, staring at the blank screen, Goodboy explained, "There's some kind of glitch. Probably another half hour before we get the photos in."

Lola looked at her watch. "I'll be back."

She went to Kristy's office, retrieved a copy of the Capital Airport bid, then went back upstairs to the accountant's office on the second floor.

The bookkeeping area was a spacious boiler room with John Bossley's office glassed in toward the back. Two gray-haired number crunchers sat at their desks, glaring at her as she walked past. John Bossley spotted her coming toward him, but turned away.

She knocked on his glass door. Finally, he looked up with a begrudged face to beckon her in.

"Well, well, well. If it isn't the Great Goddess of Safetyville. I hear accidents are down and savings are up. I wondered how long it would take you to come up here and rub it in my face."

The book said, in most cases, a confrontation could be avoided with skillful deflection. But in the case of an adversary who had suffered public embarrassment or a perceived defeat, the only solution was to even the score. That meant allowing the adversary to feel he was now in control and winning the war.

She spoke, softly. "It would be foolish for me to think these early figures will tell the whole story. And like you said, we don't know if the savings will have much of an impact at all."

"So if it's not the safety figures, it must be Evap-X3. Did you come to remind me I fought against it tooth and nail?"

"No. In fact, I am glad you fought against it."

Bossley's head snapped. "Say again."

She explained. "If I was in charge of this company, I would want someone in your position with a level head, someone who was following the rules and trying to keep us in the black. Who wants an accountant chasing bean pies in the sky? That would be my job, yes?"

He took a deep breath. "I wish someone could make Kristy see it that way."

"Believe me. She already does. Ms K depends on you. She trusts you a lot."

He motioned her to a chair in front of his cluttered desk. "Have a seat. Since I can't figure out why you're here, maybe I should let you tell me."

Lola sat down in the low, flimsy chair. "I need your help. This is the bid for the Capital Airport project. We are one of the two companies left. They want to ask us some questions tomorrow at 2:00 pm. Then, they will make the decision."

"Okay, what does that have to do with me?"

"These questions will be financial questions, way over my head. There are only two people who can answer them properly, Ms K and you. With Ms K being ... unavailable...."

"You want me to attend this meeting?"

"Yes. You have the knowledge to put our company in the best light."

He sighed. "No one has ever asked me to represent this company before."

"Ms K has never been missing in the Death Valley desert before."

"What did Henry say?"

"I did not ask Henry. He has placed this matter in my hands."

He thought about it a while. "I'll need some time to prepare."

She immediately stood up. "Then I will get out of your office right now." As she walked toward the door, she turned back. "There is one more thing."

"Yes?" He waited with suspicious eyes.

"I need to apologize to you for overstepping my bounds.

I authorized a repair on a blower machine, trying to save the company $35,000 in completion penalties. I should've checked with you first."

Bossley reached into a stack and pulled out the Mayberry Tool Repair invoice. "This $401 saved us $35,000?"

"Yes. I hope their little company won't suffer because of me."

"Hey, I can't gripe about a trade off like that. Good catch on your part. I'll get this Mayberry check cut and mailed out today."

"Thank you so much." Lola headed back down the hallway.

In Goodboy's office, the satellite photos were already on the screen. Goodboy was on the phone with an FAA official.

"Okay, but you're still telling me what you *don't* know," he growled. "I can see the wreckage on the screen. But where's the rest of the plane?"

Fat Pat turned to Lola. "They're showing us blurred shots at the base of some mountains in Washington County outside of Springdale, Utah. It's just a few scraps of metal."

"Disintegrated! No way." Goodboy continued to press the official. "I'm telling you there's a lot more of the plane somewhere in those mountains."

When Goodboy got off the phone, he was visibly upset. "What do they take us for, idiots? Even if a plane flies directly into a mountain, there's wreckage for miles."

"What about the rescue teams?" asked Lola.

"Oh, they're in there now, apparently hovering over a single piece of the cockpit. The problem is, with all that rain and fog, nobody wants to drop down too deep into those godforsaken mountain gullies. I just wish I was there to make them grow some Kahunas, fan out and do their job."

"Maybe the weather will get better for them, yes?" Lola

spoke, wishfully.

"They can't afford to wait on the weather. I mean, that's a hellish patch of geography out there. You got rattlesnakes, mountain lions, scorpions, wolves. The longer they're out there, the less their chances for survival, and that's assuming they survived the crash in the first place."

"They survived. I know they did," insisted Lola.

"Then we better get them out of there before it's too late."

Fat Pat shook her head. "I guess we need a miracle."

Goodboy gazed at the photos again. "The way this whole thing is shaping up, I don't think we can afford anything less."

Lola left the room too abruptly to say goodbye. A few minutes later, she was in her car, driving toward Litchfield.

In the dark corridors of her mind was a secret place, a horrible place where unwieldy miracles took flight. The cost of each miracle was astronomical and nonnegotiable. Not even the Mauretanians understood the life-and-death exchange rate doled out by the old Baobab tree. But then, what difference would it have made if they did?

Like Lola, they, too, had been prisoners of desperation, no different from the junkies on the streets of Juárez. The drug dealer named his price and everybody had to pay. But with the tree, who paid and how much, was still a mystery hidden in the seams of a dark, invisible world.

For a long while Lola sat in her car outside the U-Haul storage facility, trying not to go inside. That's when her cell phone rang.

Goodboy's weary voice came over the speaker. "There's good news and bad news. I'll give you both, but only if you're up to it."

"I'mmmm, I'm ready."

"The bad news is, they finally got some people on the ground. They found the pilot and one of the technicians from Bean

Systems. Neither one survived the crash."

Lola took a deep breath. "What's the good news?"

"I think it's obvious. They didn't fine Kristy and the others, or the rest of the plane. That means we still have a chance."

"Tell me the truth," she pleaded. "Do you really believe we have a chance?"

He paused for what seemed an eternity. "Lola, I can't afford not to believe. There's too much at stake here, and I'm not just talking about Kristy's life or the company or all the people that will be affected. I'm talking about a principle that's embedded in our very existence; the belief that if you give all you have to give and do the right thing, good things will come in the end."

"I understand; I think I understand."

Goodboy continued. "I'm good at keeping secrets. But I'm going to let you in on something. Kristy has been told on more than one occasion she manages with too much generosity; that she gives her employees too much in bonuses and perks and that she should hold back more for rainy days. That makes good business sense, good capitalistic self preservation sense. But it doesn't line up with what's in her heart. You understand what I'm saying?"

Lola nodded, at that moment, not cognizant of his inability to see her through the phone.

"She could've played it safe and protected herself. But when we ran out of money on this Evap-X3 project, she mortgaged her house, borrowed on her personal savings and 401k's, and poured everything she had into the company to keep it afloat. Now we're standing on the verge of millions. Does it make sense for her to be smashed up and scattered in bits and pieces along the ridge of some lonely mountainside?"

"No," Lola quickly agreed.

"Then, I have to believe it hasn't happened and it's not going to happen. I have to believe that through God's grace or the alignment of the planets or the phenomenal luck of some drunken Leprechaun, good things will come in the end. Otherwise, what's the use?"

When Lola got off the phone, she began to cry. She was crying for the decision that was already in her heart. She didn't have a drunken Leprechaun. What she had was far more deadly ... a chest of splintered wood that could change the course of destiny for those willing to pay the price.

As she entered the storage facility, she was thinking, *How much this time?*

It didn't matter. Her robotic, trance-like, hyper-analytic, self-induced methodical mode had finally kicked in. Like the Mauretanians before her and the junkies on the street in Juárez and all the prisoner of desperation throughout the world, she was going to pay. She had to. How else were good things going to come in the end?

Carter Blue Airlines Flight 6336 lifted off from Springfield's Capital Airport at 7:48 am. It was only twenty minutes late, compared to the one hour delay that morning flights invariably logged in ... late, no matter the season, passenger load or weather conditions. There was something about the heavy business travel and gate preferences and runway protocol that always pushed Carter Blue to the back of the line.

Steve Swanson was too worn down to agonize over the decision management had made to sell off preferential gate positions to other airlines in exchange for built-in customer complaints and flight delays. After a grueling twenty-two hour schedule, hop-scotching across the eastern seaboard and up to Canada and back, Swanson needed every ounce of concentration to keep the Bombardier CRJ900's nose pointing toward the puffy clouds and blue sky.

Things would've been a lot better, grabbing the four hours of sleep in the Philadelphia International crew lounge as he had planned. But some adventurous jackass had gone to a cheap

Chinese buffet and ordered himself a serious dose of food poisoning. Management had asked Swanson to ferry an empty plane to Springfield, then fly the Thursday morning schedule to Las Vegas.

Besides the *fly till you die* motto in the cockpit, most pilots embraced another implacable saying regarding requests from management: *Just don't say no.*

Moving up the ladder meant being perceived as a team player. Swanson didn't know how he could refuse to ferry the plane to Springfield in a critical time of need.

To get through the ten and a half hour day still ahead of him, Swanson made up a little song in his head:

Hey, hey, hey ... Just ten and a half hours away.

You kept me from my wife and kid so sweet overtime you're going to have to pay.

And then, he would briefly close his eyes and see the $8,800 paycheck being deposited into his account.

When they landed at O'Hare International in Chicago, he changed the song: *Hey, hey, hey ... Just nine hours away.* At Milwaukee's General Mitchell Airport, with a two hour layover, he changed the song again: *Hey, hey, hey ... Just seven hours away.*

The little song not only helped him to whittle down the hours, but kept him from hearing the small voice in the back of his head that had told him not to take the schedule at all.

In the movies they'd say, "*I've got a bad feeling about this one.*" And yet, they'd go anyway. Swanson didn't have a bad feeling about the flight, but rather, the entire operation. Carter Blue pushed its pilots to the limit. Sooner or later, someone would have to pay.

Flying out of Milwaukee, headed for Denver International Airport, Swanson got a new plane, a larger Bombardier CRJ1000, and a new first officer, Janie Lacour. A ninety day rookie from

Houston, Texas, she was short and stocky with tomboyish features and dark, owl eyes. She came from a distinguished line of pilots. Her father was a decorated USAF pilot in Viet Nam, her grandfather, a P-47 Thunderbolt ace in World War II. Flying was in Janie's blood. So was talking.

From the time she entered the cockpit, she became a nonstop chatterbox, telling her life story and how her country and western singer boyfriend had run off with her younger sister.

Swanson suspected the man ran off just to have a little peace and quiet. It was either that or tie a huge gag over her mouth and lock her in the closet.

There were FAA rules about unnecessary chatter in the cockpit, especially during critical phases of the flight. On their approach to Denver International, Swanson finally had to admonish her to hold it down. Her answer to his request came back laced with the same arrogance as the earlier ones had, "Yeah, yeah, I know."

In Denver, the passenger manifest bloated to ninety-two, a few passengers shy of the CRJ1000's one hundred seat capacity. Thursday was a great day to get to Las Vegas and get a jump on the weekend crowd. Swanson was thinking it was an even better day to get back to his family in Toledo and get some much needed rest.

Climbing over Denver's snow-capped mountains on the final leg to McCarran International in Las Vegas, Swanson changed his song again: *Hey, hey, hey ... Just two hours away.* That's when he heard a loud band and intermittent vibrations, coming from the port side engine.

Janie's eyes widened. "What was that?"

Swanson didn't answer. In the back of his mind, he tried to recall the documentation he had read about the early software glitches connected to the control-by-wire rudder system. The plane was new, the documentation, scarce. And with so many flying hours packed into his week, his brain was too fried to regurgitate the critical details about minor malfunctions before the aircraft's

FAA certification.

Cruising at 520 miles per hour at 35,000 feet, Swanson turned on the autopilot.

"I'm going to walk to the back, maybe pinpoint the noise," he informed her. "DON'T change anything." It was his polite way of forbidding her from messing with the controls.

The Bombardier CRJ1000 was a next generation engineering masterpiece with advanced integrated avionics, a terrain collision avoidance system, digital weather radar system and integrated autopilot and flight management systems. The display control consoles were loaded with hundreds of gauges and buttons for fire detection, external lights, multiple engine ignition switches, advanced hydraulics and anti-icing protection. The center pedestal contained the redesigned spoiler levers, thrust levers, flap selectors, a radio tuning unit, audio control, aileron and rudder trim.

To the experienced pilot, the aircraft was a gift from heaven. To a three-month rookie, it was a nightmare from hell.

As soon as Swanson left the cockpit, Janie unstrapped her belt and reached over the console to retrieve the operating manuals and flight tutorials. They were located in a rack on the Captain's side, near the floor. Stretched out in such an awkward position, her elbow inadvertently brushed a controller on the console. Though she thought it was a thrust lever, she couldn't be sure. She had never been inside a CRJ1000. All she knew was the engines sounded differently now, as if there was a greater aerodynamic drag.

With the older CRJ700's, which she had flown many times, the sound would've been associated with reverse thrusters and the reduction of speed after touchdown. But with the new, totally integrated flight management system, the engines made all kinds of computer-initiated sounds ... adjusting for this, compensating for that. The plane was so sophisticated, it could almost fly itself.

Ironically, that was the very argument she had used to convince her supervisor to pencil her into the schedule. The pencil had turned into ink when a more experienced pilot, originally scheduled for the flight, was grounded in Memphis due to bad weather. It was just the break she needed to finally get on board.

Janie would've been perfectly content to let the magnificent, state-of-the-art aircraft fly itself, except for one small detail ... smoke. She could see a thin gray haze, drifting in from the lighting system just above her seat.

Unintended deployment of thrust reversers was a very serious emergency situation. If she had done what she was afraid she had done, the plane was slowing down, perhaps, to a point in which it over-stressed the system and induced an engine stall. There was no way the autopilot was going to handle such a catastrophic event.

If there was anything she had learned from her father and grandfather, it was not being afraid to take control. There were ninety-two passengers depending on her quick thinking. There were two previous generations of flyers, demanding she demonstrate the same impeccable courage they had.

She had heard the order given by Captain Swanson. But this was a different situation now. She turned off the autopilot and took full control.

How could she have known the brief plumes of smoke were nothing more than the handiwork of Carter Blue's laxidasical ground crew? Some careless maintenance mechanic had left a small candy wrapper in the compartment over the cockpit area. The wrapper had flopped around until it landed on a hot spot over the lights and melted in a trail of chocolate smoke. The smoke, in conjunction with the new engine sound and earlier bang was enough to give an experienced pilot the jitters. But for a three-month rookie, it was the prelude to a nervous breakdown.

During her months of training, an old veteran pilot from Kentucky had plastered her mind with one indelible rule: *Don't let one engine bring you down.*

He explained, "Modern-day aircraft are designed to fly on one engine if necessary. If you've got a bad apple, don't let it spoil the whole bushel."

She had seen the smoke, heard the bang and felt the loud vibrations. An engine on fire could lead to an entire plane on fire. In the back of her mind, there was only one responsible thing to do ... shut the bad-apple port engine down.

Swanson was headed back down the aisle toward the cockpit, when a young boy stopped him. No more than nine years old with frizzy blond hair and an excited smile, he inquired, "Are you the Captain?"

Swanson mustered a customer-friendly smile. "Yes. Yes I am."

"Then who's flying the plane?"

Swanson thought to himself, *a know-it-all motor mouth,* but answered, "My trustworthy sidekick".

The boy grinned, proudly. "I'm going to be a pilot one day."

"Well that's wonderful news. I'm sure you'll be a good one."

Swanson was about to walk off when the boy asked, "Can I have your autograph?"

Swanson wasn't used to people asking for his autograph. But, because he loved kids and relished the thought of telling his wife he had reached celebrity status, he reluctantly agreed.

The boy plowed around in the purse of the woman sleeping next to him and pulled out a pencil and paper. "That's my mother, Helen Stodomiere. I'm Joey, Jr. and my father and big sister are in the back. We have a kinda funny name like my grandmother. We're going to see her today."

As Swanson handed the signed paper and pencil back to the young boy, he felt the plane quiver, then heard the port engine shut off.

"Is there something really important I need to know about being a good pilot?" The boy inquired as Swanson was leaving.

"Yes. Never leave a rookie in charge." Swanson hurried toward the front.

Halfway down the aisle, a businessman stuck his head out. "Is everything alright?" Before Swanson could answer, the starboard engine shut down.

When Swanson finally opened the cockpit door, all kinds of alarms were going off. Override warnings flashed in red on three of the digital screens. The upper console was lit up like a Christmas tree.

Swanson hopped into the captain's seat. "What the hell have you done?"

With both engines gone, the plane was already losing altitude. The flight management system had initiated some kind of countdown that showed only fifty seconds left.

"I think I turned off the wrong engine," she whimpered. It was as close to accurate as she had been all day.

"Why on God's green earth would you do something so-" He was interrupted by another alarm.

His overworked mind finally began to realize why the sophisticated flight management system had started a countdown. He had only so many seconds left to safely initiate an emergency restart. Somehow, Janie had overridden the anti-stall device, forcing the plane into a dangerously low airspeed and angle of attack. There were just seconds left before the aircraft reached a point of negative lift and fell from the sky.

Desperately trying to regain speed, Swanson pitched the nose of the plane downward. If he could force enough wind through the blades in the turbine engines, he could try a rare windmill restart. It was a long shot. But it was the only shot he had.

At 20,000 feet, Swanson was gliding at 380 miles per hour, more than enough speed to try the restart. Over and over, he walked through the procedure. Over and over, the engines refused to respond. Even with the help of four small auxiliary powered assist units, the engines only whined like two disobedient brats.

Swanson finally turned to Janie and verbalized his nightmarish conclusion. "We've got core lock. These engines are done."

Janie's face turned blood red. Even a three-month rookie understood what core lock meant.

Veterans and rookies alike were fully aware that when an engine abruptly shut down at a high altitude, parts of the core had a tendency to cool at different rates and warp out of shape. Engine components often misaligned and no longer operated in sync. Seals broke and intricate metal pieces fused together. All that was left was a useless heap of titanium and steel.

Janie knew what core lock meant. It meant the airplane was no longer an airplane, but a heavy metal glider, headed for the ground.

Swanson contacted Air Traffic Control. "This is Captain Swanson of Carter Blues Airlines, Flight 6336. We have an emergency. Apparent flameout on both engines. Please advise on diversion airports currently available."

Janie looked at the list of nearby airports on the digital readout, and pointed to the two most feasible options. "Salt Lake International and Cedar City Regional."

The Air Traffic Controller concurred.

Swanson knew that Salt Lake City offered better emergency landing support. But observing the plane's rapid decent, Swanson didn't think he could make it that far. The Cedar City Regional Airport was the shoe-in choice for line-of-sight distance and speed. There was just one problem ... mountains.

As a boy, Swanson's class had gone on a hiking trip in Utah's Zion National Park. There were beautiful rivers, canyons and forests, unique plants and endangered animals, and blistering deserts that stretched for miles. But the one thing Swanson remembered most were the towering mountain regions in and around the park. The Panamint Mountain range was one of the highest in America. He would need to glide over its daunting peaks to reach the Cedar City Airport.

As they approached the jagged peaks, the sunlight glistened off the colorful rocks, presenting them as beautiful diamond steeples. The depressurized air was cool and fresh like a winter breeze, filtered by Alpines and Christmas snow. The passengers, who had been screaming in the back, now sat quietly subdued.

Swanson glanced over at Janie, her face, filled with sorrow and guilt. "You know the first time I flew into Baltimore, I missed the runway and almost tore down the tower."

She pushed out a modest smile. "How did you avoid it?"

"It happened to be one of those little 200's and I was able to recover in time."

"I guess, maybe, that's where they should've kept me ... flying the 200's."

"Don't be so hard on yourself," he reprimanded. "You did what you thought was best."

She looked at the mountains and back at the screens. "We're not going to make it, are we?"

He didn't answer. With mountains on all sides, they both knew the answer.

Swanson kept going over the details in his mind. There was something odd and inexplicable about the events that had led them to that point in time. It was almost as if the crash was meant to be.

A few seconds before the plane plunged into the mountainside, Swanson's mind switched to autopilot and changed the little song for him:

Hey, hey, hey ... We all died today.

Thursday morning, Lola awakened to the sound of whispering. Both, Johnny and Ruby, were standing over her bed.

She sat up straight, her head still swirling from the deep, asphyxiating sleep that had smothered her the night before. "What happened? What's wrong?"

They both looked over at the alarm clock. The green display had just changed to 10:05 am.

"We're checking on you, Babygirl. You're usually out of here by 7:00 am."

Her groggy eyes swelled with panic. "Oh my God! I'm late for work!"

Ruby stroked Lola's matted hair. "Did you have a bad night, Lolita?"

"How could she not have a bad night with all that loud racket," said Johnny.

"Racket?"

"Yeah, out in the woods. There must've been a thousand dogs or coyotes or something out there. You could hear them growling all night."

Ruby shook her head. "Not dogs. They roared like animals in the jungle."

Johnny shook his head. "I tried to tell your mama there's no circus in town. Maybe, it's some of those new cats the zoo brought in from overseas."

"The city zoo is on the other side of town, Daddy. We couldn't hear the animals way out here."

He grabbed his chin like Sherlock Holmes. "Unless ... some of them big slick African bastards escaped and the zoo people ain't telling nobody. I better not find out that's the case or I'll sue the hell out of them."

Ruby spotted a small chest sitting atop Lola's dresser. "Is that a new jewelry box, Lolita?"

Johnny cackled, loudly. "No, that's her prized treasure chest. The antique dealers didn't want it. The pawn shops didn't want it. Can't believe she's still hanging on to it."

Ruby strolled around to the other side of the bed. "May I look at it?"

"No, don't touch it!" Lola snapped.

A stark silence engulfed the room.

Johnny grimaced. "I think you need to have a little bit more respect for your mother."

Ruby placed her finger over his lips. "It's okay. I have been with child a few times myself. These things are expected."

"Sorry, Mama. It's just, I really need to get ready for work," Lola explained.

On their way out, Johnny tossed a brown envelope on her bed. "That's your little charity boy's ID package. I'm looking for all my money back just like we agreed."

An hour later, Lola sped down Interstate-55 on her way to work. Aware of her mother's curiosity, she had taken precautions not to leave the chest behind. She had tucked it safely away in her trunk. She hoped to return it to the Litchfield storage bin before the day was gone.

All the way into the office, she scanned the radio stations, searching for any indication of the damage she had caused. Besides a small apartment fire and a busload of children stuck in a construction ditch, it appeared no major tragedies had occurred. Maybe, the tree would give her a break this time. Maybe, the life-and-death exchange rate took into account the horrible toll on humanity the first wish had extracted. Maybe, the Juba Chest had been decommissioned by some great Mauertanian Spirit Man in the hereafter and didn't hear her desperate plea at all.

Who was she kidding? Even her mother and father had heard the ancient executioners, crying out from the forest. Something was stirring in the metaphysical world, something diabolically connected to her precious tiny pieces of bark.

If she could only remember the murky dreams that had paraded through her mind. Maybe, they would offer a clue about the events to come.

At a stop light a few miles from the office, an ice cream truck pulled up next to her. She gazed at the colorful promotion of delicious frozen treats, painted on the side panel. There was tangy grape and watermelon swirl and chocolate delight. But what caught her attention were the new blue bomb ice cream bars ... sleek blue bars on a stick that glistened with blueberry flavor.

Loving sweets and being pregnant at the same time, the craving should've overwhelmed her. Instead, Lola wanted to puke.

Gradually, she realized the blue, cylinder-shaped ice cream bars reminded her of the shiny, metallic blue caskets in her dreams. She had seen four of them lined up, side by side, in what appeared to be a pool of blood. The people standing near the caskets were looking at her with angry faces.

That was as much as she could remember. The rest was too fuzzy, too painful to pursue. She quickly shut down that part of her mind and quarantined it with a DO-NOT-ENTER sign.

Inside the RedFish Complex, she went straight to Goodboy's office. His elbows rested, precariously, on his desk, his exhausted face, buried in his hand. Looking up at her, his sad eyes telegraphed the latest news.

"The weather's cleared, but so far, not a trace of the plane. They're calling off the search this afternoon."

"How can they just give up?!!!" she protested.

"You have to remember. This whole thing started Monday night. This is Thursday. An insignificant little company plane doesn't command those kinds of resources."

"What can we do?" asked Lola.

He shook his head. "Right now, keep praying for a miracle. Tomorrow, we'll have to start looking at things in a whole different way."

For most of the day, the building was unusually quiet, the silence of a mausoleum before the next body was brought in. Then, just before closing time, the drama began to unfold.

Lola was on the phone in Kristy's office, trying to convince Johnny to make his doctor's appointment. That's when she observed two employees hurry past the glass window.

"I've got to go, Daddy."

She quickly followed them into the employee lounge. A crowd had already gathered. Their terrified faces were glued to the television screen.

A white-haired CNN news correspondent stood in front of

an airport entrance.

"IF YOU'RE JUST JOINING US, THIS WORD IN FROM THE NATIONAL TRANSPORTATION SAFETY BOARD. A CATER BLUE AIRLINES COMMERCIAL JET CARRYING NINETY-TWO PASSENGERS AND FOUR CREW MEMBERS HAS CRASHED IN THE MOUNTAINS JUST OUTSIDE OF CEDAR CITY, UTAH. I'M STANDING HERE IN FRONT OF THE CEDAR CITY REGIONAL AIRPORT WHERE THE PLANE HAD BEEN DIVERTED FOR AN EMERGENCY LANDING. APPARENTLY, FLIGHT 6336, ORIGINATING OUT OF SPRINGFIELD, MISSOURI, EXPERIENCED SOME SORT OF MECHANICAL PROBLEMS AND WAS UNABLE TO REACH THE DIVERSION AIRPORT HERE IN CEDAR CITY."

Jeff, one of the Evap-X3 technicians, looked at Lola. "Utah. Isn't that where Ms K's plane went down?"

Lola nodded, cautiously, saying nothing.

"I mean, come on. Do they have some kind of gremlin in those mountains, pulling airplanes out of the sky?" A lady from HR speculated.

No one answered.

Goodboy walked in and stood behind Lola. "Are you getting all of this?"

She nodded again.

The CNN correspondent invited an older, ruddy faced man with a thin mustache to stand next to him.

"I HAVE WITH ME RETIRED AIR FORCE COLONEL CHARLES BATES, THE LEAD NTSB OFFICIAL OVERSEEING THIS SEARCH AND RESCUE OPERATION. COLONEL BATES, CAN YOU BRING US UP TO DATE ON WHERE YOU ARE WITH THIS RESCUE?"

The colonel cleared his throat, quite eager to make his appearance on national television.

"WE'VE DISPATCHED MULTIPLE SEARCH AND RESCUE TEAMS TO THE AREA AND CONTINUE TO AUGMENT OUR EFFORT. AS WE SPEAK, BESIDES THE TWO BLACKHAWK SEARCH HELICOPTERS CURRENTLY ON LOCATION, WE HAVE THREE ADDITIONAL ASSIST HELICOPTERS IN ROUTE FROM THE CAMP WILLIAMS UTAH NATIONAL GUARD BASE IN RIVERTON. THEY'RE VERY FAMILIAR WITH THIS AREA. WE BELIEVE THEIR EXPERTISE WILL ENHANCE OUR EFFORT."

The CNN correspondent pulled back the microphone.

"I KNOW YOU'RE VERY BUSY OVERSEEING THIS CRITICAL OPERATION. BUT I HAVE ONE MORE QUESTION FOR NOW. WITH THE EVIDENCE YOU HAVE SO FAR, IS THERE A GENERAL FEELING ABOUT THE CAUSE OF THIS TERRIBLE TRAGEDY?"

"WAY TOO EARLY." The Colonel acknowledged. "WE KNOW FROM THE PILOT'S COMMUNICATIONS WITH THE CONTROL TOWER THE AIRCRAFT EXPERIENCED SOME KIND OF MECHANICAL DIFFICULTY. BEYOND THAT, WE'LL HAVE WAIT AND SEE."

Lola left the room as quickly as she could. She found the first stall in the ladies restroom and began to throw up.

Is there a general feeling about what caused this terrible tragedy? She could hear the news correspondent's question, unraveling the threats of her consciousness.

She knew the cause. So did the old Baobab tree. So did the great cloud of witnesses in heaven, looking down on murderers, carrying out their wicked deeds. The exchange rate had been set, the price, paid in full. Now, it was a matter of waiting to see if the perennial pieces of bark could deliver one more time.

Kristy Cutler was drifting in and out of consciousness when the loud explosion rocked the mountainside. With no more food or water, and the inside of the plane, reeking with the smell of death, unconsciousness was a precious refuge that transported her away from the gruesome realities of life.

She could dream of walking along a sandy beach, watching the roll of the blue-green surf, feeling the cool breeze, slithering through her hair. But most often, her attempt to escape took her to dark places, haunted by inexplicable circumstances ... wolves, sitting in the seats around her, ordering cocktails to go with their impending meal of human carcasses; or armies of maggots, crawling out of the unflushable restroom toilet.

The most vivid dream had come the previous night when she imaged an old African woman, surrounded by lions and tigers, holding on to the tail of the plane, keeping it from going over the cliff.

She had never been to Africa. Even though she realized the dreamscape was a supernatural highway that any intruder could travel, the images were totally surreal and unfamiliar. But if imaginary sojourners in shadowy dreams could keep her from sliding down the steep ramp of death, then kudos to her mind for concocting such a masterful ploy.

There was no doubt in her mind the plane would eventually go over. But with the wolves coming back day and night, Phillip kept telling her their chances for survival were better if they waited until the very last minute to leave.

Neither one of them knew whether the last minute would be too late. But with the loud sonic boom and the vibrations that nudged the fuselage closer to the edge, they both knew the last minute would be soon.

A short while after the explosion, Barlow looked at her with budding calculation. "I don't know what that was. But it just took away some precious equilibrium. If I had to guess, I'd say our little play house is going over in the next few hours."

She stared at him, quizzically. "Do you have a plan? Or is this your way of saying goodbye?"

"I have a plan, but it's risky."

She glanced at the open mouth of the plane, stretching into the abyss. "Compared to what?"

He took a deep breath, gathering his thoughts. "You remember when the Dell laptops had the problem with exploding lithium batteries?"

She nodded.

"With enough heat applied to the pressurized container that houses the electrochemically charged metals, they'll still explode."

"You're beginning to sound like my Evap-X3 technicians. But go on."

"We both brought laptops. If I can tie the two batteries together and make them explode next to the lip of this fire extinguisher,

I believe I can get the canister to explode and knock a bigger hole in the back of the plane."

She thought about it. "You said it was risky."

"Yes. We could set the entire plane on fire, including the jet fuel that's still in the engines. The explosion could jar the plane away from the rocks and send it over before we manage to get out. If we get out with no fire extinguisher, the wolves will probably have a field day. Do I need to go on?"

She quietly surveyed their options.

"There's something about sitting around and dying like senior citizens in an old folks home that just doesn't appeal to me. I'd rather try."

An hour later, Barlow had rigged the two batteries together, inside a metal ice container, and chained them to the mouth of the fire extinguisher. He and Kristy tore up strips of paper, clothing, and plywood from the liquor bar and soaked the concoction in alcohol from the first aid kit. Barlow opened the restroom door, placed the homemade bomb next to a jagged hole in the lower ridges, lit the cloth fuse and slammed the door.

There was something about their movement that attracted the wolves back. There were four this time, sticking their noses in the cracks, sniffing for a taste of human delight.

Barlow remembered something. There was an inflatable raft and a flare gun in a cabinet beneath the bar. He slid across the seats, retrieved the raft and ripped the flare gun out. In what seemed a millisecond to her, he had retreived the gun and gotten back to Kristy. He was holding her body close to the floor when the explosion finally went off.

The two-step battery-canister reaction sounded like an old pistol ... click, pow!!! ... but in supersonic motion. The restroom door blew off. And just as Barlow had predicted, the plane started its deadly slide.

They scrambled toward the huge hole in the fuselage.

Like a bully on a hockey league ice rink, Barlow pushed Kristy through the opening. He dove out behind her, flare gun in hand.

They watched in amazement as the old burnt cigar rumbled over the cliff. It seemed an eternity before the loud crashed echoed up the mountain's steep wall.

The explosion had driven the wolves into the underbrush. But Barlow knew they wouldn't stay away for long.

He pointed to a stair-step rock formation leading to a high knoll. "We've got to find a high place, maybe a tree or those rocks." He grabbed her by the arm. "Come on!"

Hovering high above the cliff in an Army Blackhawk UH-60, Lieutenant Max Walker, a rugged, black, razor-headed soldier's soldier, was on the radio with the Cedar City control tower. The crew had lowered him down on a cable into a deep ravine. There, he had observed the Carter Blue crash site first hand.

"Nothing but twisted metal and mangled body parts," he had sadly reported. With nightfall quickly approaching, and his knowledge of the treacherous terrain, he recommended they resume the rescue/retrieval operations the following morning.

That's when the pilot tapped him on the shoulder and pointed to the ground. "We've got survivors down there. But I don't know for how long."

Lieutenant Walker watched a man and a woman, running toward some rocks, a pack of seven or eight wolves in hot pursuit. The man turned and shot some type of orange flare which momentarily slowed them down. But within seconds, the hungry creatures had resumed the chase.

"Get me down there right now," ordered Lieutenant Walker.

Barlow heard the distant flapping above their heads, but didn't have time to look up. The wolves were a few yards away and closing. That's when he heard the repeated gun shots. The lead wolf tumbled forward in a puddle of blood. Then, a second one went down.

The pilot looked over at Lieutenant Walker, firing his pistol like a wild-west trick shooter. "I think that was an endangered species you just shot."

Lieutenant Walker blew the smoke from his barrel. "Well, in animal heaven, he's not endangered any more. Take me down as close as you can."

The gunshots and loud rotation of the helicopter blades drove the rest of the wolf pack back into the forest. Lieutenant Walker lowered a basket for Kristy, then for Barlow. Once they were on board, Kristy began to cry, hysterically. Barlow comforted her in his arms.

Lieutenant Walker inquired, "How'd you manage to get that far away from the crash site?"

Barlow explained, "That *was* the crash site until the fuselage went over the cliff."

"That can't be," said Lieutenant Walker. "The Carter Blue wreckage is at least two miles away."

Kristy and Barlow gave each other a puzzled stare. "Carter Blue???"

****

Lola, Goodboy and a handful of employees were still watching the television screen when the CNN correspondent came back on.

"WE'RE UPDATING OUR STORY NOW WITH A REMARKABLE TWIST OF EVENTS RELATING TO THE CATER BLUE AIRLINES CRASH. EARLIER IN THIS EXCLUSIVE BROADCAST FROM THE CEDAR CITY REGIONAL AIRPORT, WE REPORTED THE INITIAL ASSESSMENT BY CREW MEMBERS ON THE

GROUND THAT THERE WAS LITTLE HOPE RESCUERS WOULD FIND ANY SURVIVORS. BUT IN AN UPDATED REPORT, WE HAVE LEARNED THAT TWO SURVIVORS ARE BEING FLOWN HERE FROM THE CRASH SITE. AN EMERGENCY AMBULANCE IS STANDING BY TO TAKE THEM TO A NEARBY HOSPITAL."

Goodboy shook his head. "Thank God, at least somebody made it."

The newsman continued.

"NOW HERE'S THE VERY BIZARRE TWIST TO THIS WHOLE RESCUE OPERATION. THESE SURVIVORS ARE NOT FROM THE CARTER BLUE CRASH. I REPEAT. THESE SURVIVORS WERE NOT ON THAT CARTER BLUE AIRLINER THAT WENT DOWN EARLIER. IF YOU'LL REMEMBER, THIS WEEK, A SMALLER CESSNA JET REGISTERED TO THE GIANT INTERNET COMPANY, BEAN SYSTEMS, ALSO ORIGINATING OUT OF SPRINGFIELD, WENT DOWN IN THOSE SAME MOUNTAINS. SEARCH TEAMS HAD PRETTY MUCH GIVEN UP ON FINDING ANY SURVIVORS FROM THAT CRASH ... UNTIL A FEW MINUTES AGO."

Goodboy looked at Lola. "Did he say what I thought he said?"

Lola was speechless.

"Wait. Turn up the volume," ordered Fat Pat. "The helicopter is coming in."

The CNN newsman had the cameraman zoom in on the helicopter as it landed.

"THE MEDIA WAS NOT ALLOWED ON THE RUNWAY. BUT WE'LL SHOW YOU WHAT WE CAN FROM THIS ANGLE. AS YOU CAN SEE, A MAN AND A WOMAN, AND SOME MILITARY PERSONNEL ARE EMERGING FROM THE HELICOPTER RIGHT NOW."

Someone shouted from the back of the RedFish employee lounge. "That's Ms K!!!!!!!!!!"

The entire room erupted in euphoria. People applauded and cried and rolled on the floor. Goodboy grabbed Lola and gave her a huge hug.

"There's our miracle," he said, with tears in his eyes. "That's the only ending that made sense."

In the ambulance, Kristy looked over at Barlow. "What time is the stockholder's meeting tomorrow?"

"It starts at 8:00 am?"

"No, I mean our presentation on Evap-X3," she clarified.

"One, maybe, 1:15 pm. Why do you ask?" And then he saw the anticipation in her eyes. "Surely, you're not thinking about trying to-"

"I feel we owe it Herman and Otis. They died for this moment, you know. I'd like to put their contribution into the official written records. I want to go on that stage and call their names."

"Kristy," he tried to reason with her. "We're headed to a hospital in the backwoods of Utah. But for all practical purposes, we should be headed to a morgue. We're beaten up, dehydrated, traumatized by wolves. We both smell like chimpanzees. How are we going to be in San Francisco by tomorrow, ready to go on stage?"

She smiled, admiringly. "Unfortunately, I've had the chance to watch you operate. You always find a way."

He took a deep breath. "I don't even have a phone to contact anybody."

She nodded her head at one of the young EMS attendants. "He does."

Barlow looked at the attendant. "Please tell this lady that

cell phone on your belt is for official use only, and even if it wasn't, you really don't like strangers using your personal cell."

He removed the phone from the case and handed it to Barlow. "After what you two have been through, you can use my phone any day."

"Thanks a lot! "

At 8:00 am the next morning, in a parking lot across from the hospital, Kristy and Barlow crammed into an old Black Hawk scout helicopter Bradley Bean had sent. A few minutes later, they were buzzing over the Mojave Desert.

Barlow explained over the noisy rotors. "Do you remember the war movie, *Black Hawk Down*?"

Kristy nodded, affirmatively.

"Bradley liked the movie so much, he bought one of the original helicopters off the set."

"What did he do with it?" she asked.

"You're in it."

She peered down at the blistering desert floor. "Is this thing safe?"

"Probably not. It was mostly meant to be a conversation piece in the back yard of his mansion. But what can you say on such short notice?"

"Phillip! That's the desert down there. We could crash again."

"Don't worry, my dear. This time, I brought plenty of sun block."

****

The Intercontinental San Francisco Hotel was a magnificent translucent blue tower that soared thirty-two stories into the sky. Barlow pointed it out as the old Black Hawk whisked them over the city, finally landing on the restricted helipad atop the Bank of America Data Center.

As they rode the elevator to the first floor, Barlow explained, "Bank of America is going to catch hell for allowing us to land in the city. Local residents have voted to close these helipads for safety reasons. Now here we are, dropping in like unwanted Gooney Birds."

"Why did they let us land?" asked Kristy.

"They had a choice. Either let us land or Bradley would pull all of his money out of the bank."

A black limousine was parked in front of the bank building. The driver hustled them into the back seat and drove like a madman to the hotel. In a large, elegant suite on the thirtieth floor, no less than ten handlers waited for their arrival. There were custom tailors, high fashion dress designers, makeup artists, fragrance specialists, cue card makers, press consultants, and food and dietary experts.

With Kristy on one side of the room and Barlow on the other, it was like the simultaneous prep of two drunken prizefighters, sobering up to enter the ring. When the two of them emerged from the mayhem, Barlow had been custom fitted into a $2,000 blue Gieves & Hawkes wool suit. Kristy dawned a Cristóbal Balenciaga sculptured designer dress of almost the same color.

When they headed across the street to the Moscone West Convention Center, Barlow whispered to her, "I don't know which was worse, those handlers or the wolves. But seeing you in that dress makes it all worthwhile."

"You're not such a shabby crash victim yourself," she complimented.

"Are you ready for this?"

"As ready as I'll ever be," she replied.

He looked into her sparkling blue eyes. "After this is over, I'd like to take you to dinner, maybe, discuss that silver lining."

She pulled him close to her. "You can take me anywhere you want to take me. Just so we don't have to fly."

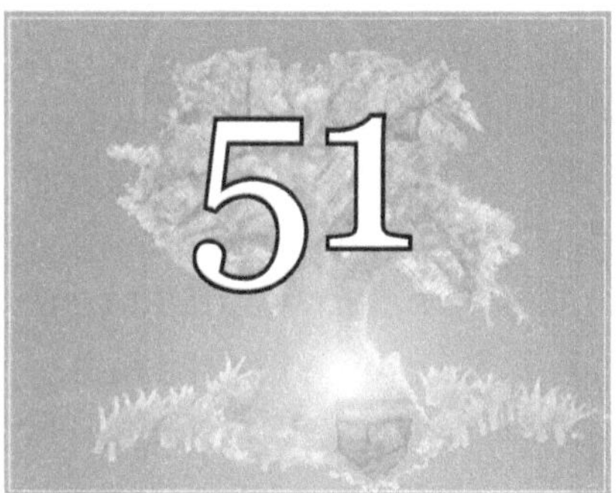

Lola suspected there was something Dr. Fox wasn't telling her.

After a romantic night at Nicholas' grandmother's house, getting reacquainted with the affectionate embrace of her husband-to-be, Lola had gotten up early and gone into the clinic to repeat some previous prenatal tests. The long, jackhammer syringe that had ousted Nicholas from the room was back again, along with several new procedures relating to unspecified irregularities.

Unspecified irregularities....

Lola didn't like the sound of that. Dr. Fox took pride in knowing her patients. She had never used big words like that before, at least, not with Lola. And why couldn't the tests have waited until her scheduled appointment a week from then?

Goodboy had told her to maintain a level head, not just about work, but everything. Having lost a child, prematurely, he was well aware of the negative effects anxiety and stress could have. Lola didn't want to reach his level of awareness. Despite the many years since his tragic ordeal, she could still see the pain in his eyes.

Besides, she had a big day ahead of her.

It was Johnny's 50th birthday. She and Nicholas were going over to the lake house to help him celebrate. He didn't need his daughter's worried face depressing him, especially if it pertained to his grandchild. He'd end up wanting to shoot somebody.

Lola decided to forego all of the murky medical speculation about the doctor's request and just wait and see.

Nicholas' grandmother's house was like a beautiful country cottage, stark white with blue window shutters, a front porch, an old fashioned chain link swing and a white picket fence all around. The three spacious bedrooms, custom oak paneling and shiny hardwood floors were a reminder of the post WWII boom days when life was sweet and promise filled the air.

When Lola turned into the driveway, she saw Nicholas standing on the porch, soaking in the sun and remembering his days in the neighborhood.

He pointed to a wood frame house across the street. "Two bullies lived over there, Joe and Bobart. Every time I came to stay with my grandmother, they'd take my bike, or try to beat me up. Joe got killed in the Gulf War and I hear Bobart has multiple sclerosis. I wonder if I could find Bobart, and while he's in his wheelchair, beat him down to the ground?"

"Such a big brave *peleón*," she declared. "Wanting to beat up a man in a wheelchair."

"I wouldn't do it. But I was standing here thinking how awesome the mind is. It remembers everything we do, everything that's done to us. Seems like it was just yesterday I was making a mad dash to the park a few blocks away before those blood thirsty hooligans came outside."

She kissed him on his cheek. "Sometimes it is best not to remember what we have done. It will only slow us down."

He quickly changed gears. "How was the doctor's office?"

"Fine. She moved next week's appointment out two weeks. All of the test results should be back by then."

"You did tell her I was willing to come this time, but you wouldn't let me?"

"No, because then, who would we have to bash around?"

At that moment, Lola's cell phone rang.

"Lolita?"

"Yes, Mama, it's me."

"Can you pick up fifty candles for your father's cake?"

"I will, Mama."

"Okay, two o'clock. Don't be late" ... which meant be thirty minutes late.

Lola hung up, then turned to Nicholas. "I can't believe how good my mother's English is getting. Buying that little translator box was a great idea."

"Actually, your father bought it. But I'll take credit for the idea. At this low, jobless point in my life, I'll take anything that swells my ego."

"How about this? You're a natural problem solver. I knew that the first day I met you."

He scratched his chin, approvingly. "My ego is listening. Go on."

"My book says I should sleep with a problem solver every night."

"It did?" His face perked up.

"No. But there's room in the back for notes. I'll just pencil it in."

On the way to the lake house, Nicholas' truck radio was tuned to a popular talk station. When the announcer mentioned the Carter Blue plane crash, Lola reached over and turned it off.

Nicholas glanced at her, curiously. "Everyone in town's been talking about those strange plane crashes. So far, I haven't heard your take on it."

"If it's all the same to you, I'd rather not talk about it. This week has been so stressful. I'd just like to let my mind relax."

"Sure. I just thought since you had the inside story, you'd have more to say," he pressed.

"Okay, I'll say this. Things happen for a reason. You hope it's for a good reason. The main thing is Ms K is safe and will be returning next week."

They were both silent for a while. Finally, he rolled down his window and pointed to a sign. "Look! Snippy, pregnant, she-devil bitches wanted. Apply within."

Lola tried to appear serious, but shook with laughter. "That sign did not say that. And I am going to tell my daddy what you called me."

Johnny couldn't have cared less what he called her. He was too busy coercing them to load the candles on his cake so he could blow them out and chug down a big hunk.

"I'm half a century old. I don't know how much longer I'll be on this earth. I'd like to get a piece of cake before I go to my grave. Is that too much for a black man to ask in this great country of ours?"

And then he began to sing his old slavery song.

"Hold on, Daddy!" Lola finally got all the candles lit. She placed the huge white-icinged, cream-filled monstrosity on the counter. They all started singing happy birthday.

Johnny didn't wait. Before they could finish, he took a deep breath and blasted the cake with a blizzard of wind and spit. All of the candles went out. They all began to cheer and applaud.

Half way through his first double decker slice, his jaws, churning like a giant cement mixer, he paused to open his cards. There were three: One from each, Ruby, Lola and Nicholas.

Ruby's card was brief but heart-wrenching:

It's your birthday, but my happiest day. In fact, being with you, everyday is my happiest day........I love you.

Lola reached over and handed him a small red gift-wrapped box. "Open it. It goes with Mama's card."

He opened it to find a new red and pink silk negligee with black straps.

"Wowwww!" he shouted.

Ruby smiled. "Since it is too little for you to wear, I guess I will be forced to step into the plate."

"Step up to the plate," Lola corrected.

"Don't back-talk your mama," he scolded her. "And answer this one question." He was still gawking at the scant piece of lingerie.

"What question, Daddy?"

"How long before this party is over and you deadbeats leave the premises?"

"We're not going anywhere," declared Lola, handing him the two cards from her and Nicholas. "Read them together."

He opened Nicholas' card first. It was all handwritten:

I feel privileged to be a part of your birthday celebration. It's not often you get a chance to meet the great artist who painted the masterpiece. Lola is your masterpiece and mine to be. Not a day goes by without her mentioning all that you have poured into her. Thank you and Ms Ruby for her. And thank you for welcoming me into the family. P.S. ... As you know, Lola can be quite stubborn and unruly. From time to time, I may need to borrow your cane.

Everyone was laughing. Johnny reached over and handed Nicholas his black walking cane. "My advice is to get you some practice licks in right now, knowemsayin'?"

Lola grabbed the cane from Nicholas. "Daddy! You're supposed to be on my side."

Johnny opened Lola's card, also handwritten:

You didn't have to take me in, but you did. You didn't have to love me and protect me and keep me, but you did. You didn't have to make me welcome to all that you had, but you did. You didn't have to do right by my mother, but you did. You did because you have a big heart, the same heart you have passed on to me and I will pass on to your grandchild. Thank you for making me the proudest daughter on this side of the Rio Grande.... I love you.

Johnny tightened his lips, trying to fight back his emotions.

Lola handed Johnny another wrapped box. "This is from me and Nicholas."

He opened it to find a new Apple iPhone with multiple, attachable gadgets.

"Lola says you look at a lot of pictures and video," said Nicholas. "This is your best bet."

Johnny smiled with approval. "I've heard about these and seen Babygirl treat hers like a gold bar from the Mint. How long will it take to teach me to use it?"

Nicholas slid over on the sofa next to him. "It's pretty simple. We can start right now."

As they rummaged through the box for batteries and chargers, Lola stepped into the bathroom and made a call. When she returned, they had the phone up and running.

A few minutes later, the phone rang. Johnny's eyes narrowed. "You pressing some kind of remote?"

"No, Daddy," Lola explained. "It's ringing. You must have

a call."

Johnny pressed the button. "Hehh-Hello?"

"Johnny?" His brother's voice came on the line.

"ArchieV? Is that you?"

"In the flesh."

"Why you disgusting old slug! How'd you get this number?"

"Your daughter said I'd better talk to you before the people at the graveyard found out you escaped."

"It's been a long time, man. How you been?" Johnny headed up the stairs to the roof, the phone pressed tightly against his ear.

Lola looked at Ruby. "They have not talked for ten years or so. He's very active in the church and said something about Daddy's line of work, and well, things got out of hand."

Nicholas frowned. "You never really told me what kind of work your father was in."

"For a long time he worked for the Mafia," she casually informed him.

Nicholas chuckled at Lola's witty sense of humor. But no one else was laughing.

Realizing she was serious, he swallowed hard and pressed on his palpitating heart. "You know, I really don't like talking shop on the weekend."

Minutes later, Johnny came down from the balcony. "That was my older brother. When my father ran off, he was the only father I knew."

And for the first time, Johnny began to cry.

He sat on the sofa, trying to compose himself.

Finally, he forced out a piece of his heart. "You don't know what all of this means. I spent years running from a family, fool that I was. Now, I can't image my life without one. Thanks. Thanks for everything." And then he went into the bathroom to finish out his cry.

When he finally returned, he reminded them, "This coming Friday, I'm taking your mother to BIG EASY Burgers. I hear they've put in a dance floor, a domino and bingo section, and added some new Cajun recipes straight from the heart of New Orleans. I'm buying. You two are welcome to come."

Lola thought for a moment. "Sorry, Daddy. They're having a big Welcome Home dinner for Ms. K Friday night. Maybe another time?"

Nicholas perked up. "I love Cajun food. What time are you going?"

Lola pinched hard on his ear. "No way! You are going with me. It's the first time I get a chance to show off my fiancé and the reason my stomach is poking out like this. I'm getting tired of those old ladies in human resources whispering under their breath."

Johnny stuck out his chest. "You tell them ole biddies you carrying Johnny Howard's grandchild. And if they don't put a lid on it, I'll come over there and bash in their heads like watermelons."

****

A few miles down Interstate-55, Silas Penrow plotted his own brand of head-bashing. Cooped up in an old storage shed where, for almost six weeks, he had observed Johnny's discrete activities, he was now ready to make his move.

Penrow had never been on a case this long, especially one that had taken him on so many unexpected twists and turns. He had killed a goofy Cadillac salesman and a drunk Texas clown. He had been shot in the face with nails and in the back with bullets. He had escaped from a sadistic hospital nurse, been chased by a killer tornado and led on a wild goose chase by the tar baby and his girlfriend, all over the countryside.

He was supposed to be like Magnum PI, breaking into

exclusive high-rise offices, snooping around in million dollar corporate files. Instead, he found himself homesteading in an abandon storage shack, eating sardines and crackers and watching the old gravel road for Johnny's Deville to come rolling out of the forest.

Although he was out of money, he had the good sense not to ask the mob for an advance. And although Raymond had killed DeLeon for dragging his feet and making mistakes, he seemed content to give Penrow ample time to get things right this time.

The good news was that Penrow had watched Johnny long enough to observe a pattern. Each Friday night, Johnny and his girlfriend went out to eat somewhere. Penrow was betting this Friday they'd do the same.

He had already called Raymond and requested the backup he needed. Now, it was just a matter of pulling it all together and then watching the big tar baby go down.

The week seemed to fly by.

On Monday Lola received word from the Springfield Airport Authority that RedFish had won the bid. When she went up to John Bossley's office to thank him for attending the airport meeting, he was already waiting for her. As soon as she walked into his office, he handed her a box of chocolates and a card.

"Open it!" he ordered with a big smile.

The card was a one-liner: *WHEN I'M WRONG, I'M WRONG.*

"I'm not sure who I thought you were. But you're not that person," he said. "I wanted to apologize."

"Chocolates!" Lola's eyes sparkled. "You really know how to seduce a pregnant woman. Thanks. And thanks for representing the company at the airport meeting. We won the job, you know."

"I suspected we would. The guy at the meeting ... Jay Potter?"

"I received the message from him, yes," she said.

"He's an old friend of Kristy's. When he walked me out, he pretty much let the cat out of the bag. He even mentioned that Trippple-Saw had tried to push their way in at the last minute."

Lola attempted to look surprised. "Trippple-Saw?"

"Yeah. It was laughable. Seems their bid was all bloated and out of whack. I can't tell you how good it feels to see their rumps on the ground for a change."

Good job, Shannon! Lola thought to herself. The little pointed-nosed spy was probably somewhere on an idiot stick, roasting over an open flame.

Lola spent most of the day lining up resources for the airport job. That afternoon, on her way to her car, she spotted Raúl in the parking lot.

She beckoned him over.

"Come give your baby-mama a hug," she teased.

"Don't play with me," he warned. "Fat women are getting raped every day."

She looked at her reflection in the car window. "Ahh mama mia. It is true. Too bad I will not be able to get my *muy grandes* fingers into this little envelope to give you your papers."

His eyes lit up. "You got my papers?!"

"Maybe. And maybe the secret of the envelope will die with the fat woman."

"Oh, you must've misunderstood me, my pretty little fine beautiful *señorita*. I was simply talking about the awful crime in this city," he quickly regressed.

"Oh, I see. I feel so much better now." She reached into the brown envelope. "These are the papers you will need."

He stared at the birth certificate, driver's license and social security card. "These look like the real thing."

She explained. "In a way they are real. Some of these comes from government workers who run the printing machines."

He smiled. "Like foxes in the hen-house. Cool."

"You must memorize the information and use it over and over again. You are this person now, until you die ... or until they deport you."

"Or..." His mind floated for a while, soaking in the possibilities. "Until I go to Washington DC and push that amnesty law past them rednecks in Congress."

Lola cackled, loudly.

"What's wrong? You don't think I could get elected?" he asked.

"You could. I just don't think you could pass the background check."

He looked at his phony documents and they both shook with laughter.

She handed him three hundred dollars. "This will cover your books and enrollment fee at the Litchfield Education Center on Union Ave. They offer the GED, ESL and tutoring for the college entrance exam."

He handed her two hundred back. "I already have two hundred saved."

She tried to hand it back. "What about gas and meals? You'll be going there three nights a week."

"It's already handled, okay."

She shook her head. "Stupid Mexican pride."

He turned his neck from side to side like a bobble-head toy. "Takes one to know one."

He started to walk away and then turned around. "Hey Lola."

Lola was halfway into her car. "Yes."

"*Gracias, amiga*. I won't let you down."

****

Tuesday at noon, Lola walked into Goodboy's office. "You left a voicemail you needed to see me."

"Yes, have a seat. Take a load off." He pointed to one of the deep cushioned chairs in front of his desk.

"Load off?" She flopped down like a mother goose. "So I guess I look fat to you too?"

"It's the beauty of birth. That's what I used to tell my wife. And then I'd change the subject."

"It's not fair," she whined. "Men should have to carry the baby too."

"I totally agree," said Goodboy. "That's another thing I did. When my wife was pregnant, I agreed with everything she said."

"You're hopeless, just like Nicholas. Tell me what you wanted to talk about."

"You, Lola. I want to talk about you."

Lola slowly scooted up in her chair. "Yes?"

"I've been on the phone with Kristy most of the morning. She stayed in California to finish structuring our deal."

"How did it go?"

Goodboy handed Lola a sheet of paper with some confirmation number on it. "Look at the very bottom of the page."

Lola saw it, but couldn't believe it. "Does this say $10,000,000."

"Ten million," he confirmed. "That was wired into our account today. It's a deposit on a one-hundred-million-dollar deal. And that's only for one year. After that Bean Systems will have to renew, or maybe buy the patents out right."

"That's amazing!" said Lola.

"No, what's amazing is that it almost didn't happen at all. You know what pushed it over the top?"

She shook her head, "No."

"You did, Lola," he reminded her. "Well, you and your father's wiener roast. At that point, we were stuck in the mud. Do you remember?"

"Kinda."

"Here's the thing. Since you've been here, you've been a tremendous asset to this company. I've never seen anyone adapt so quickly. We're about to double, maybe even triple in size. I want to know if you've given any thought to your future."

"My future?"

"Yes. Where do you want to go? What do you want to do here? You're the Operations Manager now. But if we go national, there will be two or three Operations Managers. Kristy is going to want to move you up. But up to what?"

"I-aahh, I had not thought about it."

"That's fine," said Goodboy. "But I want you to start thinking about it. By the time you have this baby and come back, it's going to be a whole new ball game."

Lola's heart was pounding, wildly. Her future was soaring into outer space. "Thanks, Goodboy. I will give it some thought, I will."

"By the way, Kristy wanted me to pass on the new numbers for your salary." He took out a pen and paper and wrote it down.

Lola's mouth fell open. "Is this right? There must be a mistake."

"No mistake. That's $130,000 per year, plus you'll share in the bonus structure with the other teams. It begins immediately."

"Oh my God!"

"What's wrong?" inquired Goodboy.

"My fiancé. When he sees this, he's going to beat me to death."

****

On Wednesday afternoon, two ladies from the planning committee came into Kristy's office. Lola was sitting there, going through some papers. They both appeared nervous, trying to figure out who would speak first.

Lola smiled. "Can I help you ladies?"

The older lady, with streaks of gray and a withering face, spoke first. "We were just a little concerned. We've been doing all this planning for the *Welcome Home* dinner this Friday and no one's seen Ms K. Is she coming back?"

"She is on her way back right now. But it is going to take a while. She is on the AMTRAK train."

The younger woman squinted. "She's riding a train all the way from Utah?"

"Not exactly Utah. But yes, a train. After crashing in the mountains, it will probably be a while before she is ready to board a plane again."

The older lady thought about it. "I guess trains are safer, if you don't count that awful collision over in Litchfield."

The younger woman shook her head. "My husband's brother was killed in the accident ... twenty-two year old bakery truck driver. What a waste. He had his whole life ahead of him"

Lola remained silent, staring out of the window, not wanting their eyes to meet hers.

Finally, the older lady reported, "We have just one last decision to make."

"Yes."

"Toward the end of the banquet, we want to play some music and have Ms K dance."

"Not a wild disco dance or anything embarrassing," the older lady clarified. "But something salutatory, like a waltz of victory."

The younger woman threw both hands into the air with proud dramatization. "Yes. Miraculous survival. Victory over death and now, her triumphant return."

The older lady's face filled with compassion. "The problem is Ms K's husband is deceased. And as far as we know, she won't have a date. Henry will probably bring his wife. He always brings his wife to these kinds of functions. Why she has to be..." The older lady could no longer hide her crush on Henry.

The younger woman cleared her throat. "If we can stay focused long enough, we'd like to find someone to dance with Ms K? Someone with a little class who won't step all over her feet?"

Lola pondered for a while, then smiled. "I have just the person for you."

She waited until they had left, then got on the phone. "Yes, I need the number for the Bean Systems office in San Mateo, California."

****

On Thursday, Lola took a half-day off. She needed to find a dinner dress that would somehow make friends with her bulging stomach and not look like a bedtime robe. Having spent most of the week at Nicholas' grandmother's house, she also needed to get by the lake house to talk to Johnny. The throbbing in his abdomen had gotten worse. Yet, he still resisted a trip to the doctor.

Late that afternoon, Johnny and Lola stood on the lake house balcony, looking out toward the forest. Like a prize eagle, the little orphan red bird perched atop Johnny's shoulder, eating from his hand.

"It's just a matter of time before this little fellah blows this joint and starts his own family in the trees. I hope his kids don't worry the hell out of him like some human kids do."

"I'm just saying, Daddy. It wouldn't hurt to go in and, at least, find out what's wrong. Then you would know what you are dealing with."

"And then what?" he snapped. "Start taking a dozen more pills every day? Maybe, I could give them back their defective kidney and have them stick my name back on the waiting list."

"So what is your solution? Just do nothing?" she scolded him.

"My solution is to live, knowemsayin'? Take every day that's given to me and squeeze the most out of it. I've never been this happy, Babygirl. I'm not letting the doctor take that away."

"But the doctor may know of a cure for you," said Lola.

"What's in his head can stay in his head. But I'm not letting it get in my head and mess with my groove."

Recognizing his deep seated fear, Lola finally relented. "So what do you want me to tell Dr. Campbell?"

"Tell him I appreciate everything he's done. And he's welcome to any and all of my inner parts, once I stop breathing. But at this point, I got my own medical advice."

"What is that, Daddy?"

"Wash down two painkillers with a shot of Johnny Walker Red, eat a hunk of leftover birthday cake and go to bed next to the most beautiful woman in the world, the one that puts a smile on my face everyday."

It was after dark when Lola finally left the lake house, headed back to Nicholas' place. Cruising down Interstate-55 near the intersection of Southwind Drive, she would've cringed to know how dangerously close she had come to seeing Silas Penrow, face-to-face.

At a sleazy, rat-infested roadside motel, Penrow patiently waited in his black Navigator for his army of killers to arrive.

Just before 9:00 pm, a gray Lincoln pulled into the motel driveway, followed by a Durango SUV. Penrow flashed his lights, then led them to the back side of the motel where he had already reserved two rooms. Four men got out.

The black-haired Italian giants had become familiar figures to Penrow. Lofingers and the other thick-necked hulk had been present at Penrow's meeting with Raymond. During the entire meeting, they had seemed eager to find a reason to slit his throat, even appeared disappointed when Raymond sealed the deal. The other two men, slowly exiting the Durango, were new faces, if you wanted to call their stark, ruddy mugs, faces.

The driver, Bobby Tocco, was a short, stocky Detroit native with a gruesome reputation with the stiletto. Rumor had it he took great pride in cutting *snitching* tongues out before he pumped his victims full of lead.

The other man, whose recessed eye sockets and thick lips resembled a black and white clown's mask, was known around Chicago as The PineSol Guy, or in closer circles, PineX. His penchant for personal hygiene earned him the PineSol name.

The moment he got out of the Durango, he bathed his long fingers in Germ-X hand sanitizer. The X in PineX, however, didn't refer to his perennial pump bottle, as some outsiders mistakenly believed. Rather, it reflected his love for eXplosives. His black satchel was so packed with dynamite, C-4 and grenades, no one dared offer to help him carry it inside.

They all piled into the first room to discuss their strategy.

With the flimsy double beds loaded down with an odd assortment of bags and cases, Lofingers reached into his suitcase to remove two bottles of booze. Bobby Tocco went for the bourbon. Everyone else filled their plastic cups with Scotch.

By the time all of the bags were emptied, the room resembled a National Guard armory. PineX even strapped on a belt holding two huge black Pinapple grenades.

The bizarre assembly of firepower and brute skills reminded Penrow of the day all of the great hunters had come to town to kill Bolo Ash. Their mere presence had been a testament to the legendary whitetail buck's remarkable cunning and unbelievable ability to stay alive.

So it was with the tar baby from Chicago. For years, with the luck of a hundred Leprechauns carrying a thousand rabbit feet, he had somehow outmaneuvered the greatest killing machine in the world.

But now, luck had run out. The brutal ending was chiseled in each man's face. They synchronized their watches and chugged down another pre-celebratory round. This time tomorrow, the tar baby from Chicago would be staring at the ceiling in somebody's morgue.

Friday morning, there was a commotion in the hallway, and then someone started to applaud. Lola stepped out of Kristy's office in time to see her long-lost boss, bombarded by hugs and kisses and cheers. A crowd followed her down the hallway.

Kristy walked up to Lola and threw her arms around her. "Thanks, Lola. Thanks so much for holding down the fort."

Lola started to cry.

Kristy turned to the rest of the employees. "Thank you all. Thank you for your prayers and well-wishes. And thank you for believing in this company when the chips were down. I'll have more to say. But for now, I need to get back to work before Lola issues me a pink slip. See you tonight."

Inside the office, Kristy flopped down in a chair in front of her desk.

Lola sat down beside her. "How do you feel, Ms K?"

"After crashing into a mountain, hanging over a cliff for a week, negotiating terms with one of the shrewdest men on the planet and enduring a fifty hour train ride back to Springfield, I would say a stroke and long-term hospitalization would be in order."

"But you look great," Lola observed. "Is that a new hairstyle and makeup?"

"It's something the handlers pushed on me in San Francisco."

"Handlers?"

"It's a long story, Lola. For now I'll just say Midwest boredom is the most heavenly feeling in the world. It's so good to be back home."

****

It was after 5:00 pm when Lola got back to Nicholas' grandmother's house. She had intended to leave work early, allowing herself plenty of time to get dressed for the banquet. But bringing Kristy up to date on all of the changes that had transpired during her absence had taken longer than expected.

Lola found Nicholas in the bedroom closet, staring at his black, semi-formal tuxedo.

"Why do I have to wear a tuxedo to a construction company dance?" he complained.

"First of all, it's not a dance. It's a dinner. Secondly, the man at the suit shop told me this is not really a tuxedo like the ones they wear to the opera. It is a regular suit cut like a tux. It has no ... how you say ... cummerbund, just a bow tie."

"Looks like a tux to me," he argued.

"And third-"

"That's thirdly," he corrected, trying to scramble her thoughts.

"Okay, thirdly, RedFish is more than a construction

company. We just signed a $100,000,000 deal with Bean Systems in California."

"*We* signed ... *we* signed?" he tried to mock her. "How much of that was your part?"

"A hundred and thirty thousand."

He looked at her with astonishment, then grabbed a large coat hanger from the rack. "Oh hellllll no!" He tried to sound just like Johnny.

He chased her into the living room where they stumbled onto the sofa. "You're telling me they gave you a $130,000 bonus?"

"No, no," she tried to stop laughing. "It's my salary now."

"You're telling me they're paying you $130,000 a year."

"Plus bonuses," she added.

"Where are those phony documents Johnny bought? I'm turning you into the immigration people, myself."

"I thought you would be happy for us," she whined.

"Not when I'm on probation and not making a dime."

"Okay, okay. I want to make a deal," she said.

"I'm listening."

"If you promise not to be upset about my salary, I will give you one wish, anything you want."

"Anything?"

"Well, anything within my reach," she clarified.

He pondered a moment. "Let me think about that one. I'll get back to you real soon."

On the way over to the State House Inn, Nicholas turned to Lola. "I've decided on my wish."

"Yes?"

"I didn't want to say anything, but my parents are not happy with our arrangement at my grandmother's house."

"You mean, because we are not married?"

"Yes. I told them we were getting married in Oklahoma next month. But they're planning a vacation to Europe and would most likely be out of town. What I'd like to do is have our family minister marry us right here in Springfield before my parents leave."

"We will miss our jar of magical berries," she pouted.

"But, you'll do it for me?"

Lola's heart melted. "You are very kind and considerate. That is why I am marrying you." And then she smiled. "That is why I am marrying you ... in Springfield."

****

At 7:05 pm, Johnny looked at his watch. "Come on, baby, let's go. I'd like to get there before a big swarm of flies suck all the sweet Cajun juices out of my burger."

Ruby stepped out of the bedroom in a sparkling blue miniskirt and diamond-studded white blouse.

Johnny's eyes bucked. "Why didn't somebody tell me my wife wasn't feeling well and Jennifer Lopez was taking her place?"

Ruby smiled, proudly. "You like, yes?"

"OOOOHHH yeah!"

"Lolita found it while she was out shopping. She said you had a lot of friends at the burger place that would be seeing me for the first time."

For a second or two, he considered Lola's thoughtfulness. "I might have to knock a little something off your daughter's outstanding bill for this one."

"No need to. I am rewarding back her kindness with services."

"Services?"

Ruby walked Johnny over to her painting area near the window. She pointed at a new canvas. "What do you see?"

He studied the green grass and tall trees. "Looks like some kinda field."

"Look in the center."

Johnny immediately spotted the deep hole.

Ruby explained. "This is Lolita's perfect hole she dug with the big machines. You might say she found her true self in that hole, the self that America wanted to overlook."

Johnny shook his head. "I remember."

"She will hang this hole on her wall so she will always, always remember her ... how you say ... *metaforess*."

"Metamorphosis," he corrected.

"Yes, that is what our smart college daughter called it."

"This beautiful one-of-a-kind piece on her office wall?" he tried to clarify.

Ruby nodded. "I think so."

"Oh helllll no!" said Johnny. "If those people over at RedFish want a high class painting by a famous Mexican artist, hanging on their wall, they're gonna have to pay."

Ruby blushed. Hearing Johnny call her *famous* sent chills down her spine. Within the few second it took for the sensible side of her brain to kick in, even she believed him.

Every day, he whispered her usefulness into her ear, just as he had promised. He made her feel like somebody ... his somebody. Not even her back door status and life on the run could take that away.

Ruby rubbed up against him, allowing the sweet fragrance of her perfume to drown his nostrils. She kissed him on the jaw. "I love you, Johnny. Little Lolita loves you too. Maybe you will still knock a little something off her bill, yes?"

Johnny took a hard swallow. "Right now I'm thinking we forgive the whole damn debt."

The ballroom at the luxurious State House Inn was packed with friends, employees and subcontractors, alike. Local news media cameras crowded the aisles, capturing footage for their late night broadcast.

The story of the crash had garnered national attention. Some local curiosity-seekers attended just to see how the only Springfield survivor of two plane crashes looked. Something was odd and screwy and divinely inexplicable about the whole series of events. No one except Lola could say why.

Lola and Nicholas sat at a VIP table in front of the stage next to Goodboy and his lovely wife, Carolyn. Several other staff members, including John Bossley and his wife, joined them.

"So what do you, Nicholas?" asked John Bossley in a light-hearted exchange.

"I'm just a deadbeat right now," Nicholas replied.

Lola kicked him hard under the table.

"He is a manager for a national hardware chain in the Kansas City district," she tried to clean things up. "He thinks being on leave makes him a deadbeat."

Goodboy intervened. "I'd love to be a deadbeat. But my wife keeps putting these envelopes on my side of the dresser; you know, the ones that come in the mail each month letting you know they're about to cut off your electricity and water?"

"Yeah, well being a quick-thinking Springfield native, born and bred in the Midwest, I was able to solve that problem," boasted Nicholas.

John Bossley perked up. "What did you do?"

Nicholas smiled, shamelessly. "I had a garage sale and sold the dresser."

The whole table roared with laughter.

Goodboy looked at Lola. "I like him, Lola. I think he's a keeper."

****

When Johnny pulled up in front of BIG EASY Burgers in his shiny Deville, he was astounded by the changes.

The old wooden building, reminiscent of a large 7-11 Store, had been totally remodeled. The exterior sparkled with new psychedelic blue paint and handcrafted murals reflecting the good life on Bourbon Street. The tattered oak door that crunched like a sick moose each time a customer came in had been replaced by revolving glass carousel doors that blinked red, yellow and green. A thick strip of red, diamond flex carpet had been painted into the sidewalk, offering the illusion of entering a fancy New Orleans hotel.

They had even added valet parking.

Johnny flipped the young black attendant his keys ... with

a warning. "Any new scratches could result in years off your life, young man. Take care of her and I'll take care of you."

Like a proud warrior, Johnny entered the building, Ruby's arm, tucked tightly under his. A squatty, middle-aged man with a beard and dark shades shouted from behind the bar. "Oh hell. There's trouble in Litchfield."

Johnny grinned, warmly, then whispered to Ruby. "That's Bumpy, one of the owners. He used to be a New Orleans gangster. But with this burger place, he's gone totally legit."

Johnny and Ruby approached the bar. Bumpy shook Johnny's hand. "Where you been, OG? I was about to put out a missing persons alert in and around the old folks homes."

"Handling business," Johnny responded, coolly. "And waiting for you to get this dump up to code."

Bumpy threw his arms out in opposite directions. "What do you think?"

Johnny shook his head, approvingly. "Nice, my man. Max to the max."

"You ain't seen nothing yet." He pointed to a set of glass doors in the back of the room. "We've expanded. This is the main dining area. You go through those doors into the card, domino and bingo section. You go through another set of doors and you'll see the jamming room with a DJ and dance floor."

Johnny gave Bumpy a high five. "You're totally representin', baby! *Black Enterprise* front cover doings. I'm proud of you."

Bumpy smiled. "We aim to please ... which is the message I'd like to get across to this beautiful young lady you got with you. Baby, whatever offers this ole man got on the table, I'd like to triple it with a money back guarantee."

Johnny chuckled, loudly. "Too late, Bumpy. You looking at Mrs. Johnny."

Ruby stuck out her hand. "Please to meet you, Bumpy."

Bumpy clung to her hand in desperation. "Listen. Would you consider leaving him if I served you the most delicious custom-made, sizzling hot, doubled seasoned, Cajun burger this side of the Mississippi?"

She thought about it. "Maybe. Does it come with the hot peppered curly fries he's always talking about?"

"A double order for you. Plus, I'll throw in our famous Piña Colada smoothie on the house."

She looked at Johnny, then back at Bumpy. "I think it is time to get the divorce lawyers on the phone."

****

After an endless parade of well-wishers and a special proclamation from the mayor, Kristy finally stepped up to the podium. All night long, she had been dabbing her black eyeliner and fighting back the tears. But standing in front the emotionally-charged crowd, hearing the deafening cheers and wild clapping, she finally opened the watery floodgates.

A few minutes later, after composing herself, she began with the two words: *Thank you.*

She explained, "As much as I have used those two words, they still don't seem adequate. And yet, I don't know what else to say. I don't know what other words would capture the fullness in my heart.

"This has been a long journey. Although, it's not about to end, this is a good place to recount how far we've come. When my husband died and I took over the company, I didn't know much. What I did know was that I wanted to treat people fairly. In spite of all of the doubters and detractors and experts who questioned my sense of fairness, I believed that one day it would pay off. Through your tireless work and dedication to this company, you have made that belief come true. And again, all I can say is thank you.

"As we grow, expand and prosper, I hope to say thank you many more times in the future. I don't plan to change my philosophy. If anything, I want to share it with other entrepreneurs who may believe the company is more important than the people in the company. In my opinion, *people* are what make the company, and you are my people. I am so proud of you, staying the course, stepping up when the chips were down. Again, and again, all I can say is thank you. I will say it a different way in your paychecks for next month. For now, I love you, and from the depths of my heart ... THANK YOU!"

After a long round of applauds, one of the ladies on the planning committee approached the podium.

"We have a special treat planned, a dance of victory for our victorious leader. What better person to accompany her than the man who shared those challenging moments on that mountain."

Kristy's mouth dropped with revelation.

"It's my pleasure to present to you our surprise guest and dance partner extraordinaire who flew in from California just to be with us tonight. How about a round of applause for co-survivor and hero, Mr. Phillip Barlow of Bean Systems."

Barlow strutted out from his hiding place behind the silky curtains.

The lights dimmed, the soft music began, and suddenly, Kristy and Barlow were floating across the stage like Ginger Rogers and Fred Astaire.

"Pretty sneaky," Kristy whispered into his ear.

"Any excuse is a good excuse to see you again," he whispered back. "Besides, I couldn't wait around for another plane to crash. These days you're riding the train."

Kristy was smiling, crying, and holding tightly to his broad shoulders. Lola sensed something more than a dance between survivors.

She turned to Nicholas. "Do you see what I see?"

"What? That they need to get a room?"

"No," she said. "That they have already gotten one."

****

Ironically, at that very moment, Johnny and Ruby were dancing too.

They had finished off a mouthwatering serving of Cajun burgers with all the trimming, a pitcher of New Orleans Dixie Beer and some kind of new berry peach cobbler Bumpy wanted them to try.

After wandering around in the crowded card and bingo section, unable to find an available table, they had ventured into the jamming room where an old Luther Vandross classic, *Always and Forever*, was playing. Johnny held Ruby tightly in his arms and sang in her ear:

Every day love me your own special way
Melt all my heart away with a smile
Take time to tell me you really care
And we'll share tomorrow together
Oh baby, I'll always love you forever

Johnny was surprised when Ruby chimed in on the last line: *I'll always love you forever*.

He squinted. "Where'd you learn this song?"

"They used to play it in a dance hall in Mexico City. But my English wasn't too good then. And I didn't know the meaning."

"You know the meaning now?"

Her eyes watered a bit. "Every word, Johnny, because the words say what's in my heart for you."

He shook his head. "Seeing you like this, holding you close to me, reminds me of that night we danced on the party boat under the stars. Except, these fools got a roof blocking the stars out."

She mustered a serious face. "What's wrong with your people? Did they not know Johnny Howard and his lovely wife would want to see the stars again?"

"When I go back up front to the bar, I'll let Bumpy know this room needs a glass dome installed PDQ. But for now, I'm going to forget about the remodeling and concentrate on that twinkle in your eyes."

A few dances later, Johnny made his way up to the bar to refresh their drinks.

Bumpy closed the cash register and came over. "A Margarita and Johnny-Red, right?"

"You got it," Johnny confirmed. "Don't know what you're taking for that Louisiana Alzheimer's, but it's working."

They both laughed, heartily.

"How about the accommodations? Everything up to snuff?" Bumpy inquired.

"Hey, man, everything's just great," he replied.

Johnny wanted to say *perfect*. But something was bothering him, something that kept the word from coming out of his mouth. And then he realized it was the new patron that was bothering him, the big Italian guy, sitting at the end of the bar.

Johnny surveyed the entire dining hall. It harbored a mixed crowd, mostly blacks with a few white faces scattered about the room. The few white customers appear to be avid Cajun food lovers, scoffing down burgers and beer, oblivious to any cultural pressures, totally comfortable with the urban scene. The big Italian, however, seemed uneasy, certainly not a likely candidate for a relaxing drink at a black bar.

Johnny had to question himself. After spending so much time around the Chicago mob, he had a tendency to be paranoid. Like a security guard, profiling black teens in a white suburban shopping center, his initial reaction was to expect trouble. It didn't necessarily have to be that way. The Italian guy could've simply been waiting for the rest of his party to arrive, or an out-of-towner who was staying nearby and didn't know where else to go.

Johnny spoke above the crowd. "Hey, what's that new brand of Cognac you got on the top shelf?"

A few people at the bar turned to see who was asking. The Italian guy never turned, never made eye contact.

"*Pierre Ferrand,*" Bumpy replied. "You want to try it?"

"Maybe later," Johnny declined, pressing his hand against the concealed gun holster, strapped beneath his shirt.

By then, Johnny had spotted another ruddy-faced man with black hair, standing outside the door. He wasn't trying to come in; just standing there like a royal guard outside the palace gate.

Johnny slapped a twenty on the counter to pay for the drinks. In a low voice, he inquired, "Hey, Bumpy. When you remodeled this place, did the fire inspector force you to put in another exit?"

"Yeah." He pointed to an emergency door on the back wall of the dining room."

"The fire department didn't bellyache about exits in the bingo room or dance area?" Johnny pressed.

"They tried, man. We had to get a lawyer to fight it. With a door up that far, people could skip paying their tab or grab some of that expensive sound equipment and keep on stepping. We got a six month exemption. After that, who knows? Why do you ask?"

"Just curious." Johnny grabbed the drinks and headed back to the dance room.

As soon as he walked up to Ruby, she read the expression

on his face.

"What's wrong, Johnny?"

"Maybe nothing. Maybe everything." He set down the drinks and reached into his pocket. He pulled out five crisp hundred dollar bills and a credit card. "I need you to listen to every word I'm saying, you understand?"

She nodded, nervously.

"I want you to take this money and this credit card. I want you to walk out of here, calmly, like you on a Sunday picnic. There's a gas station down the street. Call a taxi and go to a nice hotel, maybe the Hilton with cameras and off-duty police security, you know, where you stayed before. You don't open the door for the maid, for room service, for nothing or nobody, you understand?" He handed her his birthday iPhone. "I'll call you when I'm done here. If you haven't heard from me by tomorrow, you call Babygirl and have her pick you up."

"What's going on? Is there someone after you in here?"

"I don't have time to explain right now. I just need you out of here and in a safe place."

"I'm not going anywhere, Johnny."

"I'm not asking you, Ruby. I'm telling you. I need you to get out of here right now," he growled.

"And I'm telling you. Wherever you go. That's where I go. I'm not leaving you."

He took a deep breath, tried to calm his nerves. "Baby, I'm just trying to protect you. I don't know how many people I'm dealing with. Could be a whole army."

"I don't care." And then, she paused a long while. "That song we just listened to: *Always and Forever*. It means just that."

The music continued to play. As the night lingered on, the dance crowd grew larger. Johnny and Ruby sat at a table near the dance floor, trying to appear unaware. It was almost an hour before

Johnny formulated his plan.

He spotted a familiar face in the crowd. BottomsUp was an ole-school playboy he had met during the poker game in which he had won the lake house.

Johnny pulled him to the side. "Hey, Bottom, I need a favor."

"Anything, but call my three aces against your flush," he joked, reminiscently. "I don't have no lake house to give you."

"No, no, nothing like that." Johnny handed BottomsUp a $50 bill and valet stub. "I need you to get that young guy in valet parking to bring my hog around back. Tell him to leave the keys in it."

"You mean, in the back alley?"

"Yeah, exactly, with the keys in it."

"If you're trying to let somebody steal it, I'll take it off your hands," BottomsUp offered.

"No, no, baby. I love that machine," said Johnny. "It's just I got my wife with me, and there's a little lady up front I used to know that could cause me some trouble. I'd just as soon avoid that scene altogether, knowemsayin'?"

He smiled. "Hey, say no more. You know I understand dealing with these crazy mixed-up gold diggers. How much time you need?"

Johnny looked at his watch. "Right now would be just fine."

Johnny turned to Ruby. "Last chance, baby. Please, you can walk out of here right now."

Ruby shook her head. "I already told you."

"Okay, then when the time comes, you need to do exactly what I just told you to do." Johnny reviewed the plan, then disappeared into the crowd.

Seconds later, Johnny strolled through the dining hall. He reached over to a vacant table and grabbed a bottle containing the restaurant's famous New Orleans red hot pepper sauce. He concealed it in his pocket.

"Hey Bumpy, where's your restroom in this new joint? You can't expect an old man with an angry prostate to hold out forever." Johnny wanted everyone to hear.

"Same place, down that hallway," Bumpy instructed.

Johnny lumbered down the hall and through the MEN's door. He stood at the urinal with his pants unzipped.

Lofingers, who had been sitting at the bar, motioned to Bobby Tocco. Leaving his post just outside the door, Bobby walked inside and over to the bar.

Lofingers leaned over. "He's taking a piss. See if you can give the tar baby some quiet time too."

Bobby walked, casually, down the hallway. When he reached the MEN's restroom door, he flipped open his eight inch stiletto, slid it up his coat sleeve and went inside.

A tall, slender young wannabe model was parked in front of the mirror, picking at his face and brushing his wavy hair. Johnny stood in front of the far urinal, whistling a tune ... his old slavery song.

"The older you get, the longer it takes," Johnny grumbled to the young model.

The model chuckled at the fragility of old age, then grabbed his brush and headed out the door. Except for the hollow beat of the music, drifting in from the ceiling, Bobby Tocco and Johnny were all alone.

Bobby glanced at the empty stalls, then headed toward the urinals. Hoping to camouflage his true intent, he began unzipping his plaid trousers. He was only a few steps away when Johnny suddenly turned and dashed the hot pepper sauce in Bobby's face.

"Auuuuuh!!!" He grabbed his eyes with one hand, still gripping the knife with the other. As he groaned in agony from the burning sensation of New Orleans' outrageous seasoning, Johnny seized his wrist and drove the shiny stiletto blade through the center of his throat.

A new song started to play in the music room, a New Orleans Cajun foot stomper. The blood spewed into the air like an oil gusher on the Louisiana coast. Bobby Tocco coughed and wheezed and sank to the floor. Johnny dragged his trembling body inside a stall and sat him up as though he was taking a crap.

Johnny whispered in his ear. “You gotta watch these spicy foods, my man. They’ll give you the runs.”

Johnny emerged from the restroom with his .357 in hand. Not wanting to spook the customers, he concealed it behind his back. On the wall, next to Bumpy’s office door, was the main fire alarm. He pulled the red lever, then headed toward the front.

Just as Johnny had instructed, Ruby had moved to the bingo section, away from the loud dance music. As soon as she heard the fire bells ringing, she walked into the dining hall and stood by the new exit door.

When Johnny emerged from the hallway, he stood next to the bar. The moment Lofingers saw him, the big Italian realized something had gone wrong.

He stood up from the bar stool, reached into his coat and pulled out a Browning automatic. Before he could take aim, however, Johnny shot him twice in the chest, sending him spiraling to the floor.

The customers in the dining hall were already spooked by the fire alarm. The wild west quick-draw and loud explosions from Johnny’s big gun set off a human stampede. Wide-eyed patrons overturned tables and chairs and trampled over unlucky drunken klutzes that had stumbled to the floor.

Amidst the pandemonium and screams of desperation, it was a miracle Johnny heard Ruby’s frantic warning. Seeing Lofingers, rising to his knees like a member of the undead, she shouted to the top of her voice. “Behind you Johnny!”

The warning came a split second too late. Lofingers fire off a single shot from his Browning, slicing a piece of Johnny's left shoulder.

If there was one thing Lofingers had learned over the years, it was that, somctimcs, victims shot back. That's why, on risky, unpredictable hits, Lofingers always wore his bulletproof vest. The two slugs from Johnny's gun had put him down but not out. Johnny's carelessness had given him a second chance.

Unfortunately for Lofingers, his second chance was short-lived. Johnny turned and fired a third bullet directly through Lofingers' skull. A woman screamed, hysterically, as hair and brain fragments splattered the wood paneled bar.

Johnny pressed hard against his bleeding shoulder, then scrambled toward Ruby and the exit door. But a second wave of panic-stricken dancers, bingo and card players pushed him back through the overturned tables in front of the bar.

That's when he heard a shot ring out from the front door.

Bumpy grimaced with pain. The sawed-off shotgun he had retrieved from behind the bar fell from his hand. He sank like an ocean liner in slow motion, his feet, sticking out from the edge of the bar.

Johnny whirled to see a third man with dark, rounded eyes, thick lips, and a huge utility belt around his waist. He was trying to get a clear shot at Johnny. But the onslaught of renegade patrons pushed him back outside.

Johnny finally reached Ruby. Seeing the splattered blood stains on his shirt, she flinched. "Are you all right, Johnny?"

"It's just a scratch. I got kidneys that hurt worse than this." He covered the pain with his familiar tough-guy veneer.

Using his oversized shoe, he kicked open the door. Just as he had requested, his trusty Deville sat in the alleyway, keys in the ignition.

Johnny started up the engine and stomped the accelerator. A hard left turn around the corner of the building would give him a straight shot to the street. In his mind, it would be the conclusion of another daring escape, a chance to cheat the blood-thirsty mob enforcers one more time.

How could he have known that Penrow, the man he had ambushed in his Litchfield apartment, was waiting around the corner to ambush him back?

As the Deville approach the corner of the building, Penrow stepped out and opened fire with a semi-auto Uzi carbine. The vicious hail of bullets broke the windshield, hitting Ruby in the chest.

Johnny slammed on the brakes and fired back through the open windshield, grazing Penrow in the leg and forcing him to retreat behind the corner of the building.

Johnny threw the big hog in reverse and stomped the accelerator again. His anger slowly mushroomed as he glanced at Ruby's beautiful diamond-studded white blouse, covered in blood.

She should've whimpered and groaned from the excruciating pain. Instead, she said three Hail Marys, then reached her trembling fingers toward the knob on the stereo. An *escaramuza* folk song called *El Ranchero* suddenly flooded the speakers. She turned up the volume to drown out the merciless sound of gunfire, ripping their world apart.

Speeding backwards up the alley, Johnny thought about an old movie he had seen in which Superman flew backwards around the earth to reverse time. If only he could slip out of the alley and into a blue suit and red cape and tamper with the clock to save the woman he loved.

Yet, the blood, streaming from her wounded chest, served as a stark reminder he wasn't Superman. He was Johnny Howard, or was it Fountain, or was it Wexler III ... a small time hustler caught up in a big time web of revenge. There was no Superman suit in which he could redeem the world. There was only his .357

magnum, an old shot-up Deville and the perpetual hope he could cheat the sleazy agents of death one more time.

Inside, an angry PineX had muscled his way back into the building. He finally reached the dining hall exit through which the tar baby had fled.

He pushed open the door and stepped into the alley. He was just in time to greet the glassy red blur of taillights, a few feet away. The big Deville slammed into his fragile body and sucked him under the wheels.

Despite the loud music, Johnny could hear the crunch of PineX's rib cage, collapsing under the weight of the back tires. By the time the front tires rolled over his lifeless body, there was nothing left but a pancake of blood.

Approaching the far west corner of the building, Johnny calculated his backward maneuver toward the street. That's when Lofingers' thick-necked companion stepped out with a Russian-made semi-auto Glock, firing like a madman.

Johnny slammed on his brakes and started forward again. But the volley of lead shattered the rear window and peppered the deep-cushioned seats.

Johnny could feel the hot stinging steel in his back and neck. As he lost control and crashed into the fence, he reached out in desperation, trying to keep Ruby's head from hitting the dash.

The darkness was closing in, the widening streams of blood, blinding his vision with an impenetrable wall of red. All he could hear was the Mexican folk song, the crack of gunfire and those perpetual, unrelenting footsteps coming his way.

Lofingers' thick-necked partner had finally stopped shooting. He approached the car slowly, cautiously, poised, if necessary, to finish the job. Penrow approached from the other end of the alley, dragging his leg from the superficial wound.

Johnny was slumped over the wheel, a bullet-riddled carcass, bleeding from head to toe. Lofingers' partner smiled at his accomplishment, and leaned toward the blown-out passenger window.

He offered a final commentary. "Well, well, well. You ain't so tough now, are you, Mr. Tar Baby?"

Johnny couldn't see. With one last breath, he raised up and shot where the sound was coming from. Like a bloody pizza pie, Lofingers' partner's entire face flew up into the night sky.

Penrow opened fire again, riddling the entire car with bullets. He then grabbed a Pineapple hand grenade off of PineX's utility belt and tossed it through the open windshield.

The old Deville rocked with a mighty blast. The metal crinkled like hot paper under a sunlit magnifying glass. Orange plumes of smoke and fire leaped out like flashes of lightning.

Of course, it was a useless gesture. Johnny and Ruby were already dead.

With the faint shrill of a hundred sirens closing in, Penrow started to limp away, distancing himself from the incredible carnage. The days of sardines and crackers were finally over. The big tar baby was no more.

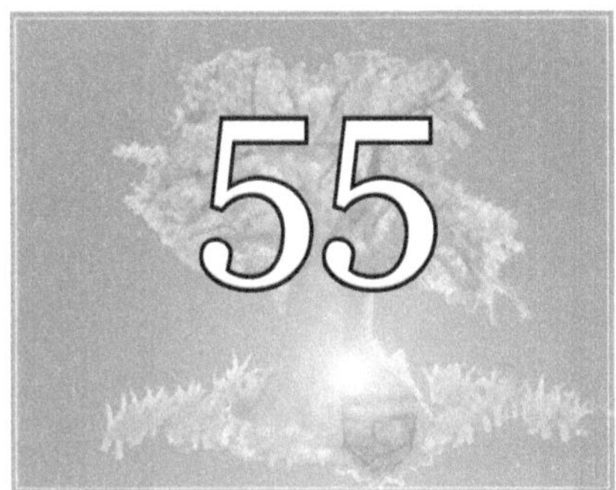

Lola didn't remember collapsing in the electronics store or being loaded into the back of the ambulance and rushed to St. John's. When she awakened Sunday morning to the bright sun, beaming through her hospital window, all she remembered was the reason she was there.

Her blurry vision finally melted into the comforting silhouette of Nicholas' fit frame, sitting by her bedside, holding her hand. He spoke in a soft voice, just above a whisper. "How are you feeling?"

She wanted to speak. But her throat was too sore from the vomit-less gagging the night before. After a few sips of water, she finally managed to reply. "I was dreaming, wasn't I? Please tell me it's not real."

He squeezed her hand, tightly. "What's real is that you've got to pull yourself together. You're seriously jeopardizing your health and the baby's health too."

"I'm trying, Nicholas. But it hurts. It hurts so bad."

They heard a light tapping at the door. Goodboy stretched his neck through the crack. "Hello?"

"I called Henry. I hope you don't mind."

Lola didn't reply.

Nicholas stood up. "Get some rest. I'll be right back."

Though Nicholas and Goodboy stepped into the hallway, Lola could hear their faint voices through a slight opening in the door.

"Her mother AND father?"

"Yes, we first heard about it Saturday morning. We were at BestBuy, looking at a high definition television. Lo and behold, all the grizzly details popped up in a newscast right there on the big screen floor model. Lola passed out."

"What are the doctors saying? Any permanent damage to her or the baby?"

"They don't think so. All the tests came back fine. But she won't eat or drink anything. That's why I called you."

"And you think I can reach her?"

"She looks up to you, Henry. She told me how you helped her get through that Allen Brothers fiasco. Now that her father's gone, you're the only father figure she has."

"I'm curious. Does anyone know what brought this on?"

Nicholas hunched his shoulders. "The news media is buzzing about a possible Mafia connection and dead hitmen from Chicago and Detroit. But you know the media. Their bread and butter is sensationalism. At this point, no one really knows for sure."

Lola knew for sure. But lying there in her hospital room, drowning under a tidal wave of pity and despair, she couldn't think of a single good reason to tell anyone. The more she told police, the more they'd dig into her background. The more they dug, the greater the chances would be that some sophisticated new supercomputer would get her deported.

The book said that one third of the time, people formed opinions based on association. What opinion would they have of her, knowing her family was associated with the Mafia?

When Goodboy came into the room, she expected to be showered with compassion and empathy. Instead, he roared at her with uncharacteristic hardness.

"Look, Chief Warrant Officer Salinas. Sometimes the ship goes down. I know. I had four children. But I lost one in Iraq and one due to a miscarriage. Seems like you're working on your miscarriage. Maybe the Iraq War will still be going on when you have another child."

"I'm not trying to have a miscarriage," she defended.

"Then act like it. Pull yourself together and get some nourishment into that baby's little hungry tummy. Stop looking back at the old ship going down. You and your child and your husband have a bright future ahead."

When Goodboy left the room, Lola was crying. But a few hours later, his stern orders took hold.

Dismissed from the hospital and on her way back to Nicholas' grandmother's house, she turned to him. "I want to go to the lake house."

Nicholas frowned. "Are you serious?"

"Yes. I need to do this while I still can."

"Do what?" he asked.

"Say goodbye," she replied. "I just need to say goodbye. Please?"

****

As Nicholas' small truck crept up the old gravel road leading to the lake house, an eerie silence filled the trees. On a bright, sunny afternoon, the birds should've been chirping, the frogs, croaking, and the fish, leaping out of the river with daredevil precision. Instead, the entire forest seemed lifeless and cold.

There was a question in the back of his mind that he was afraid to ask and she was afraid to answer: *Was the killing really over?*

The mob had been known to wipe out entire families. If they were involved, as the media had speculated, did they consider Lola a loose end?

Before they left the truck, Nicholas turned to her. "Do you feel safe being here? My father's a judge, and if we need to get a patrol car out here-"

"No. We'll be fine."

It took several hours for them to pack a few select boxes and load them on the back of the truck. Lola scavenged her room for the most important items, taking all of her clothing and accessories, but leaving her furniture and bedding behind. She had Nicholas move the refrigerator to retrieve Johnny's duffel bag. He counted $87,400 still inside.

With great care, Lola bundled two of Ruby's paintings in some plastic wrapping. She labeled one *Horse* and one *Hole* and had Nicholas load them on the truck.

Lola saved Johnny and Ruby's bedroom for last.

She found the attire they had worn to her graduation. Her mother's brown Reboso shawl made her cry. At the funeral, her mother would need something special to wear, even if the casket remained closed and nobody saw it but her.

She finally found one framed photograph of them on vacation at the TexMex County Line restaurant in San Antonio. She spoke to the picture as though they both could hear her trembling voice.

"I will miss you, not only because you were my parents, but because you were my friends. I could trust you and count on you, even when I was wrong. You made me be somebody I was not sure I could be. I hope I made you as proud of me as I was of you. I love you Daddy, knowemsayin'? Little Lolita loves you, *mama*. I will wear the shawl and bracelet you gave me until I die."

When she returned to the living room, Nicholas was standing by the front door. "I think everything's loaded."

That's when they heard the rustling inside a box on the window seal.

Lola walked over and opened the box to find the little orphaned red bird inside. He hopped out of the box and onto her shoulder.

She looked at Nicholas. "There's one more thing I need to do."

On the roof top, she placed the bird in the palm of her hand. "I know how it feels to have to grow up fast. But time does not wait for us to decide. Do not look back at the old ship going down. Find your bright future in the trees. Good luck, my little friend."

Not even sure he could fly, she slung his tubby body high into the air. He flapped and fluttered, circling the balcony a few times, clinging, futilely, to the only home he had ever known. Finally, as if the intractable messengers of time had confirmed his destiny, he soared into the forest.

He would soon let the other birds know to mind their manner and show some respect. After all, he was Johnny Howard's contribution to the new breed of red birds in the next generation to come.

After making two painfully positive identifications at the city morgue and dancing around police interrogation questions about her father's past, Lola was too emotionally drained to plan the funeral arrangements. Instead, using a portion of the money from Johnny's duffel bag, she placed the entire matter in Nicholas' capable hands. She had only one stipulation.

"I would like matching caskets. But they must not be blue."

Certainly not a blue bomb blueberry ice cream bar blue.

Nicholas found her instructions odd, but honored her request. He kept the service simple and authorized the caskets to be an exquisite dark brown.

The Bolton Funeral Home on Sixth Street was a huge two-story castle with white Roman columns guarding the front entrance. The thick green grass was freshly manicured. The sidewalk was lined with statues of Christ Jesus, timeless saints, powerful angels and other heavenly figures.

The director had already warned Nicholas. Because of the victims of the Carter Blue crash, multiple services would convene throughout the day. To avoid potential delays caused by the many funeral processions leaving for the cemetery, the Bolton limousine delivered Nicholas and Lola to the service chapel an hour early.

Chapel #5 was gracefully decorated with assorted wreaths of yellow and white roses, lilies and Gerberas. An American flag draped a wooden stand on one side of the room; a Mexican flag, on the other. A small Cadillac Deville model replica, along with Ruby's favorite *Banda el Recodo* CD occupied a table nearby. The large oil painting of Ruby's *escaramuza* horse rested on an easel next to the table.

Lola didn't expect anyone to be there. But when she and Nicholas marched in with the minister at 11:00 am and took their seat on the front row, seven people were already present.

She immediately spotted Goodboy, John Bossley and Ms K who had come to represent the company. Nicholas' parents were there. Having picked up so many to-go orders from BIG EASY Burgers, she easily recognized Bumpy, even with his wounded arm in a sling.

But there were two men she didn't recognize: One older, distinguished black man with peppered gray hair and a wrinkled face; the other, a Jamaican type with long dreadlocks and dark shades.

Nicholas' Methodist minister presided over the service. In his short obituary sermon he declared:

"I didn't know either of the dearly departed. But I do know the young family that has suffered this grievous loss. In fact, I am scheduled to marry Nicholas and Lola next month. I regret this great tragedy has brought us together, prematurely. But life is unpredictable in that way.

"What I can say to you is that God is an all-wise God and does not make mistakes. We want our loved ones to live forever, but deep in our hearts, we know better. Our greatest hope should be that we spend time wisely with each other, getting to know and love and appreciate one another, so that when this time comes, the sadness will not be complicated by regret.

"I pray that these two departed souls are resting with the Father, enjoying the fruits of their labor. But to this young family, I offer a final message: Life must go on."

Everyone, including Lola, remained tranquil and composed.

After the funeral, Lola and Nicholas stood in the hallway, thanking each person who had attended.

The older man with the peppered gray hair walked up. "You've never met me. But we did speak, briefly, on the phone. I'm ArchieV, Johnny's older brother."

Lola hugged him, tightly. "I am pleased to finally meet you. Daddy talked about you a lot."

"When I saw this thing on the national news, something told me it was him. Then the police called me, I guess from the list of numbers in his cell. I needed to come and pay my respects."

She nodded. "Thank you for coming."

"No, thank you, Lola. Thank you for putting us back in touch before he ... left us. Two old stubborn men didn't need to go out that way."

"You will join us for dinner after this is over, yes?" she offered.

"Thanks, but I have an afternoon plane to catch. I wish you well on your marriage. If you're ever in Atlanta, please look me up."

One last time he nodded his condolences, and then walked away.

The second man in the dreadlocks stood in a corner, seemingly, reluctant to approach.

Lola walked over to him. "I don't believe I've met you. I am Lola, the daughter."

He extended his hand. "I am Calypso. Your fadder and me did much business together."

Lola's expression changed. "I didn't expect any of his business associates to come."

"De thing is, he was more than a business associate. De man was my friend. I trusted him."

She paused a long while, her voice, lowered to a whisper. "Do you know who did this?"

"De Family, no doubt."

"But do you have a name?" she specified.

He removed his shades, exposing his dark, shiny eyes. "I have contacts all over de world. From time to time, information comes my way. But if I call you and tell you this thing, it will awaken de devil that is now feasting on your sorrow. Don't bodda trying to put it back to sleep."

"I want to know who killed my parents," she insisted. "I will get a pen and give you my cell number."

"Forget de pen. Just say it one time. I keep everything in my head."

As they talked, the limousine driver walked up. "Excuse me, Ms Salinas. I believe they're trying to get us out of here before the people in Chapel #3 dismiss. It's a pretty big funeral and we could get stuck behind their procession for quite a while."

Calypso nodded his head. "I wish you de best. Maybe, we will talk again."

He walked away.

Nicholas came over. "Who was that?"

"An old friend of Daddy's," she replied.

"I think our procession is ready, though it looks like we're the only ones going to the gravesite," Nicholas informed.

"That's fine," said Lola. "But I must find a restroom to relieve this pregnant bladder."

The limousine driver pointed down the hallway. "You'll see the lady's room on the left."

Lola found the restroom with no problem. On her way back, she could hear the sounds of sadness and mourning, reaching out like invisible fingers from beneath the closed chapel doors. There was reverent clapping coming from Chapel #1, perhaps a salute to the great things the deceased person had done. The people in Chapel #2 were crying, uncontrollably, perhaps, a family that had not seen tragedy up-close and personal, and now looked into the face of death for the very first time.

As she passed Chapel #3, the doors swung open. Two funeral attendants prepared the way for the caskets to be rolled out. A pair of shiny black hearses waited just outside the building. Ruby could almost touch them through the long glass windows.

The priest concluded his final remarks. "We all loved the Stodomieres. Joe, Helen, Patricia and Joey, Jr. We don't know why they were on that plane or why God called them home so soon. But if you're up there listening, we want you to know we love you and we'll miss you and..."

Lola didn't hear the rest of his commentary. Her fragile mind had been swallowed up by the sight of four metallic blue caskets, lined up next to each other on a carpet of red roses.

There was no way to deny the images from her dream. She had seen them all before.

"One day human circumstances will seduce you. And in desperation, you will turn to the chest. And it will turn to you. It will slip into the deep hollows of your mind and haunt your dreams ... haunt your very soul."

She grabbed her heart. The whole world quivered and swayed beneath her feet. She stumbled backwards against the wall and slid to the floor.

In the corner of her eye, she could see Nicholas running toward her, but not before a crowd from the chapel surrounded her.

"Lady, are you alright?" One of the attendants inquired.

She wasn't alright. She needed the caskets to disappear,

to melt away into thin air like blue bomb ice cream bars on a hot summer's day.

A bearded man with a long face and thick glasses pushed to the front of the crowd. An apparent friend of the deceased family, he looked vaguely familiar. Lola didn't recognize him until she heard his deep, condemning voice. "Now you see how it feels when death pays a visit to YOUR house."

A sudden hush fell over the crowd.

"You're responsible for this," declared Professor Broadson. "None of these people had to die."

Nicholas elbowed his way through the crowd and leaned over her. "What happened?"

"What happened is she decided to play God. That's what happened," Professor Broadson continued in a pungent discourse that sent flaming needles through Lola's heart. "I tried to warn the both of you. Did you think you could play with fire and not get burned?"

Nicholas helped Lola to her feet. "Come on. Let's get out of here."

Professor Broadson followed them outside to the limousine. He was still ranting at the top of his voice.

"What did you get for those poor souls in Litchfield? A new dress? A fancy car? I'm sure it was worth all the blood on the train tracks, all the pain and suffering you put those people through, wasn't it?"

Nicholas helped Lola into the limousine, then turned to Professor Broadson. "If you don't leave my wife alone, I'm going to-"

"What? Make another wish. Maybe, you'll wish me to have a heart attack and die so you won't have to listen to the truth?"

Nicholas stepped over and punched Professor Broadson in the face, knocking him to the ground. "No, I had something more immediate in mind."

From the ground he scolded them. "You don't know the powers you've unleashed. This is not a game of wish-and-tell.

The *Tree* will extract its recompense from all of us. You must stop this madness. Let me dispose of the chest before it's too late."

"According to you, it's already too late," Nicholas reprimanded him.

A security guard lifted the old professor up and pushed him toward the street.

He turned back. "If you care anything about her, you won't let her continue this. I can assure you it will be most lethal."

"The only thing lethal is your wild imagination," growled Nicholas. "Stay away from us or I'll have you arrested."

Nicholas climbed into the back of the limousine. Their small procession faded into the busy streets.

All the way to the gravesite and back home again, Lola couldn't stop crying. Once inside the house, Nicholas fixed her a cup of hot, lemony tea. He sat her down on the sofa with a box of tissues. "Tell me about the chest."

A new waterfall of tears streamed down. "I didn't mean to hurt anyone. Daddy was dying and I just wanted to give him a second chance."

"What did you do?"

"I made a wish he would get better."

"And..."

"And the next day, a kidney came from the train explosion."

"What makes you think the explosion had anything to do with the chest?"

"Because of Mama's purple shawl and the matador. I saw it all in a dream."

Nicholas appeared totally confused.

She explained, "Whatever you dream will come true. The chest knows. It gets into your head."

"Did you dream about the train wreck?"

"No," she admitted.

"Then you see. If the silly wish was connected to the train

wreck, you should've dreamed about the train wreck."

"It doesn't work that way."

"Okay, okay, how does it work?"

"I don't know," she whined. "I think maybe the dream is like a receipt you get at the grocery store. It is not the groceries or the money you pay. It is ... how you say ... a connnfaa...."

"Confirmation," he assisted.

"Yes. A confirmation the purchase was paid in full."

"And then the dream comes true?"

"Yes," she affirmed. "When you see the things of your dream, you know the chest knew before it happened that it was going to happen. The chest knows everything."

"And controls everything ... is that what you're saying?"

She winced. "Yes, maybe."

"You remind me of Professor Broadson. You make the chest sound like God."

And then Nicholas went on to explain that the professor had called him a few months after the cruise. Some thoughtless employee had given him Nicholas' number at the Kansas City store.

"The professor told me he had returned to the Stonehenge in Morocco and made a startling discovery, something he had overlooked during all of his previous visits. In a small, hidden chamber, he had found religious symbols that made ancient references to the *Universal Consciousness*.

What is this thing?" asked Lola. "This *Universal Consciousness*?"

"It's the belief that all things, all beings, all forms of matter are made of pure energy and that all energy in the universe is connected. The professor quoted the writings as saying the self of every self and soul of every soul in sacred unity as one."

Lola frowned. "I still do not get it."

"It's the belief that a thought is pure energy that can instigate an action that is also pure energy that affects our entire world which is also pure energy. All of this energy flows from a single source fully capable of manipulating the entire chain."

Lola stared at Nicholas with the innocent eyes of a child. "Do you believe this? Could this *Universal Consciousness* be true?"

He took a while to answer. "The thing is, this *Universal Consciousness* does the same thing as God. I'm not the Christian crusader that Dr. Fox is. But I believe in one God and not by another name. I can't wrap my Methodist mind around the idea that God is a sacred tree or a chest full of wood."

"But I have wished on the chest," she reminded him. "I have seen its power."

He walked over to the refrigerator and pulled out a Heinekens. "Tell me about your second wish."

"I had to save Ms K. She wasn't coming home. She was going to die out there."

"So you wished for her to be found?"

Lola nodded. "Yes, and the next day they found her. But they found her because they were looking for the other plane."

"What was your grocery receipt on this one?"

"The four blue caskets," she said. "Didn't you see them?"

"No. I just remember you telling me you didn't want blue caskets."

"But they were there, in the chapel. Four of them, side by side. That's what frightened me and made me fall."

He sipped on his beer a very long time, allowing the possibilities to flow through his mind. "Okay, okay, I think you and Professor Broadson are drinking from the same Tequila bottle. But for the sake of argument, let's say the chest is causing these things to happen. How do we stop these things from happening?"

"By not wishing," she explained. "Nothing happens unless you wish on the chest."

"Today, Professor Broadson spoke of a third wish. Have

you made it?"

"No," she declared. "And I don't plan to."

"So if we call up this madman and give him the chest, that should solve our little black magic Mauretanian mystery, right?"

Lola dropped her head. "Not for the ones who have already died."

"Listen. Stop beating yourself up over a wild theory some addle-brained professor has concocted to amuse himself during retirement. Pretty soon, we'll have a flying saucer landing on our front lawn, with BigFoot getting out and knocking on the door."

She thought for a moment. "I do not know this BigFoot."

"Just know he's a figment of the imagination, like this Mauretanian curse thing."

"So you believe nothing I have told you?"

"I believe you believe, Lola. That's why tomorrow, we're going to get this Juba Chest out of our lives."

"Fine. We can pick it up at the storage center when I get off from work," she agreed.

"Work!" He chuckled with amusement.

"Yes, I need to get back. Ms K will never get caught up without me."

"Forget it. You aren't going anywhere."

"But I missed last week."

"And you'll be missing this week too. I already talked to Henry about it. He says, after all you've been through, if you show up, he'll throw you in the brig."

She frowned. "I do not know of this brig."

"It's a cold, dark place where they beat pregnant women who refuse to listen to reason."

"Both of you are mean and very worthless *matóns*," she pouted.

"And you..." He thought for a minute. "I guess you would be our newest member of the Nicholas Hartman deadbeat club. Welcome aboard!"

Early Monday morning, Lola's cell phone rang. Dr. Fox's nurse was on the other end.

"Dr. Fox wanted me to see if you could come in today. Your test results are back and she has a cancellation at 3:00 pm."

Lola agreed. If she couldn't go into work, she might as well make use of the time.

In a small conference room next to Dr. Fox's office, Lola and Nicholas waited, patiently, for the doctor to return from the hospital. One of her patients had had an unexpected delivery, which the nurse explained, was typical for physicians specializing in prenatal care.

At 3:45 pm, Dr. Fox walked into the conference room. She carried a thick folder in one hand, some pamphlets and CD's in the other.

"I'm so sorry. Sometimes triplets have a mind of their own. I hope I didn't keep you waiting too long?"

"No, we are deadbeats now," Lola announced. "We have plenty of time."

Nicholas explained. "She doesn't like the idea of motherhood over company-hood. In her best interest, we're taking the week off."

"I like a man who takes charge." Dr. Fox raised her clenched fist. "Power to the anthropoids."

Lola gave them a sour gaze.

Dr. Fox's face slowly changed into a more serious expression. "Nothing's easy for a physician. But some things are so much harder than others. This afternoon, we're going to have to deal with one of those harder things."

"What thing do you speak of, Doctor?" Lola anxiously inquired.

"Talking to wonderful couples like you about major challenges faced in a pregnancy."

"Challenges?" Nicholas straightened up in his chair.

"Let me show you something."

Dr. Fox reached for a remote on the conference table. She pointed it to a slide projector that had already been cued.

The first slide showed a long-faced, scraggly haired English gentleman, wearing a white researcher's smock and holding up a test tube.

Dr. Fox cleared her throat. "This is Dr. John Hilton Edwards, a London-born geneticist credited with the discovery of Trisomy 18, a genetic disorder later named Edwards syndrome for its discoverer."

She clicked to the second slide which showed a complicated diagram of chromosomes and cell division timetables. "Edwards syndrome is caused by the presence of an extra 18th chromosome. In other words, we end up with three copies of chromosome 18 in a fetus instead of two. Edwards syndrome is the second most common autosomal trisomy. Down syndrome is the first. This Edwards syndrome only happens in about one in three thousand births."

Nicholas was getting a sick feeling in his stomach, but said nothing.

When Dr. Fox clicked to the third slide, Lola's heart slid up to her throat and made her gag. The picture was that of three newborn babies. The first had an abnormally large, distorted skull. The second had a triangular mouth and malformed ears. The third child had big club feet and webbing of the toes.

Dr. Fox continued. "There are over a hundred and thirty abnormalities associated with Edwards syndrome. In those instances when the child is not stillborn, death usually occurs within six months. In general-"

"Dr. Fox," Nicholas finally interrupted. "Can you turn that off please?"

The screen went black, followed by a long, dark silence that smothered the room.

Finally, she spoke again. "Lola, I know you thought it strange when I asked you to come back for further testing. But with something like this, I had to be sure."

Lola was holding so tightly to Nicholas' arm, it cut off his circulation. "Wh-what caused this, Doctor? What did I do?"

"Nothing, Lola. You did nothing at all. Every three or four thousand pregnancies, this thing shows up. We look at the Chorionic Villus Sampling and there it is."

"So how do we cure it?" asked Nicholas.

"Unfortunately, there is no cure," the doctor sadly reported.

"Okay, okay, so what are we supposed to do?" he asked.

She pushed the folder back and set the remote on the table. An eternity passed before she spoke.

"There's a 99% chance the tests are right, which means there's a 1% chance they're wrong. Betting on the 1% is like betting the sun won't come up tomorrow. It probably will, but who knows? A giant meteorite might hit the earth during the night and blow us all to smithereens. Kazaam! There you have it. The 1% prevails."

"Let's say this meteorite isn't coming, Doctor, and we all know it. What then?" he asked.

Another eternity passed, as though she had fallen asleep with her eyes open.

"You probably know I'm a Christian from an old family of Christians. Abortion is not supposed to be in our vocabulary. But it is in mine ... God forgive me ... in two distinct instances. The first is rape. The second is when the potential for severe, dysfunctional malformation is indisputable. Of, course, in both instances, there's a down side."

"What's the downside?" he persisted.

"You take away God's opportunity to perform a miracle."

"I do not want to kill my baby," Lola finally spoke up.

"Then, if that's your decision, let us proceed. I'm going to put you on some experimental hormones. They might help, or have no effect at all. I'm putting you on bed rest for these final four weeks. No work, no strenuous exercise, no wild nights of drinking and sex. Just concentrate on being a good mother and having the best delivery you possibly can."

"Any other advice for me or her?" asked Nicholas.

"Yes. From this point on, every night before you go to bed, pray for a meteorite."

The news about the baby totally dislodged their plans to go to the storage center in Litchfield. It wasn't until the weekend when he stumbled across Johnny's obituary that Nicholas thought about the chaotic scene Professor Broadson had caused.

Sunday morning, after fixing Lola a big breakfast, he reminded her about the chest. "We said we'd give it back to the professor and get it out of our lives."

"Have you talked to Professor Broadson to see if he still wants it?" she asked.

"Oh, I'm pretty sure he wants it."

"I think we should wait until you talk to him before we remove it from the storage."

"Why? We've got a garage in the back; maybe, keep it there until we connect with him."

"I know you won't believe me. But the chest makes noises sometimes. We should not move it until the professor is ready."

"I can't find his card. But I'll go by the museum tomorrow and get his number," said Nicholas. "We'll set an appointment with him and get this thing behind us."

She was quiet for a long time. "I have a question for you."

"Yes?"

"If you knew for sure the chest could save our baby, would you ask it to?"

He shook his head with suspicion. "Oh boy. Is this one of those trick questions where the husband ends up sleeping on the couch either way?"

She smiled. "No. But it is a question you must answer with your heart."

He took a deep breath. "Okay, okay let me get this straight. Assuming the Juba Chest was real and I knew it was real, you're asking if I would make a wish on it to save our child?"

"Yes, that's what I am asking."

"Then, the answer is no."

Lola squinted with surprise. "You would not try to save our child? I don't understand."

"Do you remember seeing those small caskets at the funeral home?"

She nodded.

"Those were children that died in that crash," he reminded

her. "If the Juba Chest were real, it would mean your wish killed them. It would mean the chest is taking lives to save lives. It would mean my wish might easily take the life of someone's child to save my own. Do I have the right to do that?"

Lola stayed quiet for a while, preparing her rebuttal.

"What if you were the captain of a ship and a big flood was coming and there was only one seat left."

"I'm listening."

"Would you give it to your child, or someone else's child?" she queried.

"Ahhhh! You're killing me, Lola."

"Just answer the question and be truthful."

"Okay, okay, if I was the captain and there was one seat left, but two children needed to get on board ... I would get off the ship and give the second child my seat."

Her eyes radiated with discovery. "Yes, Nicholas, you would. You would sacrifice yourself."

She started to cry.

"What's wrong?" he asked.

"Nothing." She buried her watery eyes in a soft white terry clothe. "I love you."

Nicholas and Lola jumped into the white limousine and slammed the door. As the driver took off, Lola was laughing so hard, she slid off the seat and onto the floor.

"That was *horrible*." She summed up their wedding in a single word.

Two weeks before her scheduled delivery and a week before Nicholas' parents went on vacation, they had concocted a nightmarish wedding celebration on the fly. Working in Kansas City and being a loner at heart, Nicholas had no friends. So when he spotted Bobart, his childhood nemesis across the street, rolling up in a wheelchair to visit his ailing mother, Nicholas reminded him of his childhood abuses so he would feel guilty. That was Nicholas' manipulative ploy to get Bobart to be his best man.

Lola didn't have any friends either. So she asked Nicholas' sister to be her bridesmaid and convinced Goodboy to give her away.

Lola was never really able to find a dress that fit her bulging stomach. Lumbering down the aisle with swollen feet, she looked like a basketball with legs, wrapped in a white table cloth. Her mind was never on the wedding vows, but rather, the fear that her weak bladder would give way before she made it through the ceremony.

Hanging around the house, drinking Heinekens and munching on pizzas, Nicholas had gained weight too. Two of his brass buttons popped off his favorite suit, giving him the distinct look of a pudgy pen cushion doughboy, ready to pop open.

When Nicholas and Lola finally stood together at the altar, Lola looked back to see who was in attendance. There were only two people, sitting in the entire audience ... Nicholas' father and mother.

On the way out of the chapel, Bobart's wheelchair got caught in a crack and started to tilt. Nicholas could've caught him. But regurgitating all of those childhood memories of being bullied, Nicholas' hand somehow slipped and Bobart flipped over on the church's front porch.

They forgot the rice, so Nicholas' sister, Terri, went into the kitchen and found some Corn Flakes to throw at them as they left the church.

In the limousine, the driver turned to hear their destination. "Where to?"

They were elated to say, "Home, James." No thought was more rewarding than ending their formal fiasco and dumping their costumes into the trash.

It was a gracious performance for Nicholas' conservative Evangelical parents; But nothing Nicholas and Lola would hold sacred in plotting their family's future course.

Nicholas told Lola, "Next year I'll take you to Oklahoma, and let that Chief do some exotic buffalo hide and snake medicine stuff. After that, if our weight is back down so we don't sink the ship, I'll take you on a beautiful, romantic cruise. We can repeat our vows over the crystal blue waters of Mastic Bay and drink

Margarita's until the sun comes up."

"Who'll keep the baby?" Lola instinctively inquired.

That's when they both felt the big white invisible elephant, stampeding through the room. The real question in the back of their minds was: *Would there even be a baby?*

Dr. Fox had said if the child wasn't stillborn, there was a high probability he would die within six months. That grim reality didn't require a babysitter. It required an undertaker. And who wanted to talk about a funeral on their wedding day?

Nicholas wrapped his arm around her, stroking her shoulders in a soft, easy rhythm.

"I've learned not to worry about those things we can't control. The best thing for us to do is to just wait and see."

****

A few days after the wedding, Nicholas received a call from his boss. The assistant manager was having trouble with the inventory codes and couldn't resolve the new shipments coming in.

"This is still your store," his regional manager reminded him. "I don't want them bringing in a new manager, then when you come back in six months, you've got nowhere to go. I need you to come to Kansas City for a couple of days and straighten this out. I'll pay you as a consultant so there's no backlash from the human resources department, which has you red-flagged as suspended. But I need you to come right away."

Nicholas was on a plane the following day. But before he left, he gave Lola explicit instructions. "No driving, no working, no on-the-phone, trying to solve RedFish's problems. Just take it easy. I'll be back home in two days."

The very next morning, Lola was zipping around town,

having hot tortillas for lunch and washing them down with French-Vanilla ice cream. She waited until Goodboy went to lunch, then slipped into Kristy's office to say hello.

Kristy was smiling from ear to ear. "I'm so glad to see you, Lola. In fact, follow me."

She took Lola around to her former cubical. The whole area had been gutted.

"We're tripling the size of your work area and housing you in a glass office so you can see your people."

"My people?" She frowned.

"Yes. I'm going to be expanding your duties. You'll need the support."

As they stood there talking, Goodboy returned early from lunch. As soon as Lola spotted him, she took off down the hallway, waddling toward the door like a big runaway turkey."

"Yeah, you'd better get out of here," Goodboy shouted. "And don't come back."

****

Nicholas was about to board his afternoon flight out of Kansas City when his cell phone rang.

"My water just broke, Nicholas. It's time to go."

"Next week, Lola. This is supposed to happen next week," he reminded her.

"It's happening now, Nicholas. What should I do?"

"I'll be there in two hours. Can you wait for me?"

"I-eeee, I don't know."

"Okay, okay, if you can't wait until I get there, call a taxi. I'll meet you at the hospital."

"I don't want to get into a taxi. I have seen those movies where the taxi driver has to deliver the baby."

"Then, what do you want to do, Lola?"

"Just meet me at the hospital," she said. "I'll figure it out."

An hour later, Raúl pulled into the driveway. He was driving a 1963 metallic green classic Chevy Biscayne low-rider with chrome wheels and a huge Alpine bass speaker in the back seat. The moment they backed out of the driveway, the front end of the car reared up like a wild stallion on the run.

"I had a study date with the hottest, finest *mami chulaat* in the GED universe," he complained. "You and that Heavy-D belly owes me big time."

With the loud music blasting and the hydraulic suspension pumping up the front end at every stop light, Lola was a nervous, nauseated wreck. He finally agreed to turn down the music. However, the suspension system had an electrical short and was essentially out of control.

"Do something!" she pleaded with him.

"You get a chance to see how the working-class Chicanos live, you-know-whatta-mean? None of that soft, executive-suite living, baby. Down here, we do it fast and raw."

"Raúl, if you do not stop this thing from bucking, I will have this baby right here in your front seat!" she threatened.

His eyes widened. "Naw, naw, you can't do that. These are custom hydraulic barber shop chairs, special ordered out of San Jose. They don't even make them anymore."

"Uooooh," she groaned at the next stop light. "I can feel it coming, afterbirth and all!"

He reached under the dash and snatched a handful of wires from their socket. The car slowly leveled to the ground. "Okay, okay, chill out. We're almost there."

Inside St John's emergency room, a nurse waited with a

wheelchair. She whisked Lola off to the third floor and began preparations for the delivery.

When Nicholas walked into her room, she was already 100% effaced. A nurse handed him some blue scrubs. "We're about ten minutes away."

Lola was screaming, loudly. "I need more pain medicine. *Mucho, de forma rápida!*"

But the nurse shook her head. "By the time it gets into her system, the baby will be here."

The delivery room was a glassed-in white sterile area with several long steel framed tables with adjustable backrests and silver stirrups growing out of the bottom.

Lola lay on the middle table. Two doctors and a nurse stood over her. Her knees perturbed over the silver stirrups, high into the air.

Dr. Fox shouted at her with a fiery voice. "Come on, Lola, you can do better than that. Push harder!"

Lola groaned and cried; her eyeballs rolled back in her head. She gripped Nicholas' hand like a steel vice, as if transferring some of the unfathomable pain to him.

As a young boy, he had heard about the miracle of birth. But he never knew a miracle required so much suffering. There were women all over the world, enduring the trauma of repopulating the universe. John F. Kennedy's mother had done it; Hitler's mother too. There was no way to know what bright star or demented soul would crawl out from the dark, bloody mucus inside the womb. The only certainty was the terrible pain tied to his or her arrival.

Dr. Fox had warned them. But neither he nor Lola were truly prepared. Would a dead clump of meat and bones flop out like a steak, ready for the grill? Or would a hideous little red face emerge with cleft lips, missing ears and pink intestines protruding from its side?

"Here comes the head," the doctor announced, unceremoniously.

Lola screamed again as the whole body slithered out. There was a long, poignant silence. And then came the sound of crying.

Lola slowly lifted her head toward the doctors, observing the shock on their faces. They seemed puzzled, perhaps, trying to figure out what form of mercy killing would be best for her little circus freak.

An eight-minute eternity passed before Dr. Fox clamped the umbilical cord. Another three minutes before the other doctor made the cut. The nurse took the baby over to a table, cleaned it up, bundled it in a warm blanket and brought it back to Lola.

Dr. Fox smiled for the first time during the entire delivery. "Congratulations, Lola. You are the proud mother of a very alert and healthy seven pound baby girl. All I can say is, God is still in the miracle business."

Lola's heart was still pounding, but for a different, glorious reason now. She swaddled the beautiful little baby girl in her arms, mindful not to crush her fragile frame. She finally turned to Nicholas. "Did you hear what Dr. Fox said ... alert and healthy?"

Nicholas couldn't hear her. He had fainted on the floor.

It was almost midnight before Lola returned to her room. There, she and Nicholas discussed how their meteorite had miraculously fallen to earth.

"Dr. Fox told me in all of her years as a physician, she had never seen such a reversal of the prognosis. And, she had never been so happy to be wrong," added Nicholas.

"Do you think we did the right thing by naming the baby Lolita Diane?" questioned Lola. "It's not very American, you know."

"I think it's appropriate," he insisted. "Since Ruby called you Lolita, it keeps the memory of your mother fresh and alive. And it pays tribute to you, the one who believed and didn't give up."

"But you didn't give up either."

He dropped his head. "Honestly, when Dr. Fox showed us those pictures, I don't think anybody in the room had the courage to go through with the pregnancy, except you."

"We had to try, Nicholas. We just had to."

Nicholas could see the exhaustion in her eyes. "I'm going to let you get some rest. I'll be back first thing in the morning."

"Try to get back in time to see me breast feed her," Lola requested.

He smiled, naughtily. "Why? So I can feel left out while she's having all the fun?"

Lola shook her head with disgust. "Stupid men."

****

When Nicholas returned to his grandmother's house, he, too, was exhausted. After lying around the house for weeks, two days at the store had pushed his feeble stamina to the limit. Unpacking his suitcase, simmering under a hot shower and guzzling down a mouthful of pizza, he was finally ready for bed.

Lola was a bad sleeper, especially, during her pregnancy. She kicked and rolled and flung her body all over the bed. The covers looked like the aftermath of a tornado. It didn't surprise him the bedspread was half way to the floor.

As he straightened the linen and fluffed the pillows, he heard an odd crunch, like sitting on a bag of Fritos that someone had left on the sofa. He lifted the pillow to find three small chips of wood, hand-sickled shavings from an old tree. He immediately recognized the pieces as bark from the chest ... Lola's Juba Chest.

He took a deep breath, surrendering to the darkness of

his thoughts. He slowly sank onto the edge of the bed, buried his forehead in his hands and languished in silence. His whole world spiraled down to hell.

When is it a good time to call your wife a sneaky, deceiving, bald-faced liar? Is it the first day she brings the baby home from the hospital, or the first few weeks when she's overwhelmed by breast-feeding and dirty diapers and crying all night, or the third month when she's trying to get acclimated to a grueling schedule of working all day, while wifing and mothering all night?

The fact that Lola had lied to him about the chest had become a festering sore beneath Nicholas' skin. And yet, the more he thought about confronting her, the more complicated the task had become.

In the first place, the chest should've been long gone.

Nicholas had gone to the museum to get a contact number for Professor Broadson, only to find the professor had left on a Cuban archaeological expedition and wouldn't be back for five months. Though Nicholas didn't give much credence to the claim the chest made strange noises, with the professor gone, there was no need to rush to Litchfield and bring it home.

There was something else, something more paradoxical and self-revealing in his need to confront her. It hinged on a simple question: Did he believe in the chest, himself?

The same question reared its ugly head during a private counseling session with his Methodist minister.

"You're saying you don't believe in the chest, but she does, right?" Sitting behind his desk in the church's pastoral office, the minister tried to clarify.

Nicholas nodded.

"So what bothers you the most: the fact she believes in the chest or that she lied about using it?"

"I, I guess both," he admitted. "I mean, if she believes it actually wreaks havoc on society and causes these great tragedies to happen, why would she use it? I mean, that seems pretty callous, doesn't it?"

The minister was careful not to take sides.

"I'm an avid reader, not just of Bible doctrine, but revelations about our society and humankind's evolution within it. I read about the crash of Uruguayan Air Force Flight 571 back in 1972. Decent, civilized people, faced with bitter cold and starvation, started eating the dead passenger to stay alive. My first thought was how callous and primitive. But what God eventually showed me was the power of desperation and what it will make people do."

"Are you saying it's okay because she was desperate?" asked Nicholas.

"Not at all. I'm saying don't condemn her for what you might've done under the same circumstance. We all have a tendency to ignore the rules when it comes to the ones we love."

Nicholas suddenly found himself thinking about the nepotism rule he had broken to provide insurance for his half sister. "So, maybe, I can put her on probation and see if she does something like this again?"

"Or maybe you could forgive her and start fresh like God does with us each and every day. The truth about the chest will eventually come out. Either she'll owe you an apology or, God forbid, you'll owe her one. Believe me, these things always work themselves out."

It was a few weeks before Christmas when the chest came up again. RedFish had shut down for the month, allowing Lola to stay home with the baby. Nicholas was just finishing his treadmill routine when his cell phone went off.

With the baby crying and the washer and dryer churning from the hallway, he stepped onto the front porch to take the call.

A few minutes later, he came back inside with a perplexed look on his face.

"What's wrong, Nicholas?" And then she interrupted him before he could explain. The washer had started to grind and shake and make strange noises.

She shouted in frustration. "Here we go again."

"When did this start?" he asked.

"A few days ago. I thought you knew."

He walked over, unplugged the machine and opened the back casing that concealed the motor. He tampered with a few wires, adjusted a setting and plugged it up again. When the machine started up, it ran like new.

Lola finished feeding the baby, then put her down for an afternoon nap.

"I fixed us some grilled chicken salads and *caldo* soup," said Lola. "Come sit with me. I want to hear about the call."

At the dining room table, Nicholas explained, "That was my new regional manager."

"New?"

"Yes. My old manager went with Home Depot. The rumor is she got an offer she couldn't refuse."

"What about the new manager?" she queried.

"He's a Kansas City native, a real go-getter. My suspension is up and he's ready for me to come back."

She studied his face. "You do not look happy about it."

"I don't know. When I went to fix the inventory codes, it just didn't feel the same. Maybe it's me. I just got the impression Bishop Hardware was changing."

"For better or worse?"

"Well, here's an example. The new manager wants me to fly in for a regional meeting. But he hasn't offered to pick up the cost of my ticket. In the old days, that would've been automatic. Plus, a buddy of mine told me they now require managers to work every Saturday. It used to be every other Saturday. Plus, the paperwork has about doubled and the company cars are no longer automatic. You have to prove yourself worthy."

"You don't have to go back, Nicholas," she reminded him. "We have enough money in the bank for you to take your time and find the job you want."

"Are you kidding? I wouldn't think of leaving you and the baby. It's just that, well, I'm not sure I want to work for corporate America again. It's gotten to be such a rat race, such a profit over people affair."

She smiled. "It doesn't surprise me."

"What do you mean?"

"From the first day I met you, you seemed to get the most enjoyment out of fixing things. Look how easy it was for you to fix our washer. And remember how you opened my chest."

"Your King Juba Chest ... I can't say that's the smartest thing I've ever done."

"You see our baby, all bright-eyed and happy. She's crawling really good now, like a little Mexican, ducking the gunfire in Juárez. She's got two more teeth. And believe it or not, she's trying to say words. I do not think this would be without the chest."

"What are you saying, Lola?"

"I have not been truthful with you, and it has been eating me inside. There's something I must tell you."

"What?" He wanted to hear it come out of her mouth.

"I made a final wish on the chest. It was the only way to save our baby."

"Lola, I thought we agreed we would take our chances."

She paused a long while. "I saw our chances as only a mother can see them, Nicholas. I felt our chances deep inside my womb. Believe me, it was horrible. It was all that Dr. Fox had predicted and more."

"So you jeopardized the lives of other again so we could come out on top?"

"Not this time, I promise. No one else will be harmed."

"How can you be so sure?"

"Because this time, I understand how the tree works. It let me understand. It let me see it face-to-face."

"Okay, well understand this," he declared. "We're getting rid of that chest as soon as the professor gets back. I don't want you going near it ... and if you do, Lola-"

"I won't. I promise you." She immediately got up, removed the storage key and access card from her purse and handed it to him. "I'm through with it."

He paused a long while. "Not saying I believe all this hocus-pocus, wish-upon-a-tree nonsense, but I'm curious. What was your grocery receipt?"

She smiled, nonchalantly. "Silly animals chasing me, that's all."

Silly, indeed. The first time Lola had brought the chest home to her Litchfield apartment, she had dreamed the Allen brothers dropped her off in the woods where she had been chased by lions. The new dream was almost identical. It was enough to make Lola wake up laughing at the stupid Texas rednecks. She thanked her lucky stars for her new life at RedFish and pushed the remnants of

Allen Brothers Construction out of her mind.

Later that afternoon, Nicholas' parents came over to get their beloved grandchild. They were fascinated by her lovely dimples, spiky brown hair and new front teeth.

In the living room near the white flocked Christmas tree, Nicholas' father held her high in the air, just above the dazzling ornaments. "Lolita Diane, you're going to be a Supreme Court Justice one day. Some of them are very old and wear diapers too."

"Thanks for letting us keep her for the weekend," said Nicholas' mother. "We have a lot of exciting things planned."

Seemingly bored by the itinerary, Nicholas' father turned up his lips. "A Barney Show and slip-slide? That's exciting? Heck, when I was that age, I was riding motorcycles."

"He means they put a picture of some hot wheels on the side of his crib," Nicholas' mother clarified.

They all chuckled.

"No candy or junk food," Lola warned them.

Nicholas' mother winked her eye at her husband. "We wouldn't think of it."

Once they had backed out of the driveway, Lola turned to Nicholas. "We have a free weekend. What do you want to do?"

"How about we go to the boat races on Lake Lou Yaeger?"

"Sure. But that's tomorrow, Saturday. What do you want to do this afternoon?" she pressed.

He hunched his shoulder. "I don't know. Any ideas?"

Lola's eyes lit up. "I have a great idea."

An hour later, they pulled up in front of the Mayberry Tool Repair Shop on Lenox Ave. The building was freshly painted and the pot holes in the driveway were gone.

Two construction workers came out of the door, talking to each other. "The old man knows his stuff, I'll give him that."

Lola looked at Nicholas. "This is the old guy I was telling

you about. He helped me with my nail gun. I think he was about to close down, but I got our company to let him do all of our repairs. Now, a few other companies are coming to him. I heard he's getting a little backed up."

"So what does that have to do with us?"

"I just wanted you to meet him. You are the hot shot retail manager from Bishop Hardware. Maybe, you can give him a few pointers on how to keep up with his workload."

Lola and Nicholas entered the old wood-framed shack and fought through the clutter. At the front counter, wearing a red and white Santa's hat, the old man leaned over a paint sprayer, jiggling the trigger.

He looked up with a smile. "Well, if it isn't the Seeko 2000 lady. Back to pick up some bandages for your injured crew?"

Lola smiled, coyly. "I am happy to inform you no nail gun injuries in three weeks."

"Outstanding! Except I happen to know RedFish shut down exactly three weeks ago for the holidays."

Lola started laughing. "You cannot blame a lady for trying to put her best foot forward."

"As far as I'm concerned, you can put your foot, leg, arm, chin ... anything you want forward in my shop. You've earned the right."

She turned to Nicholas. "I want you to meet my husband, Nicholas Hartman. Nicholas, this is Harry Mayberry, the man that keeps RedFish up and running."

Nicholas could barely shake his hand for staring at the paint sprayer. "That's a Wagner 414T Spray Tech, isn't it?"

"In fact it is," Harry confirmed. "The trigger's been jamming on the remodeling crew working that Rochester development job. They don't know why, and so far, I don't either."

"It's the glue," Nicholas reported. "The glue gets hot under the on-off switch casing and drips onto the trigger housing. We had to send quite a few of those back under a national recall."

Harry perked up. "You're in the repair business?"

"Not exactly. I manage a hardware store."

"Then you might've tangled with this other monstrosity." He reached under the counter to retrieve a huge black and red chain saw.

Nicholas chuckled. "Oh boy, Homelite 105. Run for your life."

"This guy from the old Litchfield sawmill swears up and down he's turned this thing off several times and it just kept going."

"He's not lying. These babies seem to have a mind of their own."

"Yeah, but I can't duplicate what he says is happening to him," Harry admitted. "Which means I can't fix it. And I don't send anything out of here unless it's fixed."

"There's a trick to it," said Nicholas. "It has to run a long time, until the wiring gets hot. Then if you turn it over-"

Lola cleared her throat. "Sorry, but I have been promised some French-Vanilla ice cream. We are not going to let an old broken chain saw get in the way, right Nicholas?"

"Right, right." He looked at Harry. "What time do you open on Monday?"

"Seven-thirty, senior citizen's time, which is about ten till eight."

"If you like, I can come by around nine to take a look at that saw?"

"I'd appreciate that. In fact, if you can fix it, you can pocket the repair fee. I'm sick of this thing hanging around."

A few minutes later at the ice cream shop, Nicholas gazed at Lola with budding revelation. "You think you're clever, don't you?"

She smiled, innocently. "What do you mean, Nicholas?"

"You knew I'd fall in love with that place. That's why you took me over there."

She took a few succulent licks from her ice cream cone. "I do not have the slightest idea what you mean. You're a big-time Penn State business graduate with a promising future in corporate America. Why would you want to go some place that makes you happy?"

Kristy finally made the announcement in February. She and Phillip Barlow were planning a huge June wedding inside the translucent blue towers of the Intercontinental San Francisco Hotel. It wasn't going to be just a wedding, but a grand appreciation ceremony and sentimental look back at their frantic return to civilization after eluding certain death on the Utah mountainside. Key members of the rescue team, along with Otis Redden's and Herman Johnson's family members were being flown in at Kristy's expense.

There was only one problem for Lola. She couldn't go.

Kristy explained. "Henry is going to give me away, just as he did at your wedding. That means I'll be there and Henry will be there and who's going to run the company? The only person I trust is you."

When Lola returned home that night, she told Nicholas, "I'm going to be the CEO of RedFish in June. That's all I've got to say."

He squinted. "What?

"Well, acting CEO," she clarified. "And that's all I've got to say."

"That's great."

"It-it-it is?" she stuttered, expecting him to respond in a jealous rage.

"Yes. One day I hope you move up to the point where you own your own company, just like me. And that's all I've got to say."

She grabbed the big coat hanger from the closet and started chasing him around the house.

As it turned out, Harry had asked him to come in as a partner.

"It didn't hurt that I landed a $4,000 sale yesterday from a diesel company down the street. I was just talking to this guy at the sandwich counter and the next thing I know, he's bringing us a ton of pumps and circuit breakers to overhaul."

"That is good, I guess." Lola was still in shock.

Nicholas punched some numbers into his Smartphone. "I think we're going to need some part-time help. Is that young Raúl guy you sponsored at the college as sharp as you say?"

"Raúl?! Oh no, you're not stealing our employee!"

"This is America, Dollface. White men with deep pockets rule ... which reminds me. How much do we have in the bank? I need to come to the table with a $10,000 deposit to seal this deal."

She started laughing. "Let me get this into my mind. You want me to finance your plan to steal our employees? Is that right?"

"Look at it this way. The next time we go to a RedFish function, you'll either be going with an up-and-coming Bill Gates style entrepreneur, or a deadbeat. Either way, I plan to publicize my status to ALL your coworkers so they know the caliber of man you've married."

"You wouldn't?"

"I can hear them talking now: *Do you know that Lola's*

deadbeat husband asked me for a joint to ease his troubled mind. He can't keep a job, you know. Plus, they say he's a bad father and...."

"Okay, okay, take the money," she relented. "But you'd better start showing a profit *rápida, Señor.* And you'd better leave Raúl alone. He works for RedFish and that's that."

To drown her out, Nicholas started singing Johnny's old slavery song: NOBODY KNOWS THE TROUBLE IZZ SEEN, NOBODY KNOWS BUT JESUS....

****

A few weeks later, Nicholas came home with a notebook full of documents. His face beamed with intrigue.

Lola sat at the table, going through papers of her own.

"What are you doing right now?" he asked.

She picked up a calendar and circled a few dates. "Your sister wants to keep Lolita Diane again. But they're having some kind of clown show and kid festival at her nursery those two days. I'm trying to find another date for your sister. Why?"

"Because I need your undivided attention."

Lola pushed everything aside. "I'm listening."

"Tell me about this nail gun, the one the Taiwanese guy invented."

"Harry is the expert. Why didn't *he* tell you?" she asked.

"He did, at least, he started. He had to leave early again today. He's getting up in age and he's got these health issues. Don't ask me what. I mean, he's heavy on sugar and he knows it's bad. Beyond that, wouldn't say."

"So you're in business with a sick partner? Is that good?"

"Sick and old," Nicholas confirmed. "Actually, I think that

was the whole idea behind the partnership. He wants the Mayberry name to continue. His son doesn't give a hoot about repairs. So he's really glad I came along. He hopes I'll keep the tradition going."

"I am so sorry for him. He is a very nice man."

"Don't worry. I'll take care of him, no matter what. Now, exactly what did he tell you about the nail gun?"

"He said it was *magnífico*, the best he had ever seen."

"If he's right, what would that mean to RedFish?"

"It would cut down on injuries and give us more production. It would give us an advantage over other companies."

"How many do you think Ms K would buy?"

"Depending on the price, maybe one hundred," Lola estimated. "Why do you ask these things?"

"Okay, listen to me and I want you to hear me out," he demanded with an intensifying tone. "What if Mayberry Tools owned the patent to the gun and sold a million nationwide?"

"But that is not fair. The gun should belong to us," she whined.

"Why? Because you were out there looking for a better gun and bumped into Harry? Do you know how many safety managers across the United States are out there looking for a better nail gun? Tell me why RedFish should get it."

She thought about it. "Because..."

"Right. *Because*. Because you're there and you love Ms K and Henry and because RedFish gave you a chance. Blah-blah-blah, strike up the violins. I'm asking you to think bigger than that."

"How big?"

"Big enough to appreciate the beauty of this deal. Here's what I have in mind. Say Mayberry Tools owns the patent. We sell the gun to construction companies and hardware outlets nationwide. We give RedFish its first one hundred guns for free. And for the first year, just for using the gun and sharing your experiences with it, we give you a ten percent royalty on all sales made. That's millions of dollars for doing nothing but using the free guns and giving me positive testimonials that I can use in sales paraphernalia."

Her eyes widened. "Wow. That is fantastic, if you can pull it off. But what about the surcharge to bring it to this country?"

"I researched the Congressional Records today. The tariff expired a year ago. The idiot lobbyists haven't been paying attention, and now the coast is clear."

"So how do you plan to get control of the patent?" she asked.

I'm going to Taiwan," he declared. "I'm going to find this guy and make him an offer he can't refuse."

The island of Taiwan was a thirteen thousand square mile strip of rugged mountains, steep gorges and magnificent erosions, lying off the southeastern coast of mainland China. A heavily disputed territory, confiscated from the Empire of Japan at the end of World War II, Taiwan fostered a tense atmosphere between the Communist-backed People's Republic of China and the Republic of China, the original Benshengren immigrants who fled the mainland after losing the Chinese Civil War.

Nicholas flew into Taipei City, the largest city on the island and official capital, just before dark. A bustling, highly industrialized, densely populated metropolis on the banks of the famous Danshui River, the streets crawled with scooters and bicycles and makeshift taxis. High speed trains rumbled in the distance, merging the high tech miracles of innovation with the low tech riches of magnificently constructed temples and shrines.

He checked into the Grand Victoria Hotel, a 19th century Victorian style edifice in the safe DaJhih Miramar business district in the heart of the city. Although, on the island, the second language was English, he had arranged to meet an interpreter as soon as he arrived.

Nicholas had a knack for assessing his own weaknesses. There were so many things he didn't understand about the culture and politics of international business in Taiwan. More importantly, if he was going to find the mysterious nail gun inventor, he needed someone who knew the island in ways beyond street signs and fancy buildings.

Jimmy "Chungman" Lee was an unusually tall national Taiwan University student with shaggy black hair, a flattened face and marble gray eyes. Since his mother was American and his father, Chinese, on his website he advertised himself as a bridge between cultures. That bridge was going to cost $500 a day.

As soon as he found Nicholas, waiting in the hotel lobby, he took him across the street to a gift shop, then to a 7-11 Store to buy some cigarettes, and finally to an exclusive seafood restaurant overlooking the river.

After a couple of glasses of pearl milk tea, Chungman asked in a low voice, "Who do you work for?"

"I have my own company," Nicholas replied.

"No. Which agency ... NSA, CIA?"

Nicholas smiled, widely. "You're serious, aren't you?"

"As serious as the people following you, and please don't look around."

Nicholas suddenly realized why they had made so many pit stops. Chungman had wanted to draw out the shadowy, uninvited observers of their small international parade.

Still smiling from such an incredibly ridiculous *James Bond* miscue, Nicholas inquired, "Why would anyone think I'm a spy?"

"Young, white Caucasian from the US of A, traveling alone

with no official meetings or University lectures scheduled. Why would they think anything else?"

"Who is *they*?"

"Probably mainland intelligence," Chungman speculated. "They watch the airport to see who's coming in. Don't worry, they'll stay their distance as long as you keep your nose clean."

"And how do I do that?"

"By staying out of the company of political activists, secession sympathizers and the Men In Black."

"*Men In Black?*" Nicholas wondered what Will Smith's movie had to do with it.

"Taiwan's Military Intelligence Bureau ... MIB. But don't worry. I'll make sure you don't wander off too far. That's why you're paying me $600 a day."

Nicholas frowned. "I thought it was $500 a day?"

Chungman glanced at a stocky Asian man in a dark suit, standing by the entrance. "That's before these snap-your-neck Ninjas started following you around."

"Okay, I'm going to make this short and sweet." Nicholas pulled out a small tablet with a name written down. "I need to find this guy. His name is Lo Lee Soong. He's an inventor of sorts."

Chungman stared at the paper. "The Soong family comes from a long line of wealthy construction magnets. Your inventor boy was probably somebody's great, great, great genius grandson on that good opium."

Nicholas filled in the rest of the story about the hit-and-run and mainland China's suspicions Lo Lee was a spy for the West.

"You think you can find him?"

"Probably not," admitted Chungman. "You're talking 1970-something. I mean, the guy's got to be a thousand years old by now. Dude, why didn't you just come here for a good time. I could've hooked you up with a few party girls from the University and you could've gone back home with a smile on your face."

"Your website said you were the top gun on this island," Nicholas reminded him. "But if you're just a pimp with a party connection, I guess I'll have to go another route."

Chungman chuckled. "That's good. That's very good. I believe it's advance PSYC 103. I'm supposed to recoil at the thought of falling short of your expectations and then bust my ass to prove you wrong. NYU maybe, or Cal State, right?"

"Penn State," Nicholas corrected.

"Okay, Mr. Penn State. Here's the skinny. Pimping would be a lot easier and conducive to our health than what you're talking about. If this Soong guy was the target of a hit-and-run, ordered by the mainland, it means he had something or they thought he had something. Either way, the guy's gone underground to save his neck. The secret is still corked in the bottle and life on the Asian Peninsula remains one big tangy bowl of shark fin soup. Now, here you come with a big corkscrew."

"All I want to do is talk to the man about the nail gun."

"Spy talking to a spy about State secrets. That's what they'll see."

"Why do they have to see anything?" asked Nicholas. "If you find this guy, why can't we set up a private session where nobody's looking?"

"Arrange a private session where all these island creeps go blind? You just went up to $800 a day."

"Let's make it a flat $1000," said Nicholas. "But this has to happen within twenty-four hours. Otherwise, the whole deal's off and you don't get paid."

Chungman wrapped his thin lips around a juicy crab leg, sucking in all of its luscious Asian-Pacific flavors. "What business did you say you were in again ... loan sharking?"

Nicholas smiled, implacably. "What did your website say

... top gun on the island, a bridge between cultures for only $500 a day?"

They both chuckled, incredulously.

"Be in the hotel lobby at 3:00 pm tomorrow. If I've got something, we'll bust a bitch-cap on this suicide mission. Otherwise, I won't even show. The less they see of me with you, the better."

"Better for who?"

"For me, Dude. I'm the one that's got to live here after you're gone."

"Where's the outstanding customer service in all of this?" asked Nicholas.

"Those customer service guys are already dead or in prison on the mainland, which reminds me of a minor detail I need to pass along."

"Yes."

"For you, everything is bugged, everything is traceable. The roaming satellite that bounces your cell phone signal belongs to the Chinese government. Don't call anyone. Don't say anything you might regret. If you're not in jail by tomorrow, I'll pick you up at three ... maybe."

At 3:00 pm the next day, Nicholas stood in the hotel lobby next to the checkout counter. Although he kept telling himself he was being paranoid, he felt he was being watched by a thousand eyes. Hard-faced men peered over newspapers; cleaning people wiped the counters and ashtrays around him too long; young, seductive women passed too closely, smiling at him for no reason at all.

What was he thinking? He was a small town Midwest yokel with a wife and baby back home. There was no way he should've been wading waist-deep into a dark river, filled with intelligence spooks and mainland Ninjas. Was it too late to bail out ... *was it*?

I could probably cut my losses, forget about this mysterious nail gun guy and go back home. His mind congratulated him for finally thinking in sensible terms.

But sensibility had come too late. At that instance, the glass doors at the front entrance swung open. Two young boys dressed in red circus costumes, riding unicycles and twirling fire sticks, sailed through the door. One had a loud boom box tied to his waist, the other, a shrill-sounding whistle in his mouth.

As hotel security rushed toward them, a maid tapped Nicholas on the shoulder and pointed to the kitchen.

Nervously beating the air, Chungman beckoned. "Hurry!"

They scurried through the kitchen, out the back door and into an old, beat-up Volkswagen van. A few elaborate turns down back alleys and narrow streets finally ushered them to the open highway.

"You owe me seventy-five bucks for the distraction," he quickly announced. "I don't want it coming out of my fee."

"Was all of that necessary?" asked Nicholas.

"Is a Brown Booby Bird brown? I mean, this dude you want to meet is like an old rusty grenade with the pin already pulled. It might wait five seconds, or it might just blow up in your hand."

"You found him?"

"I found his daughter, name change and all, which is as close as you're going to get to somebody that hot."

Nicholas squinted. "Hot?"

"Your inventor boy was a straight up spook with big-time street credits with the US of A. He was like Merrill Lynch talking. And he brought some heavyweight papers to the table, including the exact location of all the mainland missiles pointed at Taiwan."

Nicholas' eyes widened. "Wow, like in the movies."

"Something like that," said Chungman. "Except over here,

there are no second takes and death scenes are permanent."

Nicholas tried to swallow the growing lump in his throat. "Sooo, ahhh, what happened?"

Chungman continued. "Somebody finally dropped a dime on him. But because of his family's investments throughout China, they didn't want a big stink. So they tried to put him down easy with a runaway car fender. But the guy survived and went underground. Nobody's seen him since."

"Are the people from the mainland still looking for him?" asked Nicholas.

"More like, looking for what he's got. Word on the street said he went down with something big."

Nicholas could feel his heart pounding. "You think this is going to be dangerous?"

Chungman laughed so intensely, the van started to swerve.

"Let's put it this way. I want all my money before you get out of this van. And I'm only going to wait an hour for you to come out. After that, I'm gone, history, baby. And by the way, you can't go back to that hotel again."

"But my ticket and passport are in my room," Nicholas explained.

Chungman laughed even harder. "If they find out you've met with this Lo Lee dude, do you really think they're going to let you catch a plane out of here?"

"What are you saying?"

"What I'm saying is we're ten minutes away. You need to decide whether you want to go through with this or not. Either way, I still want my money for the risky legwork. And if you go through with it, all bets are off on the hotel and airport. Spy meeting spy can lead to some serious lock-up, beat-up, maybe, lethal injection shoot-up."

"I keep telling you. I'm not a spy."

"Well, if you go to this meeting," warned Chungman. "You sure as hell better start acting like one."

Lola didn't like the silence that haunted her world. Nicholas hadn't called since he boarded the plane in Chicago for Taiwan. Something was wrong.

He'd better not be stuck on some stupid mountainside in the middle of nowhere, she kept thinking to herself. *I don't have any more wishes left.*

She canvassed all of the major news outlets. There were no crashes or storms or mudslides or floods that might've washed him away. There was no political unrest in Taiwan, no terrorist bombs exploding in the streets.

She called his sister and then his mother. Neither had heard from him.

At work the next day, Lola found Goodboy in his office. "What do you know about Taiwan?"

"I know it's one of the most volatile places on the globe. China has some five hundred missiles pointed at the island at all times. Japan doesn't like the economic competition. The United States has to walk a fine line to support the democratic government, and yet, avoid starting World War III with China. Do I need to say more?"

"Nicholas took a business trip to Taiwan yesterday. I haven't heard from him since."

"Probably nothing to worry about, beyond normal worrying. In that part of the world, communication networks can easily go on the blink. Give the man some breathing room, Lola. I'm sure you'll hear from him soon enough."

****

Nicholas was waiting for a response.

He had walked into a quaint little restaurant in the port city of Keelung. Surrounded by green mountainous slopes that rolled out to the East China Sea, the city was a Mecca for huge cargo ships and fishing fleets. A sparse group of rugged-looking tuna fishermen sat inside the cramped building, eating sushi and laughing, loudly, at porno magazines.

Nicholas had flopped down at a table by the window, ordered a beer, then whispered to the waitress. "Please help me. I need to talk to Jolin. It's very important."

No one had approached him. After a second beer to calm his nerves, he made a trip to the restroom. That's when a young muscular Asian man with dark eyes followed him into the smelly closet-like enclosure and pulled out a gun.

"What is your business here?" he demanded.

Just a Midwestern yokel, trying to get himself killed, he thought to himself.

"I'm a businessman from America." He fought to subdue the shakiness in his voice. "I was told Jolin could help me with a project."

"What is this project?"

"A nail gun her father invented. I want to buy the rights."

The man leered. "Your real business, before I blow your head off."

Chungman's profound warning suddenly raced through his mind.

If you go to this meeting. You sure as hell better start acting like a spy.

"I'm here to pick up the package," Nicholas reluctantly confessed.

The man bashed Nicholas across the head with the butt of the pistol, sending him to the floor.

"You have the nerve to come here six years after my uncle is dead, asking for the package? You Americans are all alike. I should blow your head off right here on the spot."

At that moment, a young Taiwanese woman in her late twenties stuck her head in the door. Her face was softly curved, adorned in blue and green mascara that accented her bright brown eyes. She spoke with obvious authority.

"No, Shih-Chang, bring him to the back."

In a small sleeping room behind the kitchen, she handed Nicholas a wet towel to nurse his bruised forehead. From the corner of the room, the man with the gun watched, anxiously awaiting the chance to finish him off.

"Who are you with?" she interrogated.

Mayberry Tool Repair he started to answer, then realized how rinky-dink that sounded.

"MTR," he finally replied.

She frowned with unawareness.

He nodded. "You don't want to know."

"You people abandoned my father. After all he had done, you left him to die, a lonely old man in a wheelchair. Why shouldn't Shih-Chang put a bullet through your heart?"

"We appreciated everything, especially the missile info," Nicholas tried to improvise. "But there was a mix-up. Our field agent was ... was fatally compromised. The information never reached the next level."

"My daughter is twelve now. We've wasted six good years of her life, waiting for you traitors to keep your word."

"I'm sorry for the delay and your father's untimely passing," he said. "I'm prepared to make you an offer that will, in some small way, compensate you for your loss."

"I want the same offer, no more, no less," she demanded.

"I-aahh, I guess with so many years gone by, it would be good to review what you understand our arrangement to be."

"I will give you my father's information. In return, you will arrange safe passage for me and my daughter to the US. We have relatives in California that will care for us."

"And the gun? Do you still have the nail gun?"

"The nail gun is here with many of my father's gadgets. But he never mentioned it as part of the arrangements."

"I'm sure he intended to protect you from some things."

"The gun is of no value to me. You can have it. But only when me and my daughter are safe."

At that instance, someone knocked on the door. A short, chubby cook whispered something in her ear.

She turned to Nicholas. "Your driver has been compromised. If he knows anything, they will know it in a few hours. How do you plan to get us out of here?"

****

Lola sat in her new glass office, interviewing a potential safety assistant, when she noticed Kristy, standing outside her door. She excused herself from the interview and stepped outside.

"You need me?"

"I think so." Kristy handed her a piece of paper. "This international fax just came in on my fax machine. But it's for you. I think it's from Nicholas."

Lola read it:

LOLA. I CAN'T USE MY CELL PHONE. AUTHORITIES MAY BE MONITORING IT. I MAY HAVE A PROBLEM GETTING OUT OF THE COUNTRY. SO, PLEASE STAY BY THE FAX JUST IN CASE I NEED YOUR HELP.

"Is he in some kind of trouble?" asked Kristy.

She sobbed, fearing in the back of her mind, the old tree was getting ready to double-cross her in the cruelest manner. "I don't know, Ms K. I don't know anything at all."

****

It had been Jolin's idea to use the fax machine. She had opened a trap door beneath a fish tank and led him down a twelve foot ladder to her father's workshop. After watching the old man send out so many clandestine messages over the fax to agents on the mainland, Japan, Hong Kong and all over the Pacific Rim, Jolin suspected their best hope of avoiding China's sophisticated eavesdropping apparatuses lay in the old fashioned low-tech white elephant machine.

The room was a thirty square foot dungeon, cluttered with lathes and grinders and welding equipment. The tables were still glazed with metal shavings from Lo Lee's last project. Diagrams and patent notices lined the wall.

"He loved this place," she remembered, pouring them a cup

of Japanese sake. "This is where he died." She pointed to an old wheelchair in the corner.

Captivated by the many gadgets and machines around the room, Nicholas shook his head in awe. "No doubt he was a brilliant man."

"Brilliant and patriotic," she noted. "I received his love of country, but his brains went to my daughter, Maggie Ji. She already has an IQ of 131; such a waste in Taiwan. Because of so much rain here in Keelung, my father used to say the mountains were crying for Maggie Ji, crying for her to be set free."

"Where is she now?" he asked.

"She'll be home from school in an hour, maybe less. You will have a plan for us by then?"

Nicholas dropped his head. "I've never been very good at lying. No reason to try now. I'm not who you think I am. I'm just a businessman here to make you an offer on the nail gun. I don't have a plan."

She got up, a flaming anger in her eyes. She walked over to a shelf containing a black carrying case the size of an old IBM typewriter. She slammed the case on the table, knocking over the cups of sake.

"Here's your stupid nail gun. Get out!"

"Listen, I didn't mean to-"

"To expose us as accessories to espionage so we can go to prison? Do you know what they'll do to me and my young daughter in jail? Please, just get out!"

"No." Nicholas refused. "I'm responsible for taking the cork off this bottle. Either, I put it back on, or we all go down together. Now tell me what information your father had that made the people on the mainland want to kill him?"

****

Lola sat in Kristy's office, staring at the fax machine, praying it would come to life and answer all of the questions swirling around in her head. She had almost given up hope, when the ping of the bell and the whine of a hundred angry mosquitoes pierced her ears.

Another message came through:

LOLA. I AM IN CONTACT WITH SOMEONE WHO HAS VERY IMPORTANT INFORMATION FOR OUR UNCLE. WE ARE ALL INDISPOSED IN KEELUNG. THE EMBASSY SUITE HOTEL IS TOO FAR AWAY. WE NEED THE SAME FIVE STAR ACCOMMODATIONS MS. K RECEIVED ON THE MOUNTAIN. PLEASE ADVISE IF HENRY CAN USE HIS CONTACTS TO MAKE THIS HAPPEN.

Lola ran upstairs to Goodboy's office to show him the message.

"Good grief! How'd he get himself into this rattlesnake den?"

"Do you understand what he's saying?" asked Lola.

"Seems he's gotten mixed up with some sort of spy network in the port city of Keelung. Evidently, these people have information for Uncle Sam. Must be somebody watching so he's trapped and can't get to the US Embassy. He's asking if I can get a rescue team in there to get him out."

"Oh my God. This is serious. Nicholas would not say he is in danger if it was not true. What can we do?"

"First of all, he needs to understand it's not like the movies. The military is just not inclined to respond to every cry for help, especially in that region of the world. One misstep and you're dodging nukes from China and North Korea."

"But we cannot just leave him there."

"I'm afraid that's exactly what they're going to do, unless he's got something that makes it worth the extraordinary risk involved in getting him out."

She looked at the fax sheet again. "It doesn't say what kind of information."

"Then, that's where we need to start."

****

Nicholas and Jolin read Goodboy's return fax:

WE CANNOT COOK THE PIE FOR YOUR FIVE STAR HOTEL STAY UNTIL WE KNOW THE INGREDIENTS. PLEASE SPECIFY HOW THIS IS GOING TO TASTE TO OUR UNCLE AND HIS GUESTS ONCE IT HAS BEEN SERVED.

Nicholas frowned "Pie? Ingredients?"

Jolin smiled. "Your Lola is asking what information we have. They need to know whether it is worthwhile."

He looked at her. "Is it? Tell me it is. I mean, if I'm going to be busting rocks in China, I'd at least want to know what sent me there."

She hesitated a while. "I don't know what it is. My father never told me."

Nicholas eyes bulged. "Come again."

"He felt, if they tortured me and I didn't know, I would have nothing to give them."

"So he took the secret to his grave?"

"Not exactly," she clarified. "He told Maggie Ji. Only she

knows. There is always a small chance they wouldn't torture a child."

Nicholas shook his head with frustration. "So you don't have a clue?"

"Yes, I have a clue. But that's all I have."

She pulled two bricks from the wall to retrieve a plastic bag with a small strip of paper. The paper had three numbers on them:

GAO-TRL-513888(LCS)
GAO-TRL-531158(LCS)
GAO-TRL-531299(LCS)

"What does this mean?" asked Nicholas.

"My father said the right people would know."

"Okay, okay, if we wait until your daughter gets home, maybe she can tell us," he contemplated.

"She won't tell you. He made her promise. She won't tell anyone until she gets to America."

****

The bell on Kristy's fax pinged again. Another message came through: *The right people will know.*

GAO-TRL-513888(LCS)
GAO-TRL-531158(LCS)
GAO-TRL-531299(LCS)

Goodboy scratched his head. "These look like government records of some kind. Could take months to figure it out."

"Months!" Lola panicked. "He could be dead by then."

"Let me try something." Goodboy jumped on the phone.

"Hey John, this is Henry. I need a favor ... No, this has nothing to do with water running on the ceiling. This could be a matter of national security ... That's right ... Listen, are you still in touch with your friends in the Big House, the one that has access to that new supercomputer? ... Let's see if we can get him to put it to work."

Goodboy and Lola waited for two hours before the call came in. As he listened, Goodboy's face turned ghostly white. When he finally hung up the phone, he stared at Lola a long, excruciating moment.

"This is big, really big. I can't even tell you what's going on. Just know they're going in after Nicholas. They're going to get him out."

****

Nicholas and Jolin were still in the basement workshop when a small bell jingled.

"That's Maggie Ji, home from school," said Jolin. "If I don't ring back, she knows to leave and go to a relative. It's our warning system."

Minutes later, Jolin brought Maggie down the steep ladder. She was a petite twelve year old with thin shoulders, big eyes and a precocious smile. She wore khaki pants, blue tennis shoes and a brightly colored blouse with flowered designs. She sported a seashell necklace around her neck and a silver bracelet on her wrist.

She eyed Nicholas, warily. "Who is he?"

"He's the man who's taking us to America," Jolin explained.

"You're late. Do they spank your legs with a ruler when

you're late in America?"

"No, I'm afraid not," he replied.

"They should," she declared with condemnation.

"Well thanks a lot, Maggie, for explaining the rules."

She turned to her mother. "Coming home, I saw some men behind the trees. They were watching our restaurant. I don't believe they're our friends."

Hoping to forestall her fears, Nicholas joshed, "Were they real, or just your imagination?"

She glared at him, harshly. "Are you real, or just my imagination?"

Jolin smiled. "You see?"

At that moment, another fax came over the old machine:

THE PIE INGREDIENTS HAVE BEEN APPROVED BY THE MASTER CHEF. CALLED THE BAKERY TO SEE WHAT TIME WOULD BE BEST TO PUT IT IN THE OVEN. EVAN IS YOUR BAKING CONSULTANT. 1-800-4534433. YOU WILL HAVE TO GIVE HIM YOUR PIE RECIPE NUMBER WHICH IS THE SAME AS THE LAST FOUR DIGITS OF YOUR SOCIALIZATION GUEST NUMBER.

Social security number, he thought to himself.

Nicholas immediately turned on his smartphone and called the number.

A friendly, customer-oriented male voice came on the line. "Yes this is Evan. How can I help you?"

"I-ah, I was told to call you?"

"Yes. Are you the guy with the *cake*?"

Nicholas recognized the trick question. "No, pie."

"For verification, can you give me your recipe number?"

"It's 9890."

"Okay, that corresponds to our records," he confirmed. "Tell me, are you cooking one pie or several pies for your uncle's event?"

"Three to be exact."

"Okay, by calling this toll-free number, we have locked in your order. You may bring the pies in for our expert inspection at 9:00 pm your time. Is that going to be too late for your uncle's event?"

"If that's the best you can do, I'll manage."

"Good, good. Now, I'd like you to keep your phone on. But if your battery is low, you can recharge it and turn it on again around 8:30 pm or so. It's important we're able to contact you at that time. You understand how pies require attention to details, don't you? Or they can end up tasting really bad?"

"I do understand."

"One more thing," he added. "Sometimes our new customers get frustrated, trying to bake for the very first time. My recommendation is to take a walk along the beach and calm your nerves. You have a beach close by, don't you?"

Nicholas looked at Jolin. She nodded, affirmatively.

"Yes, yes we do," confirmed Nicholas.

"Okay, then. Happy baking. Happy beach walking. We'll be in touch real soon. I'm sure your uncle's event will be a big success."

Hoping to preserve the life of his battery, Nicholas turned off his Smartphone. He looked at the time, then at Jolin. "We have four hours to wait. Will we be safe down here?"

Before she could answer, they heard a commotion upstairs. Jolin turned on a computer which showed a split screen of the kitchen and dining room. Brandishing guns and night sticks, several thuggish-looking Chinese men searched the closets and restrooms. With the trap door concealed by a thick rug and fish tank, Nicholas was confident they'd overlook it.

That's when one of the men came through the door with a huge German Shepherd tracking dog. The dog pushed out its long nose and began sniffing each corner of the dining room. Eventually, his hungry prowling would lead to the back room where the trapdoor was located.

"Is there another way out of here?" asked Nicholas.

"No," said Jolin.

"Yes," said Maggie Ji.

They both stared at Maggie Ji.

"Grandfather showed me. He said this day might come."

"Where, Maggie?"

She pointed to the wheelchair in the corner. "Move it, please."

Behind the chair was a large wooden Galileo grandfather clock. Maggie walked over and pushed a lever. The glass case swung open like a dollhouse door.

"It leads to the sea. That's what Grandfather told me."

Nicholas gripped the handle on the nail gun case. "Wherever it leads, it's better than staying here. Come on. Let's go."

"Wait." Maggie climbed up a small step ladder and grabbed a can of spray paint. She sprayed it all over the floor and near the bookcase. "Dogs have very sensitive noses. As long as he's sneezing, he can't pick up our scent."

"Wow, where did you learn that?" asked Nicholas.

"From one of the spy books you obviously haven't read."

He looked at Jolin. "Is that leg and ruler thing just for being late, or can it be applied as needed?"

A damp, dark cave greeted them on the other side of the old clock. Nicholas found a torch and some matches and fired up the musky air with a sparkling blaze. They followed a single trail that led deep into the mountainside, along jagged cliffs, under low ceilings and around tight corners that forced them to stoop and crawl.

Two hours later, after wandering around in circles, Nicholas mustered enough courage to admit the obvious. “I think we’re lost.”

Sitting on a rock, trying to figure a way out, Maggie Ji looked at her mother. “He‘s no *James Bond,* is he?”

“I’m sitting right here. I can hear you, young lady.”

“I’m just saying, you don’t have a compass or secret map or anything? What about a gun. Do you even have a gun?”

“I have this nail gun,” he reminded her. “Which I’m tempted to take out and fasten up a certain pair of loose lips.”

“He’s not with American Intelligence,” Jolin explained.

“True, dat.” She dipped into her bag of American slang.

“Listen, if you have any ideas about getting us out of here, I’d be glad to hear them,” said Nicholas.

“Well, if that’s your way of asking for help...”

“Maggie Ji, get on with it,” her mother scolded.

“We need to know which direction to go, right. The GPS on your phone can tell us that. Please tell me you have GPS.”

Of course I do,” he confirmed. “But you can’t pick up a satellite signal inside this mountain.”

She pointed to the cliff above them. “If you go high enough. All we need is a little crack in the formation.”

Nicholas’ eyes bucked. “Up there?”

“What’s wrong? Your mama didn’t put your climbing diaper on you today?” she mocked. “Give me your phone. I’ll do it.”

“No, I’ll do it.” Nicholas forced out a puny override. It took him a few seconds to realize he had been a victim of advance PSYC 103.

He gingerly eased his way up the rugged black wall, watching as loose rocks tumbled into the dark ravine below. It didn’t help to have a heckler like Maggie Ji in the audience, berating his feeble performance.

With both feet dangling from a high ledge, he fired up his

Smartphone. "It's working!"

"Duh!" she scoffed.

"It says south is that way," he pointed. "That's the way to the ocean."

"We see. Now please come down before something happens," ordered Jolin.

Suddenly, out of nowhere, a spooked black bat whizzed past Nicholas' head. With wild gyrations, he fanned and swiped, losing his balance and his phone. Clinging tightly to the ledge, he snaked his way down the wall, finally landing at Jolin's feet.

"Oh my goodness! Are you alright?!"

Nicholas blinked his eyes. For a split second, she looked and sounded like Lola.

"I'm-ah. I'm fine."

"Wish we could say the same for the phone." Maggie Ji stared into the ravine.

"I can't believe this!" said Nicholas. "It was your idea."

She shook her head. "I know, I know. I keep thinking you're a real spy."

It took another hour. But eventually, they found the mouth of the cave. It opened up onto a sandy white beach that stretched a half mile to the sea.

Gazing out at the shadowy paradise, they quickly discovered they were not alone. Campfires, tattered wooden markers, broken down porta-potties and scarecrow-like figures dotted the landscape. Nicholas kept waiting for zombies to run out and eat their brains.

High atop the hill, overlooking the beach, there was sporadic movement. Someone shouted through a bullhorn, a huge gun thundered in the distance, and to their horror, the first artillery shell came roaring in.

The shell exploded far short of the makeshift zombie city,

giving Nicholas a chance to pull Jolin and Maggie Ji back into the cave.

"What the hell!" Nicholas' face turned red.

Jolin finally explained, "It's the rehearsal for the Keelung Ghost Festival, the *Festival of the Dead.*"

In 1851, in the border area of Shichiouling, a major dispute had broken out between two warring factions over livestock and water resources. A monk from Ching-an Temple, the religious center for the Changchou community, had led a group to Fangting to clash with Chuanchou immigrants, causing a violent uprising and horrific bloodshed on both sides.

To commemorate the fallen souls, and honor the Old Venerable Temple where the bones had been buried, each year, the port city of Keelung and other cities throughout the island, held the Ghost Festival. The artillery blasts were part of a modern-day re-enactment of the sacred battles that had been fought so many years ago.

With a pitiful face, Jolin informed him, "They'll practice for hours."

He looked at his watch. "We don't have hours. We need to be on the beach by the ocean in ten minutes."

For the first time, Maggie Ji appeared quiet and withdrawn, holding tightly to her mother's waist. The loud artillery shells, exploding directly in front of them, was more than even a twelve year old smart aleck could take.

Don't worry," said Jolin. "It's going to be alright."

But it wasn't alright. The three of them had begun to hear voices coming from inside the cave. It didn't take a rocket scientist to realize the mainland thugs inside the restaurant had never given up. They had gotten a new dog with a new nose. And now, they were hot on Nicholas' trail.

"We can't stay here," declared Nicholas. The voices were

getting closer; the yelp of the vicious canine was just behind them, and closing fast.

Nicholas took Maggie Ji by the hand. "You scared?"

She nodded. Glassy tears of innocence streamed down her face.

"I would be too, except ... my mama made me wear these special running diapers. Not even an artillery shell can catch up. You stay with me, you're going to be fine. You understand?"

She nodded again.

"Okay, okay, we wait for the guns to fire. When they stop, we head for the sea."

The guns pounded the little zombie village with four or five rounds, then stopped.

Instantly, the petrified trio began their mad dash across the white sand. Had the bull horn general stayed true to his previous cadence, they would've made it through the zombie village in plenty of time. But something about the lack of precision and utter lack of destruction of the target made him angry. He ordered them in a loud, condemning, premature voice to try again.

The ear-piercing barrage was unrelenting. The explosions rained down on them like sickles of fire. The sand shifted so erratically, Maggie Ji lost her footing and fell to the ground.

Nicholas picked her up and brushed the sand from her eyes. "You're going to let an old man in diapers who's not even a real spy outrun you? Come on!"

They were up and running again, Jolin, a short distance behind. That's when they heard the clatter of gunfire, coming from the mouth of the cave.

The mainland thugs had spotted them, streaking across the sand. Not wanting to chance a risky chase beneath the rain of artillery fire, their desperate strategy quickly coalesced into an all-out Asian bushwack. They opened fire, spraying the three escaping traitors with a firestorm of bullets.

It worked. Jolin took a single slug in the leg and dropped to the sand.

With bullets still sizzling through the air, Nicholas went back for her.

"Don't quit on me now," he scolded her. "A true patriot would never bring shame to her father's name by quitting. Grab my neck and hold on."

As he helped her up, the voice in the bullhorn cried out again. But before they could fire, someone else did.

The grenade launcher sounded like a Black Cat rocket on the Fourth of July. When it exploded near the mouth of the cave, it disintegrated everything in its path.

Nicholas looked back just in time to see three mainland thugs splatter into small pieces. The rest of them hustled back into the cave.

Two Navy SEAL's, dressed in black wet suits, stood next to a rubber speedboat. The taller SEAL had already loaded the launcher for another shot.

The shorter, muscular SEAL assisted Maggie Ji, Jolin and Nicholas into the boat. "What happened to your phone?"

"Let's just say the bats ate it," replied Nicholas. "I'll explain later."

****

On a Navy submarine, cruising beneath the dark blue waters of the Pacific, Maggie Ji stood over Jolin's bed, inspecting the fresh bandages on her leg. "Does it hurt much?"

She smiled. "No. The bullet went right through. And they gave me something for the pain."

"Don't worry, Mother. America has the best medical treatment in the world. With the horrible food they eat, they have to."

Jolin smiled. "So I've heard, Maggie Ji. So I've heard."

Maggie turned to Nicholas, sitting in a chair on the other side of the bed. "You saved my mother and me. Not bad for a fake spy who wears diapers."

He grinned. "You didn't do so bad yourself."

She stared at the black nail gun case Nicholas gripped in his hand. "Did Grandfather leave you a secret message in there?"

"No," he said. "I'm afraid you're the only one with secrets."

She walked over to Nicholas, removed her sterling silver bracelet and handed it to him. "Now you have secrets too."

Nicholas frowned. "Huh?"

"Grandfather said give it to someone I trusted. Everything you want to know is inside."

A week after his return from Taiwan, Nicholas was lying on the sofa, bouncing Lolita Diane on his stomach. She had taken her first few steps and was beaming from all of the attention.

Nicholas was chatting with her, one of their many father-daughter talks to come.

"Of course, you've probably already heard. Your father is a big-time secret covert espionage operations spy specialist for MTR. That's Mayberry Tool Repair for those not familiar with the top secret jargon. The President keeps calling, bugging the heck out of me. The *James Bond* people want me to come on-board. Hollywood would like to do a movie, but I told them I have a business to run and a sweet little girl to rear. I can't be gallivanting all over the world, trying to save mankind. Hopefully, they'll get the message and leave me alone, knowemsayin', Baby Lolita girl?"

Lola ran into the room. "I just got off the phone with

Goodboy. He says the evening news is coming on right now."

When Lola turned to the national news channel, they saw FBI agents loading a short, thin, distinguished Asian man in his sixties into the back of one of their federal vehicles. He was handcuffed and surrounded by agents with drawn firearms.

The newsman stepped in front of the camera.

IF YOU'RE JUST JOINING US, WE HAVE A LATE BREAKING STORY THAT MANY CONSIDER A BOMB-SHELL IN INTERNATIONAL ESPIONAGE CIRCLES. THE FEDERAL BUREAU OF INVESTIGATION HAS CRACKED A MAJOR CHINESE SPY RING DATING BACK TWENTY YEARS OR MORE. CHI MU, A 62-YEAR-OLD CHINESE BORN ENGINEER HAS BEEN ARRESTED FOR ALLEGEDLY STEALING TOP SECRET MILITARY TECHNOLOGY FROM THE CALTECH NAVAL PROPULSION LAB WHERE HE HAD WORKED FOR OVER TWELVE YEARS.

MU WAS ARRESTED CARRYING A BRIEFCASE CONTAINING ENCRYPTED HARD DRIVES PERTAINING TO SUBMARINE PROPULSION SYSTEMS AND STATE-OF-THE-ART ELECTRONIC GUIDANCE SYSTEMS. FBI AGENTS REFERRED TO MU AS A PERFECT SLEEPER SPY, HAVING BEEN HERE FOR MANY YEARS AND WORKED HIS WAY UP THE SECURITY CLEARANCE LADDER. IN AN UNCONFIRMED REPORT, A DARING RESCUE MISSION IN THE PACIFIC LED TO MU'S EXPOSURE.

IF THERE IS A SILVER LINING IN THIS DARK CLOUD, IT IS THAT MU WAS APPREHENDED BEFORE BEING EXPOSED TO THE TOP SECRET GLX PROGRAM THAT IS SCHEDULED TO COME ON LINE NEXT YEAR.

THAT PROGRAM CONTAINS THE PRIMARY BLUEPRINT FOR THE US NAVY'S STRATEGIC WEAPONRY FOR THE NEXT TWENTY YEARS.

AT LEAST FOUR OTHERS SUSPECTS HAVE ALSO BEEN ARRESTED IN THIS EXTRAORDINARY PROBE. FBI OFFICIALS ARE CONFIDENT ALL INVOLVED WILL BE BROUGHT TO JUSTICE...

With budding admiration, Lola gazed at Nicholas. "Can you believe it? You helped to break up some kind of international spy ring!"

"Yeah, all because of a stupid nail gun," he said.

"How does it make you feel?"

"Mostly good. Take away the bats and dogs and bullets and artillery. But bad too."

"Why bad?" she asked.

"Because of the injustice our country dished out. I mean, this man risked his life to feed us information that strengthens our democracy and may very well have changed the course of military history. You know what we did for him?"

"No. What?"

"Danced a sleazy lobbyst dance around him. Passed a special tariff in Congress to make sure he couldn't sell his nail gun and earn a decent living in this freedom-for-all country."

Lola hunched her shoulders. "What can you do?"

"I tell you what I'm going to do," he vowed, "If I'm able to pull off this deal, I'm going to give his daughter and granddaughter a portion of the revenue. It might not be much, but it'll wash some of the dirt off our flag."

She stared at him a long time, thanking her lucky stars for the purity of his heart. “God bless America, Nicholas.”

He still had a solemn look on his face. “God forgive America too.”

The first week in June finally arrived. Kristy, having reluctantly resurrected her acquaintance with the airlines, flew out to San Francisco on Tuesday to prepare for her huge wedding celebration. Goodboy was scheduled to follow on Wednesday. For Thursday and Friday, the acting CEO of RedFish Construction Company would be Lola Salinas Hartman.

Lola was sure of it. Sooner or later, she'd wake up to find her dream of heading a big American corporation was still just that ... a dream, a ridiculous fantasy-filled frolic into never-never land.

On Thursday morning, driving into work, she pinched herself and banged her hand on the steering wheel and twisted her neck back and forth. No matter how she tried, she couldn't make the dream stop passing itself off as an extraordinary feat of reality.

How could a worthless illegal alien who had clawed her way through the grit and dirt of a hellish death hole beneath the sovereign borders of the greatest nation in the world be put in charge of a multi-million dollar corporation? How could the Donald Trumps and Karl Rove's and self-appointed demagogues of privilege have missed her daring escape from the underclass, the place where her heritage and genes and gender said she belonged?

The Klan and Tea Party and Conservative-Patriotic-Americans-for-the-Purity-of-blah-blah-blah had a name for her: *Thief.* She had slipped over the border and stolen glory and veneration belonging to the upper class, the blue-blooded Americans that were already here and pre-stamped for greatness.

And yet, how could the blue-bloods who claimed to believe in the merits of hard work and individual performance, overlook their critical role in this outlandish state of affairs. By assuming the automatic privilege of their birthright, they had gotten fat and lazy. They had inadvertently fallen sleep at the wheel.

All the way into work, she replayed the incredible voices that swirled around in the back of her mind. They were like threads of royal blue carpet that paved her way up the stairwell of success.

I'm teaching you about life, Babygirl. You gotta know your purpose....

May I see your resume? You have any degrees or certificates at all? Is that how you plan to go through life, just passing....

We're drowning here. I don't want to waste your time. And, I certainly don't want you to waste mine....

Lola, baby. You're just a safety coordinator. There's no reason you couldn't find another job in Kansas City....

About eighty percent of employees never say a word. They're hoping to end up $200 to the good. But twenty percent do say something. These are the people I want running the company....

I've figured out who you really are. You're my guardian angel. Every time I'm in trouble you're always there....

Since you've been here, you've been a tremendous asset to this company. I've never seen anyone adapt so quickly....

What is my new title, President, CEO....

I'm afraid that's my headache right now. But who knows? Keep doing what you're doing and one day it might be yours....

That Thursday morning, her new headache was already waiting. When she pulled into the parking lot, all of the office employees were standing outside of the front door.

"Don't go in there," warned Fat Pat. "We've got a bomb threat."

Lola stepped away from the door. "When did this happen?"

"The police called a few minutes ago. They're sending someone out."

Twenty minutes later, a white van pulled up to the gate. Lola signaled the security guard to let him through.

A tall, handsome man with a reddish tan, wearing white overalls with official safety decals on both shoulders, jumped out. He had a large black suitcase in his hand. "Morning. I was told you have a potential threat to your facility. I'm here to check it out."

Lola had never seen the Springfield bomb unit in operation. But her instincts told her something was not quite right.

"Are you with the police?"

He nodded. "We're a third-party contractor they use in these situations."

"Are they going to send a patrol car out?"

"I'm sure they will," he assured her. "They're waiting for me to call them with my assessment."

"What do you plan to do?"

"To go in there and do my job, ma'am. But that's not going to happen as long as I'm standing out here talking to you."

Lola kept staring at him. It finally dawned on her why he looked so familiar. She remembered him as one of the drivers for Allen Brothers Construction. Of course, that was before he suddenly became a bomb detection expert.

"If you don't mind, I'd like to see some ID," she demanded.

"Sure, no problem." He got into the truck, ransacking the glove box. Then suddenly, he cranked up the engine and sped toward the gate.

The security guard tried to stop him. But he plowed right through the wooden cross arm and headed down the street.

Lola couldn't help sniggling at the Allen brothers' stupid espionage caper.

"Hey guys, it is just a gag from one of our competitors. Nothing to worry about. You can go back inside."

Nobody moved, not until she led the way.

Lola hoped the bomb threat was not an omen of things to come. All she needed on her first day as CEO was the company to blow up.

By noon, she had settled into a more manageable routine. She called vendors, signed invoices and even gave an inspirational talk to the sales staff. She reworked the safety standards with her new assistant, settled a minor dispute in the lumber yard without having to fire anyone, and negotiated a deal with the City to widen the entrance to one of their new developments at no charge.

At the end of the day, she was exhausted. And yet, the mind-boggling realization that she had actually made it through the day, re-energized her spirit. She felt proud, soaring high with the eagles of commerce, celebrating her residency amidst the purple mountains and alabaster cities that gleamed.

That's when the call came in.

Over her iPhone, Calypso's heavy Jamaican accent was crystal clear. "Many voices in my head have spoken to me about this call. But da loudest one reminded me I gave you my word. Dat is how me and your fodda operated. Da man's word was pure gold."

"Thanks. Thanks for saying that."

"About the dawgs that did this to your fodda..."

"Yes?"

"He took dim down, your fodda did, all but one. There was a New Orleans lowlife full of liquor and pride, bragging about his deeds in Springfield. He is from da sticks outside of Nashville. I hear dis is da place he spends most of his time."

"Do you have a name?"

"Yes. His name is Silas Penrow. But be careful. Da man has killed. He will kill again."

When Lola got home that night, Nicholas was sitting at the table going through the mail.

"Here's another one," he said, holding up an envelope with two checks sticking out. "Every time we try to send my parents rent for living here, they send it back."

When she didn't respond, he stared more observantly. Recognizing the despondent expression on her face, he got up from the table and hugged her. "What's wrong? Something happened at work?"

"No everything is fine."

"I can see everything is *not* fine. You might as well tell me."

She stared at the beautiful painting on her living room wall. Ruby's *escaramuza* horse stared back at her. "I guess it is just one of those days I miss Mama and Daddy."

"Of course, that's to be expected. I miss them too. It's like the minister said. The main thing is to remember the good times you spent and how happy and proud they were of you."

She took a tissue and dabbed her eyes. "You think they are watching from heaven?"

Johnny in heaven??? Nicholas tried to imagine such a scenerio and the cost of fitting all of the angels with bullet proof vests.

He finally responded in a compassionate voice. "I'm sure they are."

"You think they can see how much I am hurting from what happened to them?"

"Probably."

She shook her head with reassurance. "Then, they will understand."

The next day at work was pleasantly uneventful. Lola spent most of her time meeting with sales reps, trying to narrow the choices for a new fleet of cement mixers the company planned to buy. Her new safety assistant, a young black girl with movie star facial features and silky black hair, came into her office that afternoon with a question.

"I looked at my payroll check today. They were supposed to take the $200 out this time, but they didn't. What do you want me to do?"

Lola smiled. "I want you to get ready for a wonderful career at RedFish. I'm going to make sure of it."

After work, on her way to her car, she spotted Raúl, coming across the parking. He walked over to her car. "I've had problems with my phone all day. I just got your message you needed to see me. What's up? You trying to coming crawling back to big daddy?"

"In your dreams, Raúl."

"That's cool, because my check can't cover you and all them babies."

"I've only got one little girl, Raúl."

"Yeah, but you know you Mexican women. Once you get started with them anchor babies, you don't know how to stop."

They both laughed.

With a serious face, Lola finally inquired, "Are you still in touch with any of your gang members?"

He dropped his head. "That's kinda like a play world I left behind, thanks to you sticking your *narizota* in my business. You know I will graduate from Lincoln Land in nine months."

"I never doubted you, Raúl. I knew you could do it."

"Why you asking about my use-to-be street bloodz?"

She handed him an envelope with $500 inside. "I don't want you getting involved with them again. But this one time I need a favor. And you can tell no one. This purchase must remain between you and me."

Silas Penrow looked at himself in the mirror. He was putting on weight. It was clear he needed to cut back on some of those Jambalaya combo platters, lobster bisques and crab cake dinners so scrumptiously soaked in butter and spices. Whenever he drove down to New Orleans to party, he guzzled them down like there was no tomorrow. Too much blubber might keep those sexy French Quarter *filles folles* away.

It was the downside of success, having a big bankroll, eating and drinking whatever he so desired. But if he had to have a problem, he preferred it to be the pot belly that came with extravagant living rather than the constipation that came with eating sardines and crackers in a storage shack outside of Litchfield.

Since bringing down the big tar baby and pocketing $80,000, he had gotten two more assignments from Raymond, pushing his earnings to almost $150,000. Not bad for a country bumpkin wanna-be from Nashville, Tennessee. DeLeon would've been proud of his young protégé ... except for the meat hook and two bullets in the back of the head that kept him from being proud of anything anymore.

Everything was going well. Penrow liked the way his private eye resume was blossoming into shape. Every experience chronicled his growing savvy and professionalism. Every experience, that is, except one.

If there was one thing that bothered Penrow, it was an unfinished job. There was a troublesome young Mexican girl in Springfield that had his face imprinted on her brain. If she ever decided to go to the police and solve the Cadillac salesman's murder, it could spell trouble. Those were the kinds of scenarios Penrow preferred to eliminate before they occurred.

The problem was logistics. It was always easier to front track than back track. Raymond had him moving forward with new cases rolling off the Mafia press each month. There was an eyewitness in Pittsburgh that had gone underground; an insurance agent in Boston that didn't want to sign off on fictitious damages to a mob-owned tugboat in Quincy Bay. There were always people who needed to be found and persuaded to see things the family's way.

That didn't leave much time for getting back to Springfield, tying up loose ends. Nevertheless, he promised himself, one day, he'd go back and close out the tar baby case for good.

If there was one thing he enjoyed over all others, it was his schizophrenic lifestyle. One day, he'd be in New York, dodging angry pedestrians and arguing with rude taxicab drivers. The next day, he'd be back home on his uncle's ranch in Nashville, riding horses and shooting squirrels. He was a country boy at heart with plans to buy the ranch from his uncle in the next few months.

It was the life of which he had always dreamed. As long as he could continue to make Raymond and the boys happy, it was a life he planned to hold on to until he died.

Leaving the ranch on a bright Wednesday morning, Penrow turned onto County Highway B and pointed his Navigator toward the local feed store. Three brown stallions and a frisky little colt ran along the white picket fence, trying to keep up with his familiar SUV. His favorite bull, Neme, was already leading a group of heifers toward the haystacks Penrow had left in the fields.

At the edge of his neighbor's driveway, a flock of hungry buzzards pecked away at what was left of a huge raccoon carcass, run over during the night. Penrow viewed the narrow eyed, sharp beak scavengers as service providers, the ultimate cleaning crew, compensating for reduced government trash-pickup services and keeping the countryside fresh and unblemished from the inevitable cycle of death.

Approaching the quiet, rural intersection at Cemetery Crossing, Penrow noticed a construction sign on the side of the road. A lone flagman in a safety hat and rubber boots, dark shades and a bright orange safety vest, stood in the middle of the highway. He waved his flag for Penrow to slow down.

Penrow dreaded the thought of all of the new developments going up around the countryside. The construction slowed down traffic, displaced the beautiful wildlife and sent an ominous signal that thousand of city slickers were on the way.

The greedy real estate people promoted the idea of leaving the crowded cities and moving to the fresh air, clean lakes and glorious green amenities of the the countryside, all in the name of progress. Penrow, however, hated that kind of progress. He wished the yuppies, fleeing the city, would simply find another place to go.

As the flagman waved his vehicle to an abrupt halt, Penrow could already hear the useless story the guy was about to tell. Some oversized dragline hauler was up ahead, blocking the whole highway, stuck halfway between a sinkhole and a muddy ditch.

Seeing the flagman approached his SUV, Penrow rolled down his window. "Okay, who screwed up this time?"

When the flagman removed his dark glasses, Penrow suddenly realized. He wasn't a HE, but a SHE; Not just any SHE, but the SHE he had tried to kill back in Litchfield.

With the lightning speed of a wild-west gunslinger, she snatched the nail gun from beneath her vest and began to fire. Rocket-propelled darts of steel, five, six, seven nails drove deeply into his skull. Blood streamed from the side of his face like cracks in the side of a flooded dam.

Penrow tried desperately to remove the nails from his eye. But unlike before, the daggers had gone too deep.

"How do you like the new-and-improved model?" she taunted. "Sleek? More powerful? It was made in Taiwan, you know."

In excruciating pain, Penrow threw his head against the steering wheel. The nails in his chin set off a fire storm along the nerve endings beneath his gums.

"Ooohhhh!" he shouted.

"Quiet, please! I am trying to answer your question," she announced. "Who screwed up? You screwed up when you killed my mother and father. You did not leave much for me to bury. But that's okay; you know what they say? What goes around, comes around ... you lowlife scumbag."

She threw a rock against his forehead and walked away.

Penrow kept a spare pistol in his glove compartment. As he reached across the seat, the back of his hand brushed over the rock she had thrown. It was then he realized. It wasn't a rock at all. It was aaaaahhhh-

Raúl's powerful Russian-made, black market grenade blew the entire roof off of the Navigator. Part of Penrow's bloody head lay on the payment in front of the truck. Had he been able to see the buzzards gathering overhead, he would've understood. After all, he was a country boy. And road kill in the country was a job the ultimate cleaning crew handled very well.

"How was the Women's Business Council Conference in Atlanta?" asked Ms K, standing in the doorway of Lola's new glassed-in office.

The closing session was unexpectedly moved to a scumbag's ranch in Tennessee, she thought to herself.

"I-I-I didn't get very much out of it," she finally reported.

"And I know why."

Lola's heart fluttered. "Why?"

"Because you were too exhausted, that's why. Here we are in July and you haven't taken a vacation since we shut down last December. You didn't get a chance to go out to my wedding in San Francisco and enjoy yourself. It's just been work, work, work."

"No, really, Ms K, I feel fine," Lola reassured her.

"No. You just think you do. I want you to take a week of vacation starting next week. Then, I want you to plan another week before we break in December."

"But Ms K..."

"No buts. That's an order, Chief Brigadier Admiral Salinas, or whatever Henry calls you."

A week later, Lola sat at home, trying to enjoy her forced vacation, watching Lolita Diane climb in and out of a large cardboard box in which Nicholas had carved doorways and peepholes.

Trying to play a fun game of peak-a-boo, Lola got down on the floor and stuck her head inside one of the doorways. Lolita Diane started to giggle. Lola, however, cringed with a growing sense of claustrophobia, retreated to the couch and gulped down a bottle of spring water.

The close quarters inside the box had reminded her of the cave beneath the US border, the blackness of collapsing dirt walls and the terror of seeing her uncle buried alive. The mind was a notorious storeroom. The priest used to call it a great bear trap that never released its prey. Somewhere in its dark crevasses was a record of every mishap, contrary thought and shameful deed.

Lola had no desire to review the records, especially with the pages so thoroughly stained with blood. What alcoholic wanted to review the fatal accident he had caused while under the influence? What crack head wanted to review an abusive childhood that ushered him into a life of low self-esteem? Lola refused to look at the horrors of her past. She slid into her self-induced methodical mode and made the painful memories go away.

****

In downtown Springfield, inside Illinois Commerce Bank's colossal brick headquarters, Nicholas sat across the desk from a senior lending officer. An older man with an intense face and drooping eyelids, banged on the keyboard of his laptop, trying to make the numbers surrender to his will.

After twenty minutes or so, flipping from one screen to another, he dropped his shoulders and sighed.

"Unfortunately, the ratios are not cooperating. Has nothing to do with your credit score or business model. They both look pretty good to me."

"What's the problem then?" asked Nicholas.

"In a word ... *collateralization.* These days, you almost need a million in collateral to borrow a million. The inspectors come down on us pretty hard if we deviate from their formulas."

"That's ridiculous," said Nicholas. "If I already have a million, why do I need to borrow it from you?"

"Precisely. But the abuses of the past have a way of strangling the promise of the future. In the old days, a handshake was good enough. It's just not that way anymore."

"So I guess we're done?"

"Not quite. Our main branch in Chicago has been designated as an SBA regional center. They can do things we can't. I'm going to get some material and contact information. I'd like you to call them and explain your situation. There's a very good chance they'll be able to work with you."

The banker got up and walked over to a glass cubical with shiny black file cabinets and stacks of colorful brochures. As he rummaged through the drawers, Nicholas' inquisitive mind drifted to the conversation at the next desk.

A young blonde with heavy makeup and silver rimmed glasses was talking on the phone. "Yes, yes, for you, of course we can. You've been a customer for a long time, Professor Broadson. Your business means a lot to us."

Did she say Professor Broadson, Nicholas was thinking.

She continued, "So how's the weather in Cuba? I hear it's very beautiful there."

Nicholas got up from his chair and walked over to her desk. Waving his hand and whispering in a low voice he inquired, “Is that Professor Broadson from the Museum?”

“Hold on Professor.” She appeared irritated by the interruption. “May I ask who you are?”

“I’m a friend of the professor,” he paused. “Well, not really a friend, but he knows me. I’ve been trying to deliver an item to him since he’s been out of town.”

“What is your name, sir?”

“Nicholas Hartman?”

“Professor, do you know a Nicholas Hartman? He says he’s a friend of yours.”

Hearing his reply she looked at Nicholas. “I’m afraid he doesn’t know you, sir. I’d appreciate it if you would return to your seat. These calls are considered confidential.”

Nicholas persisted, “Just tell him it’s about the chest. We had somewhat of a misunderstanding at the funeral and I-”

“Sir, unless you return to your seat, I’m going to have to call security.”

Nicholas reached into his wallet. “Okay, but here’s my card. Please give him my number and ask him to call me. Again, this is about the chest.”

Nicholas’s banker walked up behind him. “Is Judy trying to steal my customers again?”

“No,” Nicholas reassured him. “You’d have to be pretty desperate to voluntarily become her customer.”

The banker chuckled with a concurring sparkle in his eyes. He appeared hard pressed, tactfully avoiding the urge to speak his mind. “Here’s the information you’ll need. Just call the Chicago office and tell them I sent you. I’m sure they’ll be glad to help.”

The next morning, Nicholas caught a plane to Chicago. When he called Lola to let her know he had arrived, she lectured him with the strict counsel of a mother hen. "Don't get mixed up with any spy rings, Navy SEALs and Zombie cities, Nicholas. You understand? Me and Lolita Diane need you back home, safe and sound."

Lola had just gotten off the phone with Nicholas when she heard the God Bless America ring tone she had associated with RedFish. Kristy was calling with an unsettling report. "The people from ICE called today."

"ICE?"

"Yes, U.S. Immigration and Customs Enforcement," she explained. "Gracie in HR took the call. Seems they were interested in your social security number. Do you know anything about it?"

"This is the first I've heard of it," replied Lola in a calm voice.

"Probably some government mix-up. Anyway, when you come back, get with Gracie and find out what's going on, okay?"

"I will," promised Lola.

"By the way, how's the vacation going?"

"Fine, just fine," she reported. The book said complaining would not undo an executive decision.

"Henry said if I talked to you to mention the new Children's Petting Zoo inside the Henson Robinson City Zoo on East Lake Drive. He says the ducks, goats and donkeys come right up and eat out of your hand. He thinks your daughter will really enjoy it."

"I will try it," she said. "But I am curious. What was he doing at the Petting Zoo?"

Kristy chuckled with amusement. "He called it undercover work. Some old habits never die."

"What do you mean, Ms K?"

"He found out Allen Brothers Construction was given a no-bid City contract to build a small storage facility near the Petting Zoo. Henry went over there snooping around, trying to find out how they got it and to verify the total scope of the work. I told him that's not important now. We're at another level. But you know Henry. That Navy intelligence thing is in his blood."

"That is a good thing, yes? It helped to bring my husband back home."

"Good point," she acknowledged. "By the way, how is Mr. James Bond doing?"

"He's in Chicago, trying to get funding for his business. The local banks do not seem to be interested."

"How much does he need, Lola? I'd be glad to look at his business plan."

"Thanks, Ms K, but this has to be his thing. I can't get involved too deeply."

"Male ego," she sighed. "I thought Phillip had cornered the market on that. But it looks like they all have the same disease."

They both laughed.

Kristy concluded, "I've got to run. Some people from your airport job are waiting to see me. But remember what I told you. Relax, have fun. We'll see you next week."

Nicholas' room in the Crowne Plaza Hotel on West Madison Street, high above the hustle and bustle of Chicago's downtown business district, was a welcome refuge from the sour day of rejection and disappointment. He sat on the side of the bed, replaying all of the excuses they had given him, burying his face in his hands.

How did Henry Ford get his assembly line going? Who funded bobblehead dolls? What made them think putting money behind a lousy hamburger joint like McDonald's was a good idea?

He finally decided to call Lola and give her the bad news. "I met with four people today at the so-called SBA-sanctioned branch of Illinois Commerce. I asked for $850,000 and they offered me $100,000. How am I supposed to set up a national manufacturing center for a state-of-the art nail gun for $100,000?"

"There is still some jewelry left in Daddy's duffel bag," she reminded him.

"Yes. But once we get it appraised, how long will it be before FBI agents show up at our door?"

"No one said it would be easy, Nicholas. Look at Ms K. She had to mortgage her house, stocks and bonds and all her savings to get Evap-X3 off the ground. Now, all these investors are coming around, talking about IPO's and taking the company public. They see what she sees now. But look how long it took for them to see it."

He took a deep breath. "You're right. I guess I didn't expect to be dealing with bankers with blindfolds covering their entire brain."

"Just keep believing in what you're trying to do. Me and Lolita Diane believe. Somehow, you'll figure out a way to bring home the tamales."

"Thanks, Lola. I knew there was a reason I married you. I just couldn't remember why."

"I will help you to remember this weekend. Your sister is picking up Lolita Diane and we will be all alone."

"How is little Lolita?"

"Into everything as usual. We're going to the zoo tomorrow. Maybe, if your flight gets back in time, you can join us, yes?"

"Maybe. Are you sure she won't be afraid of all those big lions and tigers and elephants?"

"No, we're going to the Petting Zoo. Goodboy says the small kids love it."

"Okay, but be careful," he advised. "I don't want some wild duck, pecking her eyes out."

"Don't worry. We will be careful."

When Lola got off the phone, she heard a noise on the front porch. She opened the door to find a small Siamese cat, cornered by a ferocious pit bull.

"Get away!" she shouted, which turned his attention on her. He remained on the front step, barking at the cat, but mostly at her.

She grabbed a can of furniture polish and sprayed his face.

He howled in anguish, then took off down the street. When she reached down to pick up the spooked cat, it let out an angry whine and scratched her on her wrist. The scar quickly whelped and started to bleed.

She hauled the squirming feline to the back door and set it down on the steps outside. "Sorry, you cannot stay in here. I have a little baby, you understand."

Heading to the kitchen sink to wash her bloody scars, she discovered she didn't have a little baby. Lolita Diane was nowhere to be found.

"Lolita!"

She hurried into the bedroom, to find her, standing over the toilet. She was sloshing her tiny arm around in the water.

"No! No that water is *sucia*!"

Little Lolita immediately started to cry.

When Lola picked her up to put her in the bathtub, she discovered Lolita's true fascination with the commode. In a split second of freedom, scientist Lolita Diane Hartman had completed her first aquatic wireless experiment. And now, like a shiny black rock, Lola's iPhone rested quietly at the bottom of the toilet.

****

Nicholas didn't have much of an appetite. After an overpriced teriyaki chicken sandwich from room service, a hot shower and a quick scan of the Wall Street Business Section, he was ready for bed.

He couldn't help thinking how fortunate he was to have a devoted wife who supported his wild dream of becoming a successful entrepreneur, not to mention his wonderful little girl who stumbled around like a drunken midget, exploring her ever-expanding world. Each day she found a new way to prick his heart and increase the depths of his unfathomable love for her. It was a love that only a parent could understand.

Earlier in the day, he had helped a lady at the bank push her son's wheelchair through the door. The boy couldn't have been more than six. His small body was racked with deformities, a head too small, shoulders, too large, a twisted face and constant drooling from the side of his mouth. He didn't speak; rather, he communicated with long, agonizing groans.

Perhaps, he had been one of those Edwards Syndrome children that had beat the odds and lived on, pass his predicted longevity. Or maybe, he had a different disease that gave him a ten or twenty or thirty year lease on life. The real question that loomed in the back of Nicholas' mind was why wasn't Lolita Diane sitting in that chair.

Her normality had set off a quiet firestorm of controversy. Doctors that specialized in chromosomal disorders called for a complete re-evaluation of the entire testing process. The only person who seemed unwavering in her explanation of Lolita Diane's miracle birth was Lola. But accepting her explanation pushed everyone down a dark alley of wishing wells and magic boxes and lucky rabbit feet.

Something had happened to make two separate batteries of sophisticated prenatal tests come back incorrect. But none of the medical experts seemed to know what. Had Nicholas been able to unravel the mystery, he would've passed it on to the woman at the bank. Perhaps lurking within his discovery would've been a miracle cure to reverse the boy's condition and take away the hopelessness in his mother's eyes.

Nicholas started to set the hotel alarm clock to catch an early flight back to Springfield. That's when his cell phone rang.

"I hope I didn't catch you at an inconvenient time. I wouldn't want to stir your anger and have you punch me in the face again."

Nicholas dropped his head with embarrassment. "I am so sorry, Professor. I shouldn't have-"

"No," he interrupted. "I'm the one who needs to apologize. When I finally calmed down and took stock of my actions, I found my ranting to be quite obnoxious. I hope you can forgive me?"

"Only if you forgive me."

"Consider it done," he concurred. And then someone came into the professor's room, speaking loudly. "Hold on."

A few minutes later, Professor Broadson came back to the phone, laughing. "I'm sorry. That was one of Cuba's many enterprising government officials. We have maybe, five or six crates of artifacts from the Arawakan Archaeological Digs in the Sierra Cristal Mountains. They assume Americans with crates are bound to be smuggling something."

"The long arm of the law is in Cuba too?"

Professor Broadson chuckled again. "Hardly. It's not that they're trying to stop us from breaking the law. They just want to collect their bribe and look the other way. Maybe, he'll spread the word to the others not to waste their time."

"I take it you enjoy hopscotching the globe, investigating these old civilizations."

"It's a childhood dream come true and a reprieve for the many holes I dug in my mother's back yard," he confessed. "I'm doing something quite meaningful. The benefit of ancient knowledge to our global society is invaluable."

"I've heard that funding pitch before," joked Nicholas. "But tell me. What is the real benefit, Professor?"

"In a nutshell, we get the opportunity to confiscate the advances of prior civilizations while avoiding the mistakes those civilizations made. Of course, we need to put an asterisk by the word: *opportunity*. Many times, we refuse to heed the warnings.

We blunder into oblivion just as they did."

"I guess I should know that already. I mean, all along, that's been your warning about the chest."

"With the Juba Chest, my warning has been resoundingly simple ... Just say no."

Nicholas paused for a moment. "I'm going to be honest, Professor. I never really bought into this Juba Chest hocus pocus theory. It just seemed too far-fetched."

"Skepticism is a normal reaction, even healthy at time. I suppose if I weren't so deeply involved, I'd feel the same way. But there are things our preconditioned minds label as far-fetched and even impossible. And yet, these things cannot be dismissed."

Nicholas' curiosity swelled. "Like what?"

"In Brazil, I've watched Shaolin Monks levitate in mid air. I've been in Himalayan caves in and around Nepal where the wind whistled through the caverns like the sound of ancient voices. Except, there was no wind, at least, no source of wind that anyone could find. Inside a cave near the town of Charama in India, there are 10,000-year old rock paintings that unmistakely depict extra-terrestrials and UFOs, humanoid beings in helmets, descending from the sky. There are many mysteries I choose not to discuss, simply because they are incredibly hard to sell and might call into question one's sanity. But with the Juba Chest, I have no choice."

"Why do you believe so strongly in this chest?"

Professor Broadson waited a long time, calculating the impact of his replied. "Because I've tried it myself."

Nicholas could feel his heart stop. "What do you mean ... tried?"

There was another long pause, longer than before, as if their connection had been severed. Finally, the professor began to tell his story.

As it turned out, Professor Broadson had met treasure hunter Russell Burrows during a time of personal strife and desperation. The professor's wife of twenty years had been diagnosed with inoperable brain cancer and had only a few months to live.

"I had taken her to the top specialists in New York, Houston and Atlanta. They all said the same thing. There was nothing they could do. Even when Burrows told me the story of the Mauertanians and handed over the artifacts, it seemed inconsequential whether the legend was true or just a bunch of archaeological bologna. The chest was missing from the collection. There was no way to verify its powers or employ its alleged remedies in my own situation."

"So what happened to make you such a strong believer?"

Professor Broadson recalled, "A few days before I delivered the collection to the museum, I discovered a single wooden chip, concealed inside one of the sacred chalices. I had seen only Burrows' crude photos of the Juba Chest, engraved on the cave walls. But my instincts told me the chip was from the old tree. I suspected the Mauertanians had set it aside, just in case some unfathomable cataclysm threatened their world."

"So what did you do?"

"I took it with me to Senegal, a small country on the west coast of Africa. My wife and I had heard about an Irish missionary named Father Zach. He was said to be doing unbelievable things ... preaching in heavenly tongues, baptizing in sacred waters and actually healing people along the Casamance River; a modern John the Baptist, if you will. We were desperate. He was our last hope."

"Did he heal her?" asked Nicholas.

"She was healed," confirmed the professor. "Although, she passed away a few years ago from a different ailment, I still have the X-rays to prove she was healed. The brain tumors miraculously disappeared without any medical explanation. But can I say, unequivocally, it was Father Zach?...."

Nicholas was suddenly reminded of the pieces of bark under Lola's pillow. "So you slept on that piece of wood? I mean, isn't that how it's done?"

The professor thought about it. "I guess you could do it

that way, like a tooth for the Fairy Godmother. Of course, I never believed in the Fairy Godmother, not with my strict tell-it-like-it-is father in the house."

"So how exactly did you ... make the connection?"

"The night before we were scheduled to see Father Zach, I clutched that tiny chip in my hand all night. I wish and prayed and begged. No doubt, you would've done the same for your wife?"

"I suppose."

"Believe me," insisted the professor. "If you had an iota of a chance to save the woman you loved, you would."

"But you don't *know* whether the wood had anything to do with it, right? It could've been a holy priest performing a miracle. I was raised in the church. I believe in miracles, don't you?"

The professor hesitated a long time. "In my heart, I know it was the tree. It showed me in a dream." And then he paused again. "I'm calling this somewhat surreal, subconscious visionary state a *dream*. But it was so much more."

Professor Broadson described his dream, an endless funeral procession, meandering down the main street of Ziguinchor, just outside his hotel window. African women with colorful headdress, sang sad songs, waved bamboo hand fans and led distraught mourners to the grave site.

Nicholas spoke with lingering skepticism. "Lola swears up and down the dreams always come true, like some kind of receipt. But come on. A bad pizza can give you dreams. Should I take that as some kind of metaphysical receipt?"

Though Nicholas couldn't see his face, he sensed through the long periods of silence that the professor was struggling with the answer.

Finally, he replied. "Have you ever heard of the *Le Joola* ferry disaster?"

"Can't say I have."

"A Senegalese government ferry capsized off the coast of Gambia, killing 1,863 people. It was the second worst non-military maritime disaster in history."

"I'm sorry to hear that. But I don't understand what-"

"My wish killed all of those innocent people," the professor confessed.

"Okay, now you're beginning to sound like Lola. Explain how the ferry disaster had anything to do with your wish."

"Because it happened the very next day, almost the exact time we went to see Father Zach."

"Come on, Professor. You're reaching again."

"Am I reaching when I tell you the ferry left from Ziguinchor, the same city we were in? Am I reaching when I tell you that three days later, just as we were preparing to leave for the States, I saw the exact funeral procession from my dream? More than six hundred crude wooden caskets, carrying women and children from the ferry accident, women that wanted to live out their lives, just like my wife."

Nicholas took a deep breath. "I'm trying to connect the dots. Really, I am. But it's just not happening."

"That's because you don't understand the Mauertanians or see them as living proof of *Universal Consciousness*. You haven't studied their culture to see the patterns."

"What patterns?"

"The disasters always originate at the point of the wish, like the point on the triangle, depicted on the chest; the point in which the *Journey of Redemption* begins. I knew your wife was somewhere in Litchfield. That's where the Ferdon Street train wreck took place. I knew she had made her second wish in Springfield because both flights were tied to the Springfield Airport."

"Okay, okay, for the sake of argument, let's say you're right about all of these patterns and points of origin and life-and-death trade-offs. What's the purpose of it all? I mean, what's the Juba Chest trying to do?"

The professor sighed. "If I told you, you wouldn't believe me."

"Try me, okay. I'm out here this far."

"I believe the old tree is trying to protect our universal society, our universal way of life."

"By killing people?!!!" erupted Nicholas. "It's protecting us by killing us off?"

"Somehow, most likely at the point of origin, the old Baobab tree developed consciousness. Maybe, it was imputed by time travelers or ancient beings, trying to create order in the universe. Or maybe it evolved through some spiritual cataclysm we do not yet understand. I don't know. I can't explain it. I just know the tree became infinitely aware of the society around it. It saw certain ... how would you say ... certain inequities and malfeasance, certain destructive practices we refused to change. So it changed them for us, using death as its ultimate leveraging power."

Nicholas sighed with frustration. "I'm sorry. I still don't understand."

"Think about a traffic light. Long before you were able to drive, you noticed that your parents stopped when it was red and proceeded when it turned green. If I asked you who put it there, you wouldn't be able to tell me. Your suspicion would be some governing body like the City or the County. The main thing is that it was placed there prior to your existence to govern your actions and protect the well being of society. Do you follow me so far?"

"Yes, go on."

"You soon discover there are consequences if you disobey. You might kill someone at the intersection. The light would most certainly allow it. But if the light had a remote camera, it would be able to see what you did. It would know you, know your tags, know your intent. There's a very good chance you'd be fined or put in jail. The light would attach consequences to abusers for the sake of the universal good."

"I'm still with you, which is a bit scary. But go on."

"In Litchfield, a lot of people were dying in emergency ambulances because they were trapped on the wrong side of the railroad crossing. If you went back fifty years and looked at the long list of people dying, eighty percent were elderly and poor. The federal, state and local government couldn't come up with the money to build an overpass because, unofficially, and perhaps, subconsciously, they deemed those people expendable. No one would say it. But the status quo was acceptable. But have you been to Litchfield lately?"

"Yes, I have," said Nicholas.

"Then, you've noticed the overpass being constructed at the Ferdon Street Crossing. Your wife made a wish and the tree granted it. But not without inflicting a lethal mandate on society that would force the universal good."

"Okay, okay, I'm beginning to understand your premise, not saying I believe it. Tell me about the plane crashes."

"The last five or six crashes in the United States have been by regional airlines like Carter Blue. These airlines are exempt from many safety rules the larger carriers have to follow. An investigator from the National Transportation Safety Board tried to blow the whistle on the lack of oversight and the flawed safety practices. You know what they did?"

"I don't have a clue."

"They threatened to fire him and, ultimately, reassigned him to a desk job. That's the bureaucratic way of saying stop meddling with the interest of powerful, profit-driven people in a capitalistic society. The Congress tried to pass several laws. But the lobbyists spread enough money around to made sure they failed. So the planes just kept falling ... until now."

Nicholas remembered a recent article. "Yes, I read about the new aviation bill coming out of the Congress."

"It's all because of the back-to-back crashes in Utah. It's the same with the *Le Joola* ferry disaster. The Senegalese government imposed new regulations against overloading ferries. Operators can go to prison for life for loading eighteen hundred passengers on a boat designed for five hundred. My wish awakened the tree, gave it eyes to see. The tree then implemented it harsh measures of correction on a society that would not correct itself. I suspect, after so many big-gun school shootings, and so many powerful people paid to look the other way, the chest is just waiting for the right time and the right wish to pay a visit to the NRA."

"Seems to me the tree is trying to do God's job," said Nicholas. "Do you consider the tree to be God?"

"I've always been taught that God is a God of love and mercy," said Professor Broadson. "If there is one thing I'm sure of, it's that the Juba Chest has no mercy. It corrects with an iron hand."

Nicholas took a deep breath, trying to consolidate his thoughts. "So this is the scenario we can expect after each wish?"

"Not each wish," he clarified. "The last one is different."

"Different, how?"

"The last wish is one of cleansing and purification. If you study the hieroglyphics that describe the Mauertanian's *Journey of Redemption*, you'll see the timetable and the price that must be paid."

"I'm afraid my hieroglyphics are a bit rusty. Can you explain what happens on the final wish?"

The professor was quiet again, recalibrating his thoughts. "The final wish is a death sentence to the wisher."

"Okay, okay, now you're really freaking me out. Please explain that."

"The tree looks at the heart of the wisher, pure energy evaluating the integrity of pure energy, self evaluating a part of self, you might say. If a person would call on the chest, again and again, despite the devastation and suffering it will surely bring to others, the chest grants the wish. But it also judges the wisher and declares him or her unfit to remain in society. It's similar to the remedy our culture imposes on serial killers."

"My wife is not a serial killer," Nicholas defended.

"Of course not," the professor agreed. "But you can see why I was so adamant at the funeral about her avoiding the final wish."

A long, noxious silence smothered their exchange. Finally, the professor mustered the words. "She *did* avoid it, didn't she?"

Nicholas didn't answer ... couldn't answer.

"Oh, my God. She did it. She made the final wish, didn't she?"

"I mean, it was over a year ago. Nothing really happened."

"I suspect something did happen," the professor corrected. "Something miraculous, something nobody could explain."

"Our baby was normal. It kind of left the doctors in shock."

"Which means the Juba Chest granted the wish."

"But Lola is fine. She hasn't been, well, removed from society."

"If you'll look at the etchings on the chest, you'll see a distinct space between the cluster of animals and the final lion's head. The Mauertanian calendar uses this type of spacing to indicate a pause or delay, as in a final period of awakening."

"A pause meaning it hasn't happened, but it's going to." Nicholas reluctantly connected all of the dots.

"This is only my crude hypothesis," admitted the professor.

"I can't accept that, Professor. I can't accept your hypothesis of a clock ticking on Lola's life."

"I'm sorry, Nicholas, I'm not trying to upset you. I hope I'm wrong about all of this."

"But what if you aren't wrong? What can I do?"

He thought about it. "Did she tell you about the dream, the night she made the final wish? What was the dream?"

Nicholas tried to remember. "Something about silly animals."

"You have any vicious animals at home, like Rottweilers or maybe a pet python the old tree could use as an executioner?"

"The zoo." Nicholas remembered Lola's impending visit.

"What did you say?"

"Lola and the baby are going to the City Zoo tomorrow."

"Please tell me you can stop her, at least, until we're able to find out more about her dream?"

"I'll call her, Professor. I'll call her right now."

Lola didn't sleep well. All night long, she kept hearing strange noises from the back yard. There was scratching at the back door accompanied by ferocious groans, the kinds of groans a little Siamese kitten couldn't make.

There was something else that Lola found unsettling. After her routine bath and feeding, Lolita Diane kept clinging to Lola's leg, wanting to be picked up. On most mornings, she roamed from one room to another, searching for something to pull down or climb upon or stick in her mouth. On this morning, however, she followed Lola wherever she went.

"Don't worry," Lola told her. "We're going to get out of here and have some fun."

Lola wanted to call Nicholas to see what time his plane was scheduled to arrive. But, thanks to Lolita's groundbreaking toilet experiment, her iPhone was nothing more than a water-soaked rock. In the old days, she would've used the house phone. But who had a house phone these days? Maybe the little old ladies down the street.

There was a wireless distributor a few miles from the City Zoo. She would stop by for a replacement phone on her way home.

****

Goodboy wasn't satisfied with the answers he had gotten from the City Manager. When confronted about the no-bid contract the City had given to Allen Brothers Construction, the Manager downplayed the scope of the job and remained vague about the capital construction budget allocated for the entire project.

"You know what's happening," Goodboy had told Kristy. "Uncle Abner's been playing golf and greasing palms. If we aren't careful, he'll get a foothold with the City and then come after our airport contract."

Goodboy had decided to go back out to the zoo to take a closer look at the construction site. He had more than enough experience to determine the true scope of the job and generate his own estimation of the cost. If the job was over the $100,000 no-bid limit, someone was going to pay.

****

Nicholas had tried to reach Lola all night long. After leaving a dozen messages, he finally called his half sister, Terri. "I need you to go by the house and tell Lola to stay home until I get there. I'll explain later."

When Terri finally reached the house, a little after 10:00 am, Lola was already gone. "Everything's locked up and her car isn't in the driveway."

"Okay, I'm boarding the plane right now," said Nicholas.

"I need you to go over to the City Zoo and see if you can find her."

"Wow, you're the third person I've heard talking about the Zoo."

"What do you mean?" quizzed Nicholas.

"Haven't you heard? They're unveiling that big cat today."

After years of being criticized for having a lackluster small-town facility, the City had embarked upon a major effort to re-energize the Henson Robinson City Zoo. The new look included exotic new animals, a Children's Petting Zoo, an expanded food court, a Ferris wheel and merry-go-round, and a small picnic area for bird lovers to eat lunch and feed the birds.

A year earlier, during the re-opening, officials had brought in a prize Serengeti lion which turned out to be very popular among local visitors. Now they were bringing in a second lion, touted as the largest in captivity throughout the entire Midwest.

"They say this thing is huge," said Terri. "I wish I could see it. But I have to be at work in thirty minutes."

"Can't you just go by and give her my message?"

"Sorry, Nicholas. You know how Bishop Hardware used to be about employees coming in late for work. Well, they've gotten worse. If they choose, they can terminate you on the spot, no warning, no nothing. A lot of people have already jumped ship. I started looking for another job last month. But nothing so far."

"I understand."

"Just keep calling, okay? I'm sure she'll eventually pick up."

****

At 11:25 am, Lola drove into the City Zoo's west parking lot on Lake Shore Drive. A modest crowd of casually dressed patrons streamed from the parking area to the main gate. By the time she found a vacant parking spot, gathered her purse and tote bag, unbuckled Lolita Diane from her car seat, loaded her into the baby stroller and made the long trek to the front gate, it was almost noon.

A Channel 20 satellite van pulled up to the front entrance. A young anchorman with wavy black hair and horn rimmed glasses jumped out, along with his camera crew.

"Is the ceremony still scheduled for noon?" The anchorman asked a nearby security guard.

"They moved it to 12:30 pm. Some kind of problems with the new kid on the block. That cat has been trouble from the very beginning."

"Great! ... well, not about the trouble. But that gives us some time to set up. Which way to the lion's den?"

A chubby man with a gray mustache, the security guard laughed. "If we were at my house, I'd show you to the guest bedroom where my mother-in-law is. But I suppose you mean the big cats."

The anchorman chuckled. "Yes. Not the human kind."

"Just follow the walkway past the black bears and orangutans, make a right at the concession stand and bingo. You're into the lions, tigers and cheetah's big cat zone."

"Thanks." The news crew began unloading their broadcast equipment.

The security guard spotted Lola, pushing the stroller through the gate. He waved at Lolita Diane. "There's a little animal lover. Are you here to see the big cat too?"

Lola paused. "We do not know this big cat you speak of."

"It's the new Serengeti lion they just brought in," he explained.

As she stood there listening to his description, a huge black crow swooped down from the trees and began flapping wildly at the back of Lola's neck. She ducked to the ground, trying to swat the bird away.

"Hey! Hey!" The security guard ran over to rescue her. The

squawking crow quickly abandoned its bizarre antics and lifted into the sky.

The security guard helped her up. "Are you okay?"

Lola was breathing, heavily. "I....I think so."

He looked at the red whelps on her arm. "Did the thing attack you?"

"No, no. "This was something else."

A tiny cat, no doubt, possessed by el diablo, she thought.

The security guard peered up into the trees and shook his head. "Wow. I've never seen that before. I can assure you he's not one of our tenants."

"Don't worry about it, I'm fine."

She checked out Lolita Diane, who quietly gnawed on a fresh carrot. She seemed oblivious to the attack, rather, more fascinated by a clown at the edge of the sidewalk, passing out balloons. Relieved little Lolita Diane had not been spooked, Lola continued through the entrance toward the Petting Zoo.

The new concession court was like a beautiful botanical garden, an elevated floor of red cobble bricks, encircled by exotic greenery and rocks that sloped downward along a water garden of lotus and lilies. Lolita Diane pointed, then shouted, "peeebooo", which was baby language for a colorful blue and yellow fantail, leaping above the water.

To Lola's surprise, Goodboy sat at a table at the edge of the courtyard, writing notes in a tablet. She rolled over to him and cleared her throat. "Sir, may I see your spying license please?"

He looked up with a smile. "I left my ID back at the office. But trust me, I'm certified."

They both chuckled.

"Ms K told me you were over here with the Allen brothers, trying to get your old job back. Is this the second interview?"

"In a way," he joked. "The first one got bogged down with

unanswered questions about company ethics. So I thought I'd try it again. Have a seat. I'll tell you all about it."

****

Nicholas' plane landed at the Springfield Capitol Airport at exactly the wrong time. Some idiot maintenance crew member had spilled jet fuel all over the runway. Incoming flights were delayed, diverted and offloaded at terminal gates a million miles from the parking lot.

As his flight sat on the tarmac, waiting its turn to deplane, he called his mother. "Have you spoken to Lola today?"

"No. Is something wrong?"

"She's not picking up her phone. When Terri stopped by to check on her, the car was gone."

"Have you done something to make that sweet little girl angry?"

"No, mother."

"Come on, I'm your mother. Be honest."

"I'm telling you, we're fine."

"Good. Your father and I were just saying the other day what a wonderful family you make. You know he had some very strong reservations in the beginning."

"Yes, I remember."

"I think it had more to do with what happened to him. You know, the whole thing with your half sister and all. He didn't want some gold-digger coming along, taking advantage of you too."

"Mom, she's not a gold-digger, never was. In fact, she's making a lot more money than I am."

"He knows that now. And I know you'll make a success of your business and turn your income situation around. By the way, how's it coming?"

"I just left Chicago, talking to some lenders. I'll have to see how it plays out."

"You know your father would be glad to make some calls for you, maybe even help with the seed money."

"Thanks, I appreciate it. But right now, I need to concentrate on finding Lola and the baby."

"Okay, Nick. I love you. Keep me informed."

****

Lola had just sat down at the table with Goodboy when she heard a strange buzzing sound. She looked up to see a huge black bumble bee, hovering above her head. Suddenly, with the speed and determination of a World War II Kamikaze pilot, the agitated insect nosedived directly into her hair.

Instantly, Goodboy stood up, racked his tablet across the top of her head and swatted it away. "What are you wearing, Bee-gucci?"

She was visibly shaken. "I, I don't know."

"Did he sting you? I mean, are you alright?"

"No."

"No, he didn't sting you, or no, you're not alright?

"Both, I think."

"Come on Master Chief Petty Officer Salinas. Stop being such a cream puff. Unless you've got a honeycomb growing out of the top of your head, you should say, *I'm fine, Admiral.*"

She glared at him with disbelief. "Since when did you become an Admiral?"

He responded with a cheshire cat grin. "Sometimes these promotions are done in secret to protect our cover."

She shook her head. Nicholas had been telling Lolita Diane he was a CIA spy.

Men....

"Okay, Admiral. Show me your findings," she requested.

Goodboy slid his tablet across the table in front of her and pointed to two squares.

"Square A is the smaller area where they're working on the other side of this courtyard. Square B is the larger area they've roped off. Whatever work they've planned for B is probably going to be more than what they're doing in A. You look at all of the equipment they've brought, there's no way the two squares are going to come in under $100,000."

"You're saying the City has issued a no-bid contract that's over the limit?"

"Exactly," he confirmed. "Which means somebody's playing ball with Uncle Abner."

"Uncle Abner..." Lola gazed, reminiscently. "You ever miss those days on the back of the truck, watching those *idiotas* make fools of themselves?"

"I'll tell you what I miss, well, besides stuffing the Allen brothers' faxes and blueprints down my overalls. I miss watching your unbelievable progress on Little Blue. Those training sessions told me something about your grit and determination. I knew you could make it if given the chance."

Lola beamed with reflection. "Do you remember my perfect hole?"

"Of course, I do."

"As soon as they finish remodeling my new office, I will hang my mother's painting of it on my wall."

"That's wonderful. By the way, if you'd like to dig a second hole, Little Blue is here at the zoo."

"Here? Right now?"

"They're using her in Square A on the other side of the courtyard."

Lola smiled, widely. "Maybe I will wait until they go to lunch and cash their checks, yes? Then Little Blue and me can be old friends again."

They both laughed with mischief, both, knowing that her career with Little Blue had been surplanted by a greater calling. Seeing them laugh, Lolita Diane started to sniggle.

"Look at her!" Goodboy slid over, lifted little Lolita out of her stroller and clutched her in his arms. "I'm going to tell you something. I suppose it's okay to mention it now."

"What?"

"I worried about this little one ... worried a lot."

"Why?"

"I don't know. I kept thinking something was wrong; or maybe something would go wrong. I know you probably got tired of me being a father hen at work. But sometimes you get these feelings. After my wife's miscarriage and losing my oldest daughter in Iraq, I've learned not to ignore them."

Edwards syndrome, Lola was thinking to herself, but responded, "You see. Not even the old Admiral spy knows everything."

He looked at Lolita who was playing with his ears. "I do know this little tyke is tired of sitting around, listening to grown ups rattle on about nothing. Let's get her up on the hill where she can slap some animals around."

The Petting Zoo was a small, rectangular barnyard enclosure, lined with gravel, dirt and hay, sitting on a man-made knoll about fifty yards from the concession stand. The brick castle front and fake draw bridge over the narrow creek bed made the young visitors feel they were entering some kind of enchanted animal Camelot. A large sign hung over the castle entrance:

WELCOME TO KING HENSON'S PRIVATE PLAYPEN. MEET THE FRIENDLIEST ANIMALS ALIVE!!!

Lolita Diane was fascinated by the colorful hodgepodge of ducks, geese, deer, goats and donkeys, playing with the other children. Some of the animals were eating right out of their hands.

Holding tightly to Goodboy's neck, Lolita pointed to a little potbellied pig that waddled over to them. Goodboy stooped to his knees so she could rub his portly pink body.

"You see," he assured Lolita Diane. "He won't hurt you."

When Lola leaned down to pet the little critter, he squealed, loudly, and ran to the other side of the yard.

Goodboy frowned. "Well, thanks a lot for breaking up the party."

"I didn't do anything," she defended.

Lolita Diane started to cry.

"Hold on now. It's going to be okay. Mama didn't mean to be a party pooper. Let's go over there and talk to the donkey."

"Why don't you guys go on," suggested Lola. "I need to find the ladies room anyway. Have fun. I'll be right back."

As Lola headed across the creek and down the ramp, she heard the familiar buzzing sound. To her surprise the bee was back, swirling around her head. Swinging, wildly, she started to run. But a gap between the wooden planks wedged around her heel and sent her tumbling to the ground.

Immediately, a stranger's strong hand reached down to help her up. "Ma'am, are you okay?"

She found herself staring into the pale face and bulging brown eyes of a man in uniform. It wasn't just any uniform, but a Captain's uniform bearing the insignia: CARTER BLUE AIRLINES.

Lola's heart pounded, wildly. "Yes, I'm fine."

"Are you sure?" he persisted. "If not, I can get one of the flight attendants to come over and help you."

Flight attendants? This was no airplane. Lola whirled around to see if there were any flight attendants behind her. When she turned back, the man was gone.

She could hear the roar of the crowd; see the faint flashes of phones and cheap box cameras, coming from the far side of the concession stand.

For a moment, she thought they were applauding for her. Yes ... of course ... She was an unknowing gage-show contestant whose clumsy retreat from a remotely controlled bumble bee had won her a prize.

But the voice over the public address system quickly vanquished any hope of such a delightfully happy ending. The eyes of the crowd were not on her, but rather, the big cat whose grand entrance was in full bloom:

AND NOW LADIES AND GENTLEMEN, HERE HE IS. THE LARGEST LION IN CAPTIVITY IN THE USA ... BRUTUS THE KING.

As she slammed the restroom door, the thunderous applauds muffled. She dumped her purse on the counter and turned on the faucet full blast. She buried here face in the cool stream, hoping that when she opened her eyes, she'd be at home in her bed, celebrating her escape from another bizarre nightmare.

Instead, her watery eyes opened to a more horrible spectacle. On the counter, right next to her purse, a gigantic black and red spider crawled right at her.

There were plenty executioners in the lush jungle. The professor's stark warning echoed through the dark chambers of her mind.

"Noooo!" She screamed and fell back against one of the stalls. The water, dripping from her face, sent her feet sliding forward. Her head slammed against the metal stall door.

With blurred eyes and a pounding headache, she looked up to see a familiar figure standing a few feet away. It was the old African women in the green flowered dress and death-head skull necklace. A huge spotted python with a slithering tongue was draped across her shoulders. Although, she never spoke, her wrinkled face was filled with compassion. She reached out her hand to Lola.

"No! No! Get away from me!" Lola scrambled to her feet and ran out of the door.

Goodboy had just sat Lolita Diane on the back of a small Shetland pony. Lola ran up to them, panic-stricken and delirious.

"I'm sorry. I must leave this place."

"What?"

"I must get out of here right now." She pulled Lolita Diane off the pony and caressed her, tightly.

"But, Lola. The girl was just beginning to have a little fun."

"I will have to explain later." She took off down the ramp.

The City Zoo was constructed like a miniature golf course in which one hole led to another. Within the Zoo, the holes were not holes, but compartments of animals, strategically arranged on peaks and valleys, giving the facility a multi-level appeal. The only constant was the central asphalt walkway, enclosed on both sides by sturdy steel railings. No matter which part of the Zoo patrons ventured into, the central walkway eventually led them to the front gate.

Lola took a shortcut over the rock garden, beneath the tall trees and through clusters of exotic plants. She reached the walkway and started to push ahead of the crowd. Though Goodboy lumbered behind her, between the sluggishness of old age and an assortment of military injuries, he couldn't keep up.

He watched with growing consternation as Lola entered the back side of the big cat zone. That's when the huge tree stump started tumbling down the hill.

The Allen brothers' Square A construction site was situated on the top level of the zoo complex, just above the big cat zone. Oblivious to the special ceremony and the hundreds of visitors below, members of the work crew went about their mundane duties, hammering away at the storage facility and a large antenna base that would one day accommodate the zoo's future *Animal Lover's* radio station.

With Henson Zoo's new multi-level design and the propensity for seasonal tornados, sweeping through the area, safety officials had deemed a mammoth oak tree that sat atop the highest hill, a potential hazard. Allen Brothers Construction had been ordered to hew it down, cut it into manageable pieces and haul it away.

The problem was, they hadn't hauled it away. The impetuous, helter-skelter work crew had procrastinated as usual and left the pilings at the edge of the site. When one of the workers accidently backed Little Blue into the pile, a huge stump dislodged and rumbled down the hill.

The steel railing along the central walkway wasn't built to withstand the tremendous impact of a ten foot log, rolling off a hill with a full head of steam. The log crashed through the railing, knocking Lola and little Lolita Diane into the lion's den on the other side.

The den was designed like a huge bathtub with cave-like stone hutches, a watering hole and steep concrete walls all around. Though the crowd had congregated toward the front of the den, they gasped in distant horror as Lola and the baby tumbled into the back.

The violent impact against the concrete floor knocked the wind out of Lola. But the maternally instinctive, sacrificial manner in which she had curled her body around her baby, left little Lolita unscathed.

The sound of her crying brought Lola to her senses. It also

attracted the attention of the two ferocious lions.

The new Serengeti lion, Brutus The King, looked like a baby dinosaur with ten inch razor claws and a head the size of a riding lawn mower. The female lion was only half as big, but tremendously fierce and already a constant challenger to her husband to be.

Brutus let out an ear-piercing roar, a warning to the two uninvited visitors that had dropped into his territory. The female lion responded with a corresponding growl. It was an official warning that a savage and deadly clock had begun ticking down.

Seeing the tragic scenario unfolding before his eyes, an alert zoo keeper ran into the freezer and returned with a bloody steak. He tossed it near the lions, hoping to buy some time.

It worked. They immediately began to fight. But how long was a small steak going to last between two vicious killers accustomed to eating an entire buffalo?

Goodboy stood at the broken railing, screaming to the top of his voice. "Lola!!! Get up, Lola!!!"

Between Goodboy's shouting and Lolita Diane crying, Lola slowly regained her wits.

She scooped up Lolita Diane and moved toward the wall. Goodboy dropped flat on his stomach and stretched over the edge of the wall. As Lola reached up to grab his hand, they quickly realized they were too far apart.

A broom-length apart, Goodboy thought to himself.

Standing up, he spotted a janitor's cart with a push broom strapped to the side. He grabbed the broom and ran back to the broken railing. Back on his belly, he stretched out over the wall, the broom, dangling from his hand.

The excessive movement attracted Brutus' attention again. He suddenly lost interest in the remaining snippets of meat and commenced a slow trot toward Lola and Lolita Diane.

"Oh, my God! Somebody do something!" An hysterical voice emanated from the crowd. But the crowd seemed paralyzed, useless spectators that could only watch and wait and suffocate in their fear.

Lola was desperately clinging to the bottom of the broom. But holding Lolita Diane in one hand and the broom in the other proved futile. Each time Goodboy tried to pull her up, Lola's hand slipped away.

"Rope! Who's got a rope?!" shouted Goodboy. But no one responded.

When the female lion saw Brutus picking up speed, she sensed it was time to join in the hunt. Soon, both animals were bearing down on Lola and her baby.

No one had to tell her. She saw the brutal executioners coming. She heard the ominous clock, somewhere in the universe, ticking her life away.

She pulled Lolita Diane's tiny arms from around her neck. She gazed at her beautiful innocence one last time. "Do not look back at the old ship going down. Find your bright future in the purple mountains and alabaster cities that gleam. Goodbye, my little Lolita. Mama loves you."

With the strength of every bone in her body, she slung Lolita high into the air ... a glorious little red bird, soaring into the bright sky. Goodboy, still flat on his stomach, clamped down on her tiny, flailing arms and reeled her in.

The last thing Lola remembered before the hot spikes of death tore into the back of her neck was Goodboy standing there, holding her child, safely, in his arms ... that, and the crowd of compassionate souls that surrounded him.

There were two Carter Blue pilots and the Stodomiere family, a gasoline truck driver and train engineers. In the middle of the crowd was the African woman in the green flowered dress.

They should've been angry, pointing their fingers of

condemnation. Instead, they stood, quietly, their faces aglow with empathy. They seemed to understand the power of human desperation. They didn't speak. But Lola could hear them saying something. They were saying: *Come with us you imperfect creature of the universe, self of every self and soul of every soul in sacred unity. Come back into the fold.*

****

Nicholas pulled up in front of the zoo and ran through the gate. A slew of emergency vehicles with flashing red lights followed close behind. A woman near the concession stand was screaming, "Oh my God! Oh my God!" Panic-stricken zoo officials ran toward the back.

When Goodboy spotted Nicholas, coming up the central walkway, he turned to two security guards. "Please stop him. He's the husband. He doesn't need to see this."

It took both security guards to restrain the force of Nicholas' raging adrenaline. Eventually, they pushed him against the wall.

"Where's my wife? Where's my baby?" he shouted.

Goodboy walked up to him. "Here's your baby."

He clutched Lolita Diane in his arms. "Where's Lola?"

Goodboy took a deep breath. "I'm sorry, Nicholas. She didn't make it. I think, somehow, she already knew this would be the day."

Nicholas was crying, wheezing, trying to catch his breath.

"Look at me," Goodboy demanded.

Nicholas finally managed to lift his head.

"That child in your arms is depending on you. You're all she's got. Now pull yourself together. Your wife gave her life for this little tyke. She'd be awfully disappointed if you weren't able to see it through."

He slowly composed himself. "How ... how did it happen?"

"It happened like it was supposed to happen," said Goodboy. "With Lola being the hero again, and saving our rear ends."

"Did she say anything?" he queried.

"She told little Lolita not to look back at the old ship going down. The rest I couldn't hear. But what she told me, she said with her life. Our Lola always found a way to overcome."

Nicholas nodded.

"More than that, Nicholas, she made me believe there's still hope for this country. A virtual nobody can come over here, work their tail off and be somebody. Isn't that what America is all about?"

Nicholas nodded again. "I suppose."

Seeing little Lolita Diane, slowly falling asleep in Nicholas' arms, Goodboy made a suggestion. "You and the little one should go home. I'll take care of things here. I'll come by later to check on you. Maybe, we can talk more then?"

"You're sure?"

"I insist."

"Thanks, Henry."

Nicholas turned around, slowly, and headed for the gate.

Just above the entrance, a huge American flag with bright stars and stripes, thrashed in the wind. He was suddenly reminded of the thousands of would-be immigrants around the world, yearning to make their new home under its glorious shadow. Some were standing in long lines outside the embassies of their native countries. Others were hiding in cargo ships and jumping fences and wading across treacherous rivers and clawing through the mud of collapsing tunnels. Despite the border patrol and electric fences and stepped-up security at every port of entry, they were coming. They were coming anyway.

Some would die in the process. But for those who made it, there was still the chance for greatness, the same chance that Lola had so wondrously exploited.

She was an incredible survivor, an extraordinary problem-solver, a mother that had made the ultimate sacrifice for her child. She was also a manipulator and a deceiver, and according to Professor Broadson, a murderer. Those were the kinds of people flooding into America.

Ironically, they were no different from the blue-bloods already here ... good people, bad people, manipulators, deceivers, problem-solvers, heroes, heroines and murderers. Somehow, amidst their collective chaos, they had failed to bring down the system. After two hundred and thirty years of stirring up the great melting pot of imperfection, the country was still strong; the flag was still flying in its perennial glory.

When Nicholas thought about all of the happiness Lola had brought into his life by coming into this country, he stopped and turned to Goodboy.

"God bless America, Henry."

Goodboy wasn't sure what Nicholas was thinking. But seeing him standing beneath the flag with little Lolita in his arms, the sun at his back and the hope of the future written on his face, Goodboy knew he agreed.

"Yes, Nicholas. For the sake of every demented soul, still believing in freedom. God bless America."

Autumn leaves had already begun to fall from the huge Dawn Redwoods in front of the Springfield State Museum. Nicholas remembered strolling along that same sidewalk with Lola, hearing the dried twigs, crunch beneath their feet. Though the memories ripped into the painful cavities of his heart, the Museum was a fitting place to meet with Professor Broadson. It was the place they had first heard about the outrageous claims of a dead treasure hunter and the power of the Juba Chest.

Nicholas carried a cardboard box under his arm. He caressed it as though it were a miniature bomb that might fall to the ground, and at any moment, explode. In many ways, the contents of the box had already exploded in their lives. That's why Lola was ... dead.

Professor Broadson sat on the concrete steps in front of the Museum, reviewing his travel plans. When he spotted Nicholas coming up the sidewalk, he stood up, then went down to meet him.

Nicholas handed him the box. "I believe this is what you're looking for. It might be a little dusty. It's been in storage for a while."

Professor Broadson peeped into the box to verify its contents. “Thank you. I regret we didn’t do this much earlier.”

“You tried, Professor. I suppose some lessons have to be learned the hard way.”

At that moment, Nicholas’ cell phone went off.

“Yes?”

There was a long pause. His attorney, Gate Mouth Fields, started to explain the terms of the settlement with Allen Brothers Construction.

Nicholas finally replied. “I want to be perfectly frank about this, Attorney Fields. No amount can compensate for my loss. But if you think $4 million is the best we can do, then take it. I don’t have the strength to drag this out.”

He paused a while longer.

“Okay, okay. I’ll come by your office tomorrow.” He hung up the phone.

Observing the pain in his eyes, Professor Broadson lingered a while, trying to give the business side of death a chance to bury itself.

“How are you adjusting?”

“Day to day and visit to visit,” Nicholas sadly confessed.

Not a single day had passed that Nicholas and little Lolita Diane had not visited Lola’s gravesite. With permission from officials of Colonial Heights Assisted Living via Goodboy’s $20,000 donation, Lola had been laid to rest in her perfect hole by the sparkling waters of Crystal Creek. Goodboy had promised Nicholas that one day the pain would subside enough for him to skip a visit or two. That would be the day his life started over.

“Indeed, you will get through this,” Professor Broadson reassured him. “The responsibilities of life will not allow us to simply give up.”

Nicholas’ thoughts turned to the profound nature of Professor Broadson’s responsibilities. “What about the chest?

What do you plan to do with it?"

"I have a place in the Himalayas. It'll be safe there."

"Safe for how long? Until some eccentric treasure hunter digs it up again?"

Professor Broadson gazed, narrowly. "In this place, there is no digging. Believe me, it'll be hidden from the world forever."

"I hope so, Professor. I hope the tree will wither and die and its callous method of fixing our society will never come up again. We have one God. We don't need another."

****THE END****

FEEDBACK

One of my personal joys in writing is the opportunity to hear directly from readers and fans. My driving philosophy is simple: "Satisfy your readers and everything else will fall into place." I am eternally grateful to know that I am achieving this goal, or that you care enough to tell me when I fall short.

Contact him at: grogan007@live.com

This is important: If you enjoyed this book, please, please leave a review. This helps future readers to make an initial decision about the book's quality, and supports my effort to provide you with the extraordinary reading experience you deserve.

BOOKS BY LEANDER JACKIE GROGAN

Orange FingerTips

Exorcism At Midnight

Baby, Put That Gun Down

Layoff Skullduggery: The Official Humor Guide

King Juba's Chest

Black Church Blues

The Blood Tears of Jesus

Help! The Bible Gobbled Up My Big Sister [Not yet released]

What's Wrong With Your Small Business Team [Nonfiction Bestseller]

www.ingramcontent.com/pod-product-compliance
Lightning Source LLC
Chambersburg PA
CBHW030430310726
48979CB00009B/1692/J

* 9 7 8 1 6 2 6 2 0 2 1 5 3 *